TOMORROW'S KIN

TOMORROW'S KIN

BOOK 1

OF THE

YESTERDAY'S KIN

TRILOGY

NANCY KRESS

TOR

A TOM DOHERTY ASSOCIATES BOOK

NEW YORK

TOMORROW'S KIN

Copyright © 2017 by Nancy Kress

A Tor Book
Published by Tom Doherty Associates
175 Fifth Avenue
New York, NY 10010

www.tor-forge.com

Tor® is a registered trademark of Macmillan Publishing Group, LLC.

The Library of Congress Cataloging-in-Publication Data is available upon request.

ISBN 978-0-7653-9029-5 (hardcover)
ISBN 978-0-7653-9031-8 (ebook)

Our books may be purchased in bulk for promotional, educational, or business use. Please contact your local bookseller or the Macmillan Corporate and Premium Sales Department at 1-800-221-7945, extension 5442, or by email at MacmillanSpecialMarkets@macmillan.com.

First Edition: July 2017

Printed in the United States of America

0 9 8 7 6 5 4 3 2 1

For Jack, as what is not?

ACKNOWLEDGMENTS

I would like to thank my agent, the wonderful Eleanor Wood; my terrific editor, Beth Meacham; my husband, Jack Skillingstead, the best of first readers; and my dear friend Dr. Maura Glynn-Thami, who saves me from so many medical errors in all my fiction.

PART ONE

We see in these facts some deep organic bond, prevailing throughout space and time. . . . This bond, on my theory, is simple inheritance.

—Charles Darwin, *The Origin of Species*

CHAPTER 1

S minus 10.5 months

The publication party was held in the dean's office, which was supposed to be an honor. Oak-paneled room, sherry in little glasses, small-paned windows facing the quad—the room was trying hard to be a Commons someplace like Oxford or Cambridge, a task for which it was several centuries too late. The party was trying hard to look festive. Marianne's colleagues, except for Evan and the dean, were trying hard not to look too envious, or at their watches.

"Stop it," Evan said at her from behind the cover of his raised glass.

"Stop what?"

"Pretending you hate this."

"I hate this," Marianne said.

"You don't."

He was half right. She didn't like parties but she was proud of her paper, which had been achieved despite two years of gene sequencers that kept breaking down, inept graduate students who contaminated samples with their own DNA, murmurs of "Lucky find" from Baskell, with whom she'd never gotten along. Baskell, an old-guard physicist, saw her as a bitch who refused to defer to rank or to back down gracefully in an argument. Many people, Marianne knew, saw her as some variant of this. The list included two of her three grown children.

Outside the open casements, students lounged on the grass in the mellow October sunshine. Three girls in cut-off jeans played Frisbee, leaping at the blue flying saucer and checking to see if the boys sitting on the stone wall were watching. Feinberg and Davidson, from Physics, walked by, arguing amiably. Marianne wished she were with them instead of at her own party.

"Oh God," she said to Evan, "Curtis just walked in."

The president of the university made his ponderous way across the room. Once he had been an historian, which might be why he reminded Marianne of Henry VIII. Now he was a campus politician, as power-mad as Henry but stuck at a second-rate university where there wasn't much power to be had. Marianne held against him not his personality but his mind; unlike Henry, he was not all that bright. And he spoke in clichés.

"Dr. Jenner," he said, "congratulations. A feather in your cap, and a credit to us all."

"Thank you, Dr. Curtis," Marianne said.

"Oh, 'Ed,' please."

"Ed." She didn't offer her own first name, curious to see if he remembered it. He didn't. Marianne sipped her sherry.

Evan jumped into the awkward silence. "I'm Dr. Blanford, visiting post-doc," he said in his plummy British accent. "We're all so proud of Marianne's work."

"Yes! And I'd love for you to explain to me your innovative process—ah, Marianne."

He didn't have a clue. His secretary had probably reminded him that he had to put in an appearance at the party: *Dean of Science's office, 4:30 Friday, in honor of that publication by Dr. Jenner in*—quick look at e-mail—in Nature, *very prestigious, none of our scientists has published there before.* . . .

"Oh," Marianne said as Evan poked her discreetly in the side: *Play nice!* "It wasn't so much an innovation in process as unexpected results from known procedures. My assistants and I discovered a new haplogroup of mitochondrial DNA. Previously it was thought that the genome of *Homo sapiens* consisted of thirty haplogroups, and we found a thirty-first."

"By sequencing a sample of contemporary genes, you know," Evan said helpfully. "Sequencing and verifying."

Anything said in upper-crust British automatically sounded intelligent, and Dr. Curtis looked suitably impressed. "Of course, of course. Splendid results. A star in your crown."

"It's yet another haplogroup descended," Evan said with malicious helpfulness, "from humanity's common female ancestor a hundred and fifty thousand years ago. 'Mitochondrial Eve.'"

Dr. Curtis brightened. There had been a TV program about Mitochondrial Eve, Marianne remembered, featuring a buxom actress in a leopard-skin sarong. "Oh, yes! Wasn't that—"

"I'm sorry, you can't go in there!" someone shrilled in the corridor outside the room. All conversation ceased. Heads swiveled toward three men in dark suits pushing their way past the knot of graduate students by the door. The three men wore guns.

Another school shooting, Marianne thought, *where can I—*

"Dr. Marianne Jenner?" the tallest of the three men said, flashing a badge. "I'm Special Agent Douglas Katz of the FBI. We'd like you to come with us."

Marianne said, "Am I under arrest?"

"No, no, nothing like that. We are acting under direct order of the president of the United States. We're here to escort you to New York."

Evan had taken Marianne's hand—she wasn't sure just when. There was nothing romantic in the handclasp, nor anything sexual. Evan, twenty-five years her junior and discreetly gay, was a friend, an ally, the only other evolutionary biologist in the department and the only one who shared Marianne's cynical sense of humor. *"Or so we thought,"* they said to each other whenever any hypothesis proved wrong. *Or so we thought* . . . His fingers felt warm and reassuring around her suddenly icy ones.

"Why am I going to New York?"

"I'm afraid we can't tell you that. But it is a matter of national security."

"*Me?* What possible reason—"

Special Agent Katz almost, but not quite, hid his impatience at her questions. "I wouldn't know, ma'am. My orders are to escort you to UN Special Mission Headquarters in Manhattan."

Marianne looked at her gaping colleagues, at the wide-eyed grad students, at Dr. Curtis, who was already figuring how this could be turned to the advantage of the university. She freed her hand from Evan's and managed to keep her voice steady.

"Please excuse me, Dr. Curtis, Dean. It seems I'm needed for something connected with . . . with the aliens."

One more time, Noah Jenner rattled the doorknob to the apartment. It felt greasy from too many unwashed palms, and it was still locked. But he knew that Emily was in there. That was the kind of thing he was always, somehow, right about. He was right about things that didn't do him any good.

"Emily," he said softly through the door, "please open up."

Nothing.

"Emily, I have nowhere else to go."

Nothing.

"I'll stop, I promise. I won't do sugarcane ever again."

The door opened a crack, chain still in place, and Emily's despairing face appeared. She wasn't the kind of girl given to dramatic fury, but her quiet despair was even harder to bear. Not that Noah didn't deserve it. He knew he did. Her fair hair hung limply on either side of her long, sad face. She wore the green bathrobe he liked, with the butterfly embroidered on the left shoulder.

"You won't stop," Emily said. "You can't. You're an addict."

"It's not an addictive drug. You know that."

"Not physically, maybe. But it is for you. You won't give it up. I'll never know who you really are."

"I—"

"I'm sorry, Noah. But— Go away." She closed and relocked the door.

Noah stood slumped against the dingy wall, waiting to see if anything else would happen. Nothing did. Eventually, as soon as he mustered the energy, he would have to go away.

Was she right? Would he never give up sugarcane? It wasn't that it delivered a high: it didn't. No rush of dopamine, no psychedelic illusions, no out-of-body experiences, no lowering of inhibitions. It was just that on sugarcane, Noah felt like he was the person he was supposed to be. The problem was that it was never the same person twice. Sometimes he felt like a warrior, able to face and ruthlessly defeat anything. Sometimes he felt like a philosopher, deeply content to sit and ponder the universe. Sometimes he felt like a little child, dazzled by the newness of a fresh morning. Sometimes he felt like a father (he wasn't), protective of the entire world. Theories said that sugarcane released memories of past lives, or stimulated the collective unconscious, or made temporarily solid the images of dreams. One hypothesis was that it created a sort of temporary, self-induced Korsakoff's syndrome, the neurological disorder in which invented selves seem completely true. No one knew how sugarcane really acted on the brain. For some people, it did nothing at all. For Noah, who had never felt he fit in anywhere, it gave what he had never had: a sense of solid identity, if only for the hours that the drug stayed in his system.

The problem was, it was difficult to hold a job when one day you were nebbishy, sweet-natured Noah Jenner, the next day you were Attila the Hun, and two days later you were far too intellectual to wash dishes or make change at a convenience store. Emily had wanted Noah to hold a job. To contribute to the rent, to scrub the floor, to help take the sheets to the laundromat. To be an adult, and the same adult every day. She was right to want that. Only—

He might be able to give up sugarcane and be the same adult, if only he had the vaguest idea who that adult was. Which brought him back to the same problem—he didn't fit anywhere. And never had.

Noah picked up the backpack in which Emily had put his few belongings. She couldn't have left it in the hallway for very long or the backpack would have already been stolen. He made his way down the three flights from Emily's walk-up and out onto the streets. The October sun shone warmly on his shoulders, on the blocks of shabby buildings, on the trash skirling across the dingy streets of New York's Lower East Side. Walking, Noah reflected bitterly, was one thing he could do without fitting in. He walked the blocks to Battery Park, that green oasis on the tip of Manhattan's steel canyons, leaned on a railing, and looked south.

He could just make out the *Embassy,* floating in New York Harbor. Well, no, not the *Embassy* itself, but the shimmer of light off its energy shield. Everybody wanted that energy shield, including his sister Elizabeth. It kept everything out, short of a nuclear missile. Maybe that, too: so far nobody had tried, although in the two months since the *Embassy* had floated there, three different terrorist groups had tried other weapons. Nothing got through the shield, although maybe air and light did. They must, right? Even aliens needed to breathe.

When the sun dropped below the horizon, the glint off the floating embassy disappeared. Dusk was gathering. He would have to make the call if he wanted a place to sleep tonight. Elizabeth or Ryan? His brother wouldn't yell at him as much, but Ryan lived Upstate, in the same little Hudson River town as their mother's college, and Noah would have to hitchhike there. Also, Ryan was often away, doing field-work for his wildlife agency. Noah didn't think he could cope with Ryan's talkative, sticky-sweet wife right now. So it would have to be Elizabeth.

He called his sister's number on his cheap cell. "Hello?" she snapped. *Born angry,* their mother always said of Elizabeth. Well, Elizabeth was in the right job, then.

"Lizzie, it's Noah."

"Noah."

"Yes. I need help. Can I stay with you tonight?" He held the cell away from his ear, bracing for her onslaught. *Shiftless, lazy, direction-less . . .* When it was over, he said, "Just for tonight."

They both knew he was lying, but Elizabeth said, "Come on then," and clicked off without saying good-bye.

If he'd had more than a few dollars in his pocket, Noah would have looked for a sugarcane dealer. Since he didn't, he left the park, the wind pricking at him now with tiny needles, and descended to the subway that would take him to Elizabeth's apartment on the Upper West Side.

CHAPTER 2

S minus 10.5 months

The FBI politely declined to answer any of Marianne's questions. Politely, they confiscated her cell and iPad and took her in a sleek black car down Route 87 to New York, through the city to lower Manhattan, and out to a harbor pier. Gates with armed guards controlled access to a heavily fortified building at the end of the pier. Politely, she was searched and fingerprinted. Then she was politely asked to wait in a small windowless room equipped with a few comfortable chairs, a table with coffee and cookies, and a wall-mounted TV tuned to CNN. A news show was covering weather in Florida.

The aliens had shown up four months ago, their ship barreling out from the direction of the sun, which had made it harder to detect until a few weeks before arrival. At first, in fact, the ship had been mistaken for an asteroid and there had been panic that it would hit Earth. When it was announced that the asteroid was in fact an alien vessel, panic had decreased in some quarters and increased in others. A ship? Aliens? Armed forces across the world mobilized. Communications strategies were formed, and immediately hacked by the curious and technologically sophisticated. Seven different religions declared the end of the world. The stock and bond markets crashed, rallied, soared, crashed again, and generally behaved like a reed buffeted by a hurricane. Governments put the world's top linguists, biologists, mathematicians, astronomers, and physicists on top-priority standby. Psychics blossomed. People rejoiced and feared and prayed and committed suicide and sent up balloons in the general direction of the moon, where the alien ship eventually parked itself in orbit.

Contact was immediate, in robotic voices that were clearly mechanical, and in halting English that improved almost immediately. The aliens, dubbed by the press "Denebs" because their ship came from the general direction of that bright blue-white star, were friendly. The xenophiles looked smugly triumphant. The xenophobes disbelieved the friendliness and bided their time. The aliens spent two months talking to the United Nations. They were reassuring; this was a peace mission. They were also reticent. Voice communication only, and through machines. They would not show themselves: "Not now. We wait." They would not visit the International Space Station, nor permit humans to visit their ship. They identified their planet, and astronomers found it once they knew where to look, by the faintly eclipsed light from its orange dwarf star. The planet was in the star's habitable zone, slightly larger than Earth but less dense, water present. It was nowhere near Deneb, but the name stuck.

After two months, the aliens requested permission to build what they called an embassy, a floating pavilion, in New York Harbor. It would be heavily shielded and would not affect the environment. In exchange, they would share the physics behind their star drive, although not the engineering, with Earth, via the Internet. The UN went into furious debate. Physicists salivated. Riots erupted, pro and con, in major cities across the globe. Conspiracy theorists, some consisting of entire governments, vowed to attack any Deneb presence on Earth.

The UN finally agreed, and the structure went into orbit around Earth, landed without a splash in the harbor, and floated peacefully offshore. After landing, it grew wider and flatter, a half dome that could be considered either an island or a ship. The US government decided it was a ship, subject to maritime law, and the media began capitalizing and italicizing it: the *Embassy*. Coast Guard craft circled it endlessly; the US navy had ships and submarines nearby. Airspace above was a no-fly zone, which was inconvenient for jets landing at New York's three big airports. Fighter jets nearby stayed on high alert.

Nothing happened.

For another two months the aliens continued to talk through their machines to the UN, and only to the UN, and nobody ever saw them. It wasn't known whether they were shielding themselves from Earth's air, microbes, or armies. The *Embassy* was surveilled by all possible means. If anybody learned anything, the information was classified except for a single exchange:

Why are you here?

To make contact with humanity. A peace mission.

A musician set the repeated phrases to music, a sly and humorous refrain, without menace. The song, an instant international sensation, was the opening for playfulness about the aliens. Late-night comics built monologues around supposed alien practices. The *Embassy* became a tourist attraction, viewed through telescopes, from boats outside the Coast Guard limit, from helicopters outside the no-fly zone. A German fashion designer scored an enormous runway hit with "the Deneb look," despite the fact that no one knew how the Denebs looked. The stock market stabilized as much as it ever did. Quickie movies were shot, some with Deneb allies and some with treacherous Deneb foes who wanted our women or gold or bombs. Bumper stickers proliferated like kudzu: I BRAKE FOR DENEBS. EARTH IS FULL ALREADY—GO HOME. DENEBS DO IT INVISIBLY. WILL TRADE PHYSICS FOR FOOD.

The aliens never commented on any of it. They published the promised physics, which only a few dozen people in the world could understand. They were courteous, repetitive, elusive. *Why are you here? To make contact with humanity. A peace mission.*

Marianne stared at the TV, where CNN showed footage of disabled children choosing Halloween costumes. Nothing about the discussion, the room, the situation felt real. Why would the aliens want to talk to her? It had to be about her paper, nothing else made sense. No, that didn't make sense either.

"—donated by a network of churches from five states. Four-year-old Amy seizes eagerly on the black-cat costume, while her friend Kayla chooses—"

Her paper was one of dozens published every year on evolutionary genetics, each paper adding another tiny increment to statistical data on the subject. Why this one? Why her? The UN secretary-general, various presidents and premiers, top scientists—the press said they all talked to the Denebs from this modern fortress, through (pick one) highly encrypted devices that permitted no visuals, or one-way visuals, or two-way visuals that the UN was keeping secret, or not at all and the whole alien-human conversation was invented. The *Embassy*, however, was certainly real. Images of it appeared on magazine covers, coffee mugs, screen savers, T-shirts, paintings on velvet, targets for shooting ranges.

Marianne's daughter Elizabeth regarded the aliens with suspicion, but then, Elizabeth regarded everyone with suspicion. It was one reason she was the youngest Border Patrol section leader in the country, serving on the New York task force along with several other agencies. She fit right in with the current American obsession with isolationism as an economic survival strategy.

Ryan seldom mentioned the aliens. He was too absorbed in his career and his wife.

And Noah—did Noah, her problem child, even realize the aliens were here? Marianne hadn't seen Noah in months. In the spring he had gone to "try life in the South." An occasional e-mail turned up on her phone, never containing much actual information. If Noah was back in New York, he hadn't called her yet. Marianne didn't want to admit what a relief that was. Her child, her baby—but every time they saw each other, it ended in recriminations or tears.

And what was she doing, thinking about her children instead of the aliens? Why did the ambassador want to talk to her? Why were the Denebs here?

To make contact with humanity. A peace mission . . .

"Dr. Jenner?"

"Yes." She stood up from her chair, her jaw set. Somebody better give her some answers, now.

The young man looked doubtfully at her clothes, dark jeans and a ten-year-old green suede blazer, her standard outfit for faculty parties. He said, "Secretary Desai will join you shortly."

Marianne tried to let her face show nothing. A few moments later Vihaan Desai, secretary-general of the United Nations, entered the room, followed by a security detail. Tall, elderly, he wore a sky-blue kurta of richly embroidered heavy silk. Marianne felt like a wren beside a peacock. Desai held out his hand but did not smile. Relations between the United States and India were not good. Relations between the United States and everybody were not good, as the country relentlessly pursued its new policy of economic isolationism in an attempt to protect jobs. Until the Denebs came, with their cosmos-shaking distraction, the UN had been thick with international threats. Maybe it still was.

"Dr. Jenner," Desai said, studying her intently, "it seems we are both summoned to interstellar conference." His English, in the musical Indian accent, was perfect. Marianne remembered that he spoke four languages.

She said, "Do you know why?"

Her directness made him blink. "I do not. The Deneb ambassador was insistent but not forthcoming."

And does humanity do whatever the ambassador insists on? Marianne did not say this aloud. Something here was not adding up. The secretary-general's next words stunned her.

"We, plus a few others, are invited aboard the *Embassy*. The invitation is dependent upon your presence, and upon its immediate acceptance."

"Aboard . . . aboard the *Embassy*?"

"It seems so."

"But nobody has ever—"

"I am well aware of that." The dark, intelligent eyes never left her face. "We await only the other guests who happen to be in New York."

"I see." She didn't.

Desai turned to his security detail and spoke to them in Hindi. An argument began. Did security usually argue with their protectees? Marianne wouldn't have thought so, but then, what did she know about UN protocol? She was out of her field, her league, her solar system. Her guess was that the Denebs were not allowing bodyguards aboard the *Embassy,* and that the security chief was protesting.

Evidently the secretary-general won. He said to her, "Please come," and walked with long strides from the room. His kurta rustled at his ankles, shimmering sky. Though not usually intuitive, Marianne could nonetheless sense the tension coming off him like heat. They went down a long corridor, trailed by deeply frowning guards, and down an elevator. Very far down—did the elevator go under the harbor? It must. They exited into a small room already occupied by two people, a man and a woman. Marianne recognized the woman: Ekaterina Zaytsev, the representative to the UN from the Russian Federation. The man might be the Chinese representative. Both looked agitated.

Desai said in English, "We await only—Ah, here they are."

Two much younger men practically blew into the room, clutching headsets. Translators. They looked disheveled and frightened, which made Marianne feel better. She wasn't the only one battling an almost overwhelming sense of unreality. If only Evan could be here, with his sardonic and unflappable Britishness. *"Or so we thought . . ."*

No. Neither she nor Evan had ever thought of this.

"The other permanent members of the Security Council are unfortunately not immediately available," Desai said. "We will not wait."

Marianne couldn't remember who the other permanent members were. The UK, surely, but who else? How many? What were they doing this October dusk that would make them miss first contact with an alien species? Whatever it was, they would regret it the rest of their lives.

Unless, of course, this little delegation never returned—killed or kidnapped or eaten. No, that was ridiculous. She was being hysterical. Desai would not go if there was danger.

Of course he would. Anyone would. Wouldn't they? Wouldn't she? Nobody, she suddenly realized, had actually asked her to go on this mission. She'd been ordered to go. What if she flat-out refused?

A door opened at the far end of the small room, voices spoke from the air about clearance and proceeding, and then another elevator. The six people stepped into what had to be the world's most comfortable and unwarlike submarine, equipped with lounge chairs and gold-braided officers.

A submarine. Well, that made sense, if plans had been put in place to get to the *Embassy* unobserved by press, tourists, and nut jobs who would blow up the alien base if they could. The Denebs must have agreed to some sort of landing place or entryway, which meant this meeting had been talked of, planned for, long before today. Today was just the moment the aliens had decided to put the plan into practice. Why? Why so hastily?

"Dr. Jenner," Desai said, "in the short time we have here, please explain your scientific findings to us."

None of them sat in the lounge chairs. They stood in a circle around Marianne, who felt none of the desire to toy with them as she had with Dr. Curtis at the college. Where were her words going, besides this cramped, luxurious submarine? Was the president of the United States listening, packed into the situation room with whoever else belonged there?

"My paper is nothing startling, Mr. Secretary-General, which is why this is all baffling to me. In simple terms"—she tried to not be distracted by the murmuring of the two translators into their mouthpieces—"all humans alive today are the descendants of one woman who lived about a hundred and fifty thousand years ago. We know this because of mitochondrial DNA, which is not the DNA from the nucleus of the cell but separate DNA found in small organelles called mitochondria. Mitochondria, which exist in every cell of your body, are the powerhouses of the cell, producing energy for cellular functions. Mitochondrial DNA does not undergo recombination and is not found in sperm cells after they reach the egg. So the mitochondrial DNA is passed down unchanged from a mother to all her children."

Marianne paused, wondering how to explain this simply, but without condescension. "Mitochondrial DNA mutates at a steady rate, about one mutation every ten thousand years in a section called the control region, and about once every thirty-five hundred years in the mitochondrial DNA as a whole. By tracing the number and type of mutations in contemporary humans, we can construct a tree of descent: which group descended from which female ancestor.

"Evolutionary biologists have identified thirty of these haplogroups. I found a new one, L7, by sequencing and comparing DNA samples with a standard human mitochondrial sample, known as the revised Cambridge Reference Sequence."

"How did you know where to look for this new group?"

"I didn't. I came across the first sample by chance and then sampled her relatives."

"Is it very different, then, from the others?"

"No," Marianne said. "It's just a branch of the L haplogroup."

"Why wasn't it discovered before?"

"It seems to be rare. The line must have mostly died out over time. It's a very old line, one of the first divergences from Mitochondrial Eve."

"So there is nothing remarkable about your finding?"

"Not in the least. There may even be more haplogroups out there that we just haven't discovered yet." She felt a perfect fool. They all looked at her as if expecting answers—*Look! A blinding scientific light illuminates all!*—and she had none. She was a workman scientist who had delivered a workmanlike job of fairly routine haplotyping.

"Sir, we have arrived," said a junior officer. Marianne saw that his dress blues were buttoned wrong. They must have been donned in great haste. The tiny, human mishap made her feel better.

Desai drew a deep, audible breath. Even he, who had lived through war and revolution, was nervous. Commands flew through the air from invisible people. The submarine door opened.

Marianne stepped out into the alien ship.

"Where's Mom? Did you call her?" Elizabeth demanded.

"Not yet," Noah said.

"Does she even know you're in New York?"

"Not yet." He wanted to tell his sister to stop hammering at him, but he was her guest and so he couldn't. Not that he'd ever been able to stand up to either of his siblings. His usual ploy had been to get them battering on each other and leave him alone. Maybe he could do that now. Or maybe not.

"Noah, how long have you been in the city?"

"A while."

"How long a while?"

Noah put his hand in front of his face. "Lizzie, I'm really hungry. I didn't eat today. Do you think you could—"

"Don't start your whining-and-helpless routine with me, Noah. It doesn't work anymore."

Had it ever? Noah didn't think so, not with Elizabeth. He tried to pull himself together. "Elizabeth, I haven't called Mom yet and I *am* hungry. Please, could we defer this fight until I eat something? Anything, crackers or toast or—"

"There's sandwich stuff in the fridge. Help yourself. I'm going to call Mom, since at least one of us should let her know the prodigal son has deigned to turn up again. She's been out of her mind with worry about you."

Noah doubted that. His mother was the strongest person he knew, followed by Elizabeth and Ryan. Together, the three could have toppled empires. Of course, they seldom were together, since they fought almost every time they met. Odd that they would go on meeting so often, when it produced such bitterness, and all over such inconsequential things. Politics, religion, funding for the arts, isolationism . . . He rummaged in Elizabeth's messy refrigerator, full of plastic containers with their lids half off, some with dabs of rotting food stuck to the bottom. God, this one was growing *mold*. But he found bread, cheese, and some salsa that seemed all right.

Elizabeth's one-bedroom apartment echoed her fridge, which was another reason she and Mom fought. Unmade bed, dusty stacks of journals and newspapers, a vase of dead flowers probably sent by one of the boyfriends Elizabeth never fell in love with. Mom's house upstate in Tannersville, and Ryan and Connie's near hers, were neat and bright. Housecleaners came weekly; food was bought from careful lists; possessions were replaced whenever they got shabby. Noah had no possessions, or at least as few as he could manage.

Elizabeth clutched the phone. She dressed like a female FBI agent— short hair, dark pantsuit, no makeup—and was beautiful without trying. "Come on, Mom, pick up," she muttered. "It's a cell, it's supposed to be portable."

"Maybe she's in class," Noah said. "Or a meeting."

"It's Friday night, Noah."

"Oh. Yeah."

"I'll try the landline. She still has one."

Someone answered the landline on the first ring; Noah heard the chime stop from where he sat munching his sandwich. Then silence.

"Hello? Hello? Mom?" Elizabeth said.

The receiver on the other end clicked.

"That's odd," Elizabeth said.

"You probably got a wrong number."

"Don't talk with your mouth full. I'm going to try again."

This time no one answered. Elizabeth scowled. "I don't like that. Someone is there. I'm going to call Ryan."

Wasn't Ryan somewhere in Canada doing fieldwork? Or maybe Noah had the dates wrong. He'd only glanced at the e-mail from Ryan, accessed on a terminal at the public library. That day he'd been on sugarcane, and the temporary identity had been impatient and brusque.

"Ryan? This is Elizabeth. Do you know where Mom is? . . . If I knew her schedule I wouldn't be calling, would I? . . . Wait, wait, will you *listen* for a minute? I called her house and someone picked up and then clicked off, and when I called back a second later, it just rang. Will you go over there just to check it out? . . . Okay, yes, we'll wait. Oh, Noah's here . . . No, I'm not going to discuss with you right now the . . . *Ryan.* For chrissake, go check Mom's house!" She clicked off.

Noah wished he were someplace else. He wished he were somebody else. He wished he had some sugarcane.

Elizabeth flounced into a chair and picked up a book. *Tariffs, Borders, and the Survival of the United States,* Noah read upside down. Elizabeth was a passionate defender of isolationism. How many desperate people trying to crash the United States borders had she arrested today? Noah didn't want to think about it.

Fifteen minutes later, Ryan called back. Elizabeth put the call on speakerphone. "Liz, there are cop cars around Mom's house. They wouldn't let me in. A guy came out and said Mom isn't dead or hurt or in trouble, and he couldn't tell me any more than that."

"Okay." Elizabeth wore her focused look, the one with which she directed border patrols. "I'll try the college."

"I did. I reached Evan. He said that three men claiming to be FBI came and escorted her to the UN Special Mission Headquarters in Manhattan."

"That doesn't make sense!"

"I know. Listen, I'm coming over to your place."

"I'm calling the police."

"No! Don't! Not until I get there and we decide what to do."

Noah listened to them argue, which went on until Ryan hung up.

Of course Elizabeth, who worked for a quasi-military organization, wanted to call the cops. Of course Ryan, who worked for a wildlife organization that thought the government had completely messed up regulations on invasive botanical species, would shun the cops. Meanwhile Mom was probably just doing something connected with her college, a UN fund-raiser or something, and that geek Evan had gotten it all wrong. Noah didn't like Evan, who was only a few years older than he was. Evan was everything that Noah's family thought Noah should be: smart, smooth, able to fit in anyplace, even into a country that wasn't his own. And how come Elizabeth's border patrols hadn't kept out Evan Blanford?

Never mind; Noah knew the answer.

He said, "Can I do anything?"

Elizabeth didn't even answer him.

Marianne had seen many pictures of the *Embassy*. From the outside, the floating pavilion was beautiful in a stark sort of way. Hemispherical, multifaceted like a buckyball (had the Denebs learned that structure from humans or was it a mathematical universal?), the *Embassy* floated on a broad platform of some unknowable material. Facets and platform were blue but coated with the energy shield, which reflected sunlight so much that it glinted, a beacon of sorts. The aliens had certainly not tried to mask their presence. But there must be hidden machinery underneath, in the part known (maybe) only to navy divers, since the entire huge structure had landed without a splash in the harbor. Plus, of course, the hidden passage through which the sub had come, presumably entailing a momentary interruption of the energy shield. Marianne knew she'd never find out the details.

The room into which she and the others stepped from the submarine was featureless except for the bed of water upon which their sub floated, droplets sliding off its sleek sides. No windows or furniture, one door. A strange smell permeated the air: disinfectant? Perfume?

Alien body odor? Marianne's heart began to beat oddly, too hard and too loud, with abrupt painful skips. Her breathing quickened.

The door opened and a Deneb came out. At first, she couldn't see it clearly; it was clouded by the same glittery energy shield that covered the *Embassy*. When her eyes adjusted, she gasped. The others also made sounds: a quick indrawn breath, a clicking of the tongue, what sounded like an actual whimper. The Russian translator whispered, "Bozhe moi!"

The alien looked almost human. Almost, not quite. Tall, maybe six two, the man—it was clearly male—had long, thin arms and legs, a deep chest, a human face but much larger eyes. His skin was coppery and his hair, long and tied back, was dark brown. Most striking were his eyes: larger than humans', with huge dark pupils in a large expanse of white. He wore dark green clothing, a simple tunic top over loose, short trousers that exposed his spindly calves. His feet were bare, and perhaps the biggest shock of all was that his feet, five-toed and broad, the nails cut short and square. Those feet looked so much like hers that she thought wildly: *He could wear my shoes*.

"Hello," the alien said, and it was not his voice but the mechanical one of the radio broadcasts, coming from the ceiling.

"Hello," Desai said, and bowed from the waist. "We are glad to finally meet. I am Secretary-General Desai of the United Nations."

"Yes," the alien "said," and then added some trilling and clicking sounds in which his mouth did move. Immediately the ceiling said, "I welcome you in our own language."

Secretary Desai made the rest of the introductions with admirable calm. Marianne tried to fight her growing sense of unreality by recalling what she had read about the Denebs' planet. She wished she'd paid more attention to the astronomy. The popular press had said that the alien star was a K-something (*K zero? K two?* She couldn't remember). The alien home world had both less gravity and less light than Earth, at different wavelengths . . . orange, yes. The sun was an orange dwarf. Was this Deneb so tall because the gravity was less? Or maybe he was just a basketball player—

Get a grip, Marianne.

She did. The alien had said his name, an impossible collection of trilled phonemes, and immediately said, "Call me Ambassador Smith." How had he chosen that—from a computer-generated list of English names? When Marianne had been in Beijing to give a paper, some Chinese translators had done that: "Call me Dan." She had assumed the translators doubted her ability to pronounce their actual names correctly, and they had probably been right. But "Smith" for a star-farer . . .

"You are Dr. Jenner?"

"Yes, Ambassador."

"We wanted to talk with you, in particular. Will you please come this way, all of you?"

They did, trailing like baby ducklings after the tall alien. The room beyond the single door had been fitted up like the waiting room of a very expensive medical specialist. Did they order the upholstered chairs and patterned rug on the Internet? Or manufacture them with some advanced nanotech deep in the bowels of the *Embassy*? The wall pictures were of famous skylines: New York, Shanghai, Dubai, Paris. Nothing in the room suggested alienness. Deliberate? Of course it was. *Nobody here but us chickens.*

Marianne sat, digging the nails of one hand into the palm of the other to quiet her insane desire to giggle.

"I would like to know of your recent publication, Dr. Jenner," the ceiling said, while Ambassador Smith looked at her from his discon-certingly large eyes.

"Certainly," Marianne said, wondering where to begin. How much did they know about human genetics?

Quite a lot, as it turned out. For the next twenty minutes Marianne explained, gestured, answered questions. The others listened silently except for the low murmur of the Chinese and Russian translators. Everyone, human and alien, looked attentive and courteous, although Marianne detected the slightly pursed lips of Ekaterina Zaytsev's envy.

Slowly it became clear that Smith already knew much of what Marianne was saying. His questions centered on where she had gotten her DNA samples.

"They were volunteers," Marianne said. "Collection booths were set up in an open-air market in India, because I happened to have a colleague working there, in a train station in London, and on my college campus in the United States. At each place, a nominal fee was paid for a quick scraping of tissue from the inside of the cheek. After we found the first L7 DNA in a sample from an American student from Indiana, we went to her relatives to ask for samples. They were very cooperative."

"This L7 sample, according to your paper, comes from a mutation that marks the strain of one of the oldest of mitochondrial groups."

Desai made a quick, startled shift on his chair.

"That's right," Marianne said. "Evidence says that Mitochondrial Eve had at least two daughters, and the line of one of them was L0 whereas the other line developed a mutation that became—" All at once she saw it, what Desai had already realized. She blinked at Smith and felt her mouth fall open, just as if she had no control over her jaw muscles, just as if the universe had been turned inside out, like a sock.

CHAPTER 3

S minus 10.5 months

Noah sat in Elizabeth's apartment, listening to his brother and sister. Ryan had just arrived and they sat together on the sagging sofa, conferring quietly, their usual belligerence temporarily replaced by shared concern. Repeated calls to their mother's cell and landline had produced nothing.

His brother had been shortchanged in the looks department. Elizabeth was beautiful in a severe way and Noah knew he'd gotten the best of his parents' genes: his dead father's height and athletic build, his mother's light-gray eyes flecked with gold. In contrast, Ryan was built like a fire hydrant: short, muscular, thickening into cylindricalness since his marriage; Connie was a good cook. At thirty, he was already balding. Ryan was smart, slow to change, secretive, humorless.

Elizabeth said, "Tell me exactly what Evan said about the FBI taking her away. Word for word."

Ryan did, adding, "What about this—we call the FBI and ask them directly where she is and what's going on."

"I tried that. The local field office said they didn't know anything about it, but they'd make inquiries and get back to me. They haven't."

"Of course not. We have to give them a reason to give out information, and on the way over I thought of two. We can say either that we're going to the press, or that we need to reach her for a medical emergency."

Elizabeth said, "I don't like the idea of threatening the feds—too potentially messy. The medical emergency might be better. We could say Connie's developed a problem with her pregnancy. First grandchild, life-threatening complications—"

Noah, startled, said, "Connie's pregnant?"

"Four months," Ryan said. "If you ever read the e-mails everybody sends you, you might have gotten the news. You're going to be an uncle." His gaze said that Noah would make just as rotten an uncle as he did a son.

Elizabeth said, "You need to make the phone call, Ryan. You're the prospective father."

Ryan pulled out his cell, which looked as if it could contact deep space. The FBI office was closed. He left a message. FBI Headquarters in DC was also closed. He left another message. Before Ryan could say, *They'll never get back to us* and so begin another argument with Elizabeth over governmental inefficiency, Noah said, "Did the Wildlife Society give you that cell for your job?"

"It's the International Wildlife Federation and yes, the phone has top-priority connections for the loosestrife invasion."

Noah ducked his head to hide his grin.

Elizabeth guffawed. "Ryan, do you know how pretentious that sounds? An emergency hotline for weeds?"

"Do you know how ignorant *you* sound? Purple loosestrife is taking over wetlands, which for your information are the most biologically diverse and productive ecologies on Earth. They're being choked by this invasive species, with an economic impact of millions of dollars that—"

"As if you cared about the United States economy! All you care about are those weeds that—"

"Agriculture depends on ecology, which in turn depends on wetlands! You can't change that even if you get the aliens to give you the tech for their energy shields. I know that's what you 'border-defense' types want but it won't—"

"Yes, it is what we want! Our economic survival is at stake, which makes Border Patrol a lot more important than a bunch of creeping flowers!"

"Great, just great. Just ignore invasive botanicals that encroach on farmland, so that eventually we can't even feed everyone who would be imprisoned in your imported alien energy fields."

"Protected, not imprisoned. The way we're protecting you now by keeping the Denebs offshore."

"Oh, you're doing that, are you? That was the aliens' decision. Do you think that if they had wanted to plop their pavilion in the middle of Times Square that your Border Patrol could have stopped them? They're a star-faring race, for chrissake!"

"Nobody said the—"

Noah shouted, which was the only way to get their attention, "Elizabeth, your cell is ringing! It says it's Mom!"

They both stared at the cell as if at a bomb, and then Elizabeth lunged for the phone. "Mom?"

"It's me. You called but—"

"Where have you been? What happened? What was the FBI—"

"I'll tell you everything. Are you and Ryan still at your place?"

"Yes. You sound funny. Are you sure you're okay?"

"Yes. No. Stay there, I'll get a cab, but it may be a few hours yet."

"But where—"

The phone went dead. Ryan and Elizabeth stared at each other. Into the silence, Noah said, "Oh yeah, Mom. Noah's here, too."

"You are surprised," Ambassador Smith had said, unnecessarily.

Courtesy had been swamped in shock. Marianne blurted, "You're *human*? From Earth?"

"Yes. We think so."

"Your mitochondrial DNA matches the L7 sequence? No, wait— your whole biology matches ours?"

"There are some differences, of course. We—"

The Russian delegate stood up so quickly her chair fell over. She spat something that her translator gave as a milder, "'I do not understand how this is possible.'"

"I will explain," Smith said. "Please sit down."

Ekaterina Zaytsev did not sit. All at once Marianne wondered if the energy field enveloping Smith was weaponized.

Smith said, "We have known for millennia that we did not originate on World. There is no fossil record of us going back more than a hundred fifty thousand Earth years. The life-forms native to World are DNA based, but there is no direct genetic link. We know that someone took us from somewhere else and—"

"Why?" Marianne blurted out. "Why would they do that? And who is 'they'?"

Before Smith could answer, Zaytsev said, "Why should your planet's native life-forms be DNA based at all? If this story is not a collection of lies?"

"Panspermia," Smith said. "And we don't know why we were seeded from Earth to World. An experiment, perhaps, by a race now gone. We—"

The Chinese ambassador was murmuring to his translator. The translator, American and too upset to observe protocol, interrupted Smith.

"Mr. Zhu asks how, if you are from Earth, you progressed to space travel so much faster than we have? If your brains are the same as ours?"

"Our evolution was different."

Marianne darted in with, "How? Why? A hundred fifty thousand years is not enough for more than superficial evolutionary changes!"

"Which we have," Smith said, still in that mechanical voice that Marianne suddenly hated. Its very detachment sounded condescending. "World's gravity, for instance, is one-tenth less than Earth's, and our internal organs and skeletons have adjusted. World is warmer than Earth, and you can see that we carry little body fat. Our eyes are much larger than yours—we needed to gather all the light we can on a planet dimmer than yours. Most plants on World use a dark version of chlorophyll, to gather as many photons as possible. We are dazzled by the colors on Earth."

He smiled, and Marianne remembered that all human cultures share certain facial expressions: happiness, disgust, anger.

Smith continued, "But when I said that our evolution differed from yours, I was referring to social evolution. World is a more benign planet than Earth. Little axial tilt, many easy-to-domesticate grains, much food, few predators. We had no Ice Age. We settled into agriculture over a hundred thousand years before you did."

Over a hundred thousand years more of settled communities, of cities, with their greater specialization and intellectual cross-fertilization. While Marianne's ancestors fifteen thousand years ago had still been hunting mastodons and gathering berries, these cousins across the galaxy might have been exploring quantum physics. But—

She said, "Then with such an environment, you must have had an overpopulation problem. All easy ecological niches rapidly become overpopulated!"

"Yes. But we had one more advantage." Smith paused; he was giving the translators time to catch up, and she guessed what that meant even before he spoke again.

"The group of us seeded on World—and we estimate it was no more than a thousand—were all closely related. Most likely they were all brought from one place. Our gene pool does not show as much diversity as yours. More important, the exiles—or at least a large number of them—happened to be unusually mild-natured and cooperative. You might say, 'sensitive to other's suffering.' We have had wars, but not very many, and not early on. We were able to control the population problem, once we saw it coming, with voluntary measures. And, of course, those subgroups that worked together best, made the earliest scientific advances and flourished most."

"You replaced evolution of the fittest with evolution of the most cooperative," Marianne said, and thought: *There goes Dawkins.*

"You may say that."

"*I* not say this," Zaytsev said, without waiting for her translator. Her face twisted. "How you know you come from Earth? And how know where is Earth?"

"Whoever took us to World left titanium tablets, practically indestructible, with diagrams. Eventually we learned enough astronomy to interpret them."

Moses on the mountain, Marianne thought. *How conveniently neat!* Profound distrust swamped her, followed by profound belief. Because, after all, here the aliens were, having arrived in a starship, and they certainly looked human. Although—

She said abruptly, "Will you give us blood samples? Tissue? Permit medical scans?"

"Yes."

The agreement was given so simply, so completely, that everyone fell silent. Marianne's dazed mind tried to find the scam in this, this possible nefarious treachery, and failed. It was quiet Zhu Feng who, through his translator, finally broke the silence.

"Tell us, please, honored envoy, why you are here at all?"

Again Smith answered simply. "To save you all from destruction."

Noah slipped out of the apartment, feeling terrible but not terrible enough to stay. First transgression: If Mom returned earlier than she'd said, he wouldn't be there when she arrived. Second transgression: He'd taken twenty dollars from Elizabeth's purse. Third transgression: He was going to buy sugarcane.

But he'd left Elizabeth and Ryan arguing yet again about isolationism, the same argument in the same words as when he'd seen them last, four months ago. Elizabeth pulled out statistics showing that the United States' only option for survival, including avoiding revolution, was to retain and regain jobs within its borders, impose huge tariffs on imports, and rebuild infrastructure. Ryan trotted out different statistics proving that only globalization could, after a period of disruption, bring economic benefits in the long run, including a fresh flow of workers into a graying America. Workers, not flora or fauna. They had gotten to the point of hurtling words like "fascist" and "sloppy thinker," when Noah left.

He walked the three blocks to Broadway. It was, as always, brightly lit, but the gyro places and electronics shops and restaurants, their outside tables empty and chained in the cold dusk, looked shabbier than he remembered. Some stores were not just shielded by grills but boarded up. He kept walking east, toward Central Park.

The dealer huddled in a doorway. He wasn't more than fifteen. Sugarcane was a low-cost, low-profit drug, not worth the gangs' time, let alone that of organized crime. The kid was a freelance amateur, and God knows what the sugarcane was cut with.

Noah bought it anyway. In the nearest Greek place he bought a gyro as the price of the key to the bathroom and locked himself in. The room was windowless but surprisingly clean. The testing set that Noah carried everywhere showed him the unexpected: the sugarcane was cut only with actual sugar, and only by about 50 percent.

"Thank you, Lord," he said to the toilet, snorted twice his usual dose, and went back to his table to eat the cooling gyro and wait.

The drug took him quickly, as it always did. First came a smooth feeling, as if the synapses of his brain were filling with rich, thick cream. Then: One moment he was Noah Jenner, misfit, and the next he wasn't. He felt like a prosperous small businessman of some type, a shop owner maybe, financially secure and blissfully uncomplicated. A contented, centered person who never questioned who he was or where he was going, who fit in wherever he happened to be. The sort of man who could eat his gyro and gaze out the window without a confusing thought in his head.

Which he did, munching away, the juicy meat and mild spices satisfying in his mouth, for a quiet half hour.

Except—something was happening on the street.

A group of people streamed down Broadway. A parade. No, a mob. They carried torches, of all things, and something larger, held high . . . Now Noah could hear shouting. The thing carried high was an effigy made of straw and rags, looking like the alien in a hundred bad movies: big blank head, huge eyes, spindly pale green body. It stood in a small metal tub atop a board. Someone touched a torch to the straw and set the effigy on fire.

Why? As far as Noah could see, the aliens weren't bothering anybody. They were even good for business. It was just an excuse for people floundering in a bad economy to vent their anger—

Were these his thoughts? Noah's? Who was he now?

Police sirens screamed farther down the street. Cops appeared on foot, in riot gear. A public-address system blared, its words audible even through the shopwindow: "Disperse now! Open flame is not allowed on the streets! You do not have a parade permit! Disperse now!"

Someone threw something heavy, and the other window of the gyro place shattered.

Glass rained down on the empty tables in that corner. Noah jerked upright and raced to the back of the tiny restaurant, away from the windows. The cook was shouting in Greek. People left the parade, or joined it from side streets, and began to hurl rocks and bottles at the police. The cops retreated to the walls and doorways across Broadway and took out grenades of tear gas.

On the sidewalk outside, a small child stumbled by, crying and bleeding and terrified.

The person who Noah was now didn't think, didn't hesitate. He ran out into the street, grabbed the child, and ran back into the restaurant. He wasn't quite fast enough to escape the spreading gas. His nose and eyes shrieked in agony, even as he held his breath and thrust the child's head under his jacket.

Into the tiny kitchen, following the fleeing cook and waiter, and out the back door to an alley of overflowing garbage cans. Noah kept running, even though his agonized vision was blurring. Store owners had all locked their doors. But he had outrun the tear gas, and now a woman was leaning out of the window of her second-floor apartment, craning her neck to see through brick walls to the action two streets away. Gunfire sounded. Over its echo off the steel and stone canyons, Noah shouted up, "A child got gassed! Please—throw down a bottle of water!"

She nodded and disappeared. To his surprise, she actually appeared on the street to help a stranger, carrying a water bottle and towel. "I'm a nurse, let me have him . . . Aahh." Expertly she bathed the child's eyes, and then Noah's, just as if a battle wasn't going on within hearing, if not within sight.

"Thank you," Noah gasped. "It was . . ." He stopped.

Something was happening in his head, and it wasn't due to the sugarcane. He felt an immediate and powerful kinship with this woman. How was that possible? He'd never seen her before. Nor was the attraction romantic—she was in late middle age, with graying hair and a drooping belly. But when she smiled at him and said, "You don't need the ER," something turned over in Noah's heart. What the fuck?

It must be the sugarcane.

But the feeling didn't have the creamy, slightly unreal feel of sugarcane.

She was still talking. "You probably couldn't get into any ER anyway, they'll all be jammed. I know—I was an ER nurse. But this kid'll be fine. He got almost none of the gas. Just take him home and calm him down."

"Who . . . who are you?"

"It doesn't matter." And she was gone, backing into the vestibule of her apartment building, the door locking automatically behind her. Restoring the anonymity of New York.

Whatever sense of weird recognition and bonding Noah had felt with her, it obviously had not been mutual. He tried to shake off the feeling and concentrate on the kid, who was wailing like a hurricane. The effortless competence bestowed by the sugarcane was slipping away. Noah knew nothing about children. He made a few ineffective soothing noises and picked up the child, who kicked him.

More police sirens in the distance. Eventually he found a precinct station, staffed only by a scared-looking civilian desk clerk; probably everyone else was at the riot. Noah left the kid there. Somebody would be looking for him. Noah walked back to West End Avenue, crossed it, and headed northeast to Elizabeth's apartment. His eyes still stung, but not too badly. He had escaped the worst of the gas cloud.

Elizabeth answered the door. "Where the hell did you go? Damn it, Noah, Mom's arriving any minute! She texted!"

"Well, I'm here now, right?"

"Yes, you're here now, but of all the shit-brained times to go out for a stroll! How did you tear your jacket?"

"Dunno." Neither his sister nor his brother seemed aware that eight blocks away there had been—maybe still was—an anti-alien riot going on. Noah didn't feel like informing them.

Ryan held his phone. "She's here. She texted. I'll go down."

Elizabeth said, "Ryan, she can probably pay a cab fare and take an elevator by herself."

Ryan went anyway. He had always been their mother's favorite, Noah thought wearily. Except around Elizabeth, Ryan was affable, smooth, easy to get along with. His wife was charming, in an exaggeratedly feminine sort of way. They were going to give Marianne a grandchild.

It was an effort to focus on his family. His mind kept going back to that odd, unprecedented feeling of kinship with a person he had never seen before and probably had nothing whatsoever in common with. What was that all about?

"Elizabeth," his mother said. "And Noah! I'm so glad you're here. I've got . . . I've got a lot to tell you all. I—"

And his mother, who was always equal to anything, abruptly turned pale and fainted.

CHAPTER 4

S minus 10.5 months

Stupid, stupid—she never passed out! To the three faces clustered above her like balloons on sticks Marianne said irritably, "It's nothing—just hypoglycemia. I haven't eaten since this morning. Elizabeth, if you have some juice or something . . ."

Juice was produced, crackers, slightly moldy cheese.

Marianne ate. Ryan said, "I didn't know you were hypoglycemic, Mom."

"I'm fine. Just not all that young anymore." She put down her glass and regarded her three children.

Elizabeth, scowling, looked so much like Kyle—was that why Marianne and Elizabeth had never gotten along? Her gorgeous alcoholic husband, the mistake of Marianne's young life, had been dead for fifteen years. Yet here he was again, ready to poke holes in anything Marianne said.

Ryan, plain next to his beautiful sister but so much easier to love. Quiet, secretive—it was hard to know what Ryan was thinking, except about ecology, but easy to feel how much he cared. Everybody loved Ryan, except Elizabeth.

And Noah, problem child, she and Kyle's last-ditch effort to save their doomed marriage. Noah was drifting and, she knew without being able to help, profoundly unhappy.

Were all three of them, and everybody else on the planet, going to die, unless humans and Denebs together could prevent it?

She hadn't fainted from hypoglycemia, which she didn't have. She had fainted from sheer delayed, maternal terror at the idea that her children might all perish. But she was not going to say that to her kids. And the fainting wasn't going to happen again.

"I need to talk to you," she said, unnecessarily. But how to begin something like this? "I've been talking to the aliens. In the *Embassy.*"

"We know, Evan told us," Noah said, at the same moment that Elizabeth, quicker, said sharply, *"Inside?"*

"Yes. The Deneb ambassador requested me."

"Requested you? Why?"

"Because of the paper I just published. The aliens—did any of you read the copies of my paper I e-mailed you?"

"I did," Ryan said. Elizabeth and Noah said nothing. Well, Ryan was the scientist.

"It was about tracing human genetic diversity through mitochondrial evolution. Thirty mitochondrial haplogroups had been discovered. I found the thirty-first. That wouldn't really be a big deal, except that—in a few days this will be common knowledge but you must keep it among ourselves until the ambassador announces—the aliens belong to the thirty-first group, L7. They're human."

Silence.

"Didn't you understand what I just—"

Elizabeth and Ryan erupted with questions, expressions of disbelief, arm waving. Only Noah sat quietly, clearly puzzled. Marianne explained what Ambassador Smith—impossible name!—had told her. When she got to the part about the race that had taken humans to "World," leaving titanium tablets engraved with astronomical diagrams, Elizabeth exploded. "Come on, Mom, this fandango makes no sense!"

"The Denebs are *here,*" Marianne pointed out. "They did find us. And the Denebs are going to give tissue samples. Under our strict human supervision. They're expanding the *Embassy* and allowing in humans. Lots of humans, to examine their biology and to work with our scientists."

"Work on what?" Ryan said gently. "Mom, this can't be good. They're an invasive species."

"Didn't you hear a word I said?" Marianne said. God, if Ryan, the scientist, could not accept truth, how would humanity as a whole? "They're not 'invasive,' or at least not if our testing confirms the ambassador's story. They're native to Earth."

"An invasive species is native to Earth. It's just not in the ecological niche it evolved for."

Elizabeth said, "Ryan, if you bring up purple loosestrife, I swear I'm going to clip you one. Mom, did anybody think to ask this ambassador the basic question of why they're here in the first place?"

"Don't talk to me like I'm an idiot. Of course we did. There's a—" She stopped and bit her lip, knowing how this would sound. "You all know what panspermia is?"

"Yes," said Elizabeth.

"Of course." Ryan.

"No." Noah.

"It's the idea that original life in the galaxy"—whatever *that* actually was, all the textbooks would now need to be rewritten—"came from drifting clouds of organic molecules. We know that such molecules exist inside meteors and comets and that they can, under some circumstances, survive entry into atmospheres. Some scientists, like Fred Hoyle and Stephen Hawking, have even endorsed the idea that new biomolecules are still being carried down to Earth. The Denebs say that there is a huge, drifting cloud of spores—well, they're technically not spores, but I'll come to that in a minute—drifting toward Earth. Or, rather, we're speeding toward it, since the solar system rotates around the center of the galaxy and the entire galaxy moves through space relative to the cosmic microwave background. Anyway, ten months from now, Earth and this spore cloud will meet. And the spores are deadly to humans."

Elizabeth said skeptically, "And they know this *how*?"

"Because two of their colony planets lay in the path of the cloud and were already exposed. Both populations were completely destroyed. The Denebs have recordings. Then they sent unmanned probes to capture samples, which they brought with them. They say the samples are a virus, or something like a virus, but encapsulated in a coating that isn't like anything viruses can usually make. Together, aliens and humans are going to find a vaccine or a cure."

More silence. Then all three of her children spoke together, but in such different tones that they might have been discussing entirely different topics.

Ryan: "In ten months? A vaccine or cure for an unknown pathogen in ten months? It took the CDC six months just to fully identify the bacterium in Legionnaires' disease!"

Elizabeth: "If they're so technologically superior, they don't need us to develop any sort of 'cure'!"

Noah: "What do the spores do to people?"

Marianne answered Noah first, because his question was the simplest. "They act like viruses, taking over cellular machinery to repro duce. They invade the lungs and multiply and then . . . then victims can't breathe. It only takes a few days." A terrible, painful death. A sudden horror came into her mind: her three children gasping for breath as their lungs were swamped with fluid, until they literally drowned. All of them.

"Mom," Ryan said gently, "are you all right? Elizabeth, do you have any wine or anything?"

"No," said Elizabeth, who didn't drink. Marianne suddenly, ridiculously, clung to that fact, as if it could right the world: her two-fisted cop daughter, whose martial arts training enabled her to take down a two-hundred-fifty-pound attacker, had a Victorian lady's fastidiousness about alcohol. Stereotypes didn't hold. The world was more complicated than that. The unexpected existed—a Border Patrol section chief did not drink!—and therefore an unexpected solution could be found to this unexpected problem. Yes.

She wasn't making sense, and knew it, and didn't care. Right now, she needed hope more than sense. The Denebs, with technology an order of magnitude beyond humans, couldn't deal with the spore cloud, but Elizabeth didn't drink and therefore, together Marianne and Smith and—throw in the president and WHO and the CDC and USAMRIID, why not?—could defeat mindless space-floating dormant viruses.

Noah said curiously, "What are you smiling about, Mom?"

"Nothing." She could never explain.

Elizabeth blurted, "So even if all this shit is true, what the fuck makes the Denebs think that *we* can help them?"

Elizabeth didn't drink like a cop, but she swore like one. Marianne said, "They don't know that we can. But their biological sciences aren't much more advanced than ours, unlike their physical sciences. And the spore cloud hits Earth next September. The Denebs have twenty-five years."

"Do you believe that their biological sciences aren't as advanced as their physics and engineering?"

"I have no reason to disbelieve it."

"If it's true, then we're their lab rats! They'll test whatever they come up with on us, and then they'll sit back in orbit or somewhere to see if it works before taking it home to their own planet!"

"That's one way to think of it," Marianne said, knowing that this was exactly how a large part of the media would think of it. "Or you could think of it as a rescue mission. They're trying to help us while there's time, if not much time."

Ryan said, "Why do they want you? You're not a virologist."

"I don't know," Marianne said.

Elizabeth erupted once more, leaping up to pace around the room and punch at the air. "I don't believe it. Not any of it, including the so-called cloud. There are things they aren't telling us. But you, Mom—you just swallow whole anything they say! You're unbeliev-able!"

Before Marianne could answer, Noah said, "I believe you, Mom," and gave her his absolutely enchanting smile. He had never really become aware of the power of that smile. It conferred acceptance, forgiveness, trust, the sweet sadness of fading sunlight. "All of us believe everything you said.

"We just don't want to."

Noah was right, Marianne thought. Ryan was right. Elizabeth was wrong.

The spore cloud existed. Although technically not spores, which was the word the Deneb translator gave out; the word stuck among astronomers because it was a term they already knew. As soon as the Denebs gave the cloud's coordinates, composition, and speed to the UN, astronomers around the globe found it through spectral analysis and the dimming of stars behind it. Actually, they had known of its existence all along but had assumed it was just another dust cloud too small and too cool to be incubating stars. Its trajectory would bring it in contact with Earth when the Denebs said, in approximately ten months.

Noah was right in saying that people did not want to believe this. The media erupted into three factions. The most radical declared the "spore cloud" to be just harmless dust and the Denebs plotting, in conspiracy with the UN and possibly several governments, to take over Earth for various evil and sometimes inventive purposes. The second faction believed that the spore threat might be real but that, echoing Elizabeth, humanity would become "lab rats" in alien experiments to find some sort of solution, without benefit to Earth. The third group, the most scientifically literate, focused on a more immediate issue: They did not want the spore samples brought to Earth for research, calling them the real danger.

Marianne suspected the samples were already here. NASA had never detected shuttles or other craft going between the ship in orbit around the moon and the *Embassy*. Whatever the aliens wanted here, probably already was.

Teams of scientists descended on New York. Data was presented to the UN, the only body that Smith would deal with directly. Everyone kept saying that time was of the essence. Marianne, prevented from resuming teaching duties by the insistent reporters clinging to her like lint, stayed in Elizabeth's apartment and waited. Smith had given her a private communication device, which no one except the UN Special Mission knew about. Sometimes as she watched TV or cleaned Elizabeth's messy apartment, Marianne pondered this: An alien had given her his phone number and asked her to wait. It was almost like dating again.

Time is of the essence! Time is of the essence! A few weeks went by in negotiations she knew nothing of. Marianne reflected on the word "essence." Elizabeth worked incredible hours; the Border Patrol had been called in to help keep "undesirables" away from the harbor, assisting the Coast Guard, INS, NYPD, and whomever else the city deemed pertinent. Noah had left again and did not call.

Evan was with her at the apartment when the Deneb communication device rang. "What's that?" he said offhandedly, wiping his mouth. He had driven down from Tannersville, bringing department gossip and bags of sushi. The kitchen table was littered with tuna tataki, cucumber wraps, and hotategai.

Marianne said, "It's a phone call from the Deneb ambassador."

Evan stopped wiping and, paper napkin suspended, stared at her.

She put the tiny device on the table, as instructed, and spoke the code word. A mechanical voice said, "Dr. Marianne Jenner?"

"Yes."

"This is Ambassador Smith. We have reached an agreement with your UN to proceed, and will be expanding our facilities immediately. I would like you to head one part of the research."

"Ambassador, I am not an epidemiologist, not an immunologist, not a physician. There are many others who—"

"Yes. We don't want you to work on pathogens or with patients. We want you to identify human volunteers who belong to the haplogroup you discovered, L7."

Something icy slid along Marianne's spine. "Why? There hasn't been very much genetic drift between our . . . ah . . . groups of humans in just a hundred and fifty thousand years. And mitochondrial differentiation should play no part in—"

"This is unconnected with the spores."

"What is it connected with?" *Eugenics, master race, Nazis . . .*

"This is purely a family matter."

Marianne glanced at Evan, who was writing furiously on the white paper bag that sushi had come in: *GO! ACCEPT! ARE YOU DAFT? CHANCE OF A LIFETIME!*

She said, "A family matter?"

"Yes. Family matters to us very much. Our whole society is organized around ancestral loyalty."

To Marianne's knowledge, this was the first time the ambassador had ever said anything, to anyone, about how Deneb society was organized. Evan, who'd been holding the paper bag six inches from her face, snatched it back and wrote *CHANCE OF SIX THOUSAND LIFETIMES!*

The number of generations since Mitochondrial Eve.

Smith continued, "I would like you to put together a small team of three or four people. Lab facilities will be provided, and volunteers will provide tissue samples. The UN has been very helpful. Please assemble your team on Tuesday at your current location and someone will come to escort you. Do you accept this post?"

"Tuesday? That's only—"

"Do you accept this post?"

"I . . . yes."

"Good. Good-bye."

Evan said, "Marianne—"

"Yes, of course, you're part of the 'team.' God, none of this real."

"Thank you, thank you!"

"Don't burble, Evan. We need two lab techs. How can they have facilities ready by Tuesday? It isn't possible."

"Or so we think," Evan said.

It hadn't been possible for Noah to stay in his sister's apartment. His mother had had the TV on nonstop, every last news show, no matter how demented, that discussed the aliens or their science. Elizabeth burst in and out again, perpetually angry at everything she didn't like in the world, which included the Denebs. The two women argued at the top of their lungs, which didn't seem to bother either of them at anything but an intellectual level, but which left Noah unable to eat anything without nausea or sleep without nightmares or walk around without knots in his guts.

He found a room in a cheap boardinghouse and a job washing dishes, paid under the counter, in a taco place. Even though the tacos came filmed with grease, he could digest better here than at Elizabeth's, and anyway he didn't eat much. His wages went to sugarcane.

He became in turn an observant child, a tough loner, a pensive outsider, a friendly panhandler. Sugarcane made him, variously, mute or extroverted or gloomy or awed or confident. But none of it was as satisfying as it once had been. Even when he was someone else, he was still aware of being Noah. That had not happened before. The door out of himself stayed ajar. Increasing the dose didn't help.

Two weeks after he'd left Elizabeth's, he strolled on his afternoon off down to Battery Park. The late October afternoon was unseasonably warm, lightly overcast, filled with autumn leaves and chrysanthemums and balloon sellers. Tourists strolled the park, sitting on the benches lining the promenade, feeding the pigeons, touring Castle Clinton. Noah stood for a long time leaning on the railing above the harbor, and so witnessed the miracle.

"It's happening! Now!" someone shouted.

What was happening? Noah didn't know, but evidently someone did because people came running from all directions. Noah would have been jostled and squeezed from his place at the railing if he hadn't gripped it with both hands. People stood on the benches; teenagers shimmied up the lampposts. Figures appeared on top of the castle. A man began frantically selling telescopes and binoculars evidently hoarded for this occasion. Noah bought a pair with money he'd been going to use for sugarcane.

"Move that damn car!" someone screamed as a Ford honked its way through the crowd, into what was supposed to be a pedestrian area. Shouts, cries, more people rushing from cars to the railings.

Far out in the harbor, the Deneb *Embassy,* its energy shield dull under the cloudy sky, began to glow. Through his binoculars Noah saw the many-faceted dome shudder—not just shake but shudder in a rippling wave, as if alive. *Was* it alive? Did his mother know?

"Aaaahhhhh," the crowd went.

The energy shield began to spread. Either it had thinned or changed composition, because for a long moment—maybe ninety seconds—Noah could almost see through it. A suggestion of floor, walls, machinery . . . then opaque again. But the "floor" was growing, reaching out to cover more territory, sprouting tentacles of material and energy.

Someone on the bridge screamed, "They're taking over!"

All at once, signs were hauled out, people leaped onto the roofs of cars that should not have been in the Park, chanting began. But not much chanting or many people. Most crowded the railings, peering out to sea.

In ten minutes, the *Embassy* grew and grew laterally, silently spreading across the calm water like a speeded-up version of an algae bloom. When it hardened again—that's how it looked to Noah, like molten glass hardening as it cooled—the structure was six times its previous size. The tentacles had become docks, a huge one toward the city and several smaller ones to one side. By now even the chanters had fallen silent, absorbed in the hushed, awesome, monstrous feat of unimaginable construction. When it was finished, no one spoke.

Then an outraged voice demanded, "Did those bastards get a city permit for that?"

It broke the silence. Chanting, argument, exclaiming, pushing all resumed. A few motorists gunned their engines, futilely, since it was impossible to move vehicles. The first of the motorcycle cops arrived: NYPD, then Border Patrol, then chaos.

Noah slipped deftly through the mess, back toward the streets north of the Battery. He had to be at work in an hour. The *Embassy* had nothing to do with him.

A spore cloud doesn't look like anything at all.

A darker patch in dark space, or the slightest of veils barely dimming starlight shining behind it. Earth's astronomers could not accurately say how large it was, or how deep. They relied on Deneb measurements, except for the one fact that mattered most, which human satellites in deep space and human ingenuity at a hundred observatories was able to verify: The cloud was coming. The path of its closest edge would intersect Earth's path through space at the time the Denebs had said: early September.

Marianne knew that almost immediately following the UN announcement, madness and stupidity raged across the planet. Shelters were dug or sold or built, none of which would be effective. If air could get in, so could spores. In Kentucky, some company began equipping deep caves with air circulation, food for a year, and high-priced sleeping berths: reverting to Paleolithic caveman. She paid no more attention to this entrepreneurial survivalism than to the televised protests, destructive mobs, peaceful marches, or lurid artist depictions of the cloud and its presumed effects. She had a job to do.

On Tuesday she, Evan, and two lab assistants were taken to the submarine bay at UN Special Mission Headquarters. In the sub, Max and Gina huddled in front of the porthole, or maybe it was a porthole-like viewscreen, watching underwater fish. Maybe fish were what calmed them. Although they probably didn't need calming, Marianne, who had worked with both before, had chosen them as much for their even temperaments as for their competence. Government authorities had vetted Max and Gina for, presumably, both crime-free backgrounds and pro-alien attitudes. Max, only twenty-nine, was the computer whiz. Gina, in her midthirties and the despair of her Italian mother because Gina hadn't yet married, made the fewest errors Marianne had ever seen in sample preparation, amplification, and sequencing.

Evan said to Marianne, "Children all sorted out?"

"Never. Elizabeth won't leave New York, of course." (*"Leave? Don't you realize I have a job to do, protecting citizens from your aliens?"* Somehow they had become Marianne's aliens. And Elizabeth still distrusted them.) "Ryan took Connie to her parents' place in Vermont and he went back to his purple loosestrife in Canada."

"And Noah?" Evan said gently. He knew all about Noah; why, Marianne wondered yet again, did she confide in this twenty-eight-year-old gay man as if he were her age, and not Noah's? Never mind; she needed Evan.

She shook her head. Noah had again disappeared.

"He'll be fine, then, Marianne. He always is."

"I know."

"Look, we're docking."

They disembarked from the sub to the underside of the *Embassy*. Whatever the structure's new docks topside were for, it wasn't transfer of medical personnel. Evan said admiringly, "Shipping above us hasn't even been disrupted. Dead easy."

"Oh, those considerate aliens," Marianne murmured, too low for the sub captain, still in full-dress uniform, to hear. Her and Evan's usual semi-sarcastic banter helped to steady her: the real toad in the hallucinatory garden.

The chamber beyond the airlock had not changed, although this time they were met by a different alien. Female, she wore the same faint shimmer of energy-shield protection over her plain tunic and pants. Tall, copper-skinned, with those preternaturally huge dark eyes, she looked about thirty, but how could you tell? Did the Denebs have plastic surgery? Why not? They had everything else.

Except a cure for spore disease.

The Deneb introduced herself ("Scientist Jones"), went through the so-glad-you're-here speech coming disconcertingly from the ceiling. She conducted them to the lab, then left immediately. Plastic surgery or no, Marianne was grateful for alien technology when she saw her lab. Nothing in it was unfamiliar, but all of it was state-of-the-art. Did they create it as they had created the *Embassy,* or order it wholesale? Must be the latter—the state-of-the-art gene sequencer still bore the label ILLUMINA. The equipment must have been ordered, shipped, paid for (with what?) either over the previous months of negotiation, or as the world's fastest rush shipping.

Beside it sat a rack of vials with blood samples, all neatly labeled.

Max immediately went to the computer and turned it on. "No Internet," he said, disappointed. "Just a LAN, and . . . wow, this is heavily shielded."

"You realize," Marianne said, "that this is a minor part of the science going on aboard the *Embassy.* All we do is process mitochondrial DNA to identify L7 haplogroup members. We're a backwater on the larger map."

"Hey, we're *here,*" Max said. He grinned at her. "Too bad, though, about no *World of Warcraft.* This thing has no games at all. What do I do in my spare time?"

"Work," Marianne said, just as the door opened and two people entered. Marianne recognized one of them, although she had never met him before. Unsmiling, dark-suited, he was security. The woman was harder to place. Middle-aged, wearing jeans and a sweater, her hair held back by a too-girlish headband. But her smile was warm, and it reached her eyes. She held out her hand.

"Dr. Jenner? I'm Lisa Guiterrez, the genetics counselor. I'll be your liaison with the volunteers. We probably won't be seeing each other again, but I wanted to say hello. And you're Dr. Blanford?"

"Yes," Evan said.

Marianne frowned. "Why do we need a genetic counselor? I was told our job is to simply process blood samples to identify members of the L7 haplogroup."

"It is," Lisa said, "and then I take it from there."

"Take *what* from there?"

Lisa studied her. "You know, of course, that the Denebs would like to identify those surviving human members of their own haplogroup. They consider them family. The concept of family is pivotal to them."

Marianne said, "You're not a genetic counselor. You're a xenopsychologist."

"That, too."

"And what happens after the long-lost family members are identified?"

"I tell them that they are long-lost family members." Her smile never wavered.

"And then?"

"And then they get to meet Ambassador Smith."

"And *then*?"

"No more 'then.' The ambassador just wants to meet his six-thousand-times-removed cousins. Exchange family gossip, invent some in-jokes, confer about impossible Uncle Harry."

So she had a sense of humor. Maybe it was a qualification for billing oneself a "xenopsychologist," a profession that until a few months ago had not existed.

"Nice to meet you both," Lisa said, widened her smile another fraction of an inch, and left.

Evan murmured, "My, people come and go so quickly here."

But Marianne was suddenly not in the mood, not even for quoted humor from such an appropriate source as *The Wizard of Oz*. She sent a level gaze at Evan, Max, Gina.

"Okay, team. Let's get to work."

CHAPTER 5

S minus 9.5 months

There were four other scientific teams aboard the *Embassy*, none of which were interested in Marianne's backwater. The other teams consisted of scientists from the World Health Organization, the Centers for Disease Control, the United States Army Medical Research Institute for Infectious Diseases, the Weatherall Institute of Molecular Medicine at Oxford, the Beijing Genomics Institute, Kyushu University, and The Scripps Research Institute, perhaps the top immunology center in the world. Some of the most famous names in the scientific and medical worlds were here, including a dozen Nobel winners. Marianne had no knowledge of, but could easily imagine, the political and scientific competition to get aboard the *Embassy*. The Americans had an edge because the ship sat in New York Harbor and that, too, must have engendered political threats and counterthreats, bargaining and compromise.

The most elite group, and by far the largest, worked on the spores: germinating, sequencing, investigating this virus that could create a worldwide human die-off. They worked in negative-pressure, biosafety-level-four chambers. Previously the United States had had only two BSL4 facilities, at the CDC in Atlanta and at USAMRIID in Maryland. Now there was a third, dazzling in its newness and in the completeness of its equipment. The Spore Team had the impossible task of creating some sort of vaccine, gene therapy, or other method of neutralizing, worldwide, a pathogen not native to Earth, within ten months.

The Biology Team investigated alien tissues and genes. The Denebs gave freely of whatever was asked: blood, epithelial cells, sperm, biopsy samples. "Might even give us a kidney, if we asked nicely enough," Evan said. "We know they have two."

Marianne said, "*You* ask, then."

"Not me. Too frightful to think what they might ask in exchange."

"So far, they've asked nothing."

Almost immediately the Biology Team verified the Denebs as human. Then began the long process of finding and charting the genetic and evolutionary differences between the aliens and Terrans. The first, announced after just a week, was that all of the seventeen aliens in the *Embassy* carried the same percentage as Terrans of Neanderthal genes: from 1 to 4 percent.

"They're us," Evan said.

"Did you doubt it?" Marianne asked.

"No. But more interesting, I think, are the preliminary findings that the Denebs show so much less genetic diversity than we do. That wanker Wilcox must be weeping in his ale."

Patrick Wells Wilcox was the current champion of the Toba Catastrophe Theory, which went in and out of scientific fashion. Seventy thousand years ago the Toba supervolcano in Indonesia had erupted. This had triggered such major environmental change, according to theory proponents, that a "bottleneck event" had occurred, reducing the human population to perhaps ten thousand individuals. The result had been a great reduction in human genetic diversity. Backing for the idea came from geology as well as coalescence evidence of some genes, including mitochondrial, Y chromosome, and nuclear. Unfortunately, there was also evidence that the bottleneck event had never occurred. If the Denebs, removed from Earth well before the supervolcano, showed less diversity than Terrans, then Terran diversity couldn't have been reduced all that much.

Marianne said, "Wilcox shouldn't weep too soon."

"Actually, he never weeps at all. Gray sort of wanker. Holes up in his lab at Cambridge and glowers at the world through medieval arrow slits."

"Dumps boiling oil on dissenting paleontologists," Marianne suggested.

"Actually, Wilcox may not even be human. Possibly an advance scout for the Denebs. Nobody at Cambridge has noticed it so far."

"Or so we think." Marianne smiled. She and Evan never censored their bantering, which helped lower the hushed, pervasive anxiety they shared with everyone else on the *Embassy*. It was an anxious ship.

The third scientific team aboard was much smaller. Physicists, they worked with Scientist Jones on the astronomy of the coming collision with the spore cloud.

The fourth team she never saw at all. Nonetheless, she suspected they were there, monitoring the others, shadowy underground non-scientists unknown even to the huge contingent of visible security.

Marianne looked at the routine work on her lab bench: polymerase chain reaction to amplify DNA samples, sequencing, analyzing data, writing reports on the genetic inheritance of each human volunteer who showed up at the Deneb "collection site" in Manhattan. A lot of people showed up. So far, only two of them belonged to Ambassador Smith's haplogroup. "Evan, we're not really needed, you and I. Gina and Max can handle anything our expensive brains are being asked to do."

Evan said, "Right, then. So let's have a go at exploring. Until we're stopped, anyway."

She stared at him. "Okay. Yes. Let's explore."

Noah emerged from the men's room at the Mexican restaurant. During the midafternoon lull they had no customers except for a pair of men slumped over one table in the back. "Look at this!" the waitress said to him. She and the cook were both huddled over her phone, strange enough since they hated each other. But Cindy's eyes were wide from something other than her usual drugs, and Noah took a look at the screen of the sophisticated phone, mysteriously acquired and gifted by Cindy's current boyfriend before he'd been dragged off to Rikers for assault with intent.

VOLUNTEERS WANTED TO DONATE BLOOD

PAYMENT: $100

HUMAN NURSES TO COLLECT SMALL BLOOD SAMPLES

DENEB EMBASSY PIER, NEW YORK HARBOR

"Demonios del diablo," Miguel muttered. "¡Vampiros!" He crossed himself.

Noah said drily, "I don't think they're going to drink the blood, Miguel." The dryness was false. His heart had begun to thud. People like his mother got to see the *Embassy* up close, but not people like Noah. Did the ad mean that the Denebs were going to take human blood samples on the large dock he had seen form out of nothing?

Cindy had lost interest. "No fucking customers except those two sorry asses in the corner, and they never tip. I shoulda stood in bed."

"Miguel," Noah said, "can I have the afternoon off?"

Noah stood patiently in line at the blood-collection site. If any of the would-be volunteers had hoped to see aliens, they had been disappointed. Noah was not disappointed; after all, the ad on Cindy's phone had said *Human nurses to collect small blood samples*.

He was, however, disappointed that the collection site was not on the large dock jutting out from the *Embassy* under its glittering energy shield. Instead, he waited to enter what had once been a warehouse at the land end of a pier on the Manhattan waterfront. The line, huddled against November drizzle, snaked in loops and oxbows for several blocks, and he was fascinated by the sheer diversity of people. A woman in a fur-lined Burberry raincoat and high, polished boots. A bum in jeans with an indecent tear on the ass. Several giggling teenage girls under flowered umbrellas. An old man in a winter parka. A nerdy-looking boy with an iPad protected by flexible plastic. Two tired-looking middle-aged women. One of those said to the other, "I could pay all that back rent if I get this alien money, and—"

Noah tapped her arm. "Excuse me, ma'am—what 'alien money'?" The hundred-dollar fee for blood donation didn't seem enough to *pay all that back rent.*

She turned. "If they find out you're part of their blood group, you get a share of their fortune. You know, like the Indians with their casino money. If you can prove you're descended from their tribe."

"No, that's not it," the old man in the parka said impatiently. "You get a free energy shield like theirs to protect you when the spore cloud hits. They take care of family."

The bum muttered, "Ain't no spore cloud."

The boy said with earnest contempt, "You're all wrong. This is just—the Denebs are the most significant thing to happen to Earth, ever! Don't you get it? We're not alone in the universe!"

The bum laughed.

Eventually Noah reached Building A. Made of concrete and steel, the building's walls were discolored, its high-set windows grimy. Only the security machines looked new, and they made high-tech examinations of Noah's person inside and out. His wallet, cell, jacket, and even shoes were left in a locker before he shuffled in paper slippers along the enclosed corridor to Building B, farther out on the pier. Someone was very worried about terrorism.

"Please fill out this form," said a pretty, grim-faced young woman. Not a nurse: security. She looked like a faded version of his sister, bleached of Elizabeth's angry command. Noah filled out the form, gave his small vial of blood, and filed back to Building A. He felt flooded with anticlimactic letdown. When he had reclaimed his belongings, a guard handed him a hundred dollars and a small round object the size and feel of a quarter.

"Keep this with you," a guard said. "It's a one-use, one-way communication device. In the unlikely event that it rings, press the center. That means that we'd like to see you again."

"If you do, does that mean I'm in the alien's haplogroup?"

He didn't seem to know the word. "If it rings, press the center."

"How many people have had their devices ring?"

The guard's face changed, and Noah glimpsed the person behind the job. He shrugged. "I never heard of even one."

"Is it—"

"Move along, please." The job mask was back.

Noah put on his shoes, balancing first on one foot and then on the other to avoid touching the grimy floor. It was like being in an airport. He started for the door.

"Noah!" Elizabeth sailed toward him across a sea of stained concrete. "What the hell are you doing here?"

"Hi, Lizzie. Is this part of the New York State border?"

"I'm on special assignment."

God, she must hate that. Her scowl threatened to create permanent furrows in her tanned skin. But Elizabeth always obeyed the chain of command.

"Noah, how can you—"

A bomb went off.

A white light blinded Noah. His hearing went dead, killed by the sheer onslaught of sound. His legs wobbled as his stomach lurched. Then Elizabeth knocked him to the ground and hurled herself on top of him. A few seconds later she was up and running and Noah could hear her again: "Fucking flashbang!"

He stumbled to his feet, his eyes still painful from the light. People screamed and a few writhed on the floor near a pile of clothes that had ignited. Black smoke billowed from the clothing, setting the closest people to coughing, but no one seemed dead. Guards leaped at a young man shouting something lost in the din.

Noah picked up his shoes and slipped outside, where sirens screamed, honing in from nearby streets. The salt-tanged breeze touched him like a benediction.

A flashbang. You could buy a twelve-pack of them on the Internet for fifty bucks, although those weren't supposed to ignite fires. Whatever that protester had hoped to accomplish, it was ineffective. Just like this whole dumb blood-donation expedition.

But he had a hundred dollars he hadn't had this morning, which would buy a few good hits of sugarcane. And in his pocket, his fingers closed involuntarily on the circular alien coin.

Marianne was surprised at how few areas of the *Embassy* were restricted.

The BSL4 areas, of course. The aliens' personal quarters, not very far from the BSL 4 labs. But her and Evan's badges let them roam pretty much everywhere else. Humans rushed passed them on their own errands, some nodding in greeting but others too preoccupied to even notice they were there.

"Of course there are doors we don't even see," Evan said. "Weird alien cameras we don't see. Denebs we don't see. They know where we are, where everyone is, every minute. Dead easy."

The interior of the *Embassy* was a strange mixture of materials and styles. Many corridors were exactly what you'd expect in a scientific research facility: unadorned, clean, lined with doors. The walls seemed to be made of something that was a cross between metal and plastic, and did not dent. Walls in the personal quarters and lounges, on the other hand, were often made of something that reminded her of Japanese rice paper, but soundproof. She had the feeling that she could have put her fist through them, but when she actually tried this, the wall only gave slightly, like a very tough piece of plastic. Some of these walls could be slid open, to change the size or shapes of rooms. Still other walls were actually giant screens that played constantly shifting patterns of subtle color. Finally, there were odd small lounges that seemed to have been furnished from upscale mail-order catalogs by someone who thought anything Terran must go with anything else: earth-tone sisal carpeting with a Victorian camelback sofa, Picasso prints with low Moroccan tables inlaid with silver and copper, a Navajo blanket hung on the wall above Japanese zabutons.

Marianne was tired. They'd come to one such sitting area outside the main mess, and she sank into an English club chair beside a small table of swooping purple glass. "Evan—do you really believe we are all going to die a year from now?"

"No." He sat in an adjoining chair, appreciatively patting its wide and upholstered arms. "But only because my mind refuses to entertain the thought of my own death in any meaningful way. Intellectually, though, yes. Or rather, nearly all of us will die."

"A vaccine to save the rest?"

"No. There is simply not enough time to get all the necessary bits and pieces sorted out. But the Denebs will save some Terrans."

"How?"

"Take a selected few back with them to that big ship in the sky."

Immediately she felt stupid that she hadn't thought of this before. Stupidity gave way to the queasy, jumpy feeling of desperate hope. "Take us *Embassy* personnel? To continue joint work on the spores?" Her children—somehow she would have to find a way to include Elizabeth, Noah, and Ryan and Connie. But everyone here had family—

"No," Evan said. "Too many of us. My guess is just the Terran members of their haplogroup. Why else bother to identify them? And everything I've heard reinforces their emphasis on blood relationships."

"Heard from whom? We're in the lab sixteen hours a day—"

"I don't need much sleep. Not like you, Marianne. I talk to the

Biology Team, who talk more than anybody else to the aliens. Also I chat with Lisa Guiterrez, the genetics counselor."

"And the Denebs told somebody they're taking their haplogroup members with them before the spore cloud hits?"

"No, of course not. When do the Denebs tell Terrans anything directly? It's all smiling evasion, heartfelt reassurances. They're like Filipino houseboys."

Startled, Marianne gazed at him. The vaguely racist reference was uncharacteristic of Evan, and had been said with some bitterness. She realized all over again how little Evan gave away about his past. When had he lived in the Philippines? What had happened between him and some apparently not forgiven houseboy? A former lover? Evan's sexual orientation was also something they never discussed, although of course she was aware of it. From his grim face, he wasn't going to discuss it now, either.

She said, "I'm going to ask Smith what the Denebs intend."

Evan's smooth grin had returned. "Good luck. The UN can't get information from him, the project's chief scientists can't get information from him, and you and I never see him. Just minor roadblocks to your plan."

"We really are lab rats," she said. And then, abruptly, "Let's go. We need to get back to work."

Evan said slowly, "I've been thinking about something."

"What?"

"The origin of viruses. How they didn't evolve from a single entity and don't have a common ancestor. About the theory that their individual origins were pieces of DNA or RNA that broke off from cells and learned to spread to other cells."

Marianne frowned. "I don't see how that's relevant."

"I don't either, actually."

"Then—"

"I don't know," Evan said. And again, "I just don't know."

———

Noah was somebody else.

He'd spent his blood-for-the-Denebs money on sugarcane, and it turned out to be one of the really good transformations. He was a nameless soldier from a nameless army: brave and commanding and sure of himself. Underneath he knew it was an illusion (but he never used to know that!). However, it didn't matter. He stood on a big rock at the south end of Central Park, rain and discarded plastic bags blowing around him, and felt completely, if temporarily, happy. He was on top of the world, or at least seven feet above it, and nothing seemed impossible.

The alien token in his pocket began to chime, a strange syncopated rhythm, atonal as no iPhone ever sounded. Without a second's hesitation—he could face anything!—Noah pulled it from his pocket and pressed its center.

A woman's voice said, "Noah Richard Jenner?"

"Yes, ma'am!"

"This is Dr. Lisa Guiterrez at the Deneb *Embassy*. We would like to see you, please. Can you come as soon as possible to the UN Special Mission Headquarters, on the *Embassy* pier?"

Noah drew a deep breath. Then full realization crashed around him, loud and blinding as last week's flashbang. *Oh my God*—why hadn't he seen it before? Maybe because he hadn't been a warrior before. His mother had—*son of a bitch . . .*

"Noah?"

He said, "I'll be there."

The submarine surfaced in an undersea chamber. A middle-aged woman in jeans and blazer, presumably Dr. Guiterrez, awaited Noah in the featureless room. He didn't much notice woman or room. Striding across the gangway, he said, "I want to see my mother. Now. She's Dr. Marianne Jenner, working here someplace."

Dr. Guiterrez didn't react as if this were news, or strange. She said, "You seem agitated." Hers was the human voice Noah had heard coming from the alien token.

"I am agitated! Where is my mother?"

"She's here. But first, someone else wants to meet you."

"I demand to see my mother!"

A door in the wall slid open, and a tall man with coppery skin and bare feet stepped through. Noah looked at him, and it happened again.

Shock, bewilderment, totally unjustified recognition—he knew this man, just as he had known the nurse who washed tear gas from his and a child's eyes during the West Side demonstration. Yet he'd never seen him before, and he was an *alien*. But the sense of kinship was powerful, disorienting, ridiculous.

"Hello, Noah Jenner," the ceiling said. "I am Ambassador Smith. Welcome to the *Embassy*."

"I—"

"I wanted to welcome you personally, but I cannot visit now. I have a meeting. Lisa will help you get settled here, should you choose to stay with us for a while. She will explain everything. Let me just say—"

Impossible to deny this man's sincerity, he means every incredible word—

"—that I'm very glad you are here."

After the alien left, Noah stood staring at the door through which he'd vanished. "What is it?" Dr. Guiterrez said. "You look a bit shocked."

Noah blurted out, "I know that man!" A second later he realized how dumb that sounded.

She said gently, "Let's go somewhere to talk, Noah. Somewhere less . . . wet."

Water dripped from the sides of the submarine, and some had

sloshed onto the floor. Sailors and officers crossed the gangway, talking quietly. Noah followed Lisa from the sub bay, down a side corridor, and into an office cluttered with charts, printouts, coffee mugs, a laptop—such an ordinary looking place that it only heightened Noah's sense of unreality. She sat in an upholstered chair and motioned him to another. He remained standing.

She said, "I've seen this before, Noah. What you're experiencing, I mean, although usually it isn't as strong as you seem to be feeling it."

"Seen what? And who are you, anyway? I want to talk to my mother!"

She studied him, and Noah had the impression she saw more than he wanted her to. She said, "I'm Dr. Lisa Guiterrez, as Ambassador Smith said. Call me Lisa. I'm a genetics counselor serving as the liaison between the ambassador and those people identified as belonging to his haplotype, L7, the one identified by your mother's research. Before this post, I worked with Dr. Barbara Formisano at Oxford, where I also introduced people who share the same haplotype. Over and over again I've seen a milder version of what you seem to be experiencing now—an unexpected sense of connection between those with an unbroken line of mothers and grandmothers and great-grandmothers back to their haplogroup clan mother. It—"

"That sounds like bullshit!"

"—is important to remember that the connection is purely symbolic. Similar cell metabolisms don't cause shared emotions. But—an important 'but'!—symbols have a powerful effect on the human mind. Which in turn causes emotion."

Noah said, "I had this feeling once before. About a strange woman, and I had no way of knowing if she's my 'haplotype.'"

Lisa's gaze sharpened. She stood. "What woman? Where?"

"I don't know her name. Listen, I want to talk to my mother!"

"Talk to me first. Are you a sugarcane user, Noah?"

"What the hell does that have to do with anything?"

"Habitual use of sugarcane heightens certain imaginative and perceptual pathways in the brain. Ambassador Smith—Well, let's set that aside for a moment. I think I know why you want to see your mother."

Noah said, "Look, I don't want to be ruder than I've already been, but this isn't your business. Anything you want to say to me can wait until I see my mother."

"All right. I can take you to her lab."

It was a long walk. Noah took in very little of what they passed, but then, there was very little to take in. Endless white corridors, endless white doors. When they entered a lab, two people that Noah didn't know looked up curiously. Lisa said, "Dr. Jenner—"

The other woman gestured at a far door. Before she could speak, Noah flung the door open. His mother sat at a small table, hands wrapped around a cup of coffee she wasn't drinking. Her eyes widened.

Noah said, "Mom—why the fuck didn't you ever tell me I was adopted?"

CHAPTER 6

S minus 9.0 months

Evan and Marianne sat in his room, drinking sixteen-year-old single-malt scotch. She seldom drank but knew that Evan often did. Nor had she ever gone before to his quarters in the *Embassy,* which were identical to hers: ten-foot square room with a bed, chest of drawers, small table, and two chairs. She sat on one of the straight-backed, utilitarian chairs while Evan lounged on the bed. Most of the scientists had brought with them a few items from home, but Evan's room was completely impersonal. No art, no framed family photos, no decorative pillows, not even a coffee mug or extra doughnut carried off from the cafeteria.

"You live like a monk," Marianne said, immediately realizing how drunk she must be to say that. She took another sip of scotch.

"Why didn't you ever tell him?" Evan said.

She put down her glass and pulled at the skin on her face. The skin felt distant, as if it belonged to somebody else.

"Oh, Evan, how to answer that? First Noah was too little to understand. Kyle and I adopted him in some sort of stupid effort to save the marriage. I wasn't thinking straight—living with an alcoholic will do that, you know. If there was one stupid B-movie scene of alcoholic and wife that we missed, I don't know what it was. Shouting, pleading, pouring out all the liquor in the house, looking for Kyle in bars at two a.m. . . . anyway. Then Kyle died and I was trying to deal with that and the kids and chasing tenure and there was just too much chaos and fragility to add another big revelation. Then somehow it got too late, because Noah would have asked why he hadn't been told before, and then somehow . . . it all just got away from me."

"And Elizabeth and Ryan never told him?"

"Evidently not. We yell a lot about politics and such but on a personal level, we're a pretty reticent family." She waved her hand vaguely at the room. "Although not as reticent as you."

Evan smiled. "I'm British of a certain class."

"You're an enigma."

"No, that was the Russians. Enigmas wrapped in riddles." But a shadow passed suddenly behind his eyes.

"What do you—"

"Marianne, let me fill you in on the bits and pieces of news that came in while you were with Noah. First, from the Denebs: they're bringing aboard the *Embassy* any members of their 'clan'—that's what the translator is calling the L7 haplogroup—who want to come. But you already know that. Second, the—"

"How many?"

"How many have we identified or how many want to come here?"

"Both." The number of L7 haplotypes had jumped exponentially once they had the first few and could trace family trees through the female line.

"Sixty-three identified, including the three that Gina flew to Georgia to test. Most of the haplogroup may still be in Africa, or it may have largely died out. Ten of those want to visit the *Embassy*." He hesitated. "So far, only Noah wants to stay."

Marianne's hand paused, glass halfway to her mouth. "To *stay*? He didn't tell me that. How do you know?"

"After Noah . . . left you this afternoon, Smith came to the lab with that message."

"I see." She didn't. She had been in her room, pulling herself together after the harrowing interview with her son. Her adopted son. She hadn't been able to tell Noah anything about his parentage because she didn't know anything: sealed adoption records. Was Noah the way he was because of his genes? Or because of the way she'd raised him? Because of his peer group? His astrological sign? Theories went in and out of fashion, and none of them explained personality.

She said, "What is Noah going to *do* here? He's not a scientist, not security, not an administrator . . ." *Not anything.* It hurt her to even think it. Her baby, her lost one.

Evan said, "I have no idea. I imagine he'll either sort himself out or leave. The other news is that the biology team has made progress in matching Terran and Deneb immune system components. There were a lot of graphs and charts and details, but the bottom line is that ours and theirs match pretty well. Remarkably little genetic drift. Different antibodies, of course for different pathogens, and different bodily microorganisms—quite a lot of those, so no chance we'll be touching skin without their wearing their energy shields."

"So cancel the orgy."

Evan laughed. Emboldened by this as much as by the drink, Marianne said, "Are you gay?"

"You know I am, Marianne."

"I wanted to be sure. We've never discussed it. I'm a scientist, after all."

"You're an American. Leave nothing unsaid that can be shouted from rooftops."

Her fuzzy mind had gone back to Noah. "I failed my son, Evan."

"Rubbish. I told you, he'll sort himself out eventually. Just be prepared for the idea that it may take a direction you don't fancy."

Again that shadow in Evan's eyes. She didn't ask; he obviously didn't want to discuss it, and she'd snooped enough. Carefully she rose to leave, but Evan's next words stopped her.

"Also, Elizabeth is coming aboard tomorrow."

"*Elizabeth?* Why?"

"A talk with Smith about shore-side security. Someone tried a second attack at the sample collection site."

"Oh my God. Anybody hurt?"

"No. This time."

"Elizabeth is going to ask the Denebs to give her the energy-shield technology. She's been panting for it for Border Patrol ever since the *Embassy* first landed in the harbor. Evan, that would be a *disaster*. She's so focused on her job that she can't see what will happen if—no, *when*—the street finds its own uses for the tech, and it always does—" Who had said that? Some writer. She couldn't remember.

"Well, don't get your knickers in a twist. Elizabeth can ask, but that doesn't mean Smith will agree."

"But he's so eager to find his 'clan'—God, it's so stupid! That Korean mitochondrial sequence, to take just one example, that turns up regularly in Norwegian fishermen, or that engineer in Minnesota who'd traced his ancestry back three hundred years without being able to account for the Polynesian mitochondrial signature he carries—*nobody* has a cure plan. I mean, a pure clan."

"Nobody on Earth, anyway."

"And even if they did," she barreled on, although all at once her words seemed to have become slippery in her mouth, like raw oysters, "There's no sin . . . sif . . . significant connection between two people with the same mitochondrial DNA than between any other two strangers!"

"Not to us," Evan said.

"I was talking to Harrison about this just dayes . . . I mean yesterday . . ."

"Harrison Rice? The Nobelist? When were you talking to him?"

"I said. Yesday—yester . . . we had caffey. Coffee."

"Marianne, go to bed. You're tipsy, and we have work to do in the morning."

"It's not work that matters to protection against the shore cloud. Spore choud. *Spore cloud*."

"Nonetheless, it's work. Now go."

———

Noah stood in a corner of an *Embassy* conference room, which held eleven people and two aliens. Someone had tried to make the room festive with a red paper tablecloth, flowers, and plates of tiny cupcakes. This had not worked. It was still a utilitarian, corporate-looking conference room, filled with people who otherwise would have no conceivable reason to be together at either a conference or a party. Lisa Guiterrez circulated among them: smiling, chatting, trying to put people at ease. It wasn't working.

Two young women, standing close together for emotional support. A middle-aged man in an Armani suit and Italian leather shoes. An unshaven man, hair in a dirty ponytail, who looked homeless but maybe only because he stood next to Well-Shod Armani. A woman carrying a plastic tote bag with a hole in one corner. And so on and so on. It was the sort of wildly mixed group that made Noah, standing apart with his back to a wall, think of worshippers in an Italian cathedral.

The thought brought him a strained smile. A man nearby, perhaps emboldened by the smile, sidled closer and whispered, "They *will* let us go back to New York, won't they?"

Noah blinked. "Why wouldn't they, if that's what you want?"

"I want them to offer us shields for the spore cloud! To take back with us to the city! Why else would I come here?"

"I don't know."

The man grimaced and moved away. But—why had he even come, if he suspected alien abduction or imprisonment or whatever? And why didn't he feel what Noah did? Every single one of the people in this room had caused in him the same shock of recognition as had Ambassador Smith. Every single one. And apparently no one else had felt it at all.

But the nervous man needn't have worried. When the party and its ceiling-delivered speeches of kinship and the invitation to take a longer visit aboard the *Embassy* were all over, everyone else left. They left looking relieved or still curious or satisfied or uneasy or disappointed (*No energy shield offered! No riches!*), but they all left, Lisa still chattering reassuringly. All except Noah.

Ambassador Smith came over to him. The Deneb said nothing, merely silently waited. He looked as if he were capable of waiting forever.

Noah's hands felt clammy. All those brief, temporary lives on sugarcane, each one shed like a snakeskin when the drug wore off. No, not snakeskin; that wasn't the right analogy. More like breadcrumbs tossed by Hansel and Gretel, starting in hope but vanishing before they could lead anywhere. The man with the dirty ponytail wasn't the only homeless one.

Noah said, "I want to know who and what you are."

The ceiling above Smith said, "Come with me to a genuine celebration."

A circular room, very small. Noah and Smith faced each other. The ceiling said, "This is an airlock. Beyond this space, the environment will be ours, not yours. It is not very different, but you are not used to our microbes and so must wear the energy suit. It filters air, but you may have some trouble breathing at first because the oxygen content of World is like Earth's at an altitude of twelve-thousand feet. If you feel nausea in the airlock, where we will stay for a few minutes, you may go back. The light will seem dim to you, the smells strange, and the gravity less than you are accustomed to by one-tenth. There are no built-in translators beyond this point, and we will speak our own language, so you will not be able to talk to us. Are you sure you wish to come?"

"Yes," Noah said.

"Is there anything you wish to say before you join your birthright clan?"

Noah said, "What is your name?"

Smith smiled. He made a noise that sounded like a trilled version of "meehao," with a click on the end.

Noah imitated it.

Smith said, in trilling English decorated with a click, "Brother mine."

Marianne was not present at the meeting between Elizabeth and Smith, but Elizabeth came to see her afterward. Marianne and Max were bent over the computer, trying to account for what was a mitochondrial anomaly or a sample contamination or a lab error or a program glitch. Or maybe something else entirely. Marianne straightened and said, "Elizabeth! How nice to—"

"You have to talk to him," Elizabeth demanded. "The man's an idiot!"

Marianne glanced at the security officer who had escorted Elizabeth to the lab. He nodded and went outside. Max said, "I'll just . . . uh . . . this can wait." He practically bolted, a male fleeing mother-daughter drama. Evan was getting some much-needed sleep; Gina had gone ashore to Brooklyn to see her parents for the first time in weeks.

"I assume," Marianne said, "you mean Ambassador Smith."

"I do. Does he know what's going on in New York? Does he even care?"

"What's going on in New York?"

Elizabeth instantly turned professional, calmer but no less intense. "We are less than nine months from passing through the spore cloud."

At least, Marianne thought, *she now accepts that much.*

"In the last month alone, the five boroughs have had triple the usual rate of arsons, ten demonstrations with city permit of which three turned violent, twenty-three homicides, and one mass religious suicide at the Church of the Next Step Forward in Tribeca. Wall Street has plunged. The Federal Reserve Bank on Liberty Street was occupied from Tuesday night until Thursday dawn by terrorists. Upstate, the governor's mansion has been attacked, unsuccessfully. The same thing is happening everywhere else. Parts of Beijing have been on fire for a week now. Thirty-six percent of Americans believe the Denebs brought the spore cloud with them, despite what astronomers say. If the ambassador gave us the energy shield, that might help sway the numbers in their favor. Don't you think the president and the UN have said all this to Smith?"

"I have no idea what the president and the UN have said, and neither do you."

"Mom—"

"Elizabeth, do you suppose that if what you just said is true and the ambassador said no to the president, that my intervention would do any good?"

"I don't know. You scientists stick together."

Long ago, Marianne had observed the many different ways people responded to unthinkable catastrophe. Some panicked. Some bargained. Some joked. Some denied. Some blamed. Some destroyed. Some prayed. Some drank. Some thrilled, as if they had secretly awaited such drama their entire lives. Evidently, nothing had changed.

The people aboard the *Embassy* met the unthinkable with work, and then more work. Elizabeth was right that the artificial island had become its own self-contained, self-referential universe, every moment devoted to the search for something, anything, to counteract the effect of the spore cloud on mammalian brains. The Denebs, understanding how good hackers could be, blocked all Internet, television, and radio from the *Embassy.* Outside news came from newspapers or letters, both dying media, brought in the twice-daily mail sack and by the vendors and scientists and diplomats who came and went. Marianne had not paid attention.

She said to her enraged daughter, "The Denebs are not going to give you their energy shield."

"We cannot protect the UN without it. Let alone the rest of the harbor area."

"Then send all the UN ambassadors and translators home, because it's not going to happen. I'm sorry, but it's not."

"You're not sorry. You're on their side."

"It isn't a question of sides. In the wrong hands, those shields—"

"Law enforcement is the right hands!"

"Elizabeth, we've been over and over this. Let's not do it again. You know I have no power to get you an energy shield, and I haven't seen you in so long. Let's not quarrel." Marianne heard the pleading note in her own voice. When, in the long and complicated road of parenthood, had she started courting her daughter's agreement, instead of the other way around?

"Okay, *okay*. How are you, Mom?"

"Overworked and harried. How are you?"

"Overworked and harried." A reluctant half smile. "I can't stay long. How about a tour?"

"Sure. This is my lab."

"I meant of the *Embassy*. I've never been inside before, you know, and your ambassador"—somehow Smith had become Marianne's special burden—"just met with me in a room by the submarine bay. Can I see more? Or are you lab types kept close to your cages?"

The challenge, intended or not, worked. Marianne showed Elizabeth all over the Terran part of the *Embassy*, accompanied by a security officer whom Elizabeth ignored. Her eyes darted everywhere, noted everything. Finally she said, "Where do the Denebs live?"

"Behind these doors here. No one has ever been in there."

"Interesting. It's pretty close to the high-risk labs. And where is Noah?"

Yesterday's bitter scene with Noah, when he'd been so angry because she'd never told him he was adopted, still felt like an open wound. Marianne didn't want to admit to Elizabeth that she didn't know where he'd gone. "He stays in the Terran visitors' quarters," she said, hoping there was such a place.

Elizabeth nodded. "I have to report back. Thanks for the Cook's tour, Mom."

Harrison Rice came around the corner. Marianne said, "Just a minute—here is someone I'd like you to meet." She made the introductions. Harrison was a big, bluff Canadian who looked more like a truck driver who hunted moose than like a Nobel Prize–winner in immunology. In his fifties, still strong as a mountain, he had worked with Ebola, Marburg, Lassa fever, and Nipah, both in the field and in the lab. He exchanged pleasantries in his low-key way, but Elizabeth seemed distracted. Her eyes kept darting around the *Embassy*—looking for aliens? None appeared.

At the submarine bay, Marianne wanted to hug her daughter, but Elizabeth didn't appreciate hugs. Memory stabbed Marianne: a tiny Elizabeth, five years old, lips set as she walked for the first time toward the school bus she must board alone. It all went by so fast, and when the spore cloud hit, not even memory would be left.

She dashed away the stupid tears and headed back to work.

CHAPTER 7

S minus 8.5 months

The auditorium on the *Embassy* had the same thin, rice paper–like walls as some of the other non-lab rooms, but these shifted colors like some of the more substantial walls. Slow, complex, subtle patterns in pale colors that reminded Marianne of dissolving oil slicks. Forty seats in rising semicircles faced a dais, looking exactly like a lecture room at her college. She had an insane desire to regress to undergraduate, pull out a notebook, and doodle in the margin. The seats were filled not with students chewing gum and texting each other, but with some of the planet's most eminent scientists. This was the first all-hands meeting of the scientists aboard. The dais was empty.

Three Denebs entered from a side door.

Marianne had never seen so many of them together at once. Oddly, the effect was to make them seem more alien, as if their minor differences from Terrans—the larger eyes, spindlier limbs, greater height, coppery skin—increased exponentially as their presence increased arithmetically. Was that Ambassador Smith and Scientist Jones? Yes. The third alien, shorter than the other two and somehow softer, said through the translator in the ceiling, "Thank you all for coming. We have three reports today, two from Terran teams and one from World. First, Dr. Manning." All three aliens smiled.

Terrence Manning, head of the Spore Team, took the stage. Marianne had never met him, Nobel Prize–winners usually being as far above her scientific level as the sun above mayflies. A small man, he had exactly three strands of hair left on his head, which he tried to coax into a comb-over. Intelligence shone through his diffident, unusually formal manner. Manning had a deep, authoritative voice, a welcome contrast to the mechanical monotony of the ceiling.

From the aliens' bright-eyed demeanor, Marianne had half expected good news, despite the growing body of data on the ship's LAN. She was wrong.

"We have not," Manning said, "been able to grow the virus in cell cultures. As you all know, some viruses simply will not grow in vitro, and this seems to be one of them. Nor have we been able to infect monkeys—any breed of monkey—with spore disease. We will, of course, keep trying. The better news, however, is that we have succeeded in infecting mice."

Good and bad, Marianne thought. Often, keeping a mouse alive was actually easier than keeping a cell culture growing. But a culture would have given them a more precise measure of the virus's cytopathic effect on animal tissue, and monkeys were genetically closer to humans than were mice. On the other hand, monkeys were notoriously difficult to work with. They bit, they fought, they injured themselves, they traded parasites and diseases, and they died of things they were not supposed to die from.

Manning continued, "We now have a lot of infected mice and our aerosol expert, Dr. Belsky, has made a determination of how much exposure is needed to cause spore disease in mice under laboratory conditions."

A graph flashed onto the wall behind Manning: exposure time plotted versus parts per million of spore. Beside Marianne, Evan's manicured fingers balled into a sudden fist. Infection was fast, and required a shockingly small concentration of virus, even for an airborne pathogen.

"Despite the infected mice," Manning went on, and now the strain in his voice was palpable, "we still have not been able to isolate the virus. It's an elusive little bugger."

No one laughed. Marianne, although this was not her field, knew how difficult it could be to find a virus even after you'd identified the host. They were so tiny; they disappeared into cells or organs; they mutated.

"Basically," Manning said, running his hand over his head and dis-arranging his three hairs, "we know almost nothing about this patho-gen. Not the 'R naught'—for you astronomers, that is the number of cases that one case generates on average over the course of its in-fectious period—nor the incubation period nor the genome nor the morphology. What we do know are the composition of the coating encapsulating the virus, the transmission vector, and the resulting pathology in mice."

Ten minutes of data on the weird, unique coating on the "spores," a term even the scientists, who knew better, now used. Then Dr. Jessica Yu took Manning's place on the dais. Marianne had met her in the cafeteria and felt intimidated. The former head of the Spe-cial Pathogens branch of the National Center for Infectious Diseases in Atlanta, Jessica Yu was diminutive, fifty-ish, and beautiful in a severe, don't-mess-with-me way. Nobody ever did.

She said, "We, are, of course, hoping that gaining insight into the mechanism of the disease in animals will help us figure out how to treat it in humans. These mice were infected three days ago. An hour ago they began to show symptoms, which we wanted all of you to see before . . . well, before."

The wall behind Jessica Yu de-opaqued, taking the exposure graphic with it. Or some sort of viewscreen now overlay the wall and the three mice now revealed were someplace else in the *Embassy*. The mice oc-cupied a large glass cage in what Marianne recognized as a BSL4 lab.

Two of the mice lay flat, twitching and making short whooshing sounds, much amplified by the audio system. No, not amplified—those were desperate gasps as the creatures fought for air. Their tails lashed and their front paws scrambled. They were, Marianne realized, try-ing to *swim* away from whatever was drowning them.

"In humans," Yu continued, "we would call this ARDS—adult respiratory distress syndrome, a catchall diagnosis used when we don't know what the problem is. The mouse lung tissue is becoming heavier and heavier as fluid from the blood seeps into the lungs and each breath takes more and more effort. X-rays of lung tissue show 'whiteout'—so much fluid in the lungs increasing the radiological density that the image looks like a snowstorm. The viral incubation period in mice is three days. The time from onset of symptoms until death averages two-point-six hours."

The third mouse began to twitch.

Yu continued, her whole tiny body rigid, "As determined thus far, the infection rate in mice is a hundred percent. We can't, of course, make any assumptions that it would be the same in humans. Nor do we have any idea why some species of mice are infected but others are not. Rats are not susceptible, nor are monkeys. The medical data made available from the Deneb colonies do indicate involvement of similar metabolic pathways in Denebs to those of the mice. Those colonies had no survivors. Autopsies on the infected mice further indicate—"

A deep nausea took Marianne, reaching all the way from throat to rectum. She was surprised; her training was supposed to inure her. It did not. Before her body could disgrace her by retching, she squeezed past Evan with a push on his shoulder to indicate he should stay and hear the rest. In the corridor outside the auditorium she leaned against the wall, lowered her head between her knees, breathed deeply, and let shame overcome horror.

No way for a scientist to react to data—

The shame was not strong enough. It was her children that the horror brought: Elizabeth and Ryan and Noah, mouths open as they tried to force air into their lungs, wheezing and gasping, drowning where they lay . . . and Connie and the as-yet-unborn baby, Marianne's first grandchild. . . .

Stop. It's no worse for you than for anybody else.

Marianne stood. She dug the nails of her right hand into the palm of her left. But she could not make herself go back into the auditorium. Evan would have to tell her what other monstrosities were revealed. She made her way back to her lab.

Max sat at the computer, crunching data. Gina looked up from her bench. "Marianne—we found two more L7 donors."

"Good," Marianne said, went through the lab to her tiny office behind, and closed the door firmly. What did it matter how many L7s she found for Smith? Earth was finished. Eight and a half months left, and the finest medical and scientific brains on the planet had not even begun to find any way to mitigate the horror to come.

Gina knocked on the office door. "Marianne? Are you all right?"

Gina was the same age as Elizabeth, a young woman with her whole life still ahead of her. If she got that life. Meanwhile, there was no point in making the present even worse. Marianne forced cheerfulness into her voice. "Yes, fine. I'll be right out. Put on a fresh pot of coffee, would you please?"

S minus 7.5 months

Noah stood with his clan and prepared to lllathil.

There was no word for it in English. Part dance, part religious ceremony, part frat kegger, and it went on for two days. Ten L7s stood in a circle, all in various stages of drunkenness. When the weird, atonal music (but after two months aboard the *Embassy* it no longer sounded weird or atonal to his ears) began, they weaved in and out, making precise figures on the floor with the red paint on their feet. Once the figures had been sacred, part of a primitive religion that had faded with the rapid growth of science nurtured by their planet's lush and easy environment. The ritual remained. It affirmed family, always matrilineal on World. It affirmed connection, obligation, identity. Whenever the larger of World's moons was lined up in a certain way with the smaller, Worlders came together with their families and joyously made lllathil. Circles always held ten, and as many circles were made as a family needed. It didn't matter where you were on World, or what you were doing, when lllathil came, you were there.

His mother would never have understood.

The third morning, after everyone had slept off the celebration, came the second part of lllathil, which Marianne would have understood even less. Each person gave away one-fifth of everything he had earned or made since the last lllathil. He gave it, this "thumb" as it was jokingly called, to someone in his circle. Different clans gave different percentages and handled that in different ways, but some version of the custom held over mostly monocultural World. The Denebs were a sophisticated race; such a gift involved transfers of the Terran equivalent of bank accounts, stock holdings, real estate. The Denebs were also human, and so sometimes the gift was made grudgingly, or with anger at a cousin's laziness, or resignedly, or with cheating. But it was made, and there wasn't very much cheating. Or so said Mee^haoi, formerly known to Noah as Smith, who'd told him so in the trilling and clicking language that Noah was trying so hard to master. A rising inflection in the middle, a click at the end. "We teach our children very intensively to follow our ways," Mee^haoi said wryly. "Of course, some do not. Some always are different."

"You said it, brother," Noah said, in English, to Mee^haoi's total incomprehension.

Noah loved lllathil. He had very little—nothing, really—to give, but his net gain was not the reason he loved it. Nor was that the reason he studied World for hours every day, aided by his natural ear for languages. Once, in his brief and abortive attempt at college, Noah had heard a famous poet say that factual truth and emotional truth were not the same. "You have to understand with your belly," she'd said.

He did. For the first time in his life, he did.

His feet made a mistake, leaving a red toe print on the floor in the wrong place. No one chided him. Cliclimi, her old face wrinkling into crevasses and hills and dales, a whole topography of kinship, just laughed at him and reached out her skinny arm to fondly touch his.

Noah, not like that. Color in the lines!

Noah, this isn't the report card I expect of you.

Noah, you can't come with me and my friends! You're too little!

Noah, can't you do anything right?

When he'd danced until he could no longer stand (Cliclimi was still going at it, but she hadn't drunk as much as Noah had), he dropped onto a large cushion beside Jones, whose real name he still couldn't pronounce. It had more trills than most, and a strange tongue sound he could not reproduce at all. She was flushed, her hair unbound from its usual tight arrangement. Smaller than he was but stockier, her caramel-colored flesh glowed with exertion. The hair, rich dark brown, glinted in the rosy light. Her red tunic—everybody wore red for lllathil—had hiked high on her thighs.

Noah heard his mother's voice say, *"A hundred fifty thousand years is not enough time for a species to diverge."* To his horror, he felt himself blush.

She didn't notice, or else she took it as warmth from the dancing. She said, "Do you have trouble with our gravity?"

Proud of himself that he understood the words, he said, "No. It small amount big of Earth." At least, he hoped that's what he'd said.

Apparently it was. She smiled and said something he didn't understand. She stretched luxuriously, and the tunic rode up another two inches.

What were the kinship taboos on sex? What were any of the taboos on sex? Not that Noah could have touched her skin-to-skin, anyway. He was encased, so unobtrusively that he usually forgot it was there, in the "energy suit" that protected him from alien microbes.

Microbes. Spores. How much time was left before the cloud hit

Earth? At the moment it didn't seem important. (*Noah, you can't just pretend problems don't exist!* That had usually been Elizabeth.)

He said, "Can—yes, no?—make my"—damn it, what was the word for microbes?—"my inside like you? My inside spores?"

S minus 6.5 months

Gina had not returned from Brooklyn on the day's last submarine run. Marianne was redoing an entire batch of DNA amplification that had somehow become contaminated. Evan picked up the mail sack and the news dispatches. When he came into the lab, where Marianne was cursing at a row of beakers, he uncharacteristically put both hands on her shoulders. She looked at his face.

"What is it? Tell me quickly."

"Gina is dead."

She put a hand onto the lab bench to steady herself. "How?"

"A mob. They were frighteningly well armed, almost a small army. End-of-the-world rioters."

"Was Gina . . . did she . . ."

"A bullet, very quick. She didn't suffer, Marianne. Do you want a drink? I have some rather good scotch."

"No. Thank you, but no."

Gina. Marianne could picture her so clearly, as if she still stood in the lab in the wrinkled white coat she always wore even though the rest of them did not. Her dark hair just touched with premature gray, her ruddy face calm. Brisk, pleasant, competent. . . . What else? Marianne hadn't known Gina very well. All at once, she wondered if she knew anyone, really knew them. Two of her children baffled her: Elizabeth's endemic anger, Noah's drifty aimlessness. Had she ever known Kyle, the man he was under the charming and lying surface, under the alcoholism? Evan's personal life was kept personal, and she'd assumed it was his British reticence, but maybe she knew so little about him because of her limitations, not his. With nearly everyone else aboard the *Embassy,* as with her university department back home, she exchanged only scientific information or meaningless pleasantries. She'd had coffee a few times with Harrison Rice, but they had talked only about work. Marianne hadn't seen her brother, to whom she'd never been close, in nearly two years. Her last close female friendship had been over a decade ago.

Thinking this way felt strange, frightening. She was glad when Evan said, "Where's Max? I'll tell him about Gina."

"Gone to bed with a cold. It can wait until morning. What's that?"

Evan gave her a letter, addressed by hand. Marianne tore it open. "It's from Ryan. The baby was born, a month early but he's fine and so is she. Six pounds two ounces. They're naming him Jason William Jenner."

"Congratulations. You're a nan."

"A what?"

"Grandmum." He kissed her cheek.

She turned to cling to him, without passion, in sudden need of the simple comfort of human touch. Evan smelled of damp wool and some cool, minty lotion. He patted her back. "What's all this, then?"

"I'm sorry, I—"

"Don't be sorry." He held her until she was ready to pull away.

"I think I should write to Gina's parents."

"Yes, that's right."

"I want to make them understand—" Understand what? That sometimes children were lost, and the reasons didn't necessarily make sense. But this reason did make sense, didn't it? Gina had died because she'd been aboard the *Embassy,* died as a result of the work she did, and right now this was the most necessary work in the entire world.

She had a sudden memory of Noah, fifteen, shouting at her: *You're never home! Work is all you care about!* And she, like so many beleaguered parents, had shouted back, *If it weren't for my work, we'd all starve!*

And yet, when the kids had all left home and she could work as much as she wanted or needed without guilt, she'd missed them dreadfully. She'd missed the harried driving schedules—*I have to be at Jennifer's at eight* and *Soccer practice is moved up an hour Saturday!* She'd missed their electronics, cells and iPods and tablets and laptops, plugged into all of the old house's inadequate outlets. She'd missed the rainbow laundry in the basement, Ryan's red soccer shirts and Elizabeth's white jeans catastrophically dyed pink and Noah's yellow-and-black bumblebee costume for the second-grade play. All gone. When your children were small you worried that they would die and you would lose them, and then they grew up and you ended up losing the children they'd been, anyway.

Marianne pulled at the skin on her face and steeled herself to write to Gina's parents.

There were three of them now. Noah Jenner, Jacqui Young, Oliver Pardo. But only Noah was undergoing the change.

They lounged this afternoon in the World garden aboard the *Embassy,* where the ceiling seemed to be open to an alien sky. A strange orange shone, larger than Sol and yet not shedding as much light, creating a dim glow over the three Terrans. The garden plants were all dark in hue (*To gather as much light as possible,* Mee^hao¡ had said), large lush leaves in olive drab and avocado and asparagus. Water trickled over rocks or fell in high, thin streams. Warmth enveloped Noah even though his energy suit, and he felt light on the ground in the lesser gravity. Some nearby flower sent out a strange, musky, heady fragrance on the slight breeze.

Jacqui, an energetic and enormously intelligent graduate student, had chosen to move into the alien section of the *Embassy* in order to do research. She was frank, with both Terrans and Denebs, that she was not going to stay after she had gathered the unique data on Deneb culture that would ensure her academic career. Mee^hao¡ said that was all right, she was clan and so welcome for as long as she chose. Noah wondered how she planned on even having an academic career after the spore cloud hit.

Oliver Pardo would have been given the part of geek by any casting department with no imagination. Overweight, computer-savvy, a fan of superheroes, he quoted obscure science fiction books sixty years old and drew endless pictures of girls in improbable costumes slaying dragons or frost giants. Socially inept, he was nonetheless gentle and sweet natured, and Noah preferred his company to Jacqui's, who asked too many questions.

"Why?" she said.

"Why what?" Noah said, even though he knew perfectly well what she meant. He lounged back on the comfortable moss and closed his eyes.

"Why are you undergoing this punishing regime of shots just so you can take off your shield?"

"They're not shots," Noah said. Whatever the Denebs were doing to him, they did it by having him apply patches to himself when he was out of his energy suit and in an isolation chamber. This had happened once a week for a while now. The treatments left him nauseated, dizzy, sometimes with diarrhea, and always elated. There was only one more to go.

Jacqui said, "Shots or whatever, why do it?"

Oliver looked up from his drawing of a barbarian girl riding a lion. "Isn't it obvious?"

Jacqui said, "Not to me."

Oliver said, "Noah wants to become an alien."

"No," Noah said. "I was an alien. Now I'm becoming . . . not one."

Jacqui's pitying look said *You need help.* Oliver shaded in the lion's mane. Noah wondered why, of all the Terrans of L7 mitochondrial haplotype, he was stuck with these two. He stood. "I have to study."

"I wish I had your fluency in World," Jacqui said. "It would help my work so much."

So study it. But Noah knew she wouldn't, not the way he was doing. She wanted the quick harvest of startling data, not . . . whatever it was he wanted.

Becoming an alien. Oliver was more correct than Noah's flip answer. And yet Noah had been right, too, which was something he could never explain to anyone, least of all his mother. Whom he was supposed to visit this morning, since she could not come to him.

All at once Noah knew that he was not going to keep that appointment. Although he flinched at the thought of hurting Marianne, he was not going to leave the World section of the *Embassy*. Not now, not ever. He couldn't account for this feeling, so strong that it seemed to infuse his entire being, like oxygen in the blood. But he had to stay here, where he belonged. Irrational, but—as Evan would have said—there it was, mustn't grumble, at least it made a change, no use going on about it.

He had never liked Evan.

In his room, Noah took pen and a pad of paper to write a note to his mother. The words did not come easy. All his life he had disappointed her, but not like this.

> *Dear Mom—I know we were going to get together this*
> *afternoon but—*
> *Dear Mom—I wish I could see you as we planned but—*
> *Dear Mom—We need to postpone our visit because Ambassador*
> *Smith has asked me if this afternoon I would—*

Noah pulled at the skin on his face, realized that was his mother's gesture, and stopped. He looked longingly at the little cubes that held his language lessons. As the cube spoke World, holofigures in the cube acted out the meaning. After Noah repeated each phrase, it corrected his pronunciation until he got it right.

"My two brothers live with my mother and me in this dwelling," a smiling girl said in the holocube, in World. Two boys, one younger than she and one much older, appeared beside her with a much older woman behind them, all four with similar features, a shimmering dome behind them.

"'My two brothers live with my mother and me in this dwelling,'" Noah repeated. The World tenses were tricky; these verbs were the ones for things that not only could change, but could change without the speaker's having much say about events. A mother could die. The family could be chosen for a space colony. The older brother could marry and move in with his wife's family.

Sometimes things were beyond your control and you had no real choice.

Dear Mom—I can't come. I'm sorry. I love you. Noah

CHAPTER 8

S minus 4 months

The work—anybody's work—was not going well.

It seemed to be proceeding at an astonishing pace, but Marianne—and everyone else—knew that was an illusion. She sat in the auditorium for the monthly report, Evan beside her. This time, no Denebs were present—why not? She listened to Terence Manning enumerate what, under any other circumstances, would have been incredibly rapid triumphs.

"We have succeeded in isolating the virus," Manning said, "although not in growing it in vitro. After isolation, we amplified it with the usual polymerase processes. The virus has been sequenced and—only a few days ago!—captured on an electromicrograph image, which, as most of you know, can be notoriously difficult. Here it is."

A graphic appeared on the wall behind Manning: fuzzy concentric circles blending into each other in shades of gray. Manning ran his hand over his head, now completely bald. Had he shaved his last three hairs, Marianne wondered irrelevantly. Or had they just given up and fallen out from stress?

"The virion appears to be related to known paramyxoviruses, although the gene sequence, which we now have, does not exactly match any of them. It is a negative-sense single-stranded RNA virus. Paramyxoviruses, to which it may or may not be directly related, are responsible for a number of human and animal diseases, including parainfluenza, mumps, measles, pneumonia, and canine distemper. This family of viruses jumps species more easily than any other. From what we have determined so far, it most closely resembles both Hendra and Nipah viruses, which are highly contagious and highly virulent.

"The genome follows the paramyxovirus 'Rule of Six,' in that the total length of the genome in nucleotides is almost always a multiple of six. The spore virus consists of twenty-one genes with 21,648 base pairs. That makes it a large virus, but by no means the largest we know of. Details of sequence, structure, envelope proteins, et cetera, can be found on the LAN. I want to especially thank Drs. Yu, Sedley, and Lapka for their valuable work in identifying *Respirovirus sporii.*"

Applause. Marianne still stared at the simple, deadly image behind Manning. An unwelcome thought had seized her: The viral image looked not unlike a fuzzy picture of a not-too-well-preserved trilobite. Trilobites had been the dominant life-form on Earth for three hundred million years and comprised more than ten thousand species. All gone now. Humans could be gone, too, after a much briefer reign.

But we survived so much! The Ice Age, terrible predators, the "bottleneck event" of seventy thousand years ago that reduced *Homo sapiens* to mere thousands . . .

Manning was continuing. This was the bad news. "However, we have made little progress in figuring out how to combat *R. sporii.* Blood from the infected mice has been checked against known viruses and yielded no serological positives. None of our small number of antiviral drugs were effective, although there was a slight reaction to ribavirin. That raises a further puzzle, since ribavirin is mostly effective against Lassa fever, which is caused by an arenavirus, not a paramyxovirus." Manning tried to smile; it was not a success. "So, the mystery deepens. I wish we had more to report."

Someone asked, "Are the infected mice making antibodies?"

"Yes," Manning said, "and if we can't manage to develop a vaccine, this is our best possible path to a postexposure treatment, following the MB-003 model developed for Ebola. For you astronomers—and please forgive me if I am telling you things you already know—a successful postexposure treatment for Ebola in nonhuman primates was developed before the actual Ebola vaccine. When administered an hour after infection, MB-003 yields a one hundred percent survival rate. At forty-eight hours, the survival rate is two-thirds. MB-003 was initially developed in a mouse model and then produced in plants. That work took ten years. Then it was replaced by the vaccine, which also took decades to reach clinical trials."

Decades . . . The *Embassy* scientists had less than five months left, and there would be no clinical trials.

Maybe the Denebs knew faster ways to produce a vaccine from antibodies, exponentially increase production, and distribute the results. But the aliens weren't even at this meeting. They had surely been given all this information already, but even so—

How the hell could the aliens be anyplace more important than this?

Marianne felt ridiculous. She and Evan leaned close over the sink in the lab. Water gushed full-strength from the tap, making noise that, she hoped, covered their words. The autoclave hummed; a Bach concerto played tinnily on the computer's inadequate speaker. The whole thing felt like a parody of a bad spy movie.

They had never been able to decide if the labs, if everywhere on the *Embassy*, were bugged. Evan had said *Yes, of course, don't be daft.* Max, with the hubris of the young, had said no because his computer skills would have been able to detect any surveillance. Marianne and Gina had said it was irrelevant since both their work and their personal lives were so transparent. In addition, Marianne had disliked the implication that the Denebs were not their full and open partners. Gina had said—

Gina. Shot down, her life ended just as Jason William Jenner's had begun. And for how long? Would Marianne even get to see her grandson before everything was as over as Gina's life?

Dangerous to think this way. Their work on the *Embassy* was a thin bridge laid across a pit of despair, the same despair that had undoubtedly fueled Gina's killers.

"You know what has to happen," Marianne whispered. "Nobody's saying it aloud, but without virus replication in human bodies, we just can't understand the effect on the immune system and we're working blindly. Mice aren't enough. Even if we could have infected monkeys, it wouldn't be enough. We have to infect volunteers."

Evan stuck his finger into the flow of water, which spattered in bright drops against the side of the sink. "I know. *Everyone* knows. The request has been made to the powers that be."

"How do you know that?"

"I talk to people on the other teams. You know the laws against experimentation on humans unless there have first been proper clinical trials that—"

"Oh, fuck proper trials, this is a crisis situation!"

"Not enough people in power are completely convinced of that. You haven't been paying attention to the bigger picture, Marianne. The Public Health Service isn't even gearing up for mass inoculation or protection—Director Robinson is fighting it with claw and tusk. FEMA is divided and there's almost anarchy in the ranks. Congress just filibusters on the whole topic. And the president just doesn't have the votes to get much of anything done. Meanwhile, the masses riot or flee or just pretend the whole thing is some sort of hoax. The farther one gets from New York, the more the conspiracy theorists don't even believe there are aliens on Earth at all."

Marianne, still standing, pulled at the skin on her face. "It's all so frustrating. And the work we've been doing here—you and I and Max and Gina"—her voice faltered—"is pointless. It really is. Identifying members of Smith's so-called clan? Who cares? I'm going to volunteer myself to be infected."

"They won't take you."

"If—"

"The only way that could happen is in secret. If a subgroup on the Spore Team decided the situation was desperate enough to conduct an unauthorized experiment."

She studied his face. In the biology department at the university, Evan had always been the one who knew how to obtain travel money for a conference, interviews with Nobel Prize winners, an immediate appointment with the dean. He had the knack, as she did not, for useful connections. She said, "You know something."

"No. I don't. Not yet."

"Find out."

He nodded and turned off the water. The music crescendoed: Brandenburg Concerto No. 2, which had gone out into space on the "golden record" inside *Voyager 1*.

The secret experiment turned out to be not all that secret.

Evan followed the rumors. Within a day he had found a lab tech on the Biology Team who knew a scientist on the Spore Team who referred him, so obliquely that Evan almost missed it, to a security officer. Evan came to Marianne in her room, where she'd gone instead of eating lunch. He stood close to her and murmured in her ear, ending with, "They'll let us observe. You—What's that, then?"

The last sentence was said in a normal voice. Evan gazed at the piece of paper in Marianne's hands. She had been looking at it since she found it under her door.

"Another note from Noah. He isn't . . . he still can't . . . Evan, I need to go ashore to see my new grandchild."

Evan blinked. "Your *new* grandchild?"

"Yes. He's two months old already and I haven't even seen him."

"It's not safe to leave the *Embassy* now. You know that."

"Yes. But I need to go."

Gently Evan took the note from her and read it. Marianne saw that he didn't really understand. Young, childless, orphaned . . . how could he? Noah had not forgiven her for never telling him that he was adopted. That must be why he said he might not ever see her again; no other reason made sense. Although maybe he would change his mind. Maybe in time he would forgive her, maybe he would not, maybe the world would end first. Before any of those things happened, Marianne had to see little Jason. She had to affirm what family ties she had, no matter how long she had them. Or anyone had them.

She said, "I need to talk to Ambassador Smith. How do I do that?"

He said, "Do you want me to arrange it?"

"Yes. Please. For today."

He didn't mention the backlog of samples in the lab. No one had replaced Gina. As family trees of the L7 haplogroup were traced in the matrilineal line, more and more of Smith's "clan" were coming aboard the Embassy. Marianne suspected they hoped to be shielded or trans-ported when the spore cloud hit. She also suspected they were right. The Denebs were . . .

. . . were just as insistent on family connections as she was, risk-ing her life to see Ryan, Connie, and the baby.

Well.

A helicopter flew her directly from the large pier outside the Embassy (so that's what it was for). When Marianne had last been outside, autumn was just ending. Now it was spring, the reluctant northern spring of tulips and late frosts, cherry blossoms and noisy frogs. The Vermont town where Connie's parents lived, and to which Ryan had moved his family for safety, was less than twenty miles from the Canadian border. The house was a pleasant brick faux-Colonial set amid bare fields. Marianne noted, but did not comment on, the spiked chain-link fence around the small property, the electronic-surveillance sticker on the front door, and the large Doberman whose collar Ryan held in restraint. He had hastened home from his fieldwork when she phoned that she was coming.

"Mom! Welcome!"

"We're so glad you're here, Marianne," Connie said warmly. "Even though I suspect it isn't us you came to see!" She grinned and handed over the tiny wrapped bundle.

The baby was asleep. Dark fuzz on the top of his head, pale silky skin lightly flushed, tiny pursed pink mouth sucking away in an infant dream. He looked so much like Ryan had that tears pricked Marianne's eyes. Immediately she banished them: no sorrow, neither nostalgic nor catastrophic, was going to mar this occasion.

"He's beautiful," she said, inadequately.

"Yes!" Connie was not one of those mothers who felt obliged to disclaim praise of her child.

Marianne held the sleeping baby while coffee was produced. Connie's parents were away, helping Connie's sister, whose husband had just left her and whose three-year-old was ill. This was touched on only lightly. Connie kept the conversation superficial, prattling in her pretty voice about Jason, about the dog's antics, about the weather. Marianne followed suit, keeping to herself the thought that, after all, she had never heard Connie talk about anything but light and cheerful topics. She must have more to her than that, but not in front of her mother-in-law. Ryan said almost nothing, sipping his coffee, listening to his wife.

Finally Connie said, "Oh, I've just been monopolizing the conversation! Tell us about life aboard the *Embassy*. It must be so fascinating!"

Ryan looked directly at Marianne.

She interpreted the look as a request to keep up the superficial tone. Ryan had always been as protective of Connie as of a pretty kitten. Had he deliberately chosen a woman so opposite to his mother because Marianne had always put her work front and center? Had Ryan resented her for that as much as Noah had?

Pushing aside these disturbing thoughts, she chatted about the aliens. Connie asked her to describe them, their clothes, her life there. Did she have her own room? Had she been able to decorate it? Where did the humans eat?

"We're *all* humans, Terrans and Denebs," Marianne said.

"Of course," Connie said, smiling brilliantly. "Is the food good?"

Talking, talking, talking, but not one question about her work. Nor about the spore cloud, progress toward a vaccine, anything to indicate the size and terror of the coming catastrophe. Ryan did ask about the *Embassy,* but only polite questions about its least important aspects: how big it was, how it was laid out, what was the routine. Safe topics.

Just before a sense of unreality overwhelmed Marianne, Ryan's cell rang, and the ringing woke the baby, who promptly threw up all over Marianne.

"Oh, I'm sorry!" Connie said. "Here, give him to me!"

Ryan, making gestures of apology, took his cell into the kitchen and closed the door. Connie reached for a box of Wet Ones and began to wipe Jason's face. She said, "The bathroom is upstairs to the left, Marianne. If you need to, I can loan you something else to wear."

"It would have to be one of your maternity dresses," Marianne said. It came out more sour than she'd intended.

She went upstairs and cleaned baby vomit off her shirt and jeans with a wet towel. The bathroom was decorated in a seaside motif, with hand towels embroidered with sailboats, soap shaped like shells, blue walls painted with green waves and smiling dolphins. On top of the toilet tank, a crocheted cylinder decorated like a buoy held a spare roll of toilet paper.

Keeping chaos at bay with cute domesticity. Good plan. And then: *Stop it, Marianne.*

Using the toilet, she leafed idly through magazines stacked in a rustic basket. *Good Housekeeping, Time,* a Macy's catalog. She pulled out a loose paper with full-color drawings:

HOW TO TELL PURPLE LOOSESTRIFE FROM NATIVE PLANTS
DON'T BE FOOLED BY LOOK-ALIKES!

Purple loosestrife leaves are downy with smooth edges. Although usually arranged opposite each other in pairs, which alternate down the stalk at ninety-degree angles, the leaves may sometimes appear in groups of three. The leaves lack teeth. The flowers, which appear in mid- to late summer, form a showy spike of rose-purple, each with five to seven petals. The stem is stiff, four-sided, and may appear woody at the base of larger plants, which can reach ten feet tall. Average height is four feet. Purple loosestrife can be distinguished from the native winged loosestrife (*Lythrum alatum*), which it most closely resembles, by its generally larger size, opposite leaves, and more closely placed flowers. It may also be confused with blue vervain (pictured below), which has . . .

At the bottom of the page, someone—presumably Ryan—had hand drawn in purple ink three stylized versions of a loosestrife spike, then circled one. To Marianne it looked like a violet rocket ship unaccountably sprouting leaves.

Downstairs, Jason had been cleaned up and changed. Marianne played with him the limited games available for two-month-old babies: peekaboo, feetsies go up and down, where did the finger go? When he started to fuss and Connie excused herself to nurse him, Marianne said her good-byes and went out to the helicopter waiting in a nearby field. Neighbors had gathered around it, and Ryan was telling them . . . what? The neighbors looked harmless, but how could you tell? Always, Gina was on her mind. She hugged Ryan fiercely.

As the copter lifted and the house, the town, the countryside got smaller and smaller, Marianne tried not to think of what a failure the visit had been. Yes, she had seen her grandchild. But whatever comfort or connection that had been supposed to bring her, it hadn't. It seemed to her, perhaps irrationally, that never had she felt so alone.

When Noah woke, he instantly remembered what day it was. For a long moment, he lay still, savoring the knowledge like rich chocolate on the tongue. Then he said good-bye to his room. He would never sleep here, out of his energy suit, again.

Over the months, he had made the room as World as he could. A sleeping mat, thin but with as much give as a mattress, rolled itself tightly as soon as he sprang up and into the tiny shower. On the support wall he had hung one of Oliver's pictures—not a half-dressed barbarian princess this time, but a black-and-white drawing of plants in the World garden. The other walls, which seemed thin as rice paper but somehow kept out sound, had been programmed, at Noah's request, with the subtly shifting colors that the Worlders favored for everything except family gatherings. Color was extremely important to Worlders, and so to Noah. He was learning to discern shades that had once seemed all the same. *This* blue for mourning; *this* blue for adventure; *this* blue for loyalty. He had discarded all his Terran clothes. How had he ever stood the yellow polo shirt, the red hoodie? Wrong, wrong.

Drying his body, he rehearsed his request to Mee^haoj. He wanted to get the words exactly right.

Breakfast, like all World meals, was communal, a time to affirm ties. Noah had already eaten in his room; the energy suit did not permit the intake of food. Nonetheless, he took his place in the hierarchy at the long table, above Oliver and Jacqui and below everyone else. That was just. Family solidarity rested on three supports: inclusion, rank, and empathy. A triangle was the strongest of all geometrical figures.

"G'morning," Oliver said, yawning. He was not a morning person, and resented getting up for a breakfast he would not eat until much later.

"I greet you," Noah said in World. Oliver blinked.

Jacqui, quicker, said, "Oh, today is the day, is it? Can I be there?"

"At the ceremony? No, of course not!" Noah said. She should have known better than to even make the request.

"Just asking," Jacqui said. "Doesn't hurt to ask."

Yes, it does. It showed a lack of respect for all three supports in the triangle. Although Noah had not expected any more of Jacqui.

He did expect more of the three Terrans who took their places below Oliver. Isabelle Rhinehart, her younger sister Kayla, and Kayla's son had come into the World section of the *Embassy* only a week ago, but already the two women were trying to speak World. The child, Austin, was only three—young enough to grow up trilling and clicking World like a native. Noah gazed with envy at the little boy, who smiled shyly and then crawled onto his mother's lap.

But they could not hold Noah's interest long. This was the day!

His stomach growled. He'd been too excited to eat much of the food delivered earlier to his room. And truthfully, the vegetarian World diet was not exciting. But he would learn to like it. And what a small price to pay for . . . *everything.*

The ceremony took place in the same room, right after breakfast. The other Terrans had left. Mee^haoį changed the wall program. Now instead of subtly shifting greens, the thin room dividers pulsed with the blue of loyalty alternating with the color of the clan of Mee^haoį.

Noah knelt in the middle of the circle of Worlders, facing Mee^haoį, who held a long blue rod. *Now I dub thee Sir Noah.* . . . Noah hated, completely hated, that his mind threw up that stupid thought. This was nothing like a feudal knighting. It was more like a baptism, washing him clean of his old self.

Mee^haoį sang a verse of what he had been told was the family inclusion song, with everyone else echoing the chorus. Noah didn't catch all the trilling and clicking words, but he didn't have to. Tears pricked his eyes. It seemed to him that he had never wanted anything this much in life, had never really wanted anything at all.

"Stand, brother mine," Mee^hao¡ said.

Noah stood. Mee^hao¡ did something with the rod, and the energy shield dissolved around Noah.

Not only a baptism—an operation.

The first breath of World air almost made him vomit. No, the queasiness was excitement, not the air. It tasted strange, and with the second panicky breath he felt he wasn't getting enough of it. But he knew that was just the lower oxygen content. The *Embassy* was at sea level; the O_2 concentration of World matched that at twelve thousand feet. His lungs would adapt. His marrow would produce more red corpuscles. The Worlders had evolved for this; Noah would evolve, too.

The air smelled strange.

His legs buckled slightly, but before Llaa^moh¡, whom he had once known as Jones, could step toward him, Noah braced himself and smiled. He was all right. He was here. He was—

"Brother mine," went around the circle, and then the formalities were over and they all hugged him, and for the first time in 150,000 years, Terran skin touched the skin of humans from the stars.

CHAPTER 9

S minus 3.5 months

The security officer met Marianne and Evan in their lab and conducted them to a euchre game in the observation area outside the BSL4 lab.

From the first time she'd come here, Marianne had been appalled by the amateurishness of the entire setup. Granted, this was a bunch of scientists, not the CIA. Still, the Denebs had to wonder why euchre—or backgammon or chess or Monopoly, it varied—was being played here instead of at one of the comfortable common rooms or cafeterias. Why two scientists were constantly at work in the negative-pressure lab even when they seemed to have nothing to do. Why the euchre players paid more attention to the screens monitoring the scientists' vitals than to the card game.

Dr. Julia Namechek and Dr. Trevor Lloyd. Both young, strong, and self-infected with spore disease. They moved around the BSL4 lab in full space suits, breathing tubes attached to the air supply in the ceiling. Surely the Denebs' energy suits would be better for this kind of work, but the suits had not been offered to the Terrans.

"When?" Marianne murmured, playing the nine of clubs.

"Three days ago," said a physician whose name Marianne had not caught.

Spore disease (the name deliberately unimaginative, noninflammatory) had turned up in mice after three days. Marianne was not a physician, but she could read a vitals screen. Neither Namechek nor

Lloyd, busily working in their space suits behind glass, showed the slightest signs of infection. This was, in fact, the third time that the two had tried to infect themselves by breathing in the spores. Each occasion had been preceded by weeks of preparation. Those times, nothing had happened, either, and no one knew why. There were theories, but nothing proved.

Physicians experimenting on themselves were not unknown in research medicine. Edward Jenner had infected himself—and the eight-year-old son of his gardener—with cowpox to develop the smallpox vaccine. Jesse William Lazear infected himself with yellow fever from mosquitoes, in order to confirm that mosquitoes were indeed the transmission vector. Julio Barrera gave himself Argentine hemorrhagic fever; Barry Marshall drank a solution of *H. pylori* to prove the bacterium caused peptic ulcers; Pradeep Seth injected himself with an experimental vaccine for HIV.

Marianne understood the reasons for the supposed secrecy of this experiment. The newspapers that came in on the mail runs glowed luridly with speculations about human experimentation aboard the *Embassy*. Journalists ignited their pages with "Goebbels," "Guatemalan syphilis trials," "Japanese Unit 731." And those were the mainstream journalists. The tabloids and fringe papers invented so many details about Deneb atrocities on humans that the newsprint practically dripped with blood and body parts. The online news sources were, if anything, even worse. No, such "journalists" would never believe that Drs. Namechek and Lloyd had given spore disease to themselves and without the aliens knowing it.

Actually, Marianne didn't believe that, either. The Denebs were too intelligent, too technologically advanced, too careful. They *had* to know this experiment was going on. They had to be permitting it. No matter how benign and peaceful their culture, they were human. Their lack of interference was a way of ensuring CYA deniability.

"Your turn, Dr. Jenner," said Syed Sharma, a very formal microbiologist from Mumbai. He was the only player wearing a suit.

"Oh, sorry," Marianne said. "What's trump again?"

Evan, her partner, said, "Spades. Don't trump my ace again."

"No table talk, please," Sharma said.

Marianne studied her hand, trying to remember what had been played. She had never been a good cardplayer. She didn't like cards. And there was nothing to see here, anyway. Evan could bring her the results, if any, of the clandestine experiment. It was possible that the two scientists had not been infected, after all—not this time nor the previous two. It was possible that the pathogen had mutated, or just hadn't taken hold in these two particular people, or was being administered with the wrong vector. In the nineteenth century, a Dr. Firth, despite heroic and disgusting measures, had never succeeded in infecting himself with yellow fever because he never understood how it was transmitted. Pathogen research was still part art, part luck.

"I fold," she said, before she remembered that "folding" was poker, not euchre. She tried a weak smile. "I'm very tired."

"Go to bed, Dr. Jenner," said Seyd Sharma. Marianne gave him a grateful look, which he did not see as he frowned at his cards. Lab tech Alyssa Rosert took her place at the table and Marianne left.

Just as she reached the end of the long corridor leading from the BSL4 lab, the door opened and a security guard hurried through, face twisted with some strong emotion. Her heart stopped. What fresh disaster now? She said, "Did anything—" but before she could finish the question he had pushed past her and hurried on.

Marianne hesitated. Follow him to hear the news or wait until—

The lab exploded.

Marianne was hurled to the floor. Walls around her, the tough but thin membranelike walls favored by the Denebs, tore. People screamed, sirens sounded, pulsing pain tore through Marianne's head like a dark, viscous tsunami.

Then everything went black.

———

She woke alone in a room. Small, white, windowless, with one clear wall, two doors, a pass-through compartment. Immediately, she knew, even before she detected the faint hum of blown air: a quarantine room with negative pressure. The second door, locked, led to an operating room for emergency procedures and autopsies. The explosion had exposed her to spores from the experimental lab.

Bandages wreathed her head; she must have hit it when she fell, got a concussion, and needed stitches. Nothing else on her seemed damaged. Gingerly she sat up, aware of the IV tube and catheter and pulse oximeter, and waiting for the headache. It was there, but very faint. Her movement set off a faint gong somewhere and Dr. Ann Potter, a physician whom Marianne knew slightly, appeared on the other side of the clear glass wall.

The doctor said, her voice coming from the ceiling as if she were just one more alien, "You're awake. What do you feel?"

"Headache. Not terrible. What . . . what happened?"

"Let me ask you some questions first." She was asked her name, the date, her location, the name of the president—

"Enough!" Marianne said. "I'm fine! *What happened?*" But she already knew. Hers was the only bed in the quarantine room.

Dr. Potter paid her the compliment of truth. "It was a suicide bomber. He—"

"The others? Evan Blanford?"

"They're all dead. I'm sorry, Dr. Jenner."

Evan. Dead.

Seyd Sharma, with his formal, lilting diction. Julia Namechek, engaged to be married. Trevor Lloyd, whom everyone said would win a Nobel someday. Alyssa Rosert, who always remembered what trump was—all dead.

Evan. Dead.

Marianne couldn't process that, not now. She managed to say, "Tell me. All of it."

Ann Potter's face creased with emotion, but she had herself under control. "The bomber was dressed as a security guard. He had the explosive—I haven't heard yet what it was—in his stomach or rectum, presumably encased to protect it from body fluids. Autopsy showed that the detonator, ceramic so that it got through all our metal detectors, was probably embedded in a tooth, or at least somewhere in his mouth that could be tongued to go off."

Marianne pictured it. Her stomach twisted.

Dr. Potter continued, "His name was Michael Wendl and he was new but legitimately aboard, a sort of mole, I guess you'd call it. A manifesto was all over the Internet an hour after the explosion and this morning—"

"This morning? How long have I been out?"

"Ten hours. You had only a mild concussion but you were sedated to stitch up head lacerations, which of course we wouldn't ordinarily do but this was complicated because—"

"I know," Marianne said, and marveled at the calm in her voice. "I may have been exposed to the spores."

"You *have* been exposed, Marianne. Samples were taken. You're infected."

Marianne set that aside, too, for the moment. She said, "Tell me about the manifesto. What organization?"

"Nobody has claimed credit. The manifesto was about what you'd expect: Denebs planning to kill everyone on Earth, all that shit. Wendl vetted okay when he was hired, so speculation is that he was a new recruit to their cause. He was from somewhere Upstate and there's a lot of dissent going on up there. But the thing is, he got it wrong. He was supposed to explode just outside the Deneb section of the *Embassy*, not the research labs. His organization, whatever it was, knew something about the layout of the *Embassy* but not enough. Wendl was supposed to be restricted to sub-bay duty. It's like someone who'd had just a brief tour had told him where to go, but either they remembered wrong or he did."

Marianne's spine went cold. *Someone who'd had just a brief tour . . .*

"You had some cranial swelling after the concussion, Marianne, but it's well under control now."

Elizabeth.

No, not possible. Not thinkable.

"You're presently on a steroid administered intravenously, which may have some side effects I'd like you to be aware of, including wakefulness and—"

Elizabeth, studying everything during her visit aboard the *Embassy*: "*Can I see more? Or are you lab types kept close to your cages?*" "*Where do the Denebs live?*" "*Interesting. It's pretty close to the high-risk labs.*"

"Marianne, are you listening to me?"

Elizabeth, furiously punching the air months ago: "*I don't believe it, not any of it. There are things they aren't telling us!*"

"Marianne?"

Elizabeth, grudgingly doing her duty to protect the aliens but against her own inclinations. Commanding a critical section of the Border Patrol, a member of the joint task force that had access to military-grade weapons. In an ideal position to get an infiltrator aboard the floating island.

"Marianne! *Are* you listening to me?"

"No," Marianne said. "I have to talk to Ambassador Smith!"

"Wait, you can't just—"

Marianne had started to heave herself off the bed, which was ridiculous because she couldn't leave the quarantine chamber anyway. A figure appeared on the other side of the glass barrier, behind Dr. Potter. The doctor, following Marianne's gaze, turned, and gasped.

Noah pressed close to the glass. An energy shield shimmered around him. Beneath it he wore a long tunic like Smith's. His once pale skin now shone coppery under his black hair. But most startling were his eyes: Noah's eyes, and yet not. Bigger, altered to remove as much of the skin and expose as much of the white as possible. Within that large, alien-sized expanse of white, his irises were still the same color as her own, an un-alien light gray flecked with gold. They shared no genetic link, and yet their eyes reflected each other. Genetic chance.

"Mom," he said tenderly. "Are you all right?"

"Noah—"

"I came as soon as I heard. I'm sorry it's been so long. Things have been . . . happening."

It was still Noah's voice, coming through the energy shield and out of the ceiling with no alien inflection, no trill or click. Marianne's mind refused to work logically. All she could focus on was his voice: He was too old. He would never speak English as anything but a Middle Atlantic American, and he would never speak World without an accent.

"Mom?"

"I'm fine," she managed.

"I'm so sorry to hear about Evan."

She clasped her hands tightly together on top of the hospital blanket. "You're going. With the aliens. When they leave Earth."

"Yes."

One simple word. No more than that, and Marianne's son became an extraterrestrial. She knew that Noah was not doing this in order to save his life. Or hers, or anyone's. She didn't know why he had done it. As a child, Noah had been fascinated by superheroes, aliens, robots, even of the more ridiculous kind where the science made zero sense. Comic books, movies, TV shows—he would sit transfixed for hours by some improbable human transformed into a spider or a hulk or a sentient hunk of metal. Did Noah remember that childish fascination? She didn't understand what this adopted child, this beloved boy she had not borne, remembered or thought or desired. She never had.

He said, "I'm sorry."

She said, "Don't be," and neither of them knew exactly what he was apologizing for in the first place, nor what she was excusing him from. After that, Marianne could find nothing else to say. Of the thousands of things she could have said to Noah, absolutely none of them rose to her lips. So finally she nodded.

Noah blew her a kiss. Marianne did not watch him go. She couldn't have borne it. Instead she shifted her weight on the bed and got out of it, holding on to the bedstead, ignoring Ann Potter's strenuous objections on the other side of the glass.

She had to see Ambassador Smith, to tell him her suspicions about Elizabeth. The terrorist organization could strike again.

As soon as she told Smith, Elizabeth would be arrested. *Two children lost—*

No, don't think of it. Tell Smith.

But—*Wait.* Maybe it hadn't been Elizabeth. Surely others had had an unauthorized tour of the ship? And now, as a result of the attack, security would be tightened. Probably no other saboteur could get through. Perhaps there would be no more supply runs by submarine, no more helicopters coming and going on the wide pier. Time was so short—maybe there were enough supplies aboard already. And perhaps the Denebs would use their unknowable technology to keep the *Embassy* safer until the spore cloud hit, by which time of course the aliens would have left. There were only three months left. Surely a second attack inside the *Embassy* couldn't be organized in such a brief time! Maybe there was no need to name Elizabeth at all.

The room swayed as she clutched the side of the bed.

Ann Potter said, "If you don't get back into bed right now, Marianne, I'm calling security."

"Nothing is secure, don't you know that, you silly woman?" Marianne snapped.

Noah was lost to her. Evan was dead. Elizabeth was guilty.

"I'm sorry," she said. "I'll get back in bed." What was she even doing, standing up? She couldn't leave. She carried the infection inside her body. "But I . . . I need to see Ambassador Smith. Right now, here. Please have someone tell him it's the highest possible priority. Please."

The visit to his mother upset Noah more than he'd expected. She'd looked so small, so fragile in her bed behind the quarantine glass. Always, his whole life, he'd thought of her as large, towering over the landscape like some stone fortress, both safe and formidable. But she was just a small, frightened woman who was going to die.

As were Elizabeth, Ryan and Connie and their baby, Noah's last girlfriend, Emily, his childhood buddies Sam and Davey, Cindy and Miguel at the restaurant—all going to die when the spore cloud hit. Why hadn't Noah been thinking about this before? How could he be so selfish about concentrating on his delight in his new clan that he had put the rest of humanity out of his mind?

He had always been selfish. He'd known that about himself. Only before now, he'd called it "independent."

It was a relief to leave the Terran part of the *Embassy*, with its too-heavy gravity and glaring light. The extra rods and cones that had been inserted into Noah's eyes made them sensitive to such terrible brightness. In the World quarters, Kayla's little boy, Austin, was chasing a ball along the corridor, his energy suit a faint glimmer in the low light. He stopped to watch Noah shed his own suit.

Austin said, "I wanna do that."

"You will, someday. Maybe soon. Where's your mother?"

"She comes right back. I stay right here!"

"Good boy. Have you—Hi, Kayla. Do you know where Mee^hao¡ is?"

"No. Oh, wait, yes—He left the sanctuary."

That, Noah remembered, was what both Kayla and her sister called the World section of the *Embassy*. "Sanctuary"—the term made him wonder what their life had been before they came aboard. Both, although pleasant enough, were closemouthed about their pasts to the point of lockjaw.

Kayla added, "I think Mee^hao¡ said it was about the attack."

It would be, of course. Noah knew he should wait until Mee^hao¡ was free. But he couldn't wait.

"Where's Llaa^moh¡?"

Kayla looked blank; her World was not yet fluent.

"Scientist Jones."

"Oh. I just saw her in the garden."

Noah strode to the garden. Llaa^moh¡ sat on a bench, watching water fall in a thin stream from the ceiling to a pool below. Delicately she fingered a llo flower, without picking it, coaxing the broad dark leaf to release its spicy scent. Noah and Llaa^moh¡ had avoided each other ever since Noah's welcome ceremony, and he knew why. Still, right now his need overrode awkward desire.

"Llaa^moh¡—may we speak together?" He hoped he had the verb tense right: urgency coupled with supplication.

"Yes, of course." She made room for him on the bench. "Your World progresses well."

"Thank you. I am troubled in my liver." The correct idiom, he was certain. Almost.

"What troubles your liver, brother mine?"

"My mother." The word meant not only female parent but matri-archal clan leader, which Noah supposed that Marianne was, since both his grandmothers were dead. Although perhaps not his biologi-cal grandmothers, and to World, biology was all. There were no out-of-family adoptions.

"Yes?"

"She is Dr. Marianne Jenner, as you know, working aboard the *Embassy*. My brother and sister live ashore. What will happen to my family when the spore cloud comes? Does my mother go with us to World? Do my siblings?" But . . . how could they, unaltered? Also, they were not of his haplotype and so would belong to a different clan for lllathil, clans not represented aboard ship. Also, all three of them would hate everything about World. But otherwise they would die. All of them, dead.

Llaa^moh¡ said nothing. Noah gave her the space and time to think; one thing World humans hated about Terrans was that they replied so quickly, without careful thought, sometimes even interrupting each other and thereby dishonoring the speaker. Noah watched a small insect with multicolored wings, whose name did not come to his fevered mind, cross the llo leaf, and forced his body to stay still.

Finally Llaa^moh¡ said, "Mee^hao¡ and I have discussed this. He has left this decision to me. You are one of us now. I will tell you what will happen when the spore cloud comes."

"I thank you for your trust." The ritual response, but Noah meant it.

"However, you are under obligation"—she used the most serious degree for a word of promise—"to say nothing to anyone else, World or Terran. Do you accept this obligation?"

Noah hesitated, and not from courtesy. Shouldn't he use the information, whatever it was, to try to ensure what safety was possible for his family? But if he did not promise, Llaa^moh¡ would tell him nothing.

"I accept the obligation."

She told him.

Noah's jaw dropped. He couldn't help it, even though it was very rude. Llaa^moh¡ was carefully not looking at him; perhaps she had anticipated this reaction.

Noah stood and walked out of the garden.

"Thought," a famous poet—Marianne couldn't remember which one—had once said, "is an infection. In the case of certain thoughts, it becomes an epidemic." Lying in her bed in the quarantine chamber, Marianne felt an epidemic in her brain. What Elizabeth had done, what she herself harbored now in her body, Noah's transformation, Evan's death—the thoughts fed on her cells, fevered her mind.

Elizabeth, studying the complex layout of the *Embassy*: *"Where do the Denebs live?"* *"Behind these doors here."*

Noah, with his huge alien eyes.

Evan, urging her to meet the aliens by scribbling block letters on a paper sushi bag: *CHANCE OF SIX THOUSAND LIFETIMES!* The number of generations since Mitochondrial Eve.

Herself, carrying the deadly infection. Elizabeth, Noah, Evan, spores—it was almost a relief when Ambassador Smith appeared beyond the glass.

"Dr. Jenner," the ceiling said in uninflected translation. "I am so sorry you were injured in this attack. You said you want to see me now."

She hadn't been sure what she was going to say to him. How did you name your own child a possible terrorist, condemn her to whatever unknown form justice took among aliens? What if that meant something like drawing and quartering, as it once had on Earth? Marianne opened her mouth, and what came out were words she had not planned at all.

"Why did you permit Drs. Namechek and Lloyd to infect themselves three times when it violates both our medical code and yours?"

His face, both Terran and alien, that visage that now and forever would remind her of what Noah had done to his own face, did not change expression. "You know why, Dr. Jenner. It was necessary for the research. There is no other way to fully assess immune system response in ways useful to developing antidotes."

"You could have used your own people!"

"There are not enough of us to put anyone into quarantine."

"You could have run the experiment yourself with human volunteers. You'd have gotten volunteers, given what Earth is facing. And then the experiment could have had the advantage of your greater expertise."

"It is not much greater than yours, as you know. Our scientific knowledges have moved in different directions. But if we had sponsored experiments on Terrans, what would have been the Terran response?"

Marianne was silent. She knew the answer. They both knew the answer.

He said, "You are infected, I am told. We did not cause this. But now our two peoples can work more openly on developing medicines or vaccines. Both Earth and World will owe you an enormous debt."

Which she would never collect. In roughly two more days she would be dead of spore disease. And she still had to tell him about Elizabeth.

"Ambassador Smith—"

"I must show you something, Dr. Jenner. If you had not sent for me, I would have come to you as soon as I was informed that you were awake. Your physician performed an autopsy on the terrorist. That is, by the way, a useful word, which does not exist on World. We shall appropriate it. The doctors found this in the mass of body tissues. It is engraved titanium, possibly created to survive the blast. Secretary-General Desai suggests that it is a means to claim credit, a 'logo.' Other Terrans have agreed, but none know what it means. Can you aid us? Is it possibly related to one of the victims? You were a close friend of Dr. Blanford."

He held up something close to the glass: a flat piece of metal about three inches square. Whatever was pictured on it was too small for Marianne to see from her bed.

Smith said, "I will have Dr. Potter bring it to you."

"No, don't." Ann would have to put on a space suit and maneuver through the double airlock with respirator. The fever in Marianne's brain could not wait that long. She pulled out her catheter tube, giving a small shriek at the unexpected pain. Then she heaved herself out of bed and dragged the IV pole over to the clear barrier. Ann began to sputter. Marianne ignored her.

On the square of metal was etched a stylized purple rocket ship, sprouting leaves.

Not Elizabeth. Ryan.

"Dr. Jenner?"

"They're an invasive species," Ryan had said.

"Didn't you hear a word I said?" Marianne said. "They're not 'invasive,' or at least not if our testing confirms the ambassador's story. They're native to Earth."

"An invasive species is native to Earth. It's just not in the ecological niche it evolved for."

"Dr. Jenner?" the ambassador repeated. "Are you all right?"

Ryan, his passion about purple loosestrife a family joke. Ryan, interested in the *Embassy,* as Connie was not, asking questions about the facilities and the layout while Marianne cuddled her new grandson. Ryan, important enough in this terrorist organization to have selected its emblem from a sheet of drawings in a kitschy bathroom.

Ryan, her secretive and passionate son.

"Dr. Jenner, I must insist—"

"Yes. *Yes.* I recognize that thing. I know who—what group—you should look for." Her heart shattered.

Smith studied her through the glass. The large, calm eyes—Noah's eyes now, except for the color—held compassion.

"Someone you know."

"Yes."

"It doesn't matter. We shall not look for them."

The words didn't process. "Not . . . not look for them?"

"No. It will not happen again. The *Embassy* has been sealed and the Terrans removed except for a handful of scientists directly involved in immunology, all of whom have chosen to stay, and all of whom we trust."

"But—"

"And, of course, those of our clan members who wish to stay."

Marianne stared at Smith through the glass, the impermeable barrier. Never had he seemed more alien. Why would this intelligent man believe that just because a handful of Terrans shared a mitochondrial haplotype with him, they could not be terrorists, too? Was it a cultural blind spot, similar to the Terran millennial-long belief in the divine right of kings? Was it some form of perception, the product of divergent evolution, that let his brain perceive things she could not? Or did he simply have in place such heavy surveillance and protective devices that people like Noah, sequestered in a different part of the *Embassy,* presented no threat?

Then the rest of what he had said struck her. "Immunologists?"

"Time is short, Dr. Jenner. The spore cloud will envelop Earth in merely a few months. We must perform intensive tests on you and the other infected people."

"Other?"

"Dr. Ahmed Rafat and two lab technicians, Penelope Hodgson and Robert Chavez. They are, of course, all volunteers. They will be joining you soon in quarantine."

Rage tore through her, all the rage held back, pent up, about Evan's death, about Ryan's deceit, about Noah's defection. "Why not any of your own people? No, don't tell me that you're all too valuable—so are we! Why only Terrans? If we take this risk, why don't you? And what the fuck happens when the cloud does hit? Do you take off two days before, keeping yourselves safe and leaving Earth to die? You know very well that there is no chance of developing a real vaccine in the time left, let alone manufacturing and distributing it! What then? How can you just—"

But Ambassador Smith was already moving away from her, behind the shatterproof glass. The ceiling said, without inflection or emotion, "I am sorry."

CHAPTER 10

S minus 3 months

Noah stood in the middle of the circle of Terrans. Fifty, sixty—they had all come aboard the *Embassy* in the last few days, as time shortened. Not all were L7s; some were families of clan brothers, and these too had been welcomed, since they'd had the defiance to ask for asylum when the directives said explicitly that only L7s would be taken in. There was something wrong with this system, Noah thought, but he did not think hard about what it might be.

The room, large and bare, was in neither the World quarters nor the now-sealed part of the *Embassy* where the Terran scientists worked. The few scientists left aboard, anyway. The room's air, gravity, and light were all Terran, and Noah again wore an energy suit. He could see its faint shimmer along his arms as he raised them in welcome. He hadn't realized how much he was going to hate having to don the suit again.

"I am Noah," he said.

The people pressed against the walls of the bare room or huddled in small groups or sat as close to Noah as they could, cross-legged on the hard floor. They looked terrified or hopeful or defiant or already grieving for what might be lost. They all, even the ones who like Kayla and Isabelle had been here for a while, expected to die if they were left behind on Earth.

"I will be your leader and teacher. But first, I will explain the choice you must all make, now. You can choose to leave with the people of World, when we return to the home world. Or you can stay here, on Earth."

"To die!" someone shouted. "Some choice!"

Noah found the shouter: a young man standing close behind him, fists clenched at his side. He wore ripped jeans, a pin through his eyebrow, and a scowl. Noah felt the shock of recognition that had thrilled through him before: with the nurse on the Upper West Side of New York; when he'd met Mee^haoį. Not even Llaa^mohį, who was a geneticist, could explain that shock, although she seemed to think it had to do with certain genetically determined pathways in Noah's L7 brain coupled with the faint electromagnetic field surrounding every human skull. She was fascinated by it.

Lisa Guiterrez, Noah remembered, had also attributed it to neurological pathways, changed by his heavy use of sugarcane.

Noah said to the scowler, "What is your name?"

He said, "Why?"

"I'd like to know it. We are clan brothers."

"I'm not your fucking brother. I'm here because it's my only option to not die."

A child on its mother's lap started to cry. People murmured to each other, most not taking their eyes off Noah. Waiting, to see what Noah did about the young man. Answer him? Let it go? Have him put off the *Embassy*?

Noah knew it would not take much to ignite these desperate people into attacking him, the alien-looking stand-in for the Worlders they had no way to reach.

He said gently to the young man, to all of them, to his absent and injured and courageous mother: "I'm going to explain your real choices. Please listen."

———

Something was wrong.

One day passed, then another, then another. Marianne did not get sick. Nor did Ahmed Rafat and Penny Hodgson. Robbie Chavez did, but not very.

Harrison Rice stood with Ann Potter in front of Marianne's glass quarantine cage, known as a "slammer." He updated Marianne on the latest lab reports. In identical slammers, two across a narrow corridor and one beside her, Marianne could see the three other infected people. The rooms had been created, as if by alchemy, by a Deneb that Marianne had not seen before—presumably an engineer of some unknowable building methods. Ahmed stood close to his glass, listening. Penny was asleep. Robbie, his face filmed with sweat, lay in bed, listening.

Ann Potter said, "You're not initially viremic but—"

"What does that mean?" Marianne interrupted.

Harrison answered. "It means lab tests show that as with Namechek and Lloyd, the spores were detectable in the first samples taken from your respiratory tract. So the virus should be present in your bloodstream and so have access to the rest of your body. However, we can't find it. Well, that can happen. Viruses are elusive. But as far as we can tell, you aren't developing antibodies against the virus, as the infected mice did. That may mean that we just haven't isolated the antibodies yet. *Or* that your body doesn't consider the virus a foreign invader, which seems unlikely. *Or* that in humans but not in mice, the virus has dived into an organ to multiply until its offspring burst out again. Malaria does that. *Or* that the virus samples in the lab, grown artificially, have mutated into harmlessness, differing from their wild cousins in the approaching cloud. *Or* it's possible that none of us know what the hell we're doing with this crazy pathogen." He smiled at her, the most strained smile she had ever seen.

Marianne said, "What do the Denebs think?" Supposedly Harrison was co-lead with Deneb Scientist Jones.

"I have no idea what they think. None of us have seen any of them."

"Not seen them?"

"No. We share all our data and samples, of course. Half of the samples go into an airlock for them, and the data over the LAN. But all we get in return is a thank-you onscreen. Maybe they're not making progress, either, but at least they could tell us what they haven't discovered."

This was the frankest that Harrison had ever been with her about the Denebs. "Do we know . . . this may sound weird, but do we know that they're still here at all? Is it possible they all left Earth already?" *Noah.*

He said, "It's possible, I suppose. We have no news from the outside world, of course, so it's possible they prerecorded all those thank-yous, blew up New York, and took off for the stars. But I don't think so. If they had, they'd have at least unsealed us from this floating plastic bubble. Which, incidentally, has become completely opaque, even on the observation deck."

Marianne hadn't known there was an observation deck. She and Evan had not found it during their one exploration of the *Embassy.*

Harrison continued. "Your cells are not making an interferon response, either. That's a small protein molecule that can be produced in any cell in response to the presence of viral nucleic acid. You're not making it."

"Which means . . ."

"Probably it means that there is no viral nucleic acid in your cells."

"Are Robbie's cells making interferon?"

"Yes. Also antibodies. Plus immune responses like—Ann, what does your chart on Chavez show for this morning?"

Ann said, "Fever of hundred and one, not at all dangerous. Chest congestion, also not at dangerous levels, some sinus involvement. He has the equivalent of mild bronchitis."

Marianne said, "But why is Robbie sick when the rest of us aren't?"

"Ah," Harrison Rice said, and for the first time she heard the trace of a Canadian accent, "that's the big question, isn't it? In immunology, it always is. Sometimes genetic differences between infected hosts are the critical piece of the puzzle in understanding why an identical virus causes serious disease or death in one individual—or one group— and little reaction or none at all in other people. Is Robbie sick and you're not because of your respective genes? We don't know."

"But you can use Robbie's antibodies to maybe develop a vaccine?"

He didn't answer. She knew the second the words left her mouth how stupid they were. Harrison might have antibodies, but he had no time. None of them had enough time.

Yet they all worked on, as if they did. Because that's what humans did.

Instead of answering her question, he said gently, "I need more samples, Marianne. I'm sorry."

"Yes."

Fifteen minutes later he entered her slammer, dressed in full space suit and sounding as if speaking through a vacuum cleaner. "Blood samples plus a tissue biopsy, just lie back down and hold still, please . . ."

Weeks ago, over coffee, he had told her of an old joke among immunologists working with lethal diseases: *The first person to isolate a virus in the lab by getting infected is a hero. The second is a fool.* Well, that made Marianne a fool. So be it.

She said to Harrison, "And the aliens haven't . . . Ow!"

"Baby." He withdrew the biopsy needle and slapped a bandage over the site.

She tried again. "And the aliens haven't commented at all on Robbie's diagnosis? Not a word?"

"Not a word."

Marianne frowned. "Something isn't right here."

"No," Harrison said, bagging his samples, "it certainly is not."

Nothing, Noah thought, had ever felt more right, not in his entire life.

He raised himself on one elbow and looked down at Llaa^mohเ. She still slept, her naked body and long legs tangled in the light blanket made of some substance he could not name. Her wiry dark hair smelled of something like cinnamon, although it probably wasn't. The blanket smelled of sex.

He knew now why he had not felt the same shock of recognition at their first meeting that he had felt with Mee^haoเ and the unnamed New York nurse and surly young Tony Schrupp, the kid with the eyebrow piercing. After the World geneticists had done their work, Mee^haoเ had explained it to him. Noah felt profound relief. He and Llaa^mohเ shared a mitochondrial DNA group, but not a nuclear DNA one. They were not too genetically close to mate.

Of course, they could have had sex anyway; World had, and without cultural shame or religious prejudice, discovered birth control early on. But for the first time in his life, Noah did not want just sex. He wanted to mate.

The miracle was that she did, too. Initially he feared that for her it was mere novelty: be the first Worlder to sleep with a Terran! But it was not. Just yesterday they had signed a five-year mating contract, followed by a lovely ceremony in the garden to which every single Worlder had come. Noah had never known exactly how many were aboard the *Embassy*; now he did. They had all danced with him, every single one, and also with her. Mee^haoเ himself had pierced their right ears and hung from them the wedding silver, shaped like stylized versions of the small flowers that had once, very long ago, been the real thing.

"Is better," Noah had said in his accented, still clumsy World. "We want not bunch of dead vegetation dangle from our ears." At least, that's what he hoped he'd said. Everyone had laughed.

Noah reached out one finger to stroke Llaa^mohเ's hair. A miracle, yes. A whole skyful of miracles, but none as much as this: Now he knew who he was and where he belonged and what he was going to do with his life.

His only regret was that his mother had not been at the mating ceremony. And—yes, forgiveness was in order here!—Elizabeth and Ryan, too. They had disparaged him his entire life and he would never see them again, but they were still his first family. Just not the one that any longer mattered.

Llaa^mohi stirred, woke, and reached for him.

Robbie Chavez, still weak from *Respirovirus sporii*, nonetheless gave so many blood and tissue samples that he joked he'd lost ten pounds without dieting. It wasn't much of a joke, but everyone laughed. Some of the laughter held hysteria.

Twenty-two people remained aboard the *Embassy*. Why, Marianne sometimes wondered, had these twenty-two chosen to stay and work until the last possible second? Because the odds of finding anything that would affect the coming die-off were very low. They all knew that. Yet here they were, knowing they would die in this fantastically equipped, cut-off-from-the-world lab instead of with their families. Didn't any of them have families? Why were they still here?

Why was she?

No one discussed this. They discussed only work, which went on eighteen hours a day. Brief breaks for microwaved meals from the freezer. Briefer—not in actuality, but that's how it felt—for sleep.

The four people exposed to *R. sporii* worked outside the slammers; maintaining biosafety no longer seemed important. No one knew why those four had not sickened, or why no one else became ill. Marianne relearned lab procedures she had not performed since grad school. Theoretical evolutionary biologists did not work as immunologists. She did now.

Every day, the team sent samples data to the Denebs. Every day, the Denebs gave thanks, and nothing else.

In July, eight and a half months after they'd first been given the spores to work with, the scientists finally succeeded in growing the virus in a culture. There was a celebration of sorts. Harrison Rice produced a hoarded bottle of champagne.

"We'll be too drunk to work," Marianne joked. She'd come to admire Harrison's unflagging cheerfulness, as well as his robust body.

"On one twenty-secondth of one bottle?" he said. "I don't think so."

"Well, maybe not everyone drinks."

Almost no one did. Marianne, Harrison, and Robbie Chavez drank the bottle. Culturing the virus, which should have been a victory, seemed to turn the irritable more irritable, the dour more dour. The tiny triumph underlined how little they had actually achieved. People began to turn strange. The unrelenting work, broken sleep, and constant tension created neuroses.

Penny Hodgson turned compulsive about the autoclave: It must be loaded just so, in just this order, and only odd numbers of tubes could be placed in the rack at one time. She flew into a rage when she discovered eight tubes, or twelve.

William Parker, Nobel Laureate in medicine, began to hum as he worked. Eighteen hours a day of humming. If told to stop, he did, and then unknowingly resumed a few minutes later. He could not carry a tune, and he liked lugubrious country and western tunes.

Marianne began to notice feet. Every few seconds, she glanced at the feet of others in the lab, checking that they still had them. Harrison's work boots, as if he tramped the forests of Hudson's Bay. Mark Wu's black oxfords. Penny's Nikes—did she think she'd be going for a run? Robbie's sandals. Ann's—

Stop it, Marianne!

She couldn't.

They stopped sending samples and data to the Denebs and held their collective breath, waiting to see what would happen. Nothing did.

Work boots, oxfords, Nikes, sandals—

"I think," Harrison said, "that I've found something."

It was an unfamiliar protein in Marianne's blood. Did it have anything to do with the virus? They didn't know. Feverishly they set to work culturing it, sequencing it, photographing it, looking for it in everyone else. The protein was all they had.

It was August.

The outside world, with which they had no contact, had ceased to exist for them, even as they raced to save it.

Work boots—

Oxfords—

Sandals—

It was September.

Rain fell in the garden. Noah tilted his head to the artificial sky. He loved rainy afternoons, even if this was not really rain, nor afternoon. Soon he would experience the real thing.

Llaa^mohȷ came toward him through the dark, lush leaves open as welcoming hands. Noah was surprised; these important days she rarely left the lab. Too much to do.

She said, "Should not you be teaching?"

He wanted to say *"I'm playing hooky"* but had no idea what the idiom would be in World. Instead he said, hoping he had the tenses right, "My students I will return at soon. Why you here? Something is wrong?"

"All is right." She moved into his arms. Again Noah was surprised; Worlders did not touch sexually in public places, even public places temporarily empty. Others might come by, unmated others, and it was just as rude to display physical affection in front of those without it as to eat in front of anyone hungry.

"Llaa^mohȷ—"

She whispered into his ear. Her words blended with the rain, with the rich flower scents, with the odor of wet dirt. Noah clutched her and began to cry.

———

S minus 2 weeks

The common room outside the lab was littered with frozen food trays, with discarded sterile wrappings, with an empty disinfectant bottle. Harrison slumped in a chair and said the obvious.

"We've failed, Marianne."

"Yes," she said. "I know." And then, fiercely, "Do you think the Denebs know more than we do? And aren't sharing?"

"Who knows?"

"Fucking bastards," Marianne said. Weeks ago she had crossed the line from defending the aliens to blaming them. How much of humanity had been ahead of her in that? By now, maybe all of it.

They had discovered nothing useful about the anomalous protein in Marianne's blood. The human body contained so many proteins whose identities were not understood. But that wouldn't make any difference, not now. There wasn't enough time.

Nine, not counting him. The rest had been put ashore, to face whatever would happen to them on Earth. Noah would have much preferred to be with Llaa^moh¡, but she of course had duties. Even unannounced, departure was dangerous. Too many countries had too many formidable weapons.

So instead of standing beside Llaa^moh¡, Noah sat in his energy suit in the Terran compartment of the shuttle. Around him, strapped into chairs, sat the nine Terrans going to World. The straps were unnecessary; Llaa^moh¡ had told him that the acceleration would feel mild, due to the same gravity-altering machinery that had made the World section of the *Embassy* so comfortable. But Terrans were used to straps in moving vehicles, so there were straps.

Kayla Rhinehart and her little son.

Her sister Isabelle.

The surly Tony Schrupp, a surprise. Noah had been sure Tony would change his mind.

A young woman, five months pregnant, who *"wanted to give my baby a better life."* She did not say what her previous life had been, but there were bruises on her arms and legs.

A pair of thirty-something brothers with restless, eager-for-adventure eyes.

A middle-aged journalist with a sun-leathered face and impressive byline, recorders in her extensive luggage.

And, most unexpected, a Terran physicist, Dr. Nathan Beyon of Massachusetts Institute of Technology.

Nine Terrans willing to go to the stars.

A slight jolt. Noah smiled at the people under his leadership—he, who had never led anything before, not even his own life—and said, "Here we go."

That seemed inadequate, so he said, "We are off to the stars!"

That seemed dumb. Tony sneered. The journalist looked amused. Austin clutched his mother.

Noah said, "Your new life will be wonderful. Believe it."

Kayla gave him a wobbly smile.

Harrison said, "We did our best."

"I used to tell my kids that," Marianne said. "Just do your best, I'd say, and nobody can ask more of you than that. I was wrong."

"Well, they were kids," he said. His broad, strong face sagged with fatigue, with defeat. He had worked so hard. They had all of them worked so hard.

"Harrison," she began, and didn't get to finish her sentence.

Between one breath and the next, Harrison Rice and the lab, along with everything else, disappeared.

CHAPTER 11

S minus 0

She could not imagine where she was.

Cool darkness, with the sky above her brightening every second. It had been so long since Marianne had seen a dawn sky, or any sky. Silver-gray, then pearl, and now the first flush of pink. The floor rocked gently. Then the last of the knockout gas left her brain and she sat up. A kind of glorified barge, flat and wide with a single square rod jutting from the middle. The barge floated gently on New York Harbor. The sea was smooth as polished gray wood. In one direction rose the skyline of Manhattan; in the other, the *Embassy*. All around her lay her colleagues: Dr. Rafat, Harrison Rice and Ann Potter, lab techs Penny and Robbie, all the rest of the twenty-two people who'd still been aboard the *Embassy*. They wore their daily clothing. In her jeans and tee, Marianne shivered in a sudden breeze.

Nearby lay a pile of blankets. She took a yellow one and wrapped it around her shoulders. It felt warm and silky, although clearly not made of silk. Other people began to stir. Pink tinged the east.

Harrison came to her side. "Marianne?"

Automatically she said, because she'd been saying it so many times each day, "I feel fine." And then, "What the *fuck*?"

He said something just as pointless: "But we have two more weeks!"

"Oh my God!" someone cried, pointing, and Marianne looked up. The eastern horizon turned gold. Against it, a ship, dark and small, shot from the *Embassy* and climbed the sky. Higher and higher, while everyone on the barge shaded their eyes against the rising sun and watched it out of sight.

"They're going," someone said quietly.

They. The Denebs. *Noah*.

Before the tears that stung her eyes could fall, the *Embassy* vanished. One moment it was there, huge and solid and gray in the predawn, and the next it was just gone. The water didn't even ripple.

The metal rod in the center of the barge spoke. Marianne, along with everyone else, turned sharply. Shoulder-high, three feet on each side, the rod had become four screens, each filled with the same alien-human image and mechanical voice.

"This is Ambassador Smith. A short time from now, this recording will go to everyone on Earth, but we wanted you, who have helped us so much, to hear it first. We of World are deeply in your debt. I would like to explain why, and to leave you a gift.

"Your astronomers' calculations were very slightly mistaken, and we did not correct them. In a few hours the spore cloud will envelope your planet. We do not think it will harm you because—"

Someone in the crowd around the screen cried, *"What?"*

"—you are genetically immune to this virus. We suspected as much before we arrived, although we could not be sure. *Homo sapiens* acquired immunity when Earth passed through the cloud the first time, about seventy thousand years ago."

A graphic replaced Smith's face: the Milky Way galaxy, a long dark splotch overlapping it, and a glowing blue dot for Earth. "The rotation of the galaxy plus its movement through space-time will bring you back into contact with the cloud's opposite edge from where it touched you before. Your physicists were able to see the approaching cloud, but your instruments were not advanced enough to understand its shape or depth. Earth will be passing through the edge of the cloud for two-point-six years. On its first contact, the cloud killed every *Homo sapiens* that did not come with this genetic mutation."

A gene sequence of base pairs flashed across the screen, too fast to be noted.

"This sequence will appear again later, in a form you can record. It is found in what you call 'junk DNA.' The sequence is a transposon and you will find it complementary to the spores' genetic code. Your bodies made no antibodies against the spores because it does not consider them invaders. Seventy thousand years ago our people had already been taken from Earth or we, too, would have died. We are without this sequence, which appeared in mutation later than our removal."

Marianne's mind raced. Seventy thousand years ago. The "bottleneck event" that had shrunk the human population on Earth to a mere few thousand. It had not been caused by the Toba volcano or ferocious predators or climate changes, but by the spore cloud. As for the gene sequence—one theory said that much of the human genome consisted of inactive and fossilized viruses absorbed into the DNA. Fossilized and inactive—almost she could hear Evan's voice: *"Or so we thought . . ."*

Smith continued. "You will find that in Marianne Jenner, Ahmed Rafat, and Penelope Hodgson this sequence has already activated, producing the protein already identified in Dr. Jenner's blood, a protein that this recording will detail for you. The protein attaches to the outside of cells and prevents the virus from entering. Soon the genetic sequence will do so in the rest of humanity. Some may become mildly ill, like Robert Chavez, due to faulty protein production. We estimate this will comprise perhaps twenty percent of you. There may be fatalities among the old or already sick, but most of you are genetically protected. Some of your small rodents do not seem to be, which we admit was a great surprise to us, and we cannot say for certain what other Terran species may be susceptible.

"We know that we are fatally susceptible. We cannot alter our own genome, at least not for the living, but we have learned much from you. By the time the spore cloud reaches World, we will have developed a vaccine. This would not have been possible without your full cooperation and your bodily samples. We—"

"If this is true," Penny Hodgson shouted, "why didn't they *tell* us?"

"—did not tell you the complete truth because we believe that had you known Earth was in no critical danger, you would not have allocated so many resources, so much scientific talent, or such urgency into the work on the *Embassy*. We are all human, but your evolutionary history and present culture are very different from ours. You do not build identity on family. You permit much of Earth's population to suffer from lack of food, water, and medical care. We didn't think you would help us as much as we needed unless we withheld from you certain truths. If we were mistaken in our assessment, please forgive us."

They weren't mistaken, Marianne thought.

"We are grateful for your help," Smith said, "even if obtained fraudulently. We leave you a gift in return. This recording contains what you call the 'engineering specs' for a star drive. We have already given you the equations describing the principles. Now you may build a ship. In generations to come, both branches of humanity will profit from more open and truthful exchanges. We will become true brothers.

"Until then, ten Terrans accompany us home. They have chosen to do this, for their own reasons. All were told that they would not die if they remained on Earth, but chose to come anyway. They will become World, creating further friendship with our clan brothers on Terra.

"Again—thank you."

Pandemonium erupted on the barge: talking, arguing, shouting. The sun was above the horizon now. Three Coast Guard ships barreled across the harbor toward the barge. As Marianne clutched her yellow blanket closer against the morning breeze, something vibrated in the pocket of her jeans.

She pulled it out: a flat metal square with Noah's face on it. As soon as her gaze fell on his, the face began to speak. "I'm going with them,

Mom. I want you to know that I am completely happy. This is where I belong. I've mated with Llaa^moh¡—Dr. Jones—and she is pregnant. Your grandchild will be born among the stars. I love you."

Noah's face faded from the small square.

Rage filled her, red sparks burning. Her son, and she would never see him again! Her grandchild, and she would never see him or her at all. She was being robbed, being deprived of what was hers by *right*, the aliens should never have come—

She stopped. Realization slammed into her, and she gripped the rail of the barge so tightly that her nails pierced the wood.

The aliens *had* made a mistake. A huge, colossal, monumental mistake.

Her rage, however irrational, was going to be echoed and amplified across the entire planet. The Denebs had understood that Terrans would work really hard only if their own survival was at stake. But they did not understand the rest of it. The Deneb presence on Earth had caused riots, diversion of resources, deaths, panic, fear. The "mild illness" of the 20 percent like Robbie, happening all at once starting today, was enough to upset every economy on the planet. The aliens had swept like a storm through the world, and as in the aftermath of a superstorm, everything in the landscape had shifted. In addition, the Denebs had carried off ten humans, which could be seen as brainwashing them in order to procure prospective lab rats for future experimentation.

Brothers, yes—but Castor and Pollux, whose bond reached across the stars, or Cain and Abel?

Humans did not forgive easily, and they resented being bought off, even with a star drive. Smith should have left a different gift, one that would not let Terrans come to World, that peaceful and rich planet so unaccustomed to revenge or war.

But on the other hand—she could be wrong. Look how often she'd been wrong already: about Elizabeth, about Ryan, about Smith. Maybe, when the Terran disruptions were over and starships actually built, humanity would become so entranced with the Deneb gift that we would indeed go to World in friendship. Maybe the prospect of going to the stars would even soften American isolationism and draw countries together to share the necessary resources. It could happen. The cooperative genes that had shaped Smith and Jones were also found in the Terran genome.

But—it would happen only if those who wanted it worked hard to convince the rest. Worked, in fact, as hard at urging friendship as they had at ensuring survival. Was that possible? Could it be done?

Why are you here?

To make contact with World. A peace mission.

She gazed up at the multicolored dawn sky, but the ship was already out of sight. Only its after-image remained in her sight.

"Harrison," Marianne said, and felt her own words steady her, "we have a lot of work to do."

PART TWO

Man is always prey to his truths. Once he has
admitted them, he cannot free himself from them.

—Albert Camus

CHAPTER 12

S plus 2.6 years

Marianne stood in a small storage room somewhere in the DeBartolo Performing Arts Center at the University of Notre Dame, waiting to go on stage and staring at eight mice.

They were, of course, dead. These eight, however, looked unnervingly lifelike, superb examples of the taxidermist's art. Why were they here, meeting her gaze with their shiny lifeless eyes from behind the glass of a tiered display case? Had they been moved to this unlikely venue from another building, to sit among cardboard cartons and discouraged-looking mops, because someone could no longer bear to be reminded of what had been lost?

Sissy Tate, Marianne's assistant, stuck her head into the room. "Ten minutes, Marianne. Are those mice? Wow, it's stuffy in here."

"No windows. What about the—"

"They should have put you in the green room! Or at least a dressing room!" Sissy shook her frizzy cherry-red curls, which leaped around her head as if electrified. Two weeks ago the curls had been the same rich brown as her skin. Today's sweater, purple covered with tiny mirrors, glittered.

Marianne said, "There's a concert setting up in the big hall. No space."

"That's not the reason and we both know it. But at least you don't have to worry about the storm—this one is going to miss South

Bend. No problem." Sissy's head disappeared, and Marianne went back to contemplating mice.

Eight representatives of what had been the world's most common herbivore, now existing nowhere in the world except for a few sealed labs.

Mus musculus and *Mus domesticus,* their pointed snouts and scaly tails familiar to anyone who ever baited a mousetrap or worked in a laboratory.

A deer mouse and a white-footed mouse, almost twins, looking like refugees from a Disney cartoon.

On the second glass shelf, the shaggy, short-tailed meadow vole and its cousin, the woodland vole.

A bog lemming, its lips drawn back to show the grooves on its upper incisors.

And finally, a jumping mouse, looking lopsided with its huge hind feet and short forelimbs.

"Hey," Marianne said to the jumping mouse, of which no specimens had been saved. "Sorry you're extinct."

"You talking to a mouse?" a deep voice said behind her.

Marianne turned to Tim. "I didn't hear you come in."

"Yeah, well, I came to say we might have a problem."

"But Sissy just said—"

"No, not the storm. Your speech. But first—were you talking to those *mice?*"

At Tim's grin, Marianne felt herself flush. He often had that effect on her; she knew it; she was profoundly grateful that Tim Saunders did not. He lived with Sissy, he was fifteen years her junior, and he was not all that bright. To be so affected on a visceral level by someone so inappropriate was deeply embarrassing to Marianne. The powerful lean body, mahogany hair, bright turquoise eyes that made her feel as if she stood in a blue spotlight—none of this should set her hormones on high alert, not at her age. She was a grandmother twice over, for chrissake. And she lived with Harrison Rice, contentedly.

Contentedly but not passionately, said the rebellious part of her that was still seventeen. Marianne, a long way from seventeen, was appalled at that part of herself. Surely by now all adolescent fogs of desire should have evaporated from her emotions, from her mind, from her—

"I was not talking to the mice," she said with what she hoped was dignity.

"Sure looked like it." Another too-masculine grin. *Damn, damn, damn.* If she had to still feel the fog, why for such an obvious, even clichéd, pretty boy? Not that Tim was only that.

She said, "What's the problem with my speech?"

"The crowd for it. They look nasty."

Marianne frowned. Notre Dame was not supposed to be one of the nasty crowds. A noted research center, the university was pro-science, and although still Catholic-conservative on a few issues, had a socially liberal faculty and, mostly, student body. The university had even reimbursed her travel expenses, which few of her speech venues did. "How nasty?"

"Can't tell yet. But I'm on it." Tim left.

In the last two and a half years, Marianne had given over five hundred speeches for the Star Brotherhood Foundation, which she and Harrison had founded almost as soon as the alien ship had lifted off, taking Noah and nine other Terrans with it. The foundation's purpose was to convince the world that a spaceship should be built, using the plans that the aliens had gifted, to take to humanity to the stars.

At first, the foundation had gone well. The spore plague had been mild, with fewer Americans than expected getting sick, fewer still dying. The world's physicists, engineers, visionaries had all agreed with her. Humanity was going to the stars! Public opinion had been sharply divided, but Marianne and Harrison had been hopeful.

Then two things happened. First, morbidity and mortality reports came from Central Asia. Some anomaly in a genome common to that part of the world caused far more deaths from *R. sporii* than anywhere else. Horrific deaths, gasping for air, drowning in fluids in their lungs. There was still neither vaccine nor gene therapy for *R. sporii,* and the spores were apparently going to be present on Earth forever, affecting each new generation. Harrison's team had developed a postinfection treatment for the disease, but it was expensive and distribution in Russia and her neighbors was sporadic and spotty. Already beset by ethnic unrest, the countries of the former Soviet Union attacked each other with irrational blame. Hard-liners took leadership in half a dozen countries. Hatred of Denebs, skillfully fanned for political purposes, flourished in Russia, in Ukraine, in Kazakhstan and Turkmenistan and Uzbekistan.

Simultaneously, eight species of mice died.

Who knew that the loss of a bunch of rodents could collapse the world economy? Certainly Marianne hadn't known, but like everyone else, she learned rapidly. An ecology, as Ryan had been telling her for over a decade, was a fragile construct. Alter one major element in it, and everything else was disturbed. Those common and ubiquitous mice were—had been—a major element.

Without the mice, predators from hawks to bears did not have enough to eat. Some died; some shifted to eating such alternate prey as snakes. The snake population shrank, and their prey, such as rats and lizards, flourished. Rat-borne diseases were now rampant. Arctic wolves starved.

Without the mice to eat their seeds, some wild plants went unchecked, growing completely out of control and choking off their less hardy neighbors, which further affected their ecosystems.

Without the mice to disperse their seeds, some flora began to disappear.

Without the mice to eat insects, some species flourished, including cockroaches, some caterpillars, some beetles.

Without the mice, which in some parts of the world had eaten huge amounts of cultivated grain, farmers suddenly had bumper crops. The supply glut caused prices to plummet. Whole economies tottered.

Every market on Earth had been affected. Conspiracy theories thrived like kudzu: The Denebs were a fiction and the spore plague spread by WHO to neutralize the Russians in world politics. No, the aliens were real and were agents of the anti-Christ—see Revelations if you don't believe me! No, they were part of an interstellar cartel crushing Earth because we would be trade competition. Sometimes the Jews were part of this cartel, sometimes the Illuminati, sometimes the Russians or Chinese or Arabs. Accusations grew more bitter, small wars broke out, and the third world struggled, often unsuccessfully, to survive.

Marianne kept giving speeches. Harrison now worked with a re-search team at Columbia, desperately trying to genetically alter the few surviving mice into breeds that could survive in a world where *R. sporii* lay dormant in every meadow, every river, every rooftop. *"But,"* Marianne urged over and over, *"the aliens did not cause the spore cloud! Denebs are indeed human, our genetic brothers. Their intentions during their year on Earth had been good and their mistakes accidental. A ship should be built using the plans that the aliens had gifted to humanity, taking us to the stars."*

But the Denebs and the spore cloud had arrived more or less to-gether, and for a huge number of Americans, that was enough to "prove causation." At a speech three months ago, in Memphis, she and Sissy had been pelted with eggs and tomatoes. One rock had been thrown. After the community organizer had hustled them to safety, Marianne had learned that some of the pelters had been armed with more than rocks, although no weapons had been fired.

"You need a bodyguard," Sissy had said. "I know somebody. We can trust him." The foundation had stretched its miniscule budget to hire Tim Saunders as her bodyguard. Ex–Special Forces, he owned a small arsenal and was licensed to use it. A week later, he moved in with Sissy.

Marianne said to the stuffed *Mus musculus*, " 'Not a creature was stirring, not even a mouse.' " It didn't answer. *Mus*, she remembered, had once been nonnative to the United States. An invasive species.

Behind her, Sissy said, "You talking to those *mice*?"

"No," Marianne said.

"Well, it's time. Dr. Mendenhall's here to escort you on stage."

Marianne went to give her speech.

The Decio Mainstage Theatre held 350 seats, and all of them were filled. Marianne walked onto the stage, which featured a gorgeous proscenium arch, and stood quietly near the lectern while the dean of Sciences introduced her. The theater's excellent acoustics carried Dr. Mendenhall's words throughout the beautiful, high-ceilinged space with its polished, curving balustrades. Marianne, accustomed to much shabbier venues, wondered how the university could afford to maintain the theater so well. Their endowment must be enormous.

The students were too quiet. Many of them did not look like students.

The house lights had been left up. As she began to talk, the students neither stirred nor changed expression. She covered her three main points: The aliens were indeed human, our genetic brothers; all the scientific evidence confirmed that. Their intentions during their year on Earth had been good, their mistakes accidental, and they had *not* caused the spore cloud. The spaceship should be—

A girl's voice, clear and ringing, called from the balcony. "You might not think it was such an accident if *your* uncle died of spore disease!"

A boy stood in the third row and said, "Isn't it true the Denebs pay you to advertise this so-called spaceship?"

"Let her finish," someone else called, and the boy sat down. Marianne hoped it would still be all right, but from the corner of her eye she saw Tim standing in the wings, tense and alert.

"Finish us, is what you mean," someone shouted—an older voice, deep with maturity and disgust.

Dr. Mendenhall appeared beside Marianne and grasped the mic. "This university *will* treat its guests with courtesy. So whether you are a member of the student body or of the visiting public, you will let Dr. Jenner complete her remarks."

They did, but Marianne could feel their anger, rising in the lovely space, a noxious gas. People murmured now, an almost infrasonic drone like a muted drill. Her words didn't falter, but they sped up.

"In conclusion, let me just say that—"

Someone called, "How do you feel about your son Noah going with the aliens to World? Isn't that the real reason you're so desperate for us to go there, and why should the taxpayers fund your little family reunion?"

Mendenhall said, "Dr. Jenner has not—"

"No, I want to answer that," Marianne said. But the background drone did not stop. She raised her voice.

"Yes, my son accompanied the Denebs to their home planet, along with nine other Terrans—as I'm sure you all already know. My family, too, has been affected by the aliens. But two points need to be made here—*must* be made here. First, had the Denebs not come to Earth, many more families would have been tragically stricken than actually were. Without the work that Worlders and Terrans did together aboard the *Embassy,* we would not have had the postinfection treatment for spore plague, a treatment that saved many. Second, we should fund the spaceship to go to World not because I want to see Noah— although of course I do—but because humanity can benefit tremendously from the kind of free exchange of ideas that have already enriched our scientific understanding of—"

"*Enriched!*" The voice in the balcony was almost a shriek. And yet it seemed to Marianne that it also held a forced note, like a mediocre actor. "You think the aliens left us enriched, lady? My family's farm lost everything!"

"My father's stocks are gone!" From a seat to her left.

"The economy's in the toilet and none of us will get jobs when we graduate, because of your fucking aliens!"

"My apartment's overrun with rats!"

"Did you yourself ever *see* anybody die of spore disease?"

People were on their feet now. Some looked bewildered, students and faculty taken by surprise. Others reached into purses and bags and backpacks, and eggs and rotten fruit began to rain onto the stage. Marianne stood her ground; this had happened before. She cried, "We cannot get—" at the same moment that an outraged Dr. Mendenhall shouted, "People! People!"

The lights went out.

A shocked, disoriented moment. Then it all happened at once. Marianne heard bodies shoving, steps running toward the stage, and the sound of gunfire. Screams. Tim was on her, covering her body with his own, pulling her relentlessly to one side. He knew where he was going, even in the dark; he'd have made sure earlier of the exits. In thirty seconds Marianne was in the wings, through a fire door, hustled down a set of steps.

She gasped, "I can't just leave Dr.—"

"Forget him," Tim said grimly, "it's you they want. Come on, Marianne!"

She was out another door, she was outside, she was running across a parking lot, bent low and shielded by Tim's arm. Then she was in the car and Sissy was driving away as the first of the police cars raced toward the arts center.

"You okay?" Tim said.

"Yes, but—"

"Fucking amateurs." He was smiling: adrenaline pumping, taut body alive. "Didn't even block the exits. Not a clue how to organize a riot."

"Good thing for us," Sissy said tartly, her red curls bobbing in the rearview mirror. "Marianne, you want to go make a police report?"

"Yes," she said. "That . . . that hasn't happened before. Not so very . . . that hasn't happened."

"Folks are riled up," Tim said, without rancor. He was still grinning.

Marianne turned away and stared at the darkness rushing past the car window.

She had never seen a person die of spore disease. Only mice.

One speech in Ohio and one in Pennsylvania, neither violent. The three of them took turns driving the Ford minivan back to New York. Somewhere near Harrisburg, Marianne was at the wheel, Sissy beside her, Tim folded up in the backseat, asleep even though it was only late afternoon. Thin April sunshine cast long shadows on empty fields beside the turnpike. One long stretch was littered with downed trees; a tornado had come through here a few weeks ago. April was the start of a robust tornado season in a state that, once, had seldom experienced them.

Sissy said quietly, "You don't like this."

"April? No. I never did." Kyle had died in April, which every year brought grief not that her alcoholic husband was dead of cirrhosis, but that her main emotion had been relief. Surely a long marriage—any marriage—deserved more than that.

"Not April," Sissy said. "You don't like giving speeches. But you were a teacher."

Marianne smiled, grimly. "I lectured mostly to graduate students who were eager to hear me. Or if not eager, at least resigned—not like these speeches. Nobody in Bio 572, Theories of Punctuated Evolution, was armed."

"But you do it because you think it's important. That's really brave, Marianne."

Tears blurred the road; immediately Marianne blinked them away. Why couldn't Ryan or Elizabeth see it like that? Elizabeth, now transferred to Texas, blamed the Denebs for wrecking the economy. And Ryan . . . Marianne did not want to think about what Ryan said, or had done.

Sometimes she imagined that Sissy was her daughter. That brought more guilt; it seemed a slight to her actual daughter. But Sissy gave Marianne more understanding, more warmth, more support than anyone else.

They had met a year ago when Sissy had walked into the tiny office of the Star Brotherhood Foundation office and said, "You need me."

Marianne had been having a bad day. She looked at the fantastic figure in front of her: a small black woman with purple curls that looked fresh from a Van der Graaf generator, tight jeans, and a tee sewn densely with beer-bottle caps. She snapped, "No, I don't."

"Yes, you do. I've been at your last three speeches. You were late for one because you packed in too many appointments—you told the audience that. You got hoarse at one because you didn't bring a bottle of water and nobody supplied you. The PowerPoint didn't work right at one because nobody checked it. And look at that pile of papers on your desk—your filing system must be shit, if you have one at all. My name is Sissy Tate and I'm a top-grade administrative assistant. Here's my résumé and references. I don't care if you can't pay me much because I believe in what you're doing."

Marianne stared at Sissy. An infiltrator from one of the hate groups? It had been tried before. "Who do you work for?"

Sissy gave her a thousand-watt smile. "For you, Dr. Jenner. And brotherhood with Denebs. What's wrong with people that they cain't see how huge it is that we ain't alone in the universe?" When Sissy got excited, her correct English slipped into something else. Her intelligence and idealism, however, were unwavering. Even before the exhaustive background check, Marianne knew she would hire her. This girl had something. This girl was something.

Sissy had proved as efficient as she claimed. Their friendship, however, crossing generational and racial and educational lines, had nothing to do with Sissy's job.

In the backseat, Tim stirred. "We there yet?"

"No," Sissy said. "Go back to sleep. You're amazing, the way you sleep anywhere."

"Wish I didn't. Sleep's a waste of time."

"But how else will you dream of me?"

Tim laughed. "Pull over—my turn to drive."

They all changed places. City lights shone by the time they reached New York. The Holland Tunnel was no longer safe; the city had limited money for infrastructure repair. The Lincoln Tunnel now closed at 10:00 p.m. Tim drove over the George Washington Bridge and headed south to Columbia University.

"God, I'm tired," Marianne said.

Sissy turned to smile at Tim. Neither of them looked at all tired. Sissy was thirty-two, Tim thirty-seven. Marianne caught Sissy's half-lowered eyelids, her hand creeping toward his neck. "Marianne, we'll drop you first and bring the car back in the morning, okay?"

"Sure," Marianne said brightly. Jealousy of the night ahead of them was stupid, juvenile, contemptible. She felt old.

Harrison was awake, waiting for her in their apartment in the security-fortified area near Columbia. He sat sipping scotch and frowning at something on his tablet. "How did it go?"

"Fine. Some trouble at Notre Dame, but nothing Tim couldn't handle." She said it lightly; Harrison didn't like Tim, although he had never said so. But Marianne knew, and knew why. Harrison was the most intelligent man Marianne had ever met, decent and kind. But he was fifty-nine, spent his days in a lab, and was losing his hair. Tim was thirty-seven, worked out two hours a day at the gym, and had hair that hung thickly to his shoulders.

Nobody was above jealousy.

Moved to affection, she sat on the arm of Harrison's chair and hugged him. "I missed you. What happened here?"

"Some disturbing data." He pulled away from her, and she removed herself to another chair.

"What data? On the mice?"

"No. This study in *Nature*. Karcher is the lead researcher." He held out the tablet.

Marianne didn't take it. *Nature* was one of the most respected multidisciplinary peer-reviewed journals in the world, and James Karcher was a Nobel Laureate in medicine. But she was tired, and Harrison's tiny rejection hurt. There would be no sex tonight. Like most other nights.

More guilt. She only felt juiced up because of Tim's disturbing, utterly forbidden presence. "Tell me what Karcher says."

"It's a statistical analysis, so I suspect his postdocs did it and his name is on it mostly so it will be noticed. Which it should be. It's about a significant increase both in reported agitation and in hearing problems among children born since the spore cloud. We knew about the hearing issues, of course, but nobody has quantified the data and related it to infant agitation."

"How is that related to *R. sporii*?"

"Well, that's the point, isn't it? We know hardly anything about its genetic effects on fetuses. It's only been two and a half years, and very few infants have brain surgery or MRIs."

"Why are you especially interested?"

Harrison put the tablet onto a side table and poured himself another scotch. Marianne was startled. Harrison seldom drank more than one, and never when alone. Was this his second, or more?

"Two reasons I'm interested," he said. "First of all, Sarah is pregnant. Second, while you were gone, two more *P. maniculatus* were exposed."

Sarah was Harrison's daughter, as difficult a child as Elizabeth, and nearly forty. A dozen deer mice, *Peromyscus maniculatus,* were among the precious plague-free specimens salvaged by Columbia. In the years since, they had been bred in their negative-pressure pens; there were now plenty of mice for research. Not that it had helped much. If the mice were given spore disease, they died. If not, they lived. Nothing so far had altered that. But Harrison's tone was serious. She said, "Go on."

"It was tricky. We got two does pregnant, let them carry partway, and exposed them to *R sporii*. We let the pregnancies continue until the mice showed symptoms, then took the fetuses before the mothers died. So did all but three of the pups, and we only got a viable three because the gestation period is so short. We put them to nurse with another mouse. Communally living females will do that, you know. One of those died and we autopsied it. Really difficult, on such a small and incompletely developed brain."

"So I should imagine." Despite her tiredness, Marianne was fascinated. Between speeches she served as lab tech for Harrison, but as a theoretical geneticist, she had nothing like his polymath skill in biology. "What did the autopsy show?"

"Again, hard to be sure. But certain parts of the cortex seem enlarged. Sue is preparing slides. And the two surviving pups are just hanging on. They nurse, which is good, but they also seem agitated and edgy."

"How does a tiny mouse seem agitated?"

Harrison smiled. "The same way Sissy does. Twitchy unfocused energy."

This was unfair; Sissy's great energy was very focused except when she didn't have enough to do. Those times, she danced in place, snapped her fingers, sang off-key. Marianne had learned to keep her busy all the time. But she let Harrison's remark go; he was genuinely upset.

She said gently, "Twitchy mice don't mean that anything will be wrong with Sarah's baby. Some kids are just born very reactive, like Connie's youngest. How far along is Sarah? Has there been an ultrasound?"

"Four months, and yes. The ultrasound looks normal. I'm going to bed, Marianne. But I'm glad you're back." He drained his scotch and went into the bedroom.

"*But I'm glad you're back.*" That "but" said it all: *I'm glad you're back, but I have too much on my mind for sex.* Well, she already knew that.

She checked her e-mail, giving Harrison time to pretend to be asleep. Nothing interesting except the latest photo from Connie of Marianne's two grandsons. They stood side by side in the backyard in their little red parkas, beside a bare-branched sapling no taller than Colin. Jason's arm was around his little brother. Jason smiled; Colin looked ready to burst into tears. Only thirteen months apart—what had Connie been thinking? The boys didn't look alike. Jason was slim and brown-eyed. Colin was a little Ryan, short and round, his two-year-old face pudgy around huge gray eyes.

Ryan pulling Noah on a sled, both of their faces red with cold and excitement: "Come on, let's slide down again!" "Mommy, I love this so much!"

Marianne closed the e-mail and turned on the news. Tornados in Oklahoma and Kansas. Building of the US spaceship still halted; a conservative Congress had been arguing over funding for two years. The private firms trying to build spaceships did not give interviews, or release pictures, not since the NCWAK, No Contact with Alien Killers, had blown up Richard Branson's effort. Starvation in Africa, war in northern China, dead zones in the ocean . . .

She turned off the wall screen, poured herself a glass of Harrison's scotch, and picked up his tablet to read the article in *Nature*. She couldn't concentrate. After a while she lay down on the sofa, put her hand between her legs, and tried to not think about Tim Saunders.

CHAPTER 13

S plus 2.6 years

Some people had more smarts than sense. Not that Sissy Tate hadn't known that before she went to work for Marianne.

Look at Marianne now, bent over her messy desk, reading yet again that printout about the kids that cried all the time. Sissy had tried to read it because her sister Jasmine had just had another kid. Not that Sissy wanted to ever see Jasmine again, but word about the baby had reached Sissy through Mama. The article had been full of statistics and equations and terms that Sissy didn't understand—she'd only gone through a secretarial course—but she'd gotten the gist, which was that everybody was fucked all over again by the spore cloud. Babies cried, sure, but they only started crying all the time and never smiling if they'd been buns in the oven since the spore cloud hit.

Marianne understood the article, though. She typed some numbers from it into her computer, whose screen was already full of different numbers, and started running some program on them. The back of Marianne's head showed gray hair along the roots—Sissy would need to nag her into another appointment at Subtle Beauty. Some people didn't make the most of what they had without somebody else nagging at them all the time. Marianne was bat-shit lucky to have Sissy taking care of her.

Not that Sissy didn't know that she herself was the lucky one. She had this job, which paid about as much as flipping burgers at McDonald's but which actually accomplished something important in the world, something she could believe in. She had gotten out of the Bronx and got some education, even if (she knew this now, after visiting real colleges with Marianne) it wasn't a very good education. She had sweet, sexy Tim. And she had Marianne, who'd turned out to feel more like family than her own family ever did. And fuck anybody who said different.

Sissy sat at her own desk, whose polished surface had on it one laptop and one piece of paper, and finished making the online travel arrangements for the next speech. They'd fly, and the sponsor was even paying for three round-trip airline tickets. Tim didn't like the venue, a high-school football stadium, because it would be hard to keep Marianne safe. They expected a really big crowd. The sponsor wasn't a college this time but a pro-spaceship lobbying organization, Going to the Stars. Sissy had investigated it online. It looked legit, and not too crazy.

Not that "crazy" would stop Marianne. She was going to give her speeches no matter what. She spent three days a week in this tiny office, writing and reading science. Ecology, mostly. Which was another thing that was fucked, pretty much everywhere, and not just because of the mice. Sissy'd been reading about all the droughts in the Midwest because everybody had mismanaged all the crops.

"Damn!" Marianne said.

"What?"

"Here's an article—an autopsy report, actually—on a two-year-old who died in a car crash. The father donated the brain to—"

"He let somebody cut out his kid's *brain*?"

Marianne turned in her chair to look at Sissy and said gently, "The child was dead."

"I don't care! I wouldn't let anybody cut up my dead kid!"

"Sissy, you're a mass of contradictions. You admire science; this is how science advances. That father did a wonderful thing."

Did he? Maybe. Sometimes Sissy couldn't tell how the ideas from her old world and the ideas from her new world should line up in her mind. But the important thing was to learn all she could. Sometimes since she'd come to work for the Star Brotherhood Foundation, she felt like a flower opening up to the sun for the first time. Other days, new things felt like cold rain. She said belligerently, knowing that her belligerence was a cover for confusion, "What did the autopsy show?"

"Well, it's more what it seems to show, which is either enlarged or deformed primary auditory cortex, with unusually dense neural connections to the midbrain and brain stem."

Sissy seized on the part of this she could understand. "What do you mean, either that thing is enlarged or it's deformed? Can't they tell which?"

"Not really." Marianne swiveled her computer chair to face Sissy. "We don't know much about the parts of the brain that process sound. It's really complex, and to make it more complex, no two human cortices are the same. This might mean nothing. But Harrison's mice . . ."

"What about Harrison's mice?"

"I don't know yet. I just don't—I need to do a lot more reading. What else is on my schedule for today?"

"Fund-raising dinner in Tribeca."

"Damn. Can't I—"

"No. You have to go. This lady has money and she's willing to give us some."

Marianne glanced at her computer screen, back at Sissy, back at the screen. "How much money?"

Sissy decided to be honest. Not that she wasn't usually honest with Marianne. "Probably not that much, but—"

"Tell them I'm sick and reschedule."

"But Tim says it's important you show up so nobody thinks you're scared off because of that attack at Notre Dame."

"I *am* scared."

"I said 'scared off.' Anyway, it's too late to reschedule."

"You're a hard taskmaster, Sissy Tate."

"Tim is going to pick you up in an hour at your place so you better go home and get ready. You aren't going to wear that, are you?"

"No. I'm going to wear sackcloth and ashes and mourn my reading time."

"Little lady, you'd look good even in that rig-out and that's just the God honest truth," said a voice behind them. Sissy whirled. How had anybody gotten in here and was he armed and— But Tim stood beside the intruder, and Tim was grinning.

Sissy felt her insides draw up and back, like a rat getting ready to fight. She knew who this was. She'd seen him just yesterday on the news.

Jonah Stubbins was even taller than Tim, and about 150 pounds heavier. He was dressed in what Marianne had once called Full Sunbelt: yellow shirt, khakis, white belt and shoes, bolo tie. He seized Marianne's hand. "Dr. Jenner, I'm real glad to meet y'all!"

Sissy saw that Marianne was holding her breath. Stubbins saw it, too. He laughed. "Aw, I ain't wearing none of my product, Doc. Y'all are perfectly safe from . . . whatever. Unless a'course you don't wanna be!"

Marianne freed her hand and said icily, "I don't understand why you are here, Mr. Stubbins. Tim—"

"Sure you understand. You and me, little lady—may I call you Marianne?"

"No."

"All right. But we got interests in common. You already knew that, din't you?"

"I—"

"Don't say nothing till you hear me out. You Eastern types allus too quick to get to jawin'. I'm here to make y'all a donation. A real big one, that you don't expect. That's why your bodyguard showed me up here."

A donation. From Jonah Stubbins. Sissy looked at Marianne, who said, "I don't think so."

"Then think again. Just hear me out, little lady, that's all I ask. Right now, anyways!"

"I am not a 'little lady.' And you are not a viable donor to the foundation, however much you might think our interests align. Lastly, I'm not fooled, not amused, and not charmed by your folksy presentation. You have an MBA from Harvard, for God's sake, which you have misused to criminal levels."

Sissy caught her breath. She'd never heard Marianne be rude like that.

Stubbins did not leave. Instead he altered his body, somehow becoming less mountainous, less looming, less gaudy. He said, "That's a great relief. I do get tired of my business persona, you know. But it's even more of a relief to realize I wasn't wrong about you. You have the backbone to perhaps succeed at your foundation's mission, to sway public opinion by inches, until it reaches the tipping point. Because our interests do align, Dr. Jenner. We both want a starship built. However, I know the government can't, or won't, get the job done. No surprise there—I'm a Libertarian and we Libertarians know that government can seldom get anything right because responsibility is diffused and unaccountable. So I'm getting it done, even if it takes my entire fortune."

He waved his hand like the fortune was right there in front of him, and somehow Sissy could see it: piles of gold and diamonds and rubies like in a storybook.

Stubbins continued, "Now, you don't want to accept my donation because first, you don't like my products. That's irrelevant. Second, you're afraid that I'll want something from you, that there are strings attached to my donation. There aren't. I only want you to go on doing what you're doing. And third, you think that if you're associated with me, your cause will suffer. Well, it won't, because my donation will be completely anonymous. Not even the IRS can trace what I don't want them to.

"You know and I know—the whole word knows—that if environmental conditions on Earth trend the way they are now, with ocean pollution and superstorms and desertification, in three or four generations this planet will be almost uninhabitable. Escape from Earth is humanity's strongest hope for survival. I know you agree with me on that—your speeches quote Stephen Hawking and Freeman Dyson and Paul Davies on the subject. People like me are the only ones getting the job done. So take my anonymous donation and add your bit to a private lifeboat for humanity."

Sissy felt dazed. Some of those words were straight from Marianne's speeches. Marianne looked dazed, too. Was this devil using one of his products on them? Sissy wanted to move closer and sniff, but then the perfume might get her, too.

Marianne said, "How can I be sure your donation will really be anonymous?"

"Because I've made them before, to other groups working in my interests. You know some of the recipients." He pulled a piece of paper from a pocket. "Ask them, privately and in a place you're sure isn't bugged. Here, take the list, it's going to erase itself in a few minutes."

Marianne took the paper. "I can't give you an answer now, Mr. Stubbins. I need to consider."

"Of course. My personal phone number is at the bottom of the list. It won't erase. Only ten people in the world have that number. You're the eleventh. Also, here is the figure I'm prepared to donate anonymously to your foundation. Call me. Good-bye, Dr. Jenner. A pleasure."

He lumbered out and Tim locked the door. When he turned back to face Sissy and Marianne, his blue eyes shone like lighthouses. "It's a lot of money. You gotta take it, Marianne."

"*No*," Sissy said, and it came out almost a shout. Not that she didn't feel that strongly about it. But she lowered her voice. "I don't trust him."

Marianne gazed down at the list. Sissy, not good at reading upside down, saw only that it held six or seven names and some numbers before the names abruptly vanished and Marianne crumpled the paper in her fist.

Tim said, "Fuck me! How did it do that? Marianne, we gotta take his money."

"No," Sissy said. And again, "No."

Jonah Stubbins was an unlikely multibillionaire in a high-tech electronic age, more like P. T. Barnum than Bill Gates or Mark Zuckerberg, although Stubbins's fortune now rivaled Gates's. Stubbins had been born country-shucks poor, in the hills of Appalachia, which he'd hated enough to hike out of on the day he turned sixteen, bringing with him nothing but clothes, a rifle, and an untutored brain. Still, the meth labs of his violent kin had imbued him with three things: a hatred of poverty, a respect for chemistry, and a light regard for the law.

The next few years of his biography were murky, defying even journalists to discover where, how, and with what he had survived. But at twenty-two he enrolled in a third-rate college, tested out of most subjects, and emerged a year later with a degree in chemistry. By that time his good-ol'-boy façade was firmly in place, and he kept it through Harvard, which he attended on scholarship. He had already founded his fledgling company, and the applications committee was impressed. Nobody at Harvard liked Stubbins, not the legacy babies nor the brilliant nobodies nor the faculty. Nobody understood why he kept up his pose of illiteracy, despite stellar grades. In fact, nobody understood anything about him. But by the time he had his MBA, everybody knew who he was.

His company, like many start-ups, began in a garage. The garage belonged to the first of his many wives, who'd received it in the divorce from the first of her many husbands. The product was perfume.

"Perfume?" Carla Mae had scoffed. "What the fuck do you know about perfume?"

"Nothing a'tall," Jonah had said. "But it ain't regulated by the FDA, and the industry's going about its job ass-fuck wrong. You don't want to make people smell like flowers or fruit or beaches. You want to make 'em smell like sex. Or like what suggests sex."

A year later he brought out, in tiny cheap bottles, a musky oil called Sleep With Me. The equally cheap advertising campaign promised that wearing it would induce desire in whoever smelled you. Unlike every other perfume ad that ever existed, this one told the truth. Developed from a secret formula that Stubbins's genius for chemistry had based on human pheromones, Sleep With Me created desire as effectively as ecstasy combined with Viagra. The desire was not irresistible, of course, human beings still having enough free will to overcome lust if they really wanted to. Legions of smellers did not want to.

The second year, the company went public. The third year, it brought out a perfume that induced a desire to obey—very subtle, perhaps no more than the same effect created by an authoritative stance in a charismatic personality. But most people were not charismatic. I'm In Charge Here was just as big a success as Sleep With Me. The lawsuits began, and Stubbins hired the best lawyers he could find. So far, neither the government nor class-action suits had succeeded in getting any of his four products off the market.

Sleep With Me. I'm In Charge Here. Ain't We Got Fun! Trust Me. All patented, all ravenously bought and used and then bought again because who wouldn't want to be desired, obeyed, delighted, or trusted? Whether the "perfume" actually affected the person who smelled it or altered the natural body chemistry of the wearer was not conclusively proved, despite many attempts by scientists and many outraged articles by journalists. Perhaps the whole thing was a mass-hysteria placebo effect multiplied by a brilliant ad campaign. The public, even in a depressed economy, didn't care. They bought the small, expensive, distinctively green bottles with the outrageous names.

Stubbins put his MBA to good use, shrewdly diversifying and investing. When the spore clouds wrecked the global economy and entire countries went bankrupt, his personal economy dipped only a small amount. That was due in part, persistent rumor said, to bought congressmen and illegal lobbying and ruthless dealing with would-be competitors. Jonah Stubbins merely grinned at the allegations, and shuffled his feet, and made yet more enemies. He was forty-six years old and he owned the world.

And this was the man who now wanted to donate to the Star Brotherhood Foundation! Marianne sat at that evening's fund-raiser, which would net at most donations of a few thousand dollars, and made mechanical conversation with overdressed women and their mostly preoccupied husbands. She gave her brief after-dinner speech without really hearing her own words. Jonah Stubbins! His space-ship, constructed according to engineers' interpretations of the plans left by the Denebs, was the furthest along since domestic terrorists had blown up Branson's ship. Stubbins was serious about this. And the fig-ure he had written on the erase-o-paper was staggering. The founda-tion could create TV and Internet spots, pay for ads, hire another speech-giver. . . .

She sat down to polite applause. Conversation resumed. That man at the next table, leaning in so eagerly toward that woman—was she wearing Sleep With Me? Were either of the two women at the end of her table, who appeared to be discussing a business deal, scented with Trust Me or I'm In Charge Here? Did any of that stuff actually work? Well, yes, Sleep With Me did, there was independent-lab verification for that, but sexual-arousal hormones had been researched and stud-ied for decades. The others might just be smoke and mirrors.

But Stubbins's money was real.

"Well," she replied to whatever it was that her host had just said, "that *is* interesting. Tell me more."

Marianne sat in the front seat of the rented minivan beside Tim, who drove too fast north on Route 87 from New York to Tannersville. The college where Marianne had taught was there, and so was Ryan's home. Colin had turned two a month ago and, finally, there was to be a family celebration.

"I can drive myself," Marianne had said. "Or take the train."

"Amtrak isn't reliable," Sissy had said, "especially north of Albany. You *know* that, Marianne. Look what happened when you tried to get to Pittsburgh for that speech."

"Pittsburgh isn't north of Albany."

"Tim's driving you," Sissy said. "That's what a bodyguard does, he guards people. Am I right, Tim?"

"Always," Tim said, not looking up from the videogame on his tablet.

Sissy snorted. "Yeah, right. But I'm right this time, Marianne. Tim should drive you. Why wouldn't you want him to?"

Tim raised his blindingly blue gaze from his tablet. Sissy stared at Marianne. *Danger, danger.* She loved Sissy like a daughter. Tim's long legs sprawled across Marianne's office in black jeans and boots. He smelled of leather and masculinity.

Marianne had made herself shrug. "No reason. Okay, Tim, you drive."

Now she sat beside him, hunched over her tablet as the slowly greening spring landscape slid past. She concentrated on Harrison's research notes, and only on that.

If only mice weren't so damn tiny! Adult *Mus* weighed on average half a pound. As far as Harrison could tell, and it wasn't very far, the brains of sacrificed mice showed the same abnormal tissue growth as those of the deer mice. Which might or might not have been the same as the autopsied child, which in turn might or might not have anything to do with Karcher's statistical analysis of increased agitation among children born since the spore cloud. Many, but not all, of these children were deaf, and deafness did not ordinarily increase infant agitation. The data simply did not yet yield enough correlations.

Marianne looked up from her tablet and rubbed her eyes. Elizabeth was flying up from Texas for the birthday party. It would be the first time they had all been together since the Denebs left.

No, not all together. Noah was gone. Every time Marianne thought that, it was as if for the first time. She would never see Noah again. Was he happy, out there on an alien planet, with an alien wife? Probably Marianne would never know.

Tim said abruptly, "You should take the money."

The interruption was welcome. "Stubbins's money?"

"Yeah. We can use it. And who cares if he makes perfume? Money is money."

Curiosity overrode prudence. "Have you ever used any of his scents?"

"Once I tried I'm In Charge Here, when I was Special Forces. It didn't work too good. My CO didn't believe I was in charge." He chuckled, a low lazy sound that went straight to Marianne's primitive brain.

She said, "I'm going to take the money."

"Good. Sissy won't like it, though."

"I know."

"It'll be okay." He began whistling, and Marianne went back to Harrison's notes.

Was Ryan and Connie's youngest, Colin, among the children with hearing problems? That was one of the things she wanted to find out at this family gathering. The other thing she wanted to know from Ryan, she could never ask. Maybe Tim's presence would be useful, after all. With an outsider present, her family could not get too personal with each other. They had never done well with personal.

"Grandma! I'm three!" Jason held up three fingers of a candy-smeared hand.

"What a big boy!"

"And Colin's two!" Two little fingers.

It would be okay. Ryan, Connie, Jason, Elizabeth—they all met her, smiling, on the porch of the little house. This was just a normal family gathering, and everything would be okay.

Within the hour, none of it was okay.

Colin, the birthday boy, cried constantly, a high thin wail. Marianne walked him; Connie fed him; Jason brought him toys. Only food quieted him, and then only briefly. He looked underweight. Elizabeth, who did not like children, asked Jason to show her his sandbox, just to get out of the house. Ryan, looking strained, dressed Jason in his jacket and sent him outside with his aunt.

"She shouldn't have come," Ryan said to Marianne as they stood in the hall. In the living room, Colin cried. "Already Elizabeth's started that old drumbeat about law and order. Connie isn't up to this."

Marianne said carefully, "Connie looks really tired." The hallway rug was stained, the walls bore crayon marks, a houseplant looked dusty and parched. Connie had always been a meticulous housekeeper.

"Of course she looks tired," Ryan said. "She doesn't ever get uninterrupted sleep. Colin just cries and cries. Jason wasn't like this."

"Every child is different," Marianne said, and immediately regretted the fatuous truth. It was no help.

"Did any of us cry like this?"

"No. I guess I was lucky. Ryan, Connie looks like she's lost a lot of weight. Has she seen a doctor?"

"She has an appointment next week. Colin, too, although the doctor appointments never seem to help." He ran his hand though his hair, already going thin on top.

"If you need money for a night nurse or other household help. . . ."

"No. We don't. And I know you don't have any to spare. But thanks, Mom."

He had always been like that, reluctant to accept help. *"Me do it,"* he'd said as a little child, never belligerently but as a statement of fact. Self-contained, self-reliant. And always, always secretive.

Ryan, did you do it?

Did you aid the organization that tried to blow up the *Embassy*? She could never ask him. If he had done it, he wouldn't tell her. If he hadn't done it and she accused him, the fraying tie between them might snap for good. Instead she said, "Jason is so excited about Colin's birthday."

He smiled faintly. "Well, three—an excitable age."

"He seems to love being a big brother."

"Yes. We haven't seen any sibling rivalry at all. Jason constantly tries to console Colin."

Something small to be grateful for. Sibling rivalry with Elizabeth and Ryan had made Noah feel he could never measure up, had set him adrift. Maybe Ryan and Connie were better parents than she and Kyle had been. Well—not a very high bar.

Everyone kept conversation focused on the children. Jason ate cake and helped Colin to open his presents. Colin cried. During one of his rare exhausted periods, Marianne held him on her lap. Tears stained his tired little face. She played a game of snapping her fingers to the right, to the left, above his head. Colin tried to grab them, until he again began to cry. Whatever his upset was, the baby didn't have hearing problems.

During dinner, Colin blessedly slept. The adults, plus Jason in his booster seat, sat around the table, eating too fast, trying to get through the meal before Colin woke up. Tim had spent much of the afternoon prowling around the outside of the house, in the woods, and below the windows. Ryan and Connie were polite to him but basically uninterested. Elizabeth, however, kept glancing from Tim to Marianne. Marianne had made a big point of saying that Tim was her administrative assistant's boyfriend. It did not stop Elizabeth's glances. Conversation did not flow well.

Into a lull, Tim said, "I saw a wolf in your woods. Do you have a pack?"

"Yes," Ryan said, "down from Canada. Just this winter."

Connie said, "I worry about Jason every minute he's outside."

Jason, his mouth rosy with beets, mumbled, "Don't worry, Mama."

Tim smiled. "If there's an adult with Jason, ma'am, then wolves won't attack."

Elizabeth said, "Are you a woodsman, then?"

"Was."

"And you're licensed to carry all three weapons you have with you."

Tim's eyes narrowed. "Yes, ma'am. But I'm curious how you know there's three."

Marianne hastened to blur the battle lines before they could harden. "Elizabeth's with Border Patrol in Texas. And Tim's ex–Special Forces."

Elizabeth and Tim regarded each other even more closely, but with grudging respect. Ryan, however, frowned. Connie was still fixated on the wolves.

"Are you sure a wolf wouldn't attack an adult? I saw ours, just last week, and it looked skinny and hungry enough to eat *anything*."

Ryan said, "That's because there are no mice for them to eat. In fact, I'm surprised wolves have survived at all."

Tim said, "Wolves are survivors. They can make it no matter what happens."

"Well, no," Ryan said. "They almost didn't survive humans. By 1940 there were only a handful of wolves left in the entire United States."

"Don't matter," Tim said. "Like you said, they just retreated to Canada, ready to invade whenever the time was right. Biding their time. I hear other species do that, too. Can't stamp 'em out, so you got to live with 'em."

Ryan put down his fork and said evenly, "You're talking about purple loosestrife."

Tim said, "About what?"

Elizabeth said, "No, he's not, Ryan—not every conversation is about purple loosestrife. He's talking about Mom's aliens."

Tim said, "What's purple loosestrife?"

Marianne said, "They're not *my* aliens."

"Sure they are," Elizabeth said. "You helped make them welcome and now you want the ship built to go visiting."

Ryan, for once his sister's ally, said quietly, "She's right, Mom. The Denebs were an invasive species, and now we're reaping the consequences of having them here. You know that as well as anyone."

Jason looked from his father to his grandmother. Marianne pressed her lips together and said nothing. *Let the discussion die here.* Connie, uncomfortable with friction of any kind, said brightly, "Who'd like more cake?"

But Tim said to Ryan, "Your mom's right, you know. We should go to the stars. I mean—wow!"

Elizabeth said tightly, "No matter what the cost."

"We already paid the cost," Tim said. "So why not at least get what we paid for?"

"A great philosophy," Elizabeth said. "The Children's Crusade is already slaughtered, so why not have tea with the Saracens."

"Who?" Tim said.

Ryan said, calmly but with a little too much emphasis, "An invasive species always disrupts an ecology. In this case, the ecology is the entire globe. It may end life as we know it. What, in your opinion, Tim, is worth that?"

Tim's blue eyes glittered. "I didn't say it was worth it. I said it was done. Take an even strain, man."

Ryan said, "I'd rather you didn't tell me how to behave in my own house."

"Or more coffee!" Connie said desperately.

Elizabeth said, "The Deneb visit was a disaster. The follow-up is a disaster. Any return contact will be a disaster. That's just the fucking truth, and you, Mom, won't face it."

Jason said, "Aunt Lizzie said a bad word!"

"Yes, darling, she did," Connie said. "Elizabeth—"

"All right! I apologize for the word but not for the sentiments! Tim, you don't know what you're talking about. Come down to Texas and see what the Denebs' ecological interference has done there. If you were anything but an urban New Yorker, you'd realize the full devastation."

"I'm from Oklahoma," Tim said. "Don't patronize me."

Marianne said, "The starship—"

"Will never be built," Elizabeth said. "The plans are too different, too alien. Don't you read about the difficulties human engineers are having in interpreting them?"

"Of course I do. Don't patronize *me*, Elizabeth. Difficulties are not permanent impasses. Along with the advanced physics the Denebs gave us, we—"

"We what?" Ryan said. "Are farther ahead? The entire global ecology is becoming untenable. Invasive species—"

"We are the same species as the Denebs!" Marianne said. "The same species as Noah!"

She hadn't meant to say it. It just burst out, driven by . . . everything. They all looked at her, even Jason, from wide eyes. The silence stretched and stretched, like taut cable. Before it could snap, Elizabeth murmured, "Let's not discuss Noah. Connie, I will have more cake, thank you."

Everybody reached for food, or resumed eating, or pretended to eat. Connie said to Jason, "You ate all your beets! Good boy!"

"I like beets," Jason announced. "They're red."

"So they are," Ryan said.

"Carrots are orange."

"Clever boy!" Elizabeth said.

"Oranges are orange, too." This struck Jason as funny; he giggled.

The adults exchanged strained smiles. Marianne avoided Ryan's gaze. *Did you? Did you?*

In the next room, Colin began to wail.

All the way back to New York, after a night when Tim slept on Ryan's sofa and Marianne barely slept at all, neither of them said a word.

Grateful for this uncharacteristic tact, Marianne dozed, or gazed out the window, or turned on the radio to a station of classical music, without words. She'd had enough words. Fields and towns and boarded-up malls flew by.

One good thing: between exhaustion and worry and disappointment, Tim's nearness did not disturb her at all. Sometimes you had to be grateful for what you could get.

CHAPTER 14

S plus 3.6 years

Marianne burst into the office of the Star Brotherhood Foundation. Her face shone. Sissy half rose from her chair—what could have happened to make Marianne look like that? Not that Sissy wasn't happy to see her all lit up for a change! She said, "What is it?"

"Harrison," Marianne said. "They've bred a strain of *P. maniculatus* that was exposed to *R. sporii* without contracting it! Finally!"

"Oh, that's good," Sissy breathed.

"Fucking right it's good!"

Sissy laughed. Marianne never cursed and it would do her good to loosen up. She'd had a bad year—a really bad year, which made Sissy feel guilty because her own year had been so good. Not that Marianne's year hadn't been good professionally, because it *had*. The foundation had this great new office in Midtown Manhattan, thanks to Jonah Stubbins's money. Stubbins had kept his word about the donation being anonymous, so they hadn't had any grief over *that*. They had more speeches than ever. Marianne had been heckled just as much but not attacked, not since Notre Dame.

But her personal year—not so good. Her daughter-in-law, Connie, had died of cancer. Sissy didn't have a daughter-in-law, of course, but if she had, she'd have been devastated, just like she'd be if one of her sisters or sisters-in-law died. Not that they were all that great, especially Jasmine, but they were family. Devastated!

Marianne had gone to Connie's funeral, and so had her daughter

Elizabeth (someone else Sissy didn't much like), but since then the Jenners hadn't gotten together even once. Weird. Marianne felt it, Sissy knew she did, but she just didn't go to see either Ryan or Elizabeth, and they didn't come to see her. If it were *her* family, Sissy would have been charging over to each of them, trying to fix whatever was wrong. Even for Jasmine.

Maybe Marianne shared her grief with Harrison Rice. But Sissy had the impression that things weren't too good there, either—not that Marianne ever said anything to Sissy about it. Not Marianne's style.

So it was good to see her so happy. Sissy leaped from her chair, flipped on her music, and grabbed Marianne's hand. It felt hot. They danced and bumped to "Lovin' That Racket" until Marianne dropped, panting and sweating, into one of Stubbins's deep, cushioned chairs.

"So tell me," Sissy said.

"Well—just let me catch my breath a sec—well, it's good. You know we have the protein that gives humans, most humans anyways, immunity to the disease. Harrison isolated the gene sequence for that protein, grafted it onto a vector, and finally succeeded in incorporating it into the mouse's genome. The exposed mice show no sign of infection. It's not germ-line modification, of course, and it's almost certainly not dominant, but it's a first step toward germ-line recombination or methylation epigenetics."

Sissy, listening carefully, tried to sort this out. "You mean that Dr. Rice found the protein that protects humans from spore disease and—"

"We already had that protein, Sissy. Before the Denebs left."

Sissy wasn't sidetracked. "And put it into—deer mice?—so that now the mice breathe spores and don't die?"

"Exactly!"

"And now Dr. Rice thinks that maybe he can get mice to pass that immunity onto their babies?"

Marianne sobered a little. "That's a big step, though. Really complicated, if the gene doesn't happen to get into sperm or eggs by itself and turn up dominant."

"What are the chances of that?"

"This close to zero." Marianne held up two fingers so close together that no light passed between them. The fingers trembled. Drops of sweat shone on her forehead.

"Are you feeling all right? That looks like more than just dancing and—"

Marianne turned her head and vomited onto the floor.

"You're sick!" Sissy cried.

"Just a . . . cold . . ."

"It's not." She brought Marianne a towel from the bathroom and a glass of water, and then felt her forehead. "You've got a fever."

"It's just a cold. Sissy, stop that, you don't have to clean up after me."

"It ain't going to clean itself up," Sissy said, and knew that the words were Mama's. "Just sit there a minute, and then I'm taking you home."

"I'm not—"

"Yes, you are, so don't argue with me." Some people had more smarts than sense.

Marianne smiled faintly. "Someday you're going to make a great mother, Sissy."

"Well, I hope so." She got Marianne into the car (*"Really, I'm not an invalid!"*) and drove her home. As soon as Marianne unlocked the apartment door, she dashed into the bathroom and threw up again. Sissy waited. The shower sounded, and Sissy sat down to wait some more.

She'd been to Marianne's place before, but not often. Once, almost a year ago, Marianne had invited her and Tim to dinner. Neither had anything to say to Dr. Rice, or him to them. He was nice enough, Sissy supposed, but science was the only thing he could talk about. Not even about his little granddaughter, although Sissy tried. Marianne told her later that the baby cried all the time and Harrison thought there was something wrong with her and so didn't want to talk about it. Which left zero to talk about. The four of them never got together again, which was fine with Sissy. Dr. Rice was a great man, but he kind of had a stick up his ass. In Sissy's opinion.

The shower was still going. The apartment was neat but sort of drab. No fancy lampshades or bright pillows or any of the cute animal statues Sissy and Tim had on their coffee table, just a pile of printouts. Sissy picked up the top one.

HUMAN CLINICAL TRIAL OF T-413 ON BRODMANN AREA 22
AUDITORY FUNCTIONS: PRELIMINARY RESULTS
Property of Eli Lilly

The article was hard to read, even the little part in front called the abstract, but Sissy plowed on. A drug had been "fast-tracked" to see if anything could be done about all the crying babies and deaf babies being born. The drug didn't help the ones with bad hearing, but it calmed down the ones who cried because their hearing was too good—could hearing be too good? Well, yes, if everything felt jackhammer loud all the time. Poor babies. Only Marianne had already told Sissy that when the babies were brought into soundproof rooms and music was played loud, they *didn't* cry. Still, parts of their "auditory cortex" were too big or too deformed and nobody knew how *that* worked, just like nobody knew why a little while ago Marianne's grandson Colin had just all at once stopped crying all the time. Just stopped. Also—

Well, look at this—of course the drug stopped the babies crying! It was a kind of tranquilizer! It probably stopped them doing anything, turned them into zombie babies. . . .

"Sissy, I'm sorry, you shouldn't be reading that." Marianne stood in the doorway to the bathroom, wiping her mouth.

"No, I'm sorry! I didn't realize!" Sissy jumped up and then wasn't sure what to do next.

"It's okay." Marianne gave her that rare, sweet smile, and wobbled on her feet.

"Come on, sweetie—let's get you to bed. I think you have a flu."

"I don't have time for the flu!"

"The flu don't give a damn," Sissy said, and heard Mama again in her own voice, but now that was okay because Mama had had her good points along with the rest of her, and one of them was taking care of sick people. Just like Sissy was going to take care of Marianne now.

It wasn't flu. Maybe food poisoning, because when her stomach had emptied completely, she felt a little better. Sissy left. Marianne lay in bed, slept, woke. Much later she heard Harrison open the front door, drop his coat on a chair, and turn on the living room light. "Harrison?"

"Why are you awake?" Harrison said, silhouetted in the bedroom doorway against light from the living room.

"I don't feel well." Marianne glanced at the bedside clock: 1:42 a.m. Almost unheard of for Harrison, who rose before roosters and retired before full starlight. "Were you celebrating?"

"A bit. Look, I'll sleep on the sofa."

She'd been longing for him to hold her. Still, he couldn't afford to get ill. "All right. But first tell me more about the gene therapy on the mice."

"I told you most of it."

"You don't sound very celebratory. Is anything wrong? Did something happen?"

"Things always happen," he snapped, swaying on his feet, and now she realized what she'd missed before: He was drunk. Harrison, who could down four scotches without any external effects at all. She reached out and switched on the bedside lamp.

"What happened, Harrison?"

"All sorts of things happened tonight. Didn't you see the news? Another superstorm is taking out most of the North and South Carolina coast. There are tornadoes in Oklahoma. Babies are being born with brain deformities. Entire ecologies are still chaotic from the domino effects of losing mice. Russia is in revolution to hardliners. The economy is in the toilet. The center cannot hold. Score one for Yeats."

Now she was really alarmed. This wasn't at all like Harrison, who neither prattled nor overstated. She tried to get out of bed but her stomach lurched again. Carefully she lay back on the pillow. Equally carefully, she searched for words that would not upset him further.

"Did something specific occur tonight at the lab?"

"Not the lab, no. I just had a crashing epigany . . . *epiphany*. Must get my terms straight. Terms very important. Marianne, we were wrong."

"Wrong about what?"

"The Denebs. The foundation. We were dead, totally, hundred-eighty-degrees wrong."

She was silent, searching his face for some clue, some hint about what could have happened tonight.

"Bastards," he said, "all of them. They knew what the death of the mice would do. They knew about the fetal damage to the auditory cortex. They *knew*. Must have!"

"Why do you say that?" Fear had started to coil around her already unsteady stomach, a constrictor ready to squeeze.

"It's obvious."

"Not really. Their colony ship was wiped out so probably there were no children that their scientists could—"

"Why are you still defending them? Because your child went with them? Well, great for you. Mine is dead."

Marianne gasped and sat up again. Her insides roiled. "Sarah? Harrison—*What happened?* When? How do you know?"

"How do you shink—think—I know? Paul called me, half an hour ago. Sarah killed herself."

She tried to absorb the horror of this, and could not. She couldn't imagine anything worse. All that she could manage was, "Darling—"

"She was darling. My darling girl. I remember—" Harrison started to sob—Harrison!—and Marianne crept out of bed and stood woozily. He was remembering Sarah as a little girl or an eager bride or a happily expectant mother, and Marianne knew how deep such memories of lost children could cut. One hand on the edge of the bed, she staggered forward to put her arms around him.

He pushed her away, but without rancor, as if she were an object he didn't really see. "It was the baby. Isobelle wouldn't stop crying. Paul was no help, he never was. Never liked Paul. Crying and crying and Sarah got no sleep and she was never strong and she just couldn't take it anymore. She left a note 'I'm sorry sorry sorry'—over a hundred sorrys. A hundred. A *hundred*. If the baby had been normal . . . if the fucking Denebs had never come. . . ." He cried harder.

This wasn't Harrison. Or rather, it was, but a Harrison buried so deep that not only had Marianne never seen him before, she suspected Harrison hadn't either. Or maybe this Harrison was newly created, fashioned from pain—there were people who never really believed that terrible things could happen to them personally, until the things did. Even people as smart as Harrison. Maybe especially people as smart as Harrison, focused on work, expecting the rest of their lives to flow smoothly around the work.

What to say? She couldn't say that the Denebs had not caused the spore cloud. Harrison, of all people, knew that, and right now he didn't care. "Sweetheart, I'm so sorry. Where is—"

"Where is what? Isobelle? Paul? Me? The foundation?" His anger turned on her, and Marianne recognized that it must go somewhere. It wasn't really her that he was furious with, or even the aliens, but she was the one right here.

He said, "Isobelle is with her other grandparents. Paul is with the coroner. The foundation is shit, which you and I should have known all along. We made a mistake, Marianne. The Denebs screwed us. By not telling us everything they knew. Not warning us about everything the spores would cause. Then they bought us off with physics and starship plans that no one on Earth can make work, and even if we could it wouldn't matter because there is an entire generation of children who are either deaf or screaming with auditory damage or about to be drugged into catatonia and so unable to inherit space travel anyway.

A perfect case of genocide, Marianne, and you and I and everybody like us were just too dumb to see it."

"I don't believe that," she said. The snake had tightened around her stomach and she fought to not vomit.

"You don't want to believe it. Neither did I. But it's true—humanity's been royally fucked over."

"Harrison, love—" She took another step toward him but the vomit rose in her throat and she bolted for the bathroom. There was nothing left to throw up but her body kept trying anyway. When it was over, she felt a little better, but light-headed. Holding on to the walls, she went in search of Harrison.

He'd left the apartment. To go where? She didn't know. But it seemed urgent that she find him. Staggering back to the bedroom, she collapsed on the bed and picked up her cell.

"Hello?" His voice was rough with sleep, even deeper than usual. "Marianne?"

"Yes. Tim—I need you. Something's happened. I need you to go find Harrison for me. Please. Oh, please. Now."

At 3:00 a.m. Tim kicked the door of the apartment. Marianne, waiting, flung it open. Harrison sagged in Tim's arms. Tim's mouth was bleeding. "Found him in a bar on Amsterdam. Not the kind of place somebody like him should be."

"Was there—"

"Trouble? Yeah. But no biggie. Where do you want him?"

Harrison mumbled something unintelligible. Sodden and with Tim's blood smeared on his hair, he was barely conscious. Marianne said, "Bring him into the bedroom—or do you think he needs to go to an ER?"

"For a drunk? Nah. Long as he don't puke and breathe it in. I'll lie him on his side and you just watch him."

"She can't watch him," Sissy said, because of course Sissy had insisted on accompanying Tim, in order to be with Marianne. "She's sick. I'll watch him."

"Sure," Tim said. "We'll all stay." He lay down on the rug, his long body stretched full length, and instantly fell asleep. Sissy covered him tenderly with the sofa throw.

"You got another blanket somewhere, Marianne? You sleep on the sofa and I'll sit up with Harrison. I'm not at all tired."

She didn't look tired. Sissy's round, pretty face looked alert and concerned. Her frizzy curls, bright blond at the moment, stood around her head like a halo. Sainted mother to the world. Sissy shouldn't have to watch Harrison, but Marianne was too exhausted to argue. Her stomach felt as if she'd expelled not only its contents but the lining.

"Thanks, Sissy. I—" If she finished the sentence, she would start to sob, and she didn't want to do that.

Sissy found more blankets in the tiny coat closet, covered Marianne, and stood looking down at her. "Does Harrison do this often?"

"No." Oh God, she hadn't even told Sissy or Tim what had happened. Her illness, her frantic worry . . . Sissy didn't even know. Marianne said, "Yesterday his daughter killed herself."

Sissy drew a sharp breath. She squeezed onto the sofa beside Marianne. "How?"

"I don't know."

"Why?"

"Harrison said that Sarah's baby wouldn't stop crying and Sarah just couldn't take it anymore."

Sissy grimaced in disgust. "That's no reason to kill yourself. Plenty of babies won't stop crying and their mamas don't kill themselves. How does that help? It's just cowardlike."

"Sarah might have already had postpartum depression."

"So what? You don't kill yourself if you got kids to take care of. You just don't. You don't have that right."

Marianne said nothing. The other side of Sissy's sure confidence was a kind of arrogance that the young woman was completely unaware of. But Sissy's hand holding hers felt warm, reassuring. On the floor, Tim snored softly.

"Still," Sissy went on, "I can see how Harrison got drunk from shock. I'll watch him real carefully. But Marianne—you should face something."

"What?"

"I'm sorry to say this, but you should face it. That man is going to leave you now."

Marianne pulled her fingers from Sissy's. "No, you don't understand, he—"

"I do understand. *You* don't. I've been watching you two whenever he picks you up at the office or the airport, which incidentally isn't that often. I know, I know, he's doing important work. But he's one of those with tunnel vision, Marianne, and his tunnel just cracked wide open to the sky. He's going to panic and lash out and leave you. You need to be ready for that."

"You're wrong, Sissy."

"I hope so. Now you sleep." Sissy switched off the light and went into the bedroom to watch Harrison.

Marianne thought that sleep would be long coming, but it wasn't. One careful shift of her body on the sofa and she was out. The next morning, Tim and Sissy made breakfast that neither Marianne nor Harrison could eat. When it was clear to Sissy that both of them were done vomiting, she and Tim tactfully left.

Harrison slept most of the day. When he was awake, he wanted to be alone in the bedroom. The day after that, he spent hunched over his computer, surrounded by an invisible and impenetrable wall. The third day he flew to Indiana for Sarah's funeral. Politely, distantly, he asked Marianne to not accompany him. Even before he called her from Terre Haute, she knew what he would say.

Before he returned home, she'd moved out.

———

Tim put her furniture into storage. Sissy made a back room at the Star Brotherhood Foundation into a bedroom. The office that Jonah Stubbins had made possible had a bathroom with shower. Marianne ate her meals out, or ate what Sissy provided for her. She lost weight. She slept badly. The only thing that helped was work, and then more work. When there was nothing to work on, she read on the Internet, using Harrison's password for access to sites she could not have accessed on her own.

Karcher's initial research had spawned dozens of studies on both infants and mice, even though funding for science had all but disappeared since the Collapse. It was clear that *something* had affected the children's brains in utero, but unclear just what that something was. Humans had always varied enormously in auditory structures—and perhaps mice did, too. With something that small, it was difficult to tell. In fact, nobody was even sure what all the auditory structures were. The babies' receiving areas, on the upper temporal lobes, had increased neurons, or decreased neurons, or neurons with unexpected connections. Sometimes one end of the area was larger, sometimes the opposite end. Other brain activity in areas associated with hearing—auditory thalamus, Brodmann area, hippocampus, superior temporal gyrus— also differed from one child to the next. Some EEGs showed statistically significant enhancement in alpha-wave activity; some did not. Strange cortical behavior resulted from exposure to gamma waves.

Basically, nobody understood what was going on in these kids' heads.

What *was* understood was that a small percentage of post-spore infants was deaf, and the rest cried nearly every moment they were awake. Eli Lilly's renamed infant tranquilizer, Calminex, had not yet cleared clinical trials but already had ignited a firestorm of online controversy. Was it right to drug small children? Was it right not to drug them, when so many failed to thrive due to their constant agitation? What would be the long-term effects of that many stress hormones constantly flooding developing nervous systems? What would be the short-term effects of the drug? Would parents who used it be abusers of their children, or realistic people adjusting to circumstances?

The Eli Lilly research lab was hit with a truck bomb. The company did not discontinue trials.

"Marianne," Sissy said one afternoon at the office, "why don't you go for a walk? You've been plopped in front of that computer for three hours."

"I'm fine."

"Three solid hours. I timed it."

"I'm *fine*."

"No. You aren't. Come eat something with me. You didn't have any lunch."

Marianne clenched her jaw and kept on reading.

The ecological disruptions around the world were slowly righting themselves. Every once in a while, someone would report sightings of live mice living in the wild. None of these sightings were substantiated. Most of the time, when Marianne tracked down the reporters, they also believed in elves or Martians or demons inhabiting their basement.

Of Harrison's research on spore-resistant mice, she found nothing at all. It was secret, or incomplete, or had led nowhere. Like her and Harrison.

"It's a good thing," Sissy grumbled, "that we're going to New Mexico next week for that big speech. At least it'll get you out of that chair."

Marianne went on reading, leaning in closer to the computer screen. Trying to fill up as much of the world as possible with its digital light.

CHAPTER 15

S plus 4 years

Who could live in this heat?

"You'll like Albuquerque," Marianne had told Sissy. Sissy could tell it was a brave try at being cheerful, which Marianne definitely wasn't. "The desert is gorgeous, in an austere sort of way. And our hotel is right on the Rio Grande."

Well, Marianne was wrong. Sissy didn't like Albuquerque, not from the second she and Tim and Marianne stepped off the jetway into an airport where the AC was broken. At eleven in the morning it was ninety-one degrees outside, even hotter inside. And never mind all that shit about it being dry heat—ninety-one degrees was ninety-one degrees, and all three of them were sweating like stinky waterfalls by the time they reached the hotel.

Which did have working AC. It was cranked up so high that the sweat dried instantly and Sissy rooted in her bag for a sweater. Fortunately, she'd brought the heavy purple one with the pink sequins. The Rio Grande, visible from their sixth-floor hotel suite, didn't look like much of a river, even if Marianne did say that it was classified as "exotic" because it was a river that flowed through a desert. Sissy had seen creeks with more water in them. Also, the Rio Grande looked just as hot as everything else outdoors. Not that Sissy planned on going outdoors. Marianne's speech would be in the grand ballroom right in this hotel, which also had two restaurants and a dance club on the top floor. Sissy had brought her dance clothes. She wasn't setting foot outside.

But their suite was nice, two small bedrooms and a big central room with sofas, a bar, dining table, big wall screen. Sissy and Tim's room had a balcony outside French doors. She slung their suitcase on the bed and started to unpack.

Tim, who'd been prowling around the suite, checking locks and window ledges, strode into the room and said, "Come on, Sis. We got that desert trip this afternoon."

Sissy eyed him. Tim looked so hot—the good kind of hot!—in jeans and tight tee and a cowboy hat he'd bought first thing. Weather never bothered him, the bastard. "I'm not going on a desert trip."

"Sure you are. It'll be fun. Some professor is taking Marianne to see the—that thing. The ecoregion."

"She can see it. You can see it. I'm staying right here."

Tim put his arms around her. Even in the chilly room, his body radiated its own special heat. He crooned in her ear, "You my baby, I need my baby, my one and only baby. . . ."

"You're out of tune," Sissy said severely, "and I told you that I'm not a 'baby.'" But she knew she would go with him. When Tim was like this, there was no resisting him.

"That's my old woman," Tim said, and she swatted him, not gently. He laughed.

The car had AC, but they didn't stay in it. Marianne didn't, Tim didn't, Dr. Lopez didn't, and so that meant Sissy couldn't either. If Tim's job was to protect Marianne—not that there was anything in this empty country to protect her from!—then Sissy's was to see that Marianne didn't tire herself out, especially not too far from the car. It'd been four months since Marianne and Harrison broke up and Marianne still wasn't eating much. She'd lost thirty pounds. Not that it didn't look good on her, but her face was drawn and tired and she just never knew when she should rest. Some people had no common sense.

So Sissy clambered out of the car into the fucking awful heat, careful not to touch the hot metal of the car, blinking in the burning sunlight. The hats that Dr. Lopez gave them didn't block enough of the glare. They left the car beside the road, which had almost no other vehicles on it, and started to walk.

Marianne said to Dr. Lopez, "I see why you love this landscape."

Sissy blinked. Love *this*? The uneven ground, baked hard and dry, was dotted with dusty, spiky, unfriendly looking bushes, and not much else. Way off in the distance some hazy mountains spread across the horizon. The sky was a hard, unforgiving blue from which heat pressed down like stones.

Dr. Lopez said, "You see its austere beauty, don't you? Not everybody can."

I can't, Sissy thought. Were there spores lying here, invisible, on the hard ground? Of course there were. Marianne said that heat didn't kill them. Nothing did except radiation, and you couldn't radiate a whole planet. In Russia, where there wasn't so much genetic immunity for reasons Sissy didn't understand, almost half the babies got spore disease and died horrible deaths.

Marianne said, "Tell us about the ecoregion. As it was before the spore cloud, and as it is now."

Dr. Lopez nodded. Both graying and balding, he wasn't handsome—especially not next to Tim, who squatted nearby, poking at rocks with a stick—but he had a gentle face that Sissy immediately liked. His voice was soft and musical, even when he sounded like he was talking to a college class. "This area lies on the northern edge of the Chihuahuan Desert ecoregion, which comprises 15.2 million acres in New Mexico and is one of the three most biologically rich and diverse desert ecoregions in the world. It has approximately thirty-five hundred plant species."

Where?

"Unfortunately, the ecoregion also contains the largest assemblage of endangered cacti in America. The dominant flora is this." He waved at one of the ugly, dusty bushes. "Creosote—*Larrea tridentata*. The other two common flora are acacia and tarbush. The soil is mostly a mix of clay and caliche, overlain by a layer of decomposed granite, which results from long-term outwash from the mountains. Our fauna include a high level of local endemism of butterflies, spiders, ants, lizards, snakes, and scorpions."

Scorpions? Snakes? This just got worse and worse.

"Hey, I think I disturbed one of your little critters," Tim said. He straightened, still holding his stick. Sissy shrieked. Across the ground at his feet scuttled a two-inch-long yellow monster with dark stripes, a long tail, and ugly claws.

Dr. Lopez said quickly, "Don't try to pick that up, Mr. Saunders. Let it go. That's *Centruroides suffuses* and its sting is highly poisonous. We call it, with great respect, 'alacran de Durango.'"

Tim said, "It leaves me alone, I leave it alone."

Marianne said, "What does it eat?"

Dr. Lopez said, "Spiders, solfugids, other scorpions, an array of insect prey. You want to know if it's been affected by the mouse crisis. Only indirectly, in that the whole ecosystem is shifting. Before the spore cloud, we were having great success in bringing back the aplomado falcon, which was once wiped out here. But the falcons—beautiful birds, just beautiful—eat mostly small birds, but those need grasslands for breeding and Chihuahuan grasslands have been profoundly affected by the lack of mice. The grasslands had been prioritized for conservation by the World Wildlife Fund, but with the absence of mice have come shifts in seed distribution, die-offs of some larger mammals, upheavals in insect and bird population rations, invasive species . . ." He spread his hands, palms up, the gesture of helplessness.

Invasive species. Sissy didn't look at Marianne.

Dr. Lopez went on about sand dune lizards, lesser prairie chickens (were there greater prairie chickens?), owls, reptile collection, habitat loss. Especially habitat loss. Sissy tried to listen and learn, but she kept glancing at the ground. Was that another scorpion moving over there? A snake? The sun poured down heat like burning oil.

Finally she said, "I'm going back to the car."

Tim looked up from whatever he was examining on the ground. He did a three-sixty scan of the desert, looking for any threat to Marianne—like *what*, out here?—then said, "Okay, Sissy. I'll go with you."

Sometimes he could be really understanding.

Back at the hotel, Marianne worked furiously on her laptop, rewriting parts of her speech to include what she'd learned from Dr. Lopez. Sissy and Tim retired to their room and made very quiet love. Afterward, refreshed and happy, Sissy left him asleep, carefully put on her clothes just the same as they were before, and asked Marianne what she wanted to order from room service for dinner. Room service wasn't a thing that most foundation speech sponsors would pay for, and Sissy did not intend to let the chance go to waste. Marianne just wanted soup. For herself and Tim, she ordered chicken-fried steak and garlic mashed potatoes and crème brûlée.

"What's that noise?" Sissy said.

Marianne looked up. "What noise?"

"That," Sissy said, and a shiver ran over her.

They ate dinner to the roar of the wind. Sissy had gone back into the bedroom to wake Tim, drawn back the heavy curtains, and ducked onto the balcony. How could weather change that fast? At noon, glaring blue sky. At 6:00 p.m., low sullen clouds, racing wind, leaves and trash skirling across the parking lot.

"Tim, get up. Dinner."

He always woke as fast as he went to sleep. "Is that wind?"

"Lots of wind."

Naked, he padded to the French doors and peered out. "Wow. What does the local weather channel say?"

"I'll see."

Marianne was already checking weather on the Internet. "Rain, high winds—damn, nobody's going to come to the lecture."

"Some people will come," Sissy said, with more confidence than she felt. "Does Albuquerque get superstorms?"

"I'll check."

Tim, dressed, emerged from the bedroom. Room service brought dinner, which smelled wonderful. The wind howled louder, or at least it seemed louder to Sissy. She said to the waiter, "Have you lived here long?"

"All my life, ma'am."

Sissy dropped her voice. "Does Albuquerque get superstorms? Or tornadoes?"

"No, ma'am. I ain't never seen neither one."

"Thank you."

After he left, Marianne looked up from her tablet and said, "Monsoon season doesn't usually start in Albuquerque until August—well, this is late July. There can be heavy winter storms and severe lightning storms, but the last tornado of any impact was 1974. And it was only an F2. New Mexico lies outside of Tornado Alley. And the city hasn't ever had a superstorm."

"First time for everything," Sissy muttered.

They ate in silence except for the wind. Marianne scarcely looked up from her notes. Not that she wasn't always this focused before a speech, but at least she was eating. Her speech outfit, dress pants, and a pretty burgundy blazer that Sissy insisted she buy, hung loosely on her thinner body, but she'd refused to go shopping for something that actually fit. Tim, who always gulped his food, left to meet with hotel security and do his final check of the ballroom. He said to Marianne, "You stay here until I come for you."

She said, "Tim, it's been over a year since anybody has considered me worth attacking with so much as a banana. Don't you think you're overreacting?"

"Better safe than sorry," Tim said, winked at Sissy, and left. Instead of being reassured by the slight bulge of his shoulder holster under his jacket, Sissy felt oddly disturbed.

Snap out of it, Sissy. Mama's voice, strong in her head. And good advice. It was just the wind making her so jumpy. Sissy knew the cure for that—good common-sense facts. She left the table, turned on the wall screen, and found the local news.

". . . unusually high winds . . . moderate rains . . . travel advisory in effect . . ."

Marianne looked up sharply. "How high did they say the winds are?"

Sissy said, "Gusts up to fifty miles per hour."

Marianne frowned. Sissy said, "You have somebody you can call?" Marianne knew a lot of scientists, all kind of scientists.

"Yes, but I'm not going to call him. Not enough probability. You just leave your tablet on during the speech, Sissy, and keep an eye on the weather."

Sissy nodded, but she wasn't happy. She didn't even want to eat her crème brûlée.

She was even less happy after Tim escorted Marianne to the green room behind the ballroom and Sissy took her seat in a middle row of chairs. Most of the chairs were empty; Marianne had been right about people staying home. A raised stage had been set up at one end, with a lectern and two more empty chairs. The wall behind the stage had a little door. The ballroom had no windows and it must have rooms all around it, because all of a sudden Sissy couldn't hear the wind. An elderly couple sat next to her. They looked nice, so she leaned over and said, "Excuse me?"

"Yes?" the lady said.

"I'm not from around here and I'm just wondering—does Albuquerque get tornadoes or superstorms? There's so much wind out there!"

They both smiled. The man said, "No, miss. Oh, small ones some-times, but it's not a big problem here." It was what Marianne had already told her, and Sissy felt better. She should have eaten the crème brûlée. Maybe it would still be on the hallway cart after the speech. Almost 7:30—she settled herself more firmly on her chair.

Then they came in.

A whole group of young men—fifteen, sixteen, seventeen—which in itself was trouble because they were too old for a class trip and any-way there was no teacher or professor with them. They all wore long dark raincoats with hoods, which didn't look like gang gear but didn't look good, either. No girls with them, and the raincoats were loose enough to hide anything. Where was Tim? Had security let these guys through?

Sissy walked back to the ballroom entrance and asked the guard there, "Where is the ladies' room?" He told her, but there was some-thing about the way he held his face and body, something she couldn't name but felt as strong as the chill from a freezer door. She smiled and walked toward the ladies' room, and when she turned to open the door, he was watching her hard.

In the bathroom stall, she heard the wind howling. She called Tim on her cell. The call didn't go through. Sissy checked her tablet; the Wi-Fi had disappeared.

Sissy left the bathroom and turned the opposite direction from the ballroom. The security guard had been watching for her. He called down the corridor, "Miss! You can't go that way!" He started toward her.

Sissy ran. No place else, no hotel or college campus or community hall or anywhere else Marianne gave speeches, had ever tried to stop Sissy from going backstage. She darted into a staircase, ran up one floor instead of down, and raced toward a different stairwell. Her sense of direction had always been good. She found the corridors that brought her behind the ballroom. Another Security guard stood out-side the green room. He eyed her the same way the other one had.

"You can't go in there, Miss Tate."

He knew her name. She hadn't met with these people—had Tim for some reason shown them her picture? Why would he do that? Sissy made herself smile appealingly and held out her tablet. "I have to go in, I'm afraid. Dr. Jenner forgot her notes! She's always so forgetful!" She shook her curls at the man.

"You can't go in there."

"Well, she can't go on stage without her notes! There's a lot of numbers for her speech that she hasn't memorized. Important numbers."

He hesitated. Clearly he *wanted* Marianne on stage. Finally he said, "You go back to your seat. I'll give her the tablet."

"Okay."

She handed it to him and turned to go. When he opened the door, she darted through ahead of him.

"Hey!" He was outraged but she saw he was also hesitant; whatever was supposed to happen on stage, he didn't want Tim alerted to it. Sissy watched him pull himself together. "We got rules, but since you're already in. . . ." She had never seen anything as fake or horrible as his smile.

"Thank you," Sissy said sweetly. She closed the door behind her. Marianne and Tim stared at her. "Listen, Tim, there are some men in the ballroom, and I think that security is part of it and—"

"Tell me in order," Tim said, just as Marianne's cell, held halfway to her mouth, said in the slight vibrato of a speakerphone, "Marianne? I can't talk to you now. Sorry. Bye."

"Scott! Wait!" Marianne said. "I'm in New Mexico and I need to know if a—"

"New Mexico?" the vibrato said. "Where in New Mexico?"

"Downtown Albuquerque. Is there a storm coming? A big one?"

"How do you know that? We don't even know that for sure. GOES East is offline again, fucking ancient equipment, but everything else up near you says the situation is deteriorating. It could all go away or it could be something big gathering. I—"

"How big?"

"Don't know yet. But stay alert, okay? Is there a safe shelter where you are?"

"I—"

"Something that can withstand a major tornado?"

"Major? New Mexico doesn't—"

"Gotta go. Watch the Weather Channel!"

Sissy said, "My tablet doesn't work."

"Of course it does," Marianne said, holding up hers.

Tim said swiftly, "Yours didn't work in the ballroom? They have a jammer out there?"

"I don't know!"

"Okay, stay calm. Tell me what you saw in the ballroom."

Sissy did, finishing with, "Who did Marianne call?"

Marianne said, "Friend of mine at the Storm Prediction Center in Norman, Oklahoma. Tim, what do you think?"

"I think—"

Marianne said, "Sshhhh!" and held up her tablet. A talking head, looking tense, said, "We have just gotten word from the Storm Prediction Center in Oklahoma that a powerful storm system is forming over parts of New Mexico. Warm air drawn far northward from that Gulf of Mexico low-pressure zone is meeting colder air off the mountains and—just a moment, here comes an update, and . . . This looks like a tornado, folks, very unusual for New Mexico, centering on Albuquerque. Climate changes due to global warming have of course altered many usual—"

Marianne said to Tim, "Does the hotel have a safe shelter?"

"Just the basement. Sissy, were those guys in the ballroom carrying any signs or doing any chanting or anything to identify them?"

"No."

"Were they armed?"

"I think so."

"Fuck," Tim said. "Okay, here's what we do. We're not going out that door to the stage. You two go in that coat closet there and wait while I deal with the hallway guard."

Marianne said, "No! No violence! You don't even know for sure that there's any threat!"

There was a threat. Sissy knew it, and so did Tim. This was just Marianne being all trusting and liberal. Not that Sissy wished her to be any different, except in times like this.

"Do it," Tim said, and locked his eyes on to Marianne's. Something passed between them that Sissy didn't quite understand, but when Sissy grabbed Marianne's hand and pulled her into the closet, Marianne went.

It smelled musty, as if no one had put coats in it for a long time. Hangers rattled against Sissy's shoulders. A few minutes later, Tim opened the door. "Come on." They followed him back through the green room and into the corridor. The man Sissy had seen before lay on his stomach, very still. Sissy put her hand to her mouth.

"He's not dead," Tim whispered. "Come on!"

He led them away from the ballroom and down the service stairway Sissy had used before. One flight down, a door said EMERGENCY EXIT ONLY. ALARM WILL SOUND. Tim pushed it open and was blown back against Marianne, knocking her into the wall.

"Jesus fucking Christ!" Tim cried.

Sissy saw the twister, then, moving toward them over the city. It looked just like in the movies, a swirling black cone of wind and dirt and God-only-knew what else. The wind howled and rain lashed into the stairwell. Tim staggered to his feet. Sissy's tablet, which she hadn't even realized she was still holding, blew out of her hand and smashed against the wall. Marianne clutched hers against her.

"Come on!" Tim screamed. There was no shutting the door against that wind. They staggered after him down the next flight of stairs, the wind following them like a shrieking demon. Only Tim's great strength got the door at the bottom, which opened outward, wrenched apart. They squeezed through and the door slammed shut behind them from the force of the wind. Sissy pushed her hair off her face in time to get a confused glimpse of a cement-floored underground corridor, just before the lights went out.

"Hold hands and follow me," Tim said. Sissy groped for Marianne's hand. She must already be holding on to Tim because Sissy was tugged forward. Marianne followed. The lights went back on.

"A generator," Marianne said. "The hotel has a—"

"Quiet," Tim said. And then, "Get down!"

Sissy dropped to the floor and pulled Marianne down, too. From somewhere ahead, around some turn in the corridor, came shouting.

Tim looked around. Sissy knew what he was thinking, as clear as if the words appeared above his head in little balloons: *No place to hide.* He drew his gun and whispered, "Stay here."

"Tim—" Marianne began. Was she going to argue *now*? Sissy pinched her boss, hard. Marianne, startled, jerked her head around and then nodded.

Tim moved sideways to the end of the corridor, then motioned them to come on. Sissy and Marianne crept forward. The bare corridor turned, and around the turn was another, much wider hallway lined on both sides with maids' wheeled carts loaded with fresh towels, cleaning supplies, canvas bins for dirty linen, vacuum cleaners. At Sissy's end of the corridor was a closet; the other end led to the hotel kitchen. Tim pointed to the closet.

But when Sissy tried the door, it was locked.

Shouts erupted in the kitchen.

Then it all happened at once. Tim ducked behind the cover of a cleaning cart, dropped to a crouch, and began firing. Sissy pushed Marianne behind another cart. A spray bottle of Soft Scrub toppled over onto them, followed by a stack of towels. Sissy shook off the towels, trying to get Marianne farther behind the rack. Tim kept firing, the sounds deafening in the corridor, and then the whole building started to shake. The whole hotel!

Someone screamed.

The lights went out again.

But that didn't stop the firing, and in Sissy's mind the gunfire merged with the sudden howling of the wind—how was she hearing the wind way down in the basement?—and the clean smell of the fresh towels all around them. Marianne cried out something in the dark, and then pain shot through Sissy like nothing she had ever imagined, not that she didn't have a good imagination, and Marianne cried out again and it all went away, everything, all of it, forever.

A Force 4 tornado had hit parts of Albuquerque, where no tornado should have been. The city had had twelve minutes' warning. Roofs and walls were torn off well-constructed houses; heavy cars were lifted off the ground and thrown; trees were uprooted. Two sections of the city were uninhabitable. The winds reached two hundred miles per hour, the storm path nearly one-third of a mile wide. The Albuquerque tornado had been only part of the superstorm now raging from Texas to Minnesota. Power was out, cell towers down. There was massive flooding, hail in places, gale-force wind. From the desert site where the federal government was intermittently building its spaceship, came reports of major damage to the ship. Hundreds of people in five states whose luck or shelter-strength or warning system had failed, were now dead.

And so was Sissy.

Marianne could not take it in. She sat in the police station beside Tim. Outside, the storm had passed. She and Tim had been in this small, bare interrogation room for an hour—didn't the cops have time for homicide? She hoped they were all out rescuing people and not doing anything as mundane as stopping looters.

"Tim," she said, for perhaps the twentieth time, putting her hand on his arm. He didn't respond. Drawn completely into himself, he sat with his head down, his arms pulled tight toward his body, a man carved of stone. Every once in a while his shoulders shook in a massive convulsion, but he made no sound. Marianne knew that for him this room did not exist, she did not exist, the two men he had killed did not exist, nothing existed but Sissy's death.

They had made their initial statements to a wide-eyed rookie, the only person left behind in the police station. Sissy's body had been taken to a relatively undamaged funeral home. Marianne had no idea who were the men who'd tried to kill her and had murdered Sissy instead. What Deneb-hate group had they belonged to? What had they hoped to accomplish? Had they been apprehended? What would happen to Tim?

She would get him a good lawyer. Even if it bankrupted the foundation, she would get him off from whatever charges were filed. He'd fired in self-defense, and in defense of her and Sissy.

Oh, God . . . *Sissy*. To never see her dance around the office in her outrageous sweaters, never hear her scold Marianne about her clothes or diet, never again see the softness in her eyes when she looked at Tim . . .

A cop came into the room. Middle-aged, he looked weary, hard-eyed, competent. Tim did not so much as glance up. Marianne blinked back her tears and made herself stand. What she said now could be critical to Tim's future. The interrogation was beginning.

"Hello," she said steadily. "I'm Dr. Marianne Jenner, and this is my bodyguard, Tim Saunders, who was defending me from attack. Who are you?"

Two days spent in the police station and in court. Tim was arraigned and held until Marianne could arrange bail. Two suspects and six "persons of interest" were picked up by the police. At nine in the morning on the third day, Marianne sat in her hotel room—not the hotel downtown but a cheap one near the airport—and waited for ten o'clock, when the shuttle would take her to the damaged airport for the only flight she could find back to New York. The hour ahead felt like the arid years to come.

She had lost everything.

Sissy, the daughter of her heart.

Noah, gone to the stars.

Ryan, shut up in his grief over Connie and his implacable hatred of the Denebs.

Harrison, who'd thrown her out of his life.

The Star Brother Foundation, because she didn't see how she could go on with it. If she paid Tim's bail and a really good lawyer, she was out of funding. Out of courage, maybe even out of belief that the spaceship to World could ever be built. She could feel the dream leaving her, the last smoke from a spent fire.

Marianne sat on the bed, head bowed, unmoving, until her spine ached. It seemed to her that she might never move again. She had known pain before as an active thing, piercing and lancing her; this frozen pain was something new, and infinitely worse. Even breathing hurt.

A knock on the door. She couldn't move to open it. Another knock, louder. Then the murmur of voices. The shuttle? She couldn't break free of the icy shards of pain.

The door opened. A bellhop stuck his head in. "Dr. Jenner? This man—" He was pushed aside and Jonah Stubbins entered.

His eyes, small in the broad face atop the huge body, swept around the room. "Well, now, little lady—" He stopped, paused, and then, "Marianne, I know what happened. I need to talk to you. I have something to offer you that will, I think, matter to you.

"May I sit down?"

PART THREE

Show me a hero and I will write you a tragedy.

—F. Scott Fitzgerald

CHAPTER 16

S plus 6 years

"There is mouses down there!" Colin Jenner said.

"No," his father said in that slow, frowny way that Colin hated. Jason hated it, too. "Not here."

"Yes." Colin pointed at the ground. "Little baby mouses!"

His father tugged at both boys' hands so hard that even Jason was almost lifted off his feet.

Daddy hadn't wanted to bring them on this walk. He never wanted to bring them anyplace. He sat in the living room and stared at the television or sometimes just at the wall, which was dusty and had a big spiderweb up in the corner by the ceiling. Colin didn't think there was a spider in it, but he wasn't sure. He hoped there was. Spiders were interesting. Sometimes Daddy would get up and cook or wash their clothes, and sometimes Jason would do it. Jason was way over six and went to real school, not just preschool, and so he could do things like that.

But today Jason had begged and pleaded, and Daddy and Jason and Colin got in the car and drove to Daddy's swamp, which would have been exciting except for Daddy, who looked unhappy to be there. More unhappy.

The swamp was squishy underfoot and Colin's boots made a nice splurgly sound each time he pulled a foot out of mud. There was so much to hear! To look at, too—frogs and bugs and the purple flowers

Daddy hated and Colin sort of liked. But looking wasn't as exciting as hearing. It never was.

But after just a little time Daddy said he was tired. They left the swamp and walked the trail to the parking lot, with its broken-off sign that nobody ever fixed: REARDON WETLANDS PRESER. Colin pulled away from his father's hand, planted his muddy boots, and pointed again. "Baby mouses are down there!"

"I told you, Colin, there are no mice here. Not anymore, thanks to your grandmother's alien 'friends.'"

"I hear them! Baby mouses!"

His father grimaced, knelt, and put his hands on Colin's shoulders. "Say 'mice.' One mouse, two mice. Look, I explained all this to you, remember? You're old enough to begin to understand."

"I'm five now," Colin said, in case Daddy forgot. He seemed to forget Colin and Jason a lot.

"Yes, five. A big boy. So you can remember that all the house mice and field mice, all the ones like those in your picture book, are gone. They all got sick and died. A different kind of mouse, the deer mouse, might come and live here, but they haven't spread this far yet. And even when they do, you couldn't hear the babies way underground."

It was the most words Daddy had spoken in a long time, but they weren't *true* words. Colin stamped his foot. "There is mices down there."

Ryan Jenner stood, took both sons' hands and started toward the car. Behind them, a deer mouse sped from the cover of brush and disappeared into a tiny hole in the ground.

Daddy was wrong. Colin did understand about the mice. Grandma had explained it all on Skype. That was a while ago and Colin didn't remember all of it, but Jason did and he explained it, everything that had happened when Colin wasn't even born yet. Aliens had come from out of the stars, and Grandma and all the other scientists had helped them to not get sick. Only, after the aliens went away, a lot of mice died, like Jason's hamster last Christmas, which was really scary because Pockets had been all stiff and cold. Grandma promised that she, Colin, Jason, and Daddy wouldn't die for a long time. Mommy was already dead but that didn't count because Colin couldn't remember her and Jason could only remember a little. She'd died of cancer, which was different than what had killed mice. That was sad. Then birds and owls and even wolves died because there weren't enough mice to eat. Then there were too many bugs because there weren't enough birds to eat them.

Somehow the whole thing ended up hurting farmers and bread and fruit and money, although Colin didn't really understand that part and neither did Jason. But it was the reason people got poor and Daddy lost his job and the car was so old and the porch steps were broken and Colin was never, ever to tell anybody that they had food in the cellar and guns in the house. Not ever.

The really confusing part, though, was the aliens from the star. Grandma said they were good and hadn't meant to hurt any people or mice. They left directions for building a spaceship, a real one not like Colin's toys, which sounded really exciting except that the important people who were in charge of the world didn't have enough money to build it. And a big storm wrecked part of the spaceship, so they stopped. Grandma's job was to tell people that the spaceship should get built again and that the aliens were good.

But Daddy said the aliens were bad. Really, really bad. They killed people and mice and wrecked something called "the economy," which Colin didn't understand, and "the ecology," which he did because Daddy used to talk about it all the time, before he started staring at the wall or the TV. Ecology was how everything needed to eat everything else. Daddy said the aliens were even worse than the purple flowers.

So Colin and Jason didn't know who to believe. Grandma and Daddy were both scientists, who were the smartest people in the world.

Someday Colin was going to be a scientist, too, although Jason wanted to be an astronaut instead. When Colin was a scientist, everything would all be clear.

Meanwhile, he just listened. To everything. Nobody, he sometimes thought, knew how much he heard.

"Daddy," he said as they walked from the car to the broken porch steps, "the trees are not happy."

"Don't I know it," Daddy said.

Daddy didn't understand. Grandma, on Skype, didn't understand. Even Jason didn't understand. Jason didn't hear what Colin did.

On her birthday, Marianne saw a picture of herself on the cover of a news magazine.

She stood in line at the supermarket in Barnsville, a Canadian town west of Toronto. The town was small, the supermarket barely deserved the name, the magazine rack held only three magazines, which were a dying commodity anyway. Two were American, and *Time* had pictures of her, Harrison, Ahmed Rafat, and others who'd researched aboard the *Embassy*. The photos ringed big red letters: ARCHITECTS OF THE SPORE PLAGUE: WHERE ARE THEY NOW?

Marianne's fingers trembled as she put the magazine in her basket, along with coffee, milk, bread, cheese, and dish detergent. The clerk smiled, took her money, and did not seem to match her with the photo. At home, Marianne collapsed on her sofa and read the article and its many sidebars.

"Home" was this small rented bungalow ever since Stubbins had brought her here two and a half years ago. Canada was far less rabid about the damage the Denebs had caused to her ecology than was the United States—but then, when wasn't Canada less rabid? Something about the United States seemed to provide a fertile medium for culturing hate groups, irrational scapegoats, mass shootings, and the blame game. When Jonah Stubbins had tried to buy a TV station in the United States, there was suddenly none available. When he'd tried to buy broadcast-frequency bandwidth from the FCC, his application had been denied. A few cable companies welcomed him, but they were small and local. To get the airtime he wanted, Stubbins bought a Canadian station, from which he broadcast illegally to the United States. "I'm a goddamn Tokyo Rose," he'd said to reporters, but not to Marianne. She'd heard about it anyway.

The *Time* piece, a series of articles, began with an essay by Hugo Soltis, a popular columnist known for his anti-Deneb views:

> Seven years ago, every country on Earth fell apart. And they're still falling.
>
> Humanity managed to survive a global death toll of over fifty million people from the spore plague, the majority of victims in Central Asia. We managed to survive the die-off of eight mouse species, with all the economic havoc resulting directly and indirectly from that extinction. What we are not managing to survive, in any meaningful way, is what has happened to our most precious resource: Earth's children.
>
> Enrique Velasquez, age two, lives in Compton, California, with his parents and older sister. Enrique cries almost constantly, as he has since birth. He is underweight and has been diagnosed with "failure to thrive."
>
> Allison Porter, in Chicago, is three. For the first two and a half years of her life, she cried—"wailed, screeched, screamed," according to her parents—as much as Enrique. For the last six months, Allison has been on Calminex, the child-targeted tranquilizer from pharmaceutical giant Eli Lilly. Allison is calm now, but she moves and talks more slowly than what was once normal for three-year-olds. She has trouble learning.
>
> Jazzmyn Brown is five and a half, one of the children

in the womb when *R. sporii* struck Earth. Jazzmyn's mother, like Enrique's parents, cannot afford Calminex. Jazzmyn's mother, a drug addict, surrendered her to the Florida child-protective services, and since then Jazzmyn has been in and out of eleven foster homes. No one can cope for long with her tantrums and chaotic behavior.

Michael Worden, four, has no chaotic behavior, no nonstop crying, no daily doses of Calminex. Born deaf, he is a bright and happy little boy in Oklahoma City, where his parents and two sisters are all learning American Sign Language right along with Michael.

Are these the only choices for an entire generation of children: to be on drugs that retard development, to be born deaf, or to live an existence filled with crying, frustration, and pain? Because there *is* pain for these children; functional MRIs confirm this. An entire generation has been genetically modified in their most complicated and human part: the brain. Everyone on planet Earth knows this, and how it happened.

But what happens next? Is there any hope on the horizon? And where are the researchers who helped bring this about by cooperating so fully with the alien Denebs? Did these human scientists know what would be the consequences of the spore plague?

And if they didn't foresee it—should they have?

Most puzzling of all to many Americans: Why are at least some of them still working with those organizations, government and privately owned, who want to build a spaceship and renew contact with the aliens who did not bother to warn us of all the consequences of this plague? In this magazine's recent poll, 68 percent of randomly contacted people disapproved of the four spaceships still under construction. "We have enough problems right here!" Enrique's father says, and who should know better?

Marianne read with growing anger. To say that the scientists on the *Embassy* had "helped to bring this about"—how could a once-reputable news magazine even print that? Or blame the Denebs for failing to warn humanity about what they themselves didn't know? Or that the Denebs were aliens, when all evidence said they were human? How?

The rest of the articles were more balanced. One discussed the chemistry and side effects of Calminex. One reported on the four spaceships still under construction, including the funding and engineering problems of building an unknown structure powered by unknown physics to specs dictated by an unknown race. One article examined the world's economy, slowly recovering. One explored the ecological shifts from the mouse die-off: which animals were filling the vacated niche of fast-multiplying omnivores, how plants were adjusting.

And one traced the present activities and whereabouts of key *Embassy* research staff, those who had stayed until the very end.

Dr. Ahmed Rafat, geneticist. On staff at GlaxoSmithKline in London.

Penelope Hodgson, lab assistant. Housewife in Tempe, Arizona.

Dr. Ann Potter, physician. Retired from practice, living in Washington, DC.

Robert Chavez, lab assistant, working at the University of California at Berkeley.

Lisa Guiterrez, genetics counselor, changed her name to Lisa Garland, living and working in Chicago. She deeply regrets her involvement with the aliens, saying—

Marianne skipped to the last paragraphs.

Dr. Harrison Rice, immunologist and Nobel Laureate, living in

New York City and working at Columbia University, reportedly on brain anomalies in mice.

Dr. Marianne Jenner, evolutionary geneticist whose son Noah was allegedly kidnapped by aliens, living in Barnsville, Ontario, Canada. She creates content for the JS Network, owned by Jonah Stubbins, which feeds pro-Deneb programs and speeches and scientific statistics to American television and the Internet around the globe.

How had they found her? And how much danger was she in now? God, she'd thought that was all over and done with. She hadn't seen her children or grandchildren in two years, settling for Skype "visits" so that she didn't lead murderous nut jobs to Elizabeth or Ryan or the kids. She lived in Canada with a false passport and visa, both courtesy of Stubbins's huge and faintly illegal empire.

Maybe she needed yet another name, another passport, another place to live. Maybe she should leave the house right now and check into a motel. The article hadn't included her alias. But maybe the motel clerk would recognize her picture. Maybe she was being incredibly paranoid.

No. Sissy was dead because Marianne had not been paranoid enough. If she hadn't given those speeches for the foundation . . . No. No use thinking that way. It didn't help.

She picked up her cell to call Jonah Stubbins. Ordinarily they had very little contact; working for the same goal had not made his fake-folksy persona any less grating. This, however, was not "ordinarily." At least, over the phone she did not have to wonder if he was wearing any of his pheromone products, or if they were affecting her.

Before the call could go through, someone pounded on her door. "Marianne? Open up—I know you're in there!"

Something was wrong with Daddy. Jason said so, but Colin knew it even before that. He didn't need Jason to tell him everything! He wasn't a baby.

"Daddy?" Jason said. Daddy sat in his big red chair with the tall back, Colin standing on one side of him and Jason on the other. Daddy hadn't moved all morning, and when Colin had gone to bed last night, Daddy had been sitting in the chair just like that. He smelled bad. He looked straight at the wall so Colin looked at it, too, to see if maybe there was a spider on it. There wasn't.

"Daddy!" Jason said again. Daddy didn't look at him, even though Jason said it loud. Jason shook his arm, and then Daddy did look at him. "It's lunchtime now."

"Yes," Daddy said.

Colin said helpfully, "We had cereal for breakfast."

Jason put his face right up close to Daddy's. "You have to make lunch now. We want soup. I'm not allowed to turn on the stove, remember?"

"Yes," Daddy said, but at first he didn't get up. Then, slowly, he pushed himself out of the chair and walked into the kitchen. He walked really slow, picking up his feet only a little bit.

Colin scampered after him. "Daddy, are you sick? You should go to bed if you're sick."

Daddy started to cry. He did it with no noise at all, just big fat tears rolling down his face. He still smelled bad. Colin got scared. But Jason said sharply, "Daddy! Lunch!"

Daddy heated the soup. Colin wasn't very hungry, after all.

Marianne flung open the door to her bungalow; there was no mistaking that voice. Tim Saunders stood on the porch.

Marianne had not seen him since Albuquerque. Absolved of all charges, Tim had disappeared. He had not even thanked her or Stubbins for the high-priced lawyer or the car registered to one of Stubbins's corporations. Stubbins had grunted, "Ungrateful bastard. And abandoning you—he's interested mostly in keeping his own hide safe from the rest of them hate-mongers." Marianne knew better. Tim had known that Marianne was safe under Stubbins's professional protection, and the lack of thank-yous had not been ingratitude. Tim had disappeared into his grief for Sissy, and even the sight of Marianne would have been too much to bear.

Two and a half years had not changed him much. The long lean body stood in that same relaxed-alert way; the eyes in his tanned face burned just as blue. He was—what, now? Forty? Faint wrinkles at the corners of those amazing eyes, but only faint. "Marianne," he said, and his voice had that same gravelly depth.

"How did you find me?"

"*Time* magazine. The bastards. Are you okay? Can I come in?"

"I'm okay," she lied.

"Uh-huh." He shut and locked the door, prowled around the living room trying windows, glanced down the hallway of the little bungalow. "You can't stay here."

"Why? What do you know?"

"I don't know anything, if you mean anything definite. But this place is about as secure as a gazebo." He pronounced it "gays-bo," and Marianne didn't correct him. "You work for Stubbins, right? Why didn't he give you a safer house?"

"I didn't want a fortress. I don't use my own name. We thought— Tim, do you really think those people who . . . that group from Albuquerque will come after me?"

"Well, four of them went to prison. But no, I don't think they will. Might have trouble getting into Canada, anyway. But there are plenty of other alien-hate groups, even here. NCWAK is getting stronger all the time."

No Contact with Alien Killers. They were the one that had blown up Branson's partly built spaceship.

Tim said, "You're outed now and Stubbins ought to take better care of you."

"I was just going to call him when you showed up."

"And I'm the first to find you?"

"You are."

He gave her his old grin, and something turned over in Marianne's chest. *No, God no, not after all this time.*

Tim said, "You're going to hire me for your bodyguard again. Or Stubbins is. I see the old son of a bitch brought out another perfume. Makes you want to like strangers."

"Not exactly. But Tim, about the bodyguard issue—I don't think—"

"You got any coffee, Marianne? I could use some coffee. I been driving up here fast and furious."

Her cell rang: Stubbins. At the same time, a TV van pulled into the driveway. Instantly Tim was at the window, pulling the blinds closed, checking his holster.

"Marianne?" Stubbins said on the phone. "I just saw this damn article, and somebody's head is going to roll 'cause I didn't know about it before now. Looks like we need to move you again. And I think a bodyguard would be a good idea."

Marianne closed her eyes. "Let's talk about it, Jonah. But first, there's something else I want you to do."

"What's that?"

She glanced at Tim. He was pulling open cupboards in the kitchenette, presumably looking for coffee, but Marianne knew he heard every word.

She said into the phone, "It isn't just me who was named in that article. I want you to put a bodyguard on Harrison Rice, too. He won't allow it, but you can get one to just sort of follow him around, right? He not only worked with the Denebs right up till the end, but he's working now at Columbia on the hearing impairment in children. That's a double reason for . . ." For what? Would someone really harm Harrison because he was trying to understand what had happened to a generation of kids? No. She was being paranoid. People's thinking wasn't that twisted.

"Yeah," Stubbins said. "Good thinking."

Tim smiled at her. "You got sugar someplace?"

———

Stubbins was efficient. Within two hours a woman arrived at Marianne's door, high heels clicking up the walk past the two TV vans and two Internet reporters camped on the sidewalk. The woman, who did not offer her name and who had the bloodless demeanor of a robot, delivered papers and instructions. She made a phone call to Stubbins about Tim, then nodded at Marianne. "You can keep him."

Tim gave the woman his lazy, hyper-charged grin. She did not seem affected. She said, "One hour to pack, Dr. Jenner," and clicked her way back to her car, ignoring shouted questions from the reporters.

Exactly an hour later, a sleek black car backed into the driveway. Marianne, wearing a large hat that frustrated pictures, raised the garage door and the black car backed in as far as Marianne's battered Chevy would permit. Tim loaded suitcases into the trunk and they both climbed into the back seat. The windows were opaque and the driver blank-faced. Another man rode beside him.

Tim nodded professional approval. "Stubbins isn't taking any chances."

Marianne said nothing. She felt exposed, ridiculous, chagrined at being even more in Stubbins's debt, raw from other emotions she didn't want to examine too closely. She didn't look at Tim.

The reporters didn't give chase, which meant either they knew they were outclassed or she wasn't a big enough story. She hoped it was the latter. Tim, who had driven the entire previous night, fell asleep. She remembered that he had always had that ability, and then tried not to remember anything else.

The car deposited them at an apartment building in Toronto. The driver handed Marianne apartment keys to 3B. She said, "Does Jonah Stubbins just keep a whole series of apartments around the world for emergencies like this?" Because it was inconceivable that Stubbins himself lived here, in this respectable but slightly crumbling building from the last century, in this respectable but slightly crumbling neighborhood of a Canadian city. Neither the driver nor the bodyguard answered her. They unloaded the suitcases and drove off.

"Well," Tim said as he carried in her cases, "home sweet home."

Marianne set down her laptop case. The apartment, not as big as her abandoned bungalow in Barnesville, had two bedrooms. They opened off a living-dining-kitchen area with a large wall screen. The simple furnishings looked neither old nor brand new, as if the apartment had been put together a few years ago and used occasionally since then. A coffee stain blossomed on the arm of the beige sofa; sheets and blankets were folded neatly on the unmade beds; the few pictures on the wall were generic landscapes. The kitchen cupboards held six plates, six glasses, six cups, six sets of cutlery.

She felt a sudden, unbidden longing for another home—not for her bright little house near the college where she'd taught and researched up until seven years ago, but for the big, messy, noisy house where she had raised Elizabeth and Ryan and Noah. Children's artwork on the fridge, toys underfoot, SpaghettiOs, cereal boxes with prizes inside.

"What's wrong, Marianne?" Tim said.

"Nothing."

"Like hell. Are you scared? You're safe enough here, you know. That magazine will only be on the stands a week, and for that time I'll do the shopping and you stay inside and do . . . whatever it is you do. It'll be okay."

"I know."

"Is it Rice? You worried about him? Are you two still in touch?"

Tim's gaze was intent; his tone sounded like more than a simple request for information. Marianne said, "We're not in touch."

"Uh-huh."

Her cell rang, saving her from trying to interpret his two maddening syllables. Stubbins again. All their calls went through heavily encrypted satellite links. She answered as Tim turned away to open the fridge, which was empty.

Tim said, "You got a pencil and paper, Marianne? I better make a list. Oh, and money. I hope you got either money or a new credit card, 'cause I don't."

Stubbins said, "You arrived all right." It wasn't a question. "Now, about that new Internet content you're writing about my ship . . ."

Tim brought back groceries, including two bottles of wine and take-out Thai for dinner. Marianne drank two glasses of pinot noir, trying to calm her jitters, since talking rationally to herself hadn't worked all that well.

Tim poured her a third glass. "We got to talk."

"About what?"

"You don't look at me."

She was startled that he had noticed.

"Not directly," he said, "not ever. Why not? Do you want a different bodyguard?"

Yes.

No.

"Because if looking at me brings back too many memories about Albuquerque and about Sissy, I get that. You can ask Stubbins for somebody else."

"It isn't that." She drank off half the wine.

"Then what is it, Marianne?"

She didn't answer but did turn her head to look at him directly— *See? I can do it?* That was a mistake. She couldn't see her own face, but . . .

Tim let out a long breath. Of course he would know, he probably already knew, he was nothing if not experienced with women.

He stood up, came around the table, pulled her to her feet and kissed her.

Marianne pulled away. "No, no . . . we can't . . ."

"Why not?" He didn't let her go. His touch electrified and soothed her, both at once. How long had it been since anyone had touched her? Since Harrison. Two and a half years.

He said, "You carrying a torch for Rice?"

"No." She wasn't, not anymore. Banked embers.

"I grieved on Sissy for nearly two years," Tim said, "and then I hated myself because I stopped. Because I *could* stop. I thought it meant I was a shallow prick, or hadn't really loved her. But it don't mean that, Marianne. It's just life going on, you know?"

That speech finished her. She hadn't expected insight from him, or sensitivity—not even sensitivity expressed in clichés. Why not? After all, Sissy had loved him, and Sissy had been nobody's fool. His scent, masculine and heady, confused her. Still, she made one more try.

"I'm so much older than you—"

Tim laughed. "Who the hell cares?" He kissed her again, and then she was lost completely, drowning in him—no, not drowning, that implied something passive, she was rushing toward him, toward that blue gaze and that long hard body, rushing into the bedroom and the joy that blotted out, for a time anyway, all memory and all regret.

CHAPTER 17

S plus 6 years

For three whole days Daddy didn't get out of his tall red chair hardly at all, and there was no more milk left or cereal or cheese for sandwiches. Jason and Colin hadn't had any baths because they weren't supposed to get in the bathtub without an adult. The upstairs toilet was plugged up but the downstairs one still worked. However, Colin could smell the toilet from his bedroom and he didn't like it. His bedroom window was too stuck to open. The boys stood in the front hall and discussed all this in whispers.

"I think Daddy's sick," Jason said.

"I think he's mad at us," Colin said. "He frowns all the time and he won't talk."

"If he's sick," Jason said, "he should go to a doctor. But if he's mad, he should say why. It's not *fair*."

Colin nodded. It wasn't fair. When you were mad at somebody you were supposed to tell them why, using your indoor voice, and then ask what everybody could do to make things better. That's what Colin's preschool teacher, Ms. Rydder, said. Colin wished he was back in preschool, but it was still summer. Anyway, he couldn't go to school until he had a bath.

Jason said, "I *told* him he should go to the doctor."

"You did?" Jason was brave. Colin was a little scared of Daddy now. "What did he say?"

"He said, 'I wanna go home.'"

"But he is home."

"I know. It doesn't make sense."

Colin stood on one foot, but that didn't help. Outside, a tree said something in the rain, but that didn't help either.

Jason said, sounding just like Daddy—the old Daddy—"Stop fidgeting, Colin. We have to think what to do!"

Colin tried to think, but nothing came. He said, "Daddy's talking now."

They tiptoed into the living room. Daddy sat in his chair, talking quiet but not so quiet that Colin didn't hear him: "I wanna go home. I wanna go home." It made Colin feel spooky.

Jason pulled him back into the hall. "Okay," he said, "I know what to do. We're going to call Grandma!"

Colin frowned. "Daddy said that Grandma is doing something bad."

"She's *not*. Don't say that again! Grandma will help us. She's Daddy's mommy, and mommies help when people are sick."

Colin, having no experience with mommies, thought about this. "Okay. But do you know how to do Skype?" Daddy always set up their Skype calls with Grandma and then left the room. Sometimes it seemed to Colin that Daddy didn't like Grandma. But if she was his mommy . . . The whole thing was too confusing.

Jason said, "I think I can do Skype. Maybe."

He could. Colin, watching Jason at the computer, was full of admiration. When Colin was going to real school, he'd be able to do all these things, too.

The computer made the ringing-phone sound. "You did it, Jase!"

"Hello?" Grandma's voice said, and there she was on the screen. When Colin had been little, he'd thought that Grandma was inside the computer, but now he knew better. She was far away, and very busy, maybe or maybe not doing something bad.

"Hi, Grandma," Jason said. "Can you see me? Colin is here, too. You have to come to our house. Daddy is acting all weird. I think maybe he's really sick."

"And the toilet's broken," Colin said, in case Grandma could help with that, too.

Grandma made a sharp, high sound. "Did Daddy fall down? Is he breathing?"

"Yeah, he's breathing good," Jason said. "He's sitting in his red chair. For three days. And he says he has to go home, but he *is* home. He doesn't know I'm calling you. Should I call 911?"

A man appeared on the screen behind Grandma. He had really blue eyes. He was buttoning up a shirt. "Jason, I'm Tim, your grandmother's friend. Are you okay, son? Are you alone in the house?"

"*I'm* here," Colin said indignantly.

The man smiled. "So you are. Marianne, where are they?"

"Basville, in New York State. Between Rochester and Syracuse. Ryan moved after Connie died."

"We can be there in five hours."

Grandma said, "Don't go out of the house, Jason, Colin. We're coming as fast as we can, okay?"

"Okay," Jason said. "What color is your car?"

The man smiled. "Blue."

"I like blue," Colin said, so as to not be left out of the conversation.

Grandma said, "Do you have your father's cell phone?"

"No," Jason said. "But I can get it from his bedroom."

"You do that, Jason. Keep it turned on because I'm going to call you a lot. Meanwhile, you boys just sit and watch TV, okay?"

"Yes!" Colin said. Usually they weren't allowed much TV. Maybe this would be good. Maybe Grandma would get Daddy well again. Maybe Tim would take Jason and Colin to the swamp in his blue car. Maybe everything would be all right.

Marianne called Jason every twenty minutes on Ryan's cell, trying to keep the conversation light: *"What are you watching on TV?" "Is that a good cartoon?" "What is the Hero of Heroes doing now?"*

"They're fine," Tim said. He drove expertly along the New York State Thruway, after a too-long delay at the border crossing caused by prolonged computer checks on Tim's guns. It seemed to Marianne that she'd held her breath for the entire half hour. She didn't really know much about Tim's past, nor how the arrest in Albuquerque might have affected his legal status. Of course, the charges had been dropped. . . .

"Surprised that I'm clean, aren't you?" Tim said, when they finally drove away from Customs. "You never asked, but you thought I was a dangerous criminal with a long rap sheet."

"I don't know what you are," Marianne said tartly.

"Sure you do." He reached out and gave her shoulder a caressing squeeze.

How did this happen? Every day that she and Tim had been lovers, the situation had struck her as preposterous. He was seventeen years her junior; his most intellectual activity was computer games; she didn't love him. Nor did he love her. But nearly every night they reached for each other, her hunger fueled by long abstinence and his by, she suspected, sheer animal hypermasculinity. They gave each other considerable sensual pleasure. She had stopped worrying what he thought of her aging body. This, she knew, was helped by the surreptitious survey all women make of each other; she looked younger than her age.

And they were considerate of each other, which also helped. They stayed away from subjects that might hurt: her children, his past, Sissy, Harrison. Albuquerque. Conversation was light, and if it didn't satisfy Marianne, she never said so. Nor did he. They were careful, and tender. None of which made the situation any less preposterous.

Her cell rang. Stubbins, agitated enough to forget to shed his down-home persona, said, "What the hell do y'all think you're doing? You back in the *States*?"

"My son is in trouble, Jonah. I'm going to him."

"What kind of trouble? You got Saunders with you?"

"Yes. Ryan—"

"If it ain't one thing with you, it's some other fucking thing! You need another lawyer?"

"No. Maybe. I don't know yet. I'll call you later." She hung up and put the phone on silent. To Tim she said, "How did he know?"

Tim threw her an amused glance. "Your cell. Plus a tracker on my car and probably bugs in the house. You think Stubbins doesn't know where you are every minute? He doesn't want any more scandal anywhere near his spaceship."

"Then he shouldn't have hired me in the first place!"

"A complicated man, you told me once. This our exit?"

The house sat at the end of a country road, not far from the Reardon Wetlands Preserve. It seemed that even jobless, Ryan could not let go of his obsession with purple loosestrife. Or with aliens.

Ryan, did you— But she would never ask that.

She had a sudden piercing image of him as a small boy, her quiet and secretive middle child, looking from Elizabeth to Noah as the two shouted at each other about something or other. His fair hair, now darkened to shit brown, was always falling into his eyes. But when Ryan thought he was right, the gravitational pull of a black hole couldn't move him.

Jason ran onto the porch, Colin behind him. "Grandma!"

Marianne almost stumbled on the broken steps. On the grimy porch she knelt and gathered both of them into her arms. They were dirty and smelled bad, but underneath it was that sweet little-boy scent. And it would only last a few more years, before each became another Ryan, or Noah, or Elizabeth, all of which in various ways had broken her heart.

No more of that maudlin stuff. She had a mission here, and she was going to accomplish it. "This is my friend Tim," she told the boys. "Is Daddy inside?"

"He's sick," Jason said.

"He won't get out of his red chair," Colin said.

Tim said easily, "Let's let Grandma see to your daddy, and you two show me around. Did that big tree over there get hit by lightning?"

"Yeah!" Jason said enthusiastically. "It's all burned."

"Poor tree," Colin said.

"Show me," Tim said. "Careful of those steps. They sure need fixing."

Marianne threw him a grateful look and went into the house.

It was worse than she expected. Clinical depression, if deep enough, produced hopelessness and inertia, but this was something more. Ryan sat slumped in the grimy red wing chair, head down, shoulders sagging. He looked up when she spoke his name but didn't change expression. The first words that leaped into Marianne's mind were old-fashioned and scientifically imprecise: *nervous breakdown*. But that's what this was. Caused by grief, by guilt, by a sense of failure, by some unknowable quirk of his biology? If Jason hadn't called her, would the next step be suicide? She was looking, she knew, at pure pain, the kind that gnawed at you from inside until there was nothing left.

She fought to hold herself steady to her son's need. "Ryan, it's Mom."

He nodded but didn't speak.

"I came to help you. You need help, sweetie."

She held her breath until he nodded again, slowly. He wasn't too deep into his private hell to recognize that he could not get out alone.

"It's going to be all right," she said. "I promise you, Ryan. It's all going to be all right."

Grandma-for-real was different from Grandma-on-Skype. Colin didn't remember her for real before this visit, but Jason did. Grandma-for-real got things going.

An ambulance came to take Daddy to a hospital, so doctors could make him well again. Grandma had to go with him to sign some papers—Colin didn't understand that part, but it seemed important—and Tim wouldn't let her go alone. That was weird; Grandma was a *grown-up.* Why did Tim get to tell her what to do? They had a whispered fight about it in the kitchen, and Tim must have won because he drove Grandma in his blue car. There was nobody to stay with Colin and Jason, so they had to go, too.

While they waited for the ambulance, Grandma made them both take showers. Tim got the upstairs toilet unstuck. At the hospital Tim took them to the cafeteria for hamburgers and French fries, which was good; Colin was really hungry. The hospital was too noisy, though, in ways Colin didn't like. The swamp was better.

It was getting dark by the time they got home because they stopped at a supermarket and bought a lot of things. Even though she looked really tired, Grandma started cleaning. She made Colin and Jason help, too. Colin had to find his dirty clothes, which were almost all of them, and bring them to the laundry room to be washed after the bedsheets and pajamas got done. Jason had to do that, too, and then find the dirty dishes all over the house. Grandma told Tim, who was locking all the windows and doors, to clean the bathrooms. He said, "What?" but she gave him the same look that Colin's preschool teacher gave boys who shoved or hit, and Tim started cleaning. Colin was impressed.

He and Jason were in their washed pajamas, having milk and cookies in the kitchen, when the other noise started. Colin jumped up so fast he knocked over his milk. "Grandma, the trees are afraid!"

"Colin," Grandma said, "it's okay. I know you're scared about Daddy, but he'll be all right."

"Not me! Not Daddy! The *trees* are afraid! And the ground!"

Tim, mopping up the milk, smiled in a way that made Colin suddenly hate him. "An imaginative kid."

Grandma said, "Colin, honey, I know you're worried about your father, but the doctors at the hospital are—"

Colin stamped his foot and burst into tears. Nobody ever believed him!

Ten minutes later, the earthquake hit.

Marianne bent to pick the shards of a broken glass off the grimy kitchen floor. During the earthquake, dishes had rattled, toys fallen off shelves in the boys' room, a small rickety table overturned. No windows broke. Outside, a few branches were down, but no trees. The glass had broken only because Marianne, startled, had dropped it. She crammed the pieces into the overflowing garbage pail.

While Tim checked the car and house, trailed by Jason, Marianne brought up data on her phone.

"I told you," Colin said.

"That was indeed an earthquake, epicenter near Attica," she told Tim when he returned to the kitchen, "although this isn't supposed to be an earthquake area. Still, there's a usually inactive fault line, the Clarendon-Linden fault line, just east of Batavia and USGS says—"

Colin's words suddenly registered. Marianne said to him, "What did you say?"

"I told you!"

The little boy stood with legs apart, clad in pajamas printed with railroad cars, feet planted firmly on the kitchen floor. His bottom lip stuck out. His eyes, Marianne's own light gray, looked very clear, and he did not blink. The back of Marianne's neck prickled.

"You told me what, honey?"

"That something bad was coming. The trees were afraid. The ground was mad."

She said carefully, "How did you know that, Colin?"

"I heard them." His bottom lip receded a little; someone was actually listening to him.

"Heard them talk?"

"Trees can't talk, Grandma."

The voice of reason from a five-year-old. Marianne would have smiled, but her neck still prickled. "Then what did you hear?"

"First the ground . . . it sounded like . . . like a lot of cars. When they're far away."

"The ground rumbled?"

"Yes." He nodded, clearly pleased with the word. "The ground all rumbled. Then the trees sort of . . . they . . . it sounds like the machine the Sheehans have for Captain. To make him stop barking. The Sheehans can't hear it but dogs can. I can, too. Captain doesn't like it."

An ultrasonic emitter. And earthquake measurement depended on infrasonic. Was it possible that Colin could hear above and below the normal human range? Which, Marianne remembered dazedly, was 20 to 20,000 Hertz. How far below that was the infrasonic rumble from plate tectonics? But the trees . . . Trees didn't emit sound, did they?

Colin's little body had relaxed. He felt heard. He said confidently, "I heard the baby mouses, too. Way down in their hole. They wanted their mommy. Uh-oh—here it comes again!"

An aftershock, the slightest quiver under the floor, barely perceptible. Nothing else changed.

Unless everything had.

Her first concern was, had to be, for the boys' uneasiness over their father. Only they didn't show any. "He's in the hospital," Jason said reasonably, "and he doesn't have cancer like Mommy did. So he'll be okay."

Colin nodded. He trusted in his big brother, and Jason trusted in the universe. Or maybe they were just being practical, as children could be: Life with Grandma ran more smoothly than life with Daddy. Or maybe their fear and anger were just deeply buried, as Ryan's apparently had been, and would erupt later when Ryan came home again. Although that might be months away. His diagnosis was "clinical depression with suicidal ideation."

Marianne pushed away her own fear and anger to focus on the next concern: Where were they going to live? The boys had no passports, so Canada was out. She made another call to Stubbins, who was too busy to take it. Was he losing interest in her efforts? Another worry. Without him, she had no source of income, no way to pay Tim, nothing. Although under their intimate circumstances, paying Tim would be—

Another thing to not think about.

However, one of Stubbins's ubiquitous lieutenants relocated Marianne yet again. After evaluation, Ryan was transferred to Oakwood Gardens, a posh psychiatric hospital that Marianne at no time in her life could have afforded, discreetly located near a pleasant commuter town on the Hudson River. Tim, Marianne, and the boys drove to an anonymously furnished three-bedroom apartment, which she also could never have afforded, on the East Side of Manhattan. The boys were enrolled in a private school that usually had a waiting list longer than unspooled DNA.

Tim said, "Wow. Cute place. Small but sort of . . . you know, elegant. And Stubbins is paying for this and for Ryan's hospital, too? What is it you do for him, again?"

Not nearly enough to justify all this.

But there was no use questioning Jonah Stubbins; the sphinx was less secretive. Marianne began to unpack the boys' clothing.

Marianne and Colin took a taxi to the office building on West Fifty-Ninth, a little south of the zone patrolled by private guards hired by the West Side Protective Association. But Colin's appointment was at noon, not a popular hour for violent crime, and Tim was with them, alert as always. The building guard wanded them and had a tense exchange with Tim about his Beretta, then sent a keypad signal to Dr. Hudspeth. They waited.

The lobby held sagging chairs and a vending machine. Two large ficus plants shed yellow leaves onto the dingy tile floor. Colin said to the guard, "Those trees are thirsty."

"Yeah?" He wasn't interested.

"You should give them some water."

"The plant service went out of business."

"You should give them some water *now*. They're crying!"

The guard looked at him oddly. A voice said from the computer, "Thompson, please send them up." The elevator door opened.

In the elevator Colin said to Tim, "I don't like that man."

"Yeah, he's a prick."

Marianne frowned at Tim, who grinned back.

It was Dr. Hudspeth that Marianne didn't like. Marianne had chosen her because of her location, right across the park, and anyway how hard could it be to test a child's hearing? But Dr. Hudspeth seemed to not test many children. There were no toys in the tiny waiting room. The doctor, who smiled constantly over what seemed like too many teeth, had the excessively bright, cloying manner of adults not used to children and possibly not very fond of them.

In the examining room she said, "Now, pumpkin, just sit there—good! Great! We're going to play a little game. You like games, don't you?"

Colin gazed at her from steady gray eyes and said nothing.

"Good! Great! Here's the game: You're going to wear these earphones. I'm going to press a button on this thing here. Sometimes it will make a noise and sometimes it will not. When you hear it make a noise in your earphones, raise your finger like this. Can you do that for me, pumpkin?"

Colin nodded, impassive.

"All right, here we go!"

Marianne heard nothing. Colin raised fingers, didn't raise fingers, never changed expression. The test went on for about fifteen minutes. Dr. Hudspeth removed Colin's earphones.

"You did great! Now, you go out to the waiting room with your daddy for a few minutes while I talk to Grammy."

Colin said, "He's not my daddy. My daddy's sick and in the hospital until he gets better."

"Good! Great! You go out and sit with . . . your friend."

"He's Grandma's—"

"Colin, stay here," Marianne said hastily. *Grandma's what?*

Dr. Hudspeth said, "Well, all right, since there's no problem here. Colin's hearing is normal, in fact, quite acute. He heard right up to the limits of human hearing, at both high and low frequencies." She beamed at Marianne and glanced at her watch.

Marianne said, "What was the lowest frequency you tested? Twelve Hertz?"

The doctor looked surprised, and not entirely pleased. "Are you an engineer, Mrs. . . . ah . . ." She glanced at her tablet. "Carpenter?"

"No. Was it twelve Hertz?"

"Yes. That's the lowest frequency even children, whose hearing is more acute than ours, can hear, and then only under ideal laboratory conditions."

"Test him lower, please."

Dr. Hudspeth stared.

"Does the machine go lower than twelve Hertz?"

"Yes, but—"

"Do it."

Marianne, former teacher and lecturer, knew how to sound authoritative. Dr. Hudspeth put the earphones back on Colin.

He raised and did not raise fingers.

"Mrs. Carpenter, I don't think he understands. He's raising fingers at eight Hertz, when he might be feeling physical vibrations in the body but can't possibly—"

"Go lower."

"This audiometer doesn't go any lower!"

"Then we're done here. Thank you, Dr. Hudspeth. I'd like a printout of the results, please."

As they left the office, Dr. Hudspeth peered at the settings on her machine. Colin said, "That lady is upset."

"Don't worry about it."

"I won't. And I'm not a pumpkin."

"No," Marianne said. "You're not."

In the lobby, Colin insisted that Marianne buy a bottle of water from the vending machine. Carefully he dumped it over the ficus plants.

Marianne sat with Colin in the tiny bedroom he shared with Jason, who had protested at having to go to school when Colin got to stay home. In the kitchen Tim rattled pans, singing off-key as he made dinner. He was a surprisingly good cook, although Marianne was getting past being surprised by hidden talents in anybody. She sat cross-legged on Colin's low bed, since his small sprawled body covered the rest of the floor. He was drawing elephants on a sheet of white paper.

Marianne had the opening she wanted. "Did you know that elephants can talk to each other across long distances by making noises that people can't hear?"

Colin looked up. "My favorite book is *Brandon and the Elephant in the Basement*! I brought it in my suitcase. Do real elephants talk about how Brandon rescued the elephant from the basement?"

"Well, I don't know. I don't speak elephant."

Colin laughed and went back to his careful drawing of floppy gray ears. Marianne said, "People can't hear elephants because their noises are too low—too deep—for people's ears."

Colin said nothing.

"But I'll bet you could hear an elephant, couldn't you?"

He said, not raising his head but with a certain stiffness in his thin shoulders, "I'm not 'spozed to talk about that, Grandma."

"Says who?"

"Jason. He says everybody at school will think I'm weird."

So Jason knew about this, whatever it was, and tried to shield his little brother. "Yes. But I'm not at your school. You can talk about it with me."

She had Colin's attention. He stood up, worn gray crayon in hand, and looked searchingly at her face. "Is that true?"

It was his father's phrase: Ryan the scientist, always weighing evidence to find the singular truth he so fervently believed existed. Ryan had never accepted that truth could be many sided. Marianne kept her voice steady. "Yes, it is. You can tell me what you hear."

Relief brightened Colin's eyes. "I hear everything, Grandma."

"What everything?"

He held up his fingers, smeared with gray and green crayon, to count off. "I hear people talk. Well—duh! I hear plants. They don't talk words, but they make noises. Some are low like that ear doctor's machine near the end, some are like Captain's dog whistle, some are like people talking, only they go through the ground. I hear the ground when it's mad. Low rumbles, like before the earthquake. I hear baby mouses in the ground, sometimes, when they want their mother. Those are like dog whistles, too. If you take me to a zoo, maybe I can hear an elephant!"

Infrasonics and ultrasonics both, Marianne thought dazedly. How was that possible? *Was* that possible? How much was the imagination of a five-year-old who believed an elephant could be rescued from a basement? She would have to do some research, including on biosonics. But before that—

"Colin, if you hear all that, all the time—Do you hear it all the time?"

"Yes."

"Then how do you keep it all sorted out in your mind? Doesn't it . . . confuse you? All those noises at once like that?"

"Sometimes. But now they're in rows."

"Rows? What do you mean?"

The child stooped and brought up his box of crayons. On the bedspread beside Marianne he laid out a row of six crayons. In front of them he arranged five more, then two, then one in front of that, to which he pointed. "See, Grandma, that's you talking now. These two are Tim singing and the radio in the apartment out the window. This row is other stuff I hear but it's not in the front. Then this far stuff, back here."

Selective filters for background noise. She said, "Could you always do this, Colin?"

"I don't know."

Probably not. Marianne remembered Connie's desperate frustration during Colin's first three years of life. "He just cries and cries!" Connie had said, crying herself. Had the baby been unable to filter out the constant, multisonic noise that swamped him? But somewhere he had learned to do so. Noah, when he started school and well into the second grade, had been dyslexic, unable to see the difference between "was" and "saw." The problem had disappeared halfway through Noah's testing. "Sometimes," the tester had said, "bright children just learn to compensate."

Colin said, "Will you take me to the zoo to hear an elephant?"

The Bronx Zoo no longer had elephants, nor much of anything else. Funding cuts. But there must be an elephant somewhere.

"We'll see. But Colin, I'd like to have you do another ear test. It will—"

"No," Colin said instantly. He stuck out his bottom lip. "It's stupid."

"But it—"

"I'm sorry, Grandma," he said, abruptly sounding very adult, "but no. I hated that doctor. And it's stupid."

"This won't be a doctor. It's a man who builds bridges, and he has special machines to hear bridges. You can touch the machines."

"Really? Well . . . what about the elephant?"

They had reached a delicate stage in the negotiations. "Yes, but there aren't any elephants in New York. If we go see the bridge man, then I promise you an elephant someplace, but it might take a while."

Colin considered. "Okay."

"You said that sometime you hear mice in the ground. When was that?"

"Only one time. In the old house. Not *in* the house, outside near the swamp. Daddy didn't believe me. But I did hear them! I did!"

Internet reports of surviving mice sometimes included pictures. But the pictures could be pre–spore cloud and the sightings were as yet unsubstantiated by any scientifically reputable source. Still . . .

"Come eat before I throw it out!" Tim called.

"Careful, Grandma! Don't step on my picture!"

"Never, sweetie," Marianne said. She moved carefully around Colin's drawing of an elephant with huge, floppy ears.

CHAPTER 18

S plus 6 years

On Saturday Grandma took Colin and Jason to the bridge man. That was where the wonderful thing happened, although not because of the bridge or the man.

They went in Tim's blue car and they drove a long way out of New York, to a big field surrounded by a high fence with sharp wire on the top. The field had things all over it: machines that weren't working right now, long steel bars, heavy bags, pieces of wood. It had a big trailer and a lot of trash, but it was still a field and there were patches of grass and dirt and wildflowers. In the river stood a big cement rectangle with part of the bridge built on it. Grandma and the bridge man, whose name was Rudy, hugged and said all the things grownups say, "Good to see you again" and "How long has it been" and all that stuff. Colin and Jason didn't really listen. Tim checked out everything, looking for bad guys because that was his job.

To Colin's disappointment, they couldn't go onto the bridge. "Not safe, son," Rudy said. "Not at this stage of construction."

Instead they went into the trailer, which was just as messy as the field. Computers, dirty coffee cups, paper, machines, pizza boxes. Colin thought that Grandma didn't approve, but she didn't say anything.

"I appreciate your doing this, Rudy."

"I'm not even sure what 'this' is. You want me to test this kid like he's a *bridge*?"

"Yes."

Jason said, "Can we go outside and look at the bridge?"

"You can, with Tim. Colin stays here."

"No fair!" Colin cried, while Jason smirked.

"You can go outside too as soon as we're done," Grandma said. "Oh, there you are, Tim. Will you give Jason a tour of the construction machinery?"

Colin said, "I want to go, too!"

"Soon," Grandma said in her no-fooling-around voice. "Rudy, you have both a laser vibrometer and an ultrasonic treatment evaluator? The new portable kinds?"

"Of course, but—"

"Can you use the vibrometer to find the lowest frequency he can hear and the evaluator for the highest?"

Rudy stared, shrugged, and laughed. "You always were weird, even when we were in high school and I had that terrible crush on you. Well, okay. Why not? You want some coffee first?"

"After. So we can talk."

"Whatever you say, Marzidoats."

Grandma smiled a tiny bit. "No one has called me that for forty years."

"Time someone did. Okay, son, sit there. I'm going to point this thing out the window, at the bridge, and you raise your hand if you hear any noise. Like at the doctor, okay?"

"Yes," Colin said. At least this time there weren't earphones, and nobody was calling him "pumpkin."

A computer screen lit up, and a low rumble sounded. Colin raised his hand.

Again.

Again.

Rudy stared at the computer screen, at Colin, at Grandma. He shook his head and started to say something but Grandma said, "Wait, please," in her same no-fooling-around voice and Rudy closed his mouth.

First a lot of low sounds with one machine, then a lot of high sounds with a different machine. They were both pointed at the bridge, and Colin wondered if it could hear the noises. No—bridges weren't alive. But the bridge *was* making noises—they were clear to him, different from the noises the machines made, and not very interesting. Colin got bored.

When they finally, *finally* finished, Rudy had a funny look on his face. Grandma said, "I'll have that coffee now. Here come Tim and Jason. Colin, you can go outside with Jason, but you both stay where I can see you through this window here, which means you can see me."

"Yes, Grandma."

Tim said, "Hi, kid, tour in a minute," and went inside the trailer.

Jason said, "What did they do to you?"

"I heard the bridge make noise."

Jason nodded. He didn't think Colin was weird. "Cool. Hey, let's go climb on those big bags!"

"Grandma says we got to stay by the window."

"Oh. Well, then—I got an idea—let's pick some of those flowers for Grandma!"

"Okay." The flowers were blue, just like Tim's car, with petals sort of like squares. Rudy probably wouldn't mind if they picked some because they looked like weeds. Colin grabbed the stem of one and pulled.

It was really tough! No matter how hard he tried, he couldn't break the stem. He tried another one, but that wouldn't break. Jason couldn't do it either.

"Stupid flowers!" Jason said. "We need a scissors."

"We don't got scissors."

"No, but . . . look!" Somebody had broken a beer bottle a little ways away. It was out of sight of Grandma's window, but Jason darted over, picked up a shard of glass, and ran back before she could notice. He lay on the ground beside the plant, sawing with the glass shard. The stem parted. Colin lay down next to him, to watch—he was a little doubtful about Grandma and the sharp beer bottle—with his ear pressed hard against the dusty ground, and that's when the awesome thing happened.

"Jason!"

"What?" Jason had cut three blue flowers and was getting to his feet. "You got dirt on your face."

"Everything is talking down there!"

"Talking? With words?"

"No, not words. But everything is making noises under the ground! Not the ground noises—the grass and flowers and the trees outside the fence!"

"Really? What kind of noises?"

Colin raised his head. The noises stopped. "Some are ultra and some are infra"—new words just learned from Rudy—"and some sound like the ones plants make when they're thirsty, only coming in . . . in . . . like those guns in your video game. *Ack-ack-ack*."

"Bursts," Jason suggested.

"Yeah. Like that."

"Are they shooting at each other?"

"No. It's like . . . they're sending secret messages."

"Cool! You mean like the Internet! Do it again!"

Colin pressed his ear back onto the dirt. The noises started again. They *were* going through the dirt and Jason was right, it was like the Internet down there! All those noise e-mails going from one plant to another.

But what were they saying?

Colin arranged the sounds in rows in his head, with the ultra ones sort of like plants needing water except higher, right there in the front row. They came in bursts. Carefully he listened to the high bursts of sound until he was sure he could recognize them. He said, "Cut another flower."

Jason did. The bursts of sound in the front row got faster and louder.

"Stop cutting!"

Jason did. The frantic bursts of sound stopped.

"Jase, the flowers are upset because you're cutting them. I think they're trying to tell the flowers over there!"

Jason frowned. You mean . . . like when that frog in Daddy's swamp croaked real loud to warn the other frogs that we were coming?"

"I don't know. Maybe."

"But," Jason argued, "flowers can't jump into water and swim away. No, wait, Daddy said something once . . . wait, I got it! He said that some plants gave out clouds of bad-smelling chemicals to scare away animals that might eat them. Maybe the flowers really are telling some other plants that I'm coming!"

Grandma and Tim came out of the trailer. Jason quickly dropped the broken beer bottle on the ground behind him. Grandma said, "There you two are! What have you got?"

"Flowers," Jason said, holding them out. "For you."

"Chicory," Grandma said. "In really hard times in history, people would powder these to make coffee substitute. Thank you, boys!"

Colin looked doubtfully at the blue flowers; they didn't look anything like Maxwell House. "Grandma," he said, "can plants hurt?"

"Feel pain, you mean? No, honey, they don't have nerve endings."

That was a relief. It had troubled him.

She said, "Why do you ask?"

Colin looked up at her, knowing that he was so different from her, knowing too she liked him to tell the truth. Daddy also insisted on truth, or at least he did before he got sick. But maybe the truth didn't have to include the beer bottle, if he said everything else. That was a fair trade.

"Grandma," he said, "we—Jason and me—we got to tell you something."

Far into the night, Marianne sat at her computer, reading journals to which she had never before paid much attention.

Plants did emit sounds that indicated thirst; the sounds came from the fracturing of overdry water-conducting tubules.

Corn roots clicked regularly, right at the lower edge of human hearing. No one knew why.

Researchers had known for two decades that plants emitted sounds as short-range deterrents or attractors for insects.

Plants could "hear" sounds, too—some orchids released pollen only for the high-frequency buzz of a certain bee.

Plant-to-plant communication with sound had all kinds of evolutionary advantages over communicating chemically—sounds were faster, required less energy, could go farther. How far? Since grass roots were highly connected underground and much of the world's biomass was connected through fungi, the limits were unknown.

Sound moved easily through soil.

Other organisms without brains displayed mechanosensing, largely through changes in ion fluxes. Which plants certainly had.

Plants were influenced by nearby flora: Chili plants, to name just one, were shown as far back as 2013 to grow better near basil plants, even when the plants were isolated from sending each other chemical, touch, or light-transmitted signals.

Many mammals used infrasonics to communicate over distance: elephants, whales, hippos, rhinos, giraffes. Humans shared many gene sets with other mammals.

For over a hundred years scientists pooh-poohed the idea that bats could navigate by sound.

She got up to pour herself another glass of chardonnay. It was three in the morning but she didn't feel sleepy. Carrying her glass, she slipped into the boys' bedroom and looked down at Colin, curled into a ball in his locomotive-printed pajamas, his hair spiky on the pillow. In the dim light from the living room, he looked like a baby animal, a hedgehog or kitten.

The spore plague had activated sets of human immune-system

genes that had lain dormant for 140,000 years. What other "junk genes" had they awakened in developing fetuses?

"Marianne," Tim whispered in the doorway, "come to bed."

His bed, he meant, although they made sure to each be in their own rooms before Colin and Jason awakened. But for the first time, Marianne did not feel the surge of desire.

She left the kids' bedroom and closed the door. "Not tonight, Tim, okay? I'm pretty tired."

"Okay." His face was unreadable, but she could see the hard-on through his briefs. "Sleep well."

"You, too."

But sleep wouldn't come. It wasn't Tim she thought of, but Harrison. At Columbia, that *Time* magazine article had said, working on brain anomalies in mice. For scientific problems, Harrison had the tenacity of a pit bull. It was one of the things she'd loved about him.

Sleep was a long time coming.

"Marianne, it's Jonah Stubbins."

Of course it was. Marianne sat up groggily in bed. Christ—9:00 a.m.! The boys would be late for school. She heaved herself off the bed and threw on her robe.

"Marianne, you there?"

"Yes, but I can't talk right now. I—"

The boys were gone. A note from Tim lay on the table in his block printing: TOOK KIDS TO SCHOOL.

"Never mind, Jonah. What is it?"

"What it always is. I want you and your grandchildren to move to the ship-build site, for safety's sake. And your bodyguard, too, of course."

Something in the way Stubbins said "your bodyguard" irritated Marianne. Her personal life was private, and whatever Stubbins thought he knew—or maybe even did know—was none of his business. But she kept her temper. "I told you, I can't do that. I need to be close enough to my son's facility to visit him. And my grandsons are settled in school."

"We can helio you to Ryan whenever you want, and get a first-class tutor for the kids. I just want you to be safe, Marianne."

"And I appreciate it. But we're fine here."

"Okay. Whatever you say. I'm just offering."

"Thanks. But while I have you on the line, I want to ask—"

"Call me later. Gotta go." He cut the connection.

What had she been going to ask, anyway? *Why are you bankrolling me and my family for a copywriting job that a thousand others could do at a fraction of the cost?* Although maybe she wouldn't have asked it anyway. Marianne could probably support herself and the boys, but she could never afford Ryan's care. Much as she hated the fact, she needed Jonah Stubbins.

If she hurried, maybe she could be out of the apartment before Tim returned. And she would not bring her cell.

The taxi left her at the fortified gates of Columbia University, which she had no clearance to enter. "Look," she told the conspicuously armed guard, "just call Dr. Harrison Rice and tell him I'm here. Dr. Marianne Jenner. He'll clear me."

The guard looked skeptical. "Dr. Rice doesn't give interviews."

"I'm not a journalist. Just call him! He will be unhappy when he finds out I was here and not admitted."

"Why doesn't he know you're here? Why didn't you tell him you're coming so he could put you into the system?"

Because I didn't want to give him the chance to refuse. "Just call him, please! Dr. Marianne Jenner!"

She waited. The September air held the smoky promise of autumn. "Okay," the guard finally said. "You're cleared. It's building—"

"I know where it is."

Familiar and yet strange—it had been two and a half years since she'd been here. The Columbia campus looked less shabby. Perhaps alumni donations had increased as the economy picked up. But it was a shock to find a soldier with an AK-47 in front of the building containing Harrison's lab.

He met her in the lobby. "Marianne. Good to see you."

"Hello, Harrison."

Familiar and yet strange. They shook hands awkwardly as two sets of images played in Marianne's mind: she and Harrison drinking wine in bed, her naked leg thrown over his, both of them sated after sex, talking and talking about research. And Harrison the night Sarah had killed herself and Tim brought him home drunk, barely conscious, sodden and mumbling and stained with vomit.

"You look good," he said. Marianne doubted that was true of her—she'd dressed quickly and hardly combed her hair—but it was true of him. His hair, now completely gray, hadn't thinned much more, and his intelligent face was craggy in that handsome way aging men had and women did not. In his eyes, however, she could still see pain over Sarah, just as hers must be shadowed by Ryan and Noah.

"Thank you. Harrison, can we go somewhere to talk?"

She felt rather than saw his quick startlement, and so she added, "It's not personal. It's connected with your research. Something I think you should hear." So—now she knew. His interest in her had not renewed. Had she hoped it had? But, of course, she was with Tim.

She had his professional attention. "Come to my office."

It was the same preternaturally neat, impersonal environment she remembered so well. Harrison never kept around the framed plaques or silly mementos that other scientists did. Marianne had never even seen his Nobel medal.

In careful, precise sentences, she told him about Colin: the small earthquake on the Linden fault, Rudy's testing of Colin in infrasonic and ultrasonic ranges, what the child had told her about managing the constant bombardment of sound by "putting them in rows in my mind." As she talked, she watched his face—such a well-known face, such a stranger. She saw that he had already known about the hyper-hearing, which meant there must be other children like Colin. But his attention sharpened and he leaned forward in his chair at the "putting in rows." He had not known that.

"He taught himself to do that?"

"Yes, although I don't think it was as much self-teaching as unconscious compensation. How many more kids have you found with hyper-hearing?"

"It seems to be about five percent of the population, but it's difficult to tell because so many parents use this damn Calminex to quell sensory overload. Compensators like Colin are a small percentage of that, but Colin is the first I've heard describe the mechanism, even metaphorically."

"What progress have you made in identifying the genes and proteins involved?"

"We have the genes. Not yet how the proteins fold."

She was intensely interested in this, plus the steps his team and other teams around the world were taking to discover more. It felt so good to be talking about science again, to be straining to follow a mind better than hers.

They talked for a long time. Harrison finished with, "Marianne, more good news—the mice are returning."

"How? Where? What evidence? Or are you seeding immune specimens?"

He smiled at her eagerness, raised his hands palms up, let them drop in a gesture of humorous resignation. "Not our specimens, nor anybody else's as far as we can tell. Which means that all our breeding programs were pointless. The returning mice developed immunity to *R. sporii* all on their own, or maybe a small number always had it and now they're multiplying like—well, like mice. *Mus musculus* and *P. maniculatus* have each been captured in three states. Apparently nature will find a way."

She heard an echo of Tim talking about grief softening over time: *"It's just life going on, you know?"*

"I know," she said.

"It's all interconnected," Harrison said, as if this were a new thought. Maybe, to a mind that focused with laser intensity on one scientific problem at a time, it *was* new. "The spores, the mice, the ecology, the children, and the solutions to all four."

"I know," she said again. "Stay in touch, Harrison. I'd like to know how your research is going."

"Okay. Nice to see you again, Marianne." He turned away.

Outside her building on the East Side, Marianne took out her key to open the vestibule door. A man came up behind her, spun her around, and shoved a gun into her chest.

"Don't scream," he said quietly, "or I'll shoot."

She glanced wildly around. No one on the street, although it was midmorning on a Tuesday. A wave of nausea swept up her throat; she fought it down and tried to think.

"Here, take my purse. I won't say anything to anyone."

He didn't deign to answer this stupidity. Marianne studied him, memorizing what she could. He wore a ski mask—in September!—but she could see his eyes: deep brown. Pale thin lips, the bottom of a light-brown mustache. About two inches taller than she was, broad shoulders, thick neck, jeans and black leather boots and a light green nylon jacket zipped to the neck, clear latex gloves.

"I don't want your purse," he said. "I want you out of New York. Be gone by the end of the week, Marianne Elaine Jenner. You alien-loving motherfuckers have ruined this country and we don't want you polluting this city." He dropped something at her feet and ran.

Marianne fumbled with her key, dropped it, picked it up, shook as she put it in the lock. Only when she was inside did she realize she'd also picked up his dropped article. What if it was a bomb? No, it was just a thin piece of cloth, a patch of some sort. What if it was imbued with anthrax, or tularemia, or a genetically altered microorganism?

But she'd already touched it, so she kept it in her fingertips as she ran up two flights of stairs, avoiding the elevator from some crazy fear that either it would harm her or the patch would harm it, to her apartment. She rang the bell with her other hand.

Tim flung open the door. "Marianne! What the fuck did you— What is it? What happened?"

She told him, her voice unsteady but her movements sure as she bagged the patch in a ziplock freezer bag and then washed her hands with a surgeon's thoroughness.

Tim said, "Let me see that thing."

She held it out to him. For the first time, she saw what it was: a crudely embroidered patch of a mouse face with huge bloody fangs and the letters EFHO.

"I know these clowns, Marianne. Earth for Humans Only. Strictly small-time bullies. If they have any fancy bioweapon things on this patch, then I'm the president of the United States."

A relief. "Are you sure?"

"Positive. But what the hell were you doing outside without me? Or without your cell?"

"I forgot the cell. I needed to check something at the Museum of Natural History. Something not online."

"I thought the museum was closed."

"Not all of it. The research library is open." This was true.

"You took a cab?"

"Yes."

"And you couldn't wait for me." His blue eyes burned at her.

"I thought it was safe enough, midmorning and not that far away."

"Uh-huh. But when he attacked you, there were no people close by."

"No, Tim—I told you that. But it wasn't an attack. He didn't hurt me."

"Just threatened your life. And he knew not only where you live but also your full name, even your middle name. Which wasn't in the magazine article. How would he know it?"

"I don't know—maybe he found it on the Internet."

"But why use the whole name?"

"I don't know! Tim, you're missing the main point here!"

"I'm not missing anything." Still his eyes trained on her face, as disconcerting as gun sights. "It's just weird, is all."

"Do you think I should call the police?" She'd hoped to fly under all official radar in New York, stealth-protected by Stubbins's fake IDs and military-grade encryption programs for her computer and cell.

"No, no cops. They won't do anything and they'll blow your cover even more. Like I said, these are small-time bullies. What kind of gun?"

She had no idea. It might have been a realistic toy, for all she knew. She shook her head.

"From now on, you don't go out without me. For now, come here."

He put his arms around her. But she felt neither comfort nor desire, and that only made everything worse.

CHAPTER 19

S plus 6.2 years

Colin dreamed again about the square blue flowers. Jason was cutting them with the broken beer bottle and they were screaming at them from little mouths on the petals. Horrible! And then it was even worse because Daddy was lying deep underground where the plant Internet was and he was making noises, too. "What? What?" Colin and Jason said, because they couldn't understand what Daddy was trying to say, but he just went on making those terrible noises and Colin woke up scared in the dark.

"Jason?"

But Jason wasn't in his bed.

All at once the familiar morning sounds rushed into Colin's mind: Jason and Grandma and Tim were in the kitchen, making breakfast. Grandma's houseplants clicked in the living room; they needed watering. The building rumbled in its friendly morning way. From two stories up it was harder to hear the ground under the building, but it sounded normal, too. The screaming flowers were just a dream. Jason said dreams couldn't hurt you.

But other things could.

When Tim left Colin and Jason at their school, Jason ran ahead to his second-grade room, where the teachers put him because he was so smart, shouting to some kids he knew. Colin was in the first grade because he was smart, too, and anyways all the kids in kindergarten either couldn't hear anything or else took some drug that made them move really s-l-o-w. Colin hung back as long as he could but he had to go to his room, too, and then Paul would be waiting.

Colin knew that Mommy was dead and Daddy was in the hospital, but sometimes he pretended that Uncle Noah with his aliens had sneaked into the house and flown off with Mommy and Daddy. He knew that wasn't really true, but it *might* have been because Uncle Noah was Daddy's brother, and if Jason was dead or in the hospital, Colin would rescue him. But somehow Jason never seemed to see when Colin needed rescuing.

Paul Tyson was in third grade. His parents, he bragged on the playground, were very important. They had lots and lots of money. Paul always had the best tablet that played the best games, even if the teachers locked up all electronics in the safe except at lunchtime. Paul's tablet even had Ataka!, the really cool Russian videogame that everybody liked. It meant "Attack!"—they talked different in Russia. But Paul hated Uncle Noah's aliens; he said bad words about them all the time. And he was a bully, a word Colin hadn't even known until he started going to the Healy School.

Now Paul and two of his friends stood in the middle of the school lobby. Colin managed to get past them by walking close to a group of fifth-graders, the oldest kids in the school. They ignored him, but Colin knew from experience that at least one of them, a fierce girl with dreadlocks and shiny clothes, wouldn't let anyone bully anyone else. It was her crusade. That was a word Grandma used a lot; she had a crusade, too.

Even so, Paul deliberately stepped hard on Colin's foot. "Oops, *so* sorry," he said, and the fierce girl glared at him. Paul scurried away. From the doorway of his classroom he smiled at Colin. Colin's knees wobbled. How could a smile be so nasty?

First grade was easy, compared to all the stuff Grandma taught him and Jason. Sometimes Colin was bored. But today they were doing something exciting: drawing a zoo. Colin drew an elephant. He almost drew it in a basement, like in his favorite book, but probably zoos didn't have basements.

Then, just as he was finishing the elephant's ears, he had to go to the bathroom—really bad, and right now. Ms. Kellerman gave permission and Colin raced down the hall and into the boys' bathroom. In the stall, he heard the bathroom door open, and when he came out, Paul was blocking the exit. "Hey, Colin *Jenner*."

Colin froze. He made himself say, "My name is Colin Carpenter."

"No, it's not. And you didn't find the tracker I put on you, did you? Feel around the back of your pants."

By itself, like it wasn't even part of him, Colin's hand circled behind his body. The tracker was the size of a dime, stuck on the back of his jeans. He pulled it off and held it out to Paul. He didn't know what else to do. Paul was so big—

The older boy hit him hard and fast, right in the stomach. Colin fell to the floor. Paul raised a foot and kicked Colin in the stomach with his boot.

"Your grandma is an alien-lover. You thought nobody knows about her and your family, right? Think again, fucker. Your grandma fucks Denebs and maybe you would, too, if the cowards ever came back here. Only they better not because my mom and dad would kill them all dead. You listening to me, you piece of shit? You—"

"What is going on here!"

Black boots, blue pant legs . . . security. Maybe the bathroom had a camera? Somehow Colin staggered to his feet while Paul said meekly, "Nothing, sir."

"Nothing? You hit him!"

"I—" Paul didn't seem to have any words. Paul! A third-grader!

Colin gasped, "He . . . did hit me. But it . . . it was my fault. I called him a name." It took everything in him to keep his voice quiet, to act like his stomach didn't burn and scream, to add in his grandmother's tone, "It's over now." But he was not going to explain what Paul had said. Grandma and Tim had told Colin that nobody at the school must know Colin's real last name or about Grandma's crusade. They told Colin that over and over—but Paul knew! Colin was desperate that at least the security guard didn't know, too.

The guard studied both boys. Finally he said, "See that it is over. Now go back to your classrooms."

They did, but halfway down the hallway Paul turned to shout at the guard, "Cameras in the bathrooms are illegal! I'm telling my father about this!"

Colin slipped quietly into his classroom. His chest didn't hurt much, but his stomach did. The drawing of the zoo was finished and people were cleaning up. Colin picked up his crayons, clutching them so hard that one snapped in two, sounding just like the *pop!* that plants made when they really, really needed watering.

Even if Marianne had continued with the Star Brotherhood Foundation, its major mission became pointless. The United States government formally discontinued work on the spaceship it had been building from the Deneb engineering plans. The ship, badly damaged by the superstorm three years ago, had been the center of political problems since its beginning. Now it became a casualty of budget shortfalls, congressional delay, party politics, and virulent opposition from the voting blocs that believed anything bequeathed by the aliens could only harm humanity. Some Americans still believed that the Denebs had caused the spore cloud; a larger percentage believed that the aliens knew the cloud would wipe out mice and had not told Terrans this.

"It's so shortsighted!" Marianne raged to Tim as they watched the late-night news. "Christ, the statistics are right there! In seventy-five years—less if we keep going on the way we are—CO_2 in the atmosphere will reach seven hundred parts per million. You're looking at a devastating effect on the oceans, and possibly a near-total ecological collapse!"

"Uh," Tim said. He lounged on the sofa beside her, a beer in his hand. When she glanced at him, he added, "But we have more private spaceships building, right? Besides Stubbins."

"Yes." He should know that already. Didn't he ever follow the news?

Six years ago, everything known about space travel had become outdated. All the programs in development or nearing completion were suddenly horse-drawn barouches in a world of Ferraris. Space agencies in the US, in Russia and China and India and the European Union—all had gone into shock. Some had folded, some had stubbornly continued with "human" rocket plans, and some had fast-tracked the building of ships according to the alien plans. The EU, China, and Russia were building "Deneb" spaceships.

In the United States, the Boeing ship, half built, was stalled by fiscal problems.

SpaceX had thrown all of its resources behind a ship being built in California, now two-thirds done. Blue Origin was farther behind.

Sierra Nevada chose to continue with its old technology, on the reasonable grounds that it was comprehensible.

The newest company, Stubbins's Starship Venture, was reported to have the ship closest to completion. Although since the reports issued from Stubbins's PR machine and the site was closed to everyone else, it wasn't known how true this was. Fantastic salaries and freedom from government politics had lured some of the best talent in the world to the *Venture* building site in Pennsylvania. As CEO of his perfume company, Stubbins had had the reputation of trusting the project heads he hired to get their goals met, without looking too closely into their methods. Stubbins's word was always the final arbiter, but he listened more closely to his scientists than to his accountants, and that alone was such a novelty that he attracted people who otherwise might have shunned his unsavory reputation. If you were American and wanted to go to the stars, Jonah Stubbins looked like your best bet.

Not everybody wanted to go to the stars. The anchorwoman's next story covered an ugly, violent protest in Pittsburgh, the closest big city to the *Venture* site. Citizens to Save Earth, yet another anti-alien group, smashed windows and burned cars. A dozen people were injured.

During the last year, public attitudes toward Stubbins's ship seemed to have settled into an unexpected—by her, anyway—bimodal distribution. Marianne had expected a division along religious lines, since seven years ago the spore cloud had been demonized by fundamentalists as the End Times, or God's cleansing, or one of the Four Horsemen of the Apocalypse (usually but not always Pestilence). She also expected that those who had lost family to *R. sporii* would most oppose the expedition to World. Certainly her experiences giving lectures had created that impression.

But lecture-goers, it turned out, were not a typical sample. The bimodal distribution was neither religious nor familial. It was economic.

Those who had recovered from the economic collapse, or whose jobs had never been cut by it, mostly approved of Stubbins's private foray to the stars. They liked it because it was adventuresome, or because it wasn't costing taxpayers anything, or because it might produce new technology or additional markets for Terran products. The second group, those hardest hit by the collapse, opposed Stubbins and thought the government should stop him. These people hated the aliens and wanted no more contact with them.

There was a third group, small but very vocal online, who both hated Denebs *and* wanted Stubbins to travel to World. They wanted revenge, to hit World as hard as the spore plague had hit Earth. In this they were closer to opinion dominant in Central Asia than to most of the United States.

Tim drained his beer. Marianne twisted her lips in disgust at the TV screen. "Look at them. The destructive idiots. They have no facts, but that doesn't stop them."

"Uh," Tim said.

She turned to him. "Aren't you at least a little bit interested in all this?"

He sat up straighter on the sofa. "You know I am."

"Then why don't you act like it?"

"Not everyone feels your need to spread emotion all over every last goal, Marianne. Some people just act."

"Are you implying that I'm not acting enough?"

His eyes glittered. He crushed his beer can with one hand and thumped the can onto the coffee table. "When I came aboard the foundation it was because of Sissy, but I believed in it, too. In building the government ship. But that's over now, and you've gone from giving speeches to just writing Internet stuff praising Stubbins."

"It's a different means to the same end."

"Is it? Maybe. But just because I want us to go to the stars doesn't mean I want Stubbins to take us there." He stood and got another beer from the kitchenette.

By the time he'd returned, Marianne's face was expressionless. She said, "The group at Columbia has isolated the genes that have been spore-activated and may cause the changes to the auditory parts of the brain."

"Hey, great!"

He didn't ask anything about the genes, or what the discovery might mean. Marianne knew she was testing him, and disliked herself for doing it, and did it anyway. "Also, there are verified reports now of mice in the wild that are immune to *R. sporii.*"

"So things are looking up? That's good."

"Don't you want details?"

He drained the second beer—third? Fourth? Tim's capacity was astonishing. He said quietly, "Sure. Here's a detail I want. Did you get all these research updates from Harrison Rice?"

"Yes."

"By e-mail?"

"Some of them. Some in person."

"You went to see Rice. You two still have a thing for each other?"

"No. Not at all."

"But that's where you went when you were attacked outside this building that other time?" Tim said. "You told me you'd been to a museum library."

She said nothing, gazing at him steadily. If he got angry, this might be over. Her heart beat harder.

"You lied to me."

"Yes. I should not have. But you keep me on such a tight leash, you hem in my movements every minute, you check up on me . . . I'm not a child, and I resent being monitored constantly."

"It's my job to keep you safe. I'm doing my fucking job."

He was right. Before she could think what she wanted next, he said, "Ah, Marianne, let's not claw at each other. We're both just tired. Come to bed."

His solution to everything. But she went, from remorse at having lied to him or from obligation or from sheer confusion in her own mind. Not from desire. For the first time, the sex between them didn't work, and they ended up lying in the bed with a foot of sheet between them, neither saying anything, both alone with their thoughts.

The tree was really old.

Colin leaned against its trunk, listening, although what he really wanted to do was put his ear to the ground and listen to everything down there. But that would look weird to the other kids on the playground. It was a pretty small playground, because the Healy School was squished between big New York buildings. The playground had this tree by itself near the fence, a bunch of littler trees where the third-grade girls sat with their teacher, a basketball concrete where the third-grade boys were jumping and shouting, and some slides and stuff. The rest of the first-graders were on those. Only two classes got recess at a time because there just wasn't room. People had to wait their turn.

Maybe if Colin snuck *behind* the tree and lay down, nobody would notice him. There were bushes near there, too. The ground was muddy and cold and he would get his clothes dirty, but he really really wanted to listen to the tree and bushes. He slipped behind the bushes and lowered himself to the ground. It hurt because ever since Paul kicked him yesterday, Colin's belly had pain in it. Nonetheless, he pressed his ear hard against the muddy soil.

So much was going on down there! Clicks and rumbles and high-pitched sounds and low-pitched sounds. Some of them he'd heard before, but he didn't know what any of them meant. They weren't real sentences, of course, but they must mean *something*, like when thirsty plants made noises to want water. But these plants weren't thirsty; it'd rained really hard last night. Also, the tree branches above him were making noises. So many interesting sounds . . .

And then another one. Colin, flat on his stomach, raised his head. That hurt his belly, too. He saw black boots.

"Hey, *Jenner*. No school guard here now." Paul spoke very fast, like the words were bursting out of him. "That guard called my father, you know? You got me in trouble for sassing back and it's your fault, you piece of shit."

The tree branch above them made another sound.

Paul raised his boot to kick Colin.

Colin rolled to one side—it hurt his middle to do that!—and Paul followed him. Colin lay still and squeezed his eyes shut. *Now now NOW . . .*

The dead branch on the old tree cracked with a noise anyone could hear, and it hurled down on Paul. He screamed.

People rushed toward them, kids and teachers and a security guard. Then there were sirens and an ambulance and police—not a school guard but a real New York cop, with a gun—asking Colin questions. He kept his hands over his belly while he answered the questions. He said he and Paul were playing, and did not say that Paul had kicked him once before and was going to kick him again. What if they found out that he made Paul move to stand under the tree branch just before it was going to fall? They might put him in jail! Nobody must know what really happened, not any of it, not ever . . . Paul was not moving. "Concussion," somebody said, and Paul was taken away in the ambulance.

Colin clutched at his teacher's hand. She looked down at him, surprised and concerned, but he did it mostly because his legs felt so wobbly. Still, the pain in his middle was less now.

Don't let Paul die, Colin thought. If that happened, Colin would be a murderer, just like on TV. *Don't let Paul die!*

But. . . . don't let him come back to school soon, either.

"Colin, what's wrong?" Grandma said.

They were eating dinner, Grandma and Tim and Colin and Jason, and Jason was talking about some clay maps that his class was making in school. Or maybe not clay but something else. Colin couldn't listen very well and he couldn't eat either.

"Hey, buddy," Tim said, "do you feel all right?"

"I'm . . . good."

Jason said, "You don't look good."

"I'm . . ." Colin threw up all over his dinner plate. "It hurts!"

"What hurts?" Grandma said, jumping up. "Tim, he's sweating like a pig!"

Did pigs sweat? Colin didn't know. He started to cry, and everything got fuzzy except the picture in his head of a pig, sweating tears.

Icy needles pierced Marianne's gut as the ER doctor ran her hands over Colin. "What is it?" Marianne said. *No no no, I can't lose Colin too—*

"Spleen. It's been bleeding for a while. Did he injure it in the last twenty-four hours?"

"No! Not that I know of!"

"Grandma! A boy—" Colin fainted.

The next half hour was a blur. Then, as if it had all happened in a moment, Marianne found herself standing outside an operating room while a different doctor, dressed in blue scrubs, spoke to her in rapid sentences.

"The spleen appears to have been damaged sometime in the last few days and was slowly bleeding into itself until it stabilized. Did he complain of pain yesterday or this morning?"

"No, but he was pale and sort of weak-seeming, and then he seemed to get better. Is—"

"It takes a fairly hard blow to cause spleen injury."

He was looking at her with suspicion. All Marianne could do was shake her head.

"The initial blow caused the spleen to rupture. The peritoneal cavity is filling with blood. The operating team is going in to take out the spleen, and he is receiving a blood transfusion. He should survive this, and the effects on his life will be minimal, but you should know that we are obligated to report this to the child-protection people."

It barely registered. "But he'll be all right? He'll be all right?"

"We'll certainly do everything we can." He disappeared into the operating room. Marianne staggered to a chair in a waiting area and dropped into it, her eyes fastened to the door through which the doctor had disappeared. Tim took her hand.

It was the worst hour of her life. Ryan was damaged, Noah was gone, Elizabeth was furious at her—but they were all still alive. Marianne sat unmoving, scarcely breathing, as if her own motionlessness could keep Colin from leaving her. Jason sat pressed so close to Tim that he seemed to want to blend into him. If either of them spoke to her, she didn't hear. Her eyes remained trained, unblinking, on the door through which the surgeon would come.

He did, eventually. "Mrs. Carpenter? Colin will be fine."

Marianne could move again.

"We removed the spleen. He can function normally without it, although he may be more than usually susceptible to certain types of infection for the rest of his life. He can go home in a day or two. You'll get discharge directions."

"Let me see him."

"Not yet." The doctor disappeared, without explanation. Marianne started angrily after him, but Tim grabbed her shoulder.

"He has to wake up, Marianne. And then they want a cop or social worker to talk to him first. Because of what that first doctor said."

Child protective services. They thought Marianne, or Tim, had abused Colin. Marianne wanted to tear the hospital apart with her fists. To think that she could ever . . . And they would want to check records that didn't exist for "Colin Carpenter." This was going to be complicated.

She said wearily, "Take Jason home, Tim. I can deal with this."

"All right," Tim said, "if you promise not to leave the hospital until I get back."

"Promise." She wasn't leaving the hospital until she could take Colin with her.

When they finally let her see Colin, hours later, he lay in a recovery room, tubes stuck into his little body, an oxygen line in his nose. The woman who'd been talking to him, either a cop or a social worker, nodded and left. Colin peered out from under his white hospital blanket and said, "Did Paul die?"

"What, honey?"

"Did Paul die?"

"Who's Paul?"

"I told that lady. The nice one who gave me this." He held up a small toy airplane.

"Paul will be fine. How do *you* feel, honey? Does anything hurt?"

"I had to tell the lady. That I could hear the tree was going to fall. The police said I had to tell everything. My real name, too. I'm sorry, Grandma."

"It's all right. As long as you're okay, everything is all right."

His eyes were closing. Marianne said, "I'll be right back," but he might have already been asleep.

The social worker, joined by a cop, waited for her in the corridor. They found an empty waiting room. Marianne explained about the aliases, and the social worker told her what Colin had said.

A third-grade bully, with metal-capped boots. Kicking Colin in the bathroom, threatening to do it again under the tree, until by sheer chance a dead branch cracked and fell on him. Paul Tyson had taunted Colin, using his real last name.

"You are cleared of suspicion, Dr. Jenner," the social worker said. As if that was what mattered. "And we'll follow through with Paul's parents." Then the woman, who went around dispensing toy airplanes in return for children's truths, closed her tablet and left. The cop followed her, but only after a hard look that told Marianne exactly what were his sentiments about alien-loving *Embassy* scientists who wanted a spaceship built.

She checked on Colin once again. He was still asleep. Her cell would not work on the hospital ward. She took it outside, defying Tim's orders, and called Jonah Stubbins.

Tim and Marianne stood in the apartment's tiny kitchenette as he made coffee. It was after midnight, but Tim could drink coffee at any time of the day or night and still sleep. Marianne, nearly twenty years older, could not. Her body ached for sleep but she had to do this, now, tonight. Jason lay asleep in the boys' room, curled up in Colin's bed. She had found him holding Colin's old stuffed elephant and she'd almost burst into tears. Stress.

Tim poured hot water on cheap instant-coffee crystals; he would drink anything with caffeine. "And so Colin thinks he *made* the tree branch fall on the little shit."

"No. But he lured Paul to stand under it because he knew it would fall."

"The social worker didn't believe that."

"No, but—"

"I'm not sure I believe it, either," Tim said. "I'm more interested in how this Paul Tyson knew who Colin was. I want to talk to that kid."

"It doesn't matter how he knew," Marianne said wearily. "It only matters that our identity is out yet again. I can't keep moving like this. It's not good for the boys."

"Well, it wouldn't be good to stay here now, either. You gotta see that, Marianne."

"I do see it. Tim, I'm taking Stubbins's offer to move us all to the *Venture* building site and get a tutor for the boys. They'll be safe, and I can work just as well there."

Tim paused, coffee cup halfway to his mouth. He put the cup, undrunk, on the tiny counter. "Yeah? I thought you wanted to be close enough to see Ryan."

"I can't do both. Jason and Colin must come first."

"I get that." He picked up the coffee and drained it in one gulp, hot though it must still be. Marianne waited, knowing what was coming.

He said, "And while the boys are being tutored and you're working on your computer, what am I supposed to be doing? You won't need a bodyguard there, or the kids to be taken to school, or anything like that."

"I don't know what you could do." Actually, now that she thought about it, she wasn't sure what he did all day now. *"I'm going out,"* he would say, but where? And why hadn't she thought to ask before now? Self-focused, that's what she'd been.

"Tim—"

"You don't want me to go with you, do you?"

She said gently, "I think we both know that this relationship isn't really working. And that it never had a future."

He didn't answer, and despite her relief that he wasn't going to make a scene, her pride was bruised. Dumb, dumb! She should be glad that Tim wasn't hurt—as it was clear from his face that he was not—and that they didn't love each other. He had never felt about her the way he'd felt about Sissy, and for her the attraction had mostly been sexual. That had drained away. Stress, or acceptance of how different they were, or maybe just the passing of time.

She suddenly felt very old.

Tim said, "I'll miss those kids. Can I come see them sometimes? And what will you tell them?"

She hadn't thought that far. "Yes, of course you can come see them. We're leaving as soon as Colin can travel. Stubbins will send a car."

He moved toward her, and she tensed. But his kiss lacked all passion. "Go to bed, Marianne. You're exhausted."

She did. When she woke, in midmorning, Jason had been taken to school. Tim's things were still in his room. He wouldn't leave until Colin was discharged and Marianne and the boys safely transferred to Stubbins's protection. The innate decency of this moved Marianne. But she couldn't afford any more emotion. Hastily she dressed to go to the hospital.

One more trip before they could leave for Pennsylvania. Marianne drove alone to see Ryan. It was a lovely day, amazingly warm for November, and Ryan sat outside in an Adirondack chair. He wore his own clothes, his hair neatly combed. He gave his mother a tired smile. "Hi, Mom."

Encouraged, she said, "Hello, Ryan. How are you?"

"Fine." But a minute later his face sagged again and tears filled his eyes. "I want to go home."

Marianne took her son's hand. He said that often, always when he seemed most stressed, the words seeming to rise unbidden to his lips. They *were* unbidden, she knew now: unwilled, pushed up from some place deeper than rationality. The words were not literal. There was no specific geographical place Ryan wished to return to. He wanted to go back to the past, to the "home" where he was the child that his depression had regressed him into being, the child who was happy and cared for, the child who'd assumed happiness and order were the way the universe worked. Who had not yet been broken by an entirely different universe.

She had always thought it was Noah who was the weakest child, the drifter who belonged nowhere. She had been wrong. Noah had gone, happily, to the stars. But there was no way for Ryan to go where he wanted. Connie was dead and his beloved job with the wildlife agency gone, and the past could not come back again.

"I want to go home," he said again.

"I know, sweetheart," she said. "I know."

He said nothing for the rest of her visit. Marianne sat for an hour just holding her son's hand in the soft autumn sunlight.

CHAPTER 20

S plus 6.2 years

Jonah Stubbins was building his starship, the *Venture,* in northwestern Pennsylvania. The site made sense.

Part of the Allegheny Plateau, the area was free of hurricanes and tornadoes. Its geography shielded it from superstorms. Earthquakes were rare and mild. Before global warming had reached its present state, deep snow and ice storms had been frequent here, but no more. Creeping desertification, not yet far advanced, nonetheless had proven drying enough to cause many farmers to sell their gentle hills. Once coal had been mined here, but never in the quantities found farther east, and most lodes were played out. Stubbins had gotten huge swaths of land reasonably cheap.

Glaciers had left the entire area dotted with caves. However, unlike the clear, large caves to the east and south—once tourist attractions, now mostly closed due to lack of state funds—the majority of caves in this part of Pennsylvania had been formed by stream water forced underground during wetter times. The caves were small, twisty, and filled with mud. Clearing them out would involve large and conspicuous equipment. Stubbins was not worried about stealth attacks from underground.

Marianne's first sight of the vast compound was a strip of dirt, backed by an electrified fence topped with barbed wire reinforced by periodic guard towers. Beyond the fence lay another, wider strip of bare ground, followed by another fence, and then low cinder-block buildings. The whole thing looked like a gigantic maximum-security prison.

"Wow," Jason said from the backseat. Colin said nothing. He had, since Tim's departure, taken to sucking his thumb. Marianne, riding beside the driver of the car that Stubbins had sent for them, turned around to see how the boys were taking this.

"This is so cool!" Jason bounced in his seatbelt. "Look, Col, it's great!"

Colin took his thumb out of his mouth.

Thank heavens for Jason's upbeat nature.

They passed through the gate and drove for longer than she'd expected, past bulldozers and trucks, cinder-block outbuildings and groves of trees, trailers and barracks of raw weathered lumber. The closer they drove to the ship itself, the messier the site became. Thick cables, transformer stations, a thirty-five-ton crane. Equipment shrieked; people milled about, shouting to be heard. Marianne remembered the smooth, noiseless descent of the *Embassy* into New York Harbor and wondered if anything that clean and sleek could really emerge from this chaos.

The car stopped in front of a barracks, a long low building with no adornment, windows and doors set in straight lines regular as soldiers at drill. The doors opened directly onto the weedy dirt outside. Two women stood in front of the farthest door, one young and pretty, the other Marianne's age but much shorter and wider. "Here we are," the driver said.

The young woman held out her hand. "Dr. Jenner, I'm Allison Blake, the boys' teacher. And you two must be Jason and Colin."

"Hi," Colin said, but Jason made a little noise of disgust.

"You can't be both of our teacher 'cause I'm in second grade and Colin's in first!"

"But I am," Allison Blake said solemnly, "because I'm a super-teacher." She reached up behind her neck and released a red cape, which billowed around her. Her expression remained completely serious. After a bewildered moment, Jason laughed.

Colin did not. "Then what's your superpower?" he demanded.

"That's for you to find out. But I know yours. You can hear the ground."

Marianne blinked. What? How the hell did she know that Colin—

"You're wondering how I know that," the teacher said. "It's because I have another student who can do it, too. Would you like to meet him sometime soon?"

"Yeah!" Colin's eyes shone with wonder. Jason also looked interested. Marianne thought, not for the first time, that if Jason's temperament had included any jealousy at all, life would be even more difficult than it was now. Ever since Paul Tyson's assault, Colin had been moody and unpredictable.

Allison Blake said, "Then put your suitcases in your room here and ask your grandmother if you can come with me."

"Yes, go on," Marianne said. She was here for their safety, and she had to trust this place or she would go mad. "I'll get the cases."

Allison led the boys away. The short woman said to Marianne, "Quite a show. She's great with kids. Has to be or Jonah wouldn't have hired her. I'm Judy Taunton, deputy physicist in this medicine show. Jonah sent me to greet you."

"Where is he? And how did he know—"

"About the kids? Jonah knows everything. And the value of nothing, as Oscar Wilde so presciently said. Excuse me, I know this is a filthy and archaic habit, but I'm in desperate need." She lit a cigarette.

Marianne studied her. Judy Taunton was no more than five feet tall, solid as a cinder block, with gray hair in a buzz cut. Up close, her face looked younger than her body, and Marianne revised her estimate downward to midforties. She wore baggy jeans and a loose blue work shirt that made her look even wider than she was. The shirt was embroidered on the collar and placket with exquisite silk flowers, hand done. Judy exhaled a perfect smoke ring.

"Okay, let's get you oriented. Jonah wanted to meet you himself but spaceships are demanding bitches, so you get me. This is your suite. Not exactly the Ritz but we're practicing Taoist simplicity here, or possibly scientific socialism. Nobody else has anything better, not even His Nibs."

Judy picked up the boys' duffel bags and Marianne wheeled in her suitcase, laptop bag on her shoulder. The rest of their luggage, minimal anyway, would arrive later. The "suite" consisted of two rooms, each with a door to the outside and a connecting door of lumber so raw that fresh wood shavings lay on the floor beside it. The boys' room had two beds, a cheap chest of crude pine, a table and four chairs. Hers was exactly the same except for a double bed. There were no closets, just pegs on the wall. There were bathrooms, one per bedroom, with showers but no tub. Blinds on the windows, no curtains, plain white blankets and pillows.

Judy said, "A hospital room has more charm. At least there you get flowers in plastic vases and nurses in scrubs with little duckies on them. Most of us only use our rooms to sleep—not, however, that the work buildings have any more pizzazz. Mess is the big building with 'EATS' spray-painted all over it, courtesy of a drunken night for some construction guys. Food is served pretty much all the time, and it's not bad. Jonah doesn't want the masses to rise up in culinary revolution."

"Thanks," Marianne said. "What else should I know?"

"Oh, tons and tons. But the first thing, since I see you unpacking your laptop, is that the site is Faraday shielded."

Marianne stopped and looked at her. "What?"

"Jonah doesn't want hackers getting any information whatsoever about our progress. There's a big invisible shield, proprietary tech, over everything inside the inner fence. Nothing electronic gets in and nothing out."

Marianne put her laptop back in its case. "We're leaving."

Judy laughed. "That's everybody's first reaction. But it's not as bad as it sounds. The LAN is shielded, although I suppose eventually somebody will hack in somehow, because they always do. But there are computers in the mess with secure and encrypted underground cables and you can use those to communicate with the outside world. They're monitored, though, so any communication you send outside will be read and your web surfing will be tracked. Come on outside so I can finish this cigarette without stinking up your rooms."

Marianne followed Judy out the door. "Cell phones?"

"No." Judy stopped smiling. "Look, I know it's draconian, but Stubbins knows what he's doing. He must trust you or you wouldn't be here, and he told me I can be as open with you about project details as you can stand. I know you're a geneticist, not a physicist or an engineer. We're much farther along on the ship than Space X, the European Union, or China. India is hopeless. The Russians are our only competition and we can't afford leaks of how we're solving the problems associated with the Deneb plans. We have to be first."

"Why?" Marianne said.

Judy stared at her. "You really are a trusting soul, aren't you? Do you know what the Russian ship is called?"

"*Stremlenie*—the *Endeavor*."

"That's the public name. The top-secret project name is *Mest'*."

"I don't speak Russian."

"It means 'revenge.'"

Something tightened in Marianne's chest. "If it's top secret, how does Stubbins know that?"

"He knows. The *Venture* is private enterprise, but of course Stubbins works with Washington. Not openly, because every congressional district has way too many people who hate the Denebs, and lawmakers have this pesky need to get reelected. But Central Asia suffered more than anybody from the spore cloud. You're a geneticist— you must know that. They lost more people to the plague, and the mouse die-off affected their crop ecology the most. And the current regime is so old-school tyrannical that they might as well be czars."

"Yes." Marianne was thinking furiously. *Revenge*—against World. Against Noah, against Smith, against Marianne's half-Deneb grandchild. Against a star-faring section of humanity, who reported themselves as peaceful but who were capable of creating the technology that the Russians now wanted to use as a warship.

"Can the star drive be weaponized? *Can* it?"

Judy shrugged. "Nobody knows. It's hard to convey to a nonphysicist how alien these plans, and the physics behind them, really are. No, don't look at me like that, I know the Denebs are human, not alien. But the thinking behind their tech is so strange to us that there is speculation it isn't even theirs but came to them from somewhere else."

Marianne's mouth opened, then closed again without anything coming out.

"Just speculation," Judy said. "And here's more of the same, although this one is founded on some actual data. Did you ever wonder why the Denebs needed human scientists aboard the *Embassy*? Why not just get a few human lab-rat volunteers and work out the immunity issues by themselves? I've gone through every published article by every one of you who was aboard—Harrison Rice, Ahmed Rafat, Jessica Yu—and I got some biologist friends to do it with me. Every single breakthrough seems to have been made by Terrans, not Denebs. Don't you see what that means? It means the same thing as bringing you human scientists aboard in the first place. When it comes to genetics, *we know more than they do*. So what other science have they gotten from somebody else, and are just piggybacking on?"

Marianne found her voice. "You sound like one of the conspiracy theorists out there. Damn it, Judy, I worked with these people. I was there!"

"I know you were. And I could be dead wrong. But I'm not the only scientist saying that. And whatever I suspect, or believe, or entertain as mad fantasy, doesn't change a very real fact—*no one* knows what will happen the day we finish the ship and press the button to start her. Actually, we're all grateful it *is* a button and not some peculiar thing we wouldn't even recognize. The drive appears to harness the repulsion force of dark matter, and nobody on Earth understands that very well."

Judy took a long final drag on her cigarette, dropped it on the ground, and turned her heel on it. Then, noting Marianne's expression, she carefully picked it up, wrapped it in a tissue, and put it in her pocket. "I was on the Dark Energy Survey, incidentally, in the Strong Lensing work group, that ended up confirming the existence of dark energy. The survey got delayed because of funding problems after the collapse and also because of the totally inane . . . never mind. You aren't interested in the politics. *I'm* not even interested anymore in the stupidity of the politicians involved. The point is that dark energy exists, or at least the mathematics say it does, and it seems to power the Deneb star drive, although nobody knows how.

"We're doing things we don't understand to Terran materials, processes that make baking nobium-3-tin into superconductors look like kindergarten play. A lot of that is going on in underground bunkers. The engineers are in control and we physicists struggle to keep up, which is a dead reversal of the normal order. It's not just the blind leading the sighted, it's like the blind pushing them over cliffs. And David Chin, project chief, is cliff-diving just as much as the rest of us, although don't tell him I said so."

Marianne said, "How do you know—"

"That we're building it right? Of course we can't really be sure, not to every tiny intended tolerance—the error bar on this project is the size of Rhode Island. All of which means that nobody understands the implications of what may or may not happen when we turn it on."

"That wasn't what I was going to ask. What if "—this was a stupid question but she had to ask it—"the star drive blows up Earth?"

"Aren't you the one who keeps insisting the Denebs are our friends?"

"Yes, but if we somehow build it wrong . . . if we don't understand the plans correctly . . ."

"It won't blow up Earth," Judy said. "We think."

The physicist was grinning. Was she just playing with her? Marianne wasn't sure she believed Judy. But then Judy said something that tipped the balance.

"We know enough to know what we don't know—unlike the anti-alien yahoos out there—but we're not completely ignorant. The physics fits with quantum theories and brane theory both, once you make certain radical adjustments in your thinking, and even with general relativity. Which, God knows, quantum mechanics didn't. But the basic underlying idea for all of it seems to be that everything in the universe is interconnected in ways we hadn't expected. Quarks and galaxies and time and spores and coffee spoons and consciousness. All of it."

"That sounds religious."

"It isn't. I mean, yes, it is, but not in the way most people mean. But you know what I'm talking about, don't you?"

Judy's eyes, small and dark in her broad face, pierced Marianne. "Yes," she said quietly. "I didn't used to think so, but I do now." Since Colin's revelations to her. A lot more was interconnected than she'd ever believed.

"I thought so. But that's enough philosophy for now. You want a tour of this candy factory? Willy Wonka himself asked me to show you around."

"Yes," Marianne said again. "I want to see everything."

⋅

The spaceship camp was the coolest place ever. Jason said so, and now Colin agreed.

It had so much stuff! Trucks and bulldozers and steam shovels like in *Mike Mulligan and His Steam Shovel*, Colin's second favorite book. His favorite was still *Brandon and the Elephant in the Basement*, but probably there wasn't an elephant here. Still, like Grandma said, you couldn't have everything.

The camp had things to climb on, and Colin liked their teacher, and the spaceship was awesome. But best of all was Luke.

Mr. Stubbins brought him to Ms. Blake's classroom, which was really just a room like Colin's and Jason's bedroom only with some tables, chairs, books, and computers. Grandma was there because it was their first morning. They were doing math. Ms. Blake was showing Jason something called multiplication, making little piles of polished stones. Colin wrote numbers on paper and drew little balls to show how many the numbers were. That was babyish but Ms. Blake explained that she needed to find out how much math Colin already knew, so she could teach him new things.

"Kids, Dr. Jenner," Mr. Stubbins said, "this is Luke. He's already been here a while, but this morning he was with me at the ship. Luke, this is Jason and Colin."

Luke looked down at his sneakers, which seemed really new and clean. So were the rest of his clothes. He was big and moved slow, with crinkly hair the color of dry sand. When he raised his head, Colin saw that he looked afraid.

Mr. Stubbins said, "Say hello, Luke."

"Hello," Luke said. His voice was a little hard to understand.

"Hi," Jason and Colin said.

"Hello," Grandma said.

Luke didn't answer or even look at anyone. Grandma said to Mr. Stubbins, "Traumatized, developmentally challenged, or Asperger's?"

"All three. Be nice, Marianne."

Colin said, "Grandma is always nice!"

"So she is," Mr. Stubbins said. He talked different when he was around Grandma than he did to other people.

"A word, please," Grandma said. "You, too, Allison."

The three adults went into a corner and whispered hard at each other. Grandma waved her hands. Jason talked to Luke. "Do you live here?"

"Yes." It seemed hard for him to say the word.

"It's awesome, isn't it? Where are your parents?" Jason said.

"Dead."

"My mother is dead, too."

Still Luke didn't look at the boys. His face twisted like he had a pain. Jason said, "What's wrong?"

"Too loud."

Colin glanced out the window. All the machinery had stopped for lunch. "It's quiet in here."

Luke said, "The ground."

Colin caught his breath. This was the kid that Ms. Blake said could hear the way Colin did! Right now Colin heard not only the ground but the plants outside and the electricity fence and some water deep under the building and a whole lot of other stuff. Could Luke hear it, too?

He said, "Do you hear plants? And storms coming?"

Then, for the first time, Luke did look at him. His eyes widened. "You can hear?"

"Yes! All those things! And not only that, I can show you how to block out the noise. You need to put it in rows. . . ." Colin sat at the table and picked up the polished stones for Jason's multiplication. He told Luke about putting the noises in rows in his mind, and that Luke should practice. Luke's heavy face twisted with trying. Why was it so hard for him? And why hadn't he thought of it himself? Colin had, before he could even remember. He went over it with Luke again, and then again. Grandma and Mr. Stubbins and Ms. Blake were still whispering shouts at each other. Jason got bored and went back to the math stuff on his worksheet.

Finally Luke's eyes went round and he said, "Oh—"

"See? That's better, right?"

Luke burst into tears and grabbed Colin's hand. Colin was embarrassed but didn't pull away. Luke wasn't like Paul. He was going to be Colin's friend, and Jason's too, but Luke would be a friend who could hear the world, just like Colin did.

This really was the coolest place ever.

Sometimes it even made him forget what a bad person he was for crashing a tree branch onto Paul.

Judy and Marianne had become friends. In some mysterious way she reminded Marianne of Evan Blanford, although on the surface no two people could have been more different. Judy had given Marianne a complete tour of the *Venture*, but Marianne still understood very little about the ship being constructed on a reinforced-concrete launchpad. She was staggered by how close to completion the vessel was. A gleaming silvery cylinder with odd projections, it looked far too fragile to withstand liftoff through the atmosphere. Apparently some version of the Deneb energy shield activated during liftoff, protecting it. She was also surprised by the ship's small size. Had Smith's compatriots lived in such cramped quarters for the voyage to Earth? And could the *Venture* launch something as large and complex as the *Embassy* had been?

"No," Judy said. "We haven't found anything that would suggest that capability. What we have here is an abridged version of the alien tech. Either they didn't want to share the full monte, or they adapted everything so we poor knuckle-draggers can actually build the thing. Prometheus handing down fire but not the Franklin stove."

The more Marianne saw, the more questions she had. Three things, however, were completely clear.

First, the ship was the kind of massive, coordinated, expensive engineering effort that could only have been built by someone with complete control of the project, a fabulous fortune plus the ability to borrow even more money, and freedom from all committees, including Congress. If Stubbins was working with Washington, as Judy had said, it didn't interfere with his ability to make, modify, reverse, or implement decisions as he alone saw fit.

Second, Stubbins's staff were an eclectic lot. The only world-class physicist was David Chin, from Stanford, second in command. The rest of the physicists and astronomers, like Judy, were steady and unremarkable craftsmen who were probably not going to move humanity closer to understanding how World's star drive worked. The engineers were drawn from various enterprises, as were the workmen and tech staff. "Stubbins looked for people who really want to go to the stars themselves," Judy said. "Because of course we're all hoping to be picked for ship's crew, eventually. Also people who can be trusted completely. Stubbins wants no doubters, no betrayers, no leaks."

And might not get any. Marianne had never seen such tight security, except on the *Embassy*. She spent a fair amount of time on the computers in the mess, even though she knew her every keystroke was monitored. She found no information whatsoever about Luke, whom Stubbins said was "found in an orphanage." Luke, like Colin, was able to hear in infrasonic and ultrasonic ranges. What did Stubbins want with him? What did Stubbins want with Colin?

She couldn't ask him directly. Ever since her first morning here, when he'd come to the kids' classroom (and why do that personally?), he'd been off-site. Judy didn't know where.

"Washington, maybe," she said. "David Chin keeps everything rolling along."

They sat outside Marianne's barracks on utilitarian metal folding chairs, there being nothing as frivolous as lawn chairs available, in a gorgeous November sunset. Both women huddled in heavy sweaters but the sunset was too good to miss. Gold, red, and an orange like ripe fruit faded slowly from the western horizon. The first stars pricked the dark blue above. A short distance off, Allison supervised the three boys, who climbed on a pallet of metal girders. The children became silhouettes against the sky, and a soft breeze brought, instead of the usual machine oil and dust, a fugitive scent of wild grapes. A hawk wheeled in the sky.

"I don't see how World could be any lovelier than this," Marianne said, before she knew she was going to say anything at all. The next moment she thought of what a small percentage of Earth this represented, while so much of the rest of it was struggling, starving, flooding, rioting, or all of the above. The Internet news just got worse and worse. She didn't say any of this. Why spoil the moment?

Judy was hunched over an embroidery hoop, of all things; she said that embroidering flowers relaxed her. People were endlessly surprising in their hidden corners.

Marianne said, "How can you even see what you're doing? The light's mostly gone."

"Yeah. I've pricked my finger twice." She folded up her work and said abruptly, "Why do you think Stubbins is so hot to go to World?"

"I've wondered about that myself. I imagine he smells profit. He's proven to have a good nose for it."

"A lame pun. But profit of what kind? You know him better than I do, Marianne."

"I don't think anybody really knows him."

"Yeah. 'A grand, ungodly, godlike man,'" Judy said, making air quotes with both hands. Her embroidery slipped off her lap and fell onto the ground.

Marianne said, "I don't recognize the quote."

"Ah, you scientists. Deficient in the humanities."

"Come on, Judy—you're a scientist, too."

"Yes, but only by default. I wanted to be an English professor."

"Then why didn't you?"

"An overcrowded and underpaid field. But Melville remains my first love."

"So—Ahab," Marianne guessed.

"Correct. Ahab and our very own silver whale. As long as I don't end up being Ishmael."

"Let me ask you something," Marianne said, because she'd been wondering on and off. "Do you think Stubbins uses those pheromone concoctions of his—I'm In Charge or whatever it's called—to get people to come here and carry out his wishes?"

"You're not the first to ask. My opinion is no, but who understands where the line is between pheromonal influence and the power of suggestion? Or the lure of plain old power? It isn't—Uh-oh, visitors to the *Pequod*, escorted by the captain himself."

Three figures emerged from the dusk. Stubbins hit a wall switch behind Marianne and a floodlight shattered the sweet gloom. Marianne blinked in the sudden harsh light, waiting for her eyes to adjust. When they had, she blinked again.

Oh, the poor things!

The woman and child with Stubbins, clearly mother and daughter, were both incredibly ugly. They had sallow skin, lips so thin they almost disappeared, and small eyes set too close together. Both of their lower faces sloped back so abruptly that they seemed to have no chins. The girl, who looked about six, also had a low forehead covered with bangs, so that her nose seemed to fill her entire truncated face.

"Marianne, Judy, meet my fiancée, Belinda Parker, and her daughter Ava. We got ourselves engaged this morning."

It was a moment before Marianne could find her voice. Until three months ago, Stubbins had been married to an ex–super model, the fourth Mrs. Stubbins. All his wives except the first had been leggy blondes, so perfect in face and body that they scarcely seemed human. If Stubbins was engaged to Belinda, she must have something he desperately wanted. More money? Was he running out of funds to finish and launch the starship? But if Belinda was an heiress or ultra-rich widow, why hadn't she paid for plastic surgery for, if not herself, this pathetic child?

Manners took over. Marianne stood and held out her hand. "Congratulations, both of you. Welcome to the *Venture*, Belinda."

"Thank you." The woman, unsmiling, studied Marianne and Judy. Ava gazed down at her shoes, which looked orthopedic. Judy rose and added her congratulations, her eyes glowing with curiosity.

Stubbins said, "Ava, here comes your teacher, lil' darling. And here come your classmates. Hooboy, Ms. Blake, you're sure enough going to have your hands full now! Jason, Colin, Luke, Ava." He pointed to each as if choosing melons at a fruit stand.

The four children stared at each other. *This is not going well,* Marianne thought.

"You wanna play a video game?" Jason asked, and in his voice Marianne heard the echo of his uncle Noah, always quick to compassion. "We got *Ataka*! That means 'attack'!"

Ava said, "Nah." And then, fiercely, "I don't know how."

"I'll show you. C'mon, Luke and Colin, let's teach her."

The boys started indoors. Ava didn't move. Marianne waited for Belinda to say something like, "Go on, honey," but Belinda said nothing. Finally Stubbins said, "Go on now, lil' darlin', y'all have fun with your new lil' friends."

Ava raised her face to glare at him, then followed Jason. Belinda continued to study Marianne. Finally she said, "Yer grandkids? They can hear spirits, too, huh? What'd he promise *you* to get here? How high was yer price?"

Judy's eyes widened. Belinda raised her left hand. On the fourth finger gleamed a huge diamond, glinting in the floodlight. Belinda's misshapen face looked as fierce as her daughter's, but in the woman's eyes shone the light of pure, unadulterated crazy.

The new girl looked strange. Luke was slow in his head—Grandma had explained it carefully—and Colin was a bad person because he'd deliberately hurt Paul with that tree branch, maybe even killed him although everybody said no. Ava wasn't slow or bad—at least, if she was, he didn't know it yet—but she was really ugly. All three of them weren't normal, only Jason was. But the starship camp was a good place for people who weren't normal, because here everybody was kind. So Colin had to be kind to Ava.

"We got an extra remote," Jason said, handing it to her and plopping himself down on the floor before the big computer screen. "This game is Russian but it's not hard to understand. First you gotta pick a character . . ."

Ava hit the remote from his hand and it fell on the floor. "I don't wanna play."

"Okay, what do you wanna do?"

"I'll play. I'm just telling you I don't wanna."

Luke looked bewildered. "If you don't wanna, then why—"

"Stubbins says I have to. You was there. Are you a retard or something?"

"*Hey,*" Jason said, at the same moment that Luke said simply, "Yes."

Ava's face changed. She peered at Luke from her small eyes and then turned on Jason. "And what's wrong with *you?*"

Jason said, "You apologize to Luke!"

"It's okay," Luke said.

"No, it isn't. We don't call people derogatory names!" Jason said. Colin recognized Grandma's words.

Ava said, with unexpected meekness, "Sorry, Luke. But you're a . . . you're slow, and I'm ugly. So what's the problem, you two?"

Colin saw that Ava was making a club, like the clubs at his old school. Paul had a club at recess and he'd said that Colin couldn't belong. But Colin and Jason belonged here, and so did Luke. If Luke was in this club of people with problems, then Colin wanted to be, too. He had to tell Ava something, or she and Luke would be in the club and he and Jason would not.

"Well?" Ava demanded.

Jason said, "We don't have any problems!" Which wasn't true. Colin didn't want his brother to be a liar, and he did want to be in the club. So he said, "I hear things."

"What things? Voices? Like my mother? My mother is wacko. She hears angels and demons."

Colin blinked. But he'd started this, and he was going to finish it. "Not voices. I hear the ground."

Ava's squinty little eyes widened and her mouth fell open. One tooth was black. "Really? You're fucking with me!"

More words Grandma wouldn't like, but Colin let it go. "No. It's the truth. I can hear the ground. So can Luke. And plants, too," he added, in case the ground wasn't enough to get him into the club. As soon as he was in, he'd figure out how to get Jason in, too.

Ava swung her head to look at Luke, then back at Colin. And then she burst into sobs. She covered her face with her hands and sunk to the floor, sitting on the remote. She sobbed and sobbed, and after a moment of fright, Luke reached out with his big pale hand and patted her skinny hunched back, over and over.

CHAPTER 21

S plus 6.5 years

Two months later, the ship was nearly complete. Workmen riveted and shouted in the main compartments, engineers tested displays on the pristine bridge, everyone viewed the containers being loaded into the hold. There were a lot of these, including food, mostly freeze-dried, for twenty-one people for three months.

Marianne said to Judy, "How do you know you need three months? Or twenty-one people?"

"We don't." Judy's fingers flew over a keyboard, crunching some data incomprehensible to Marianne. They had stopped by Judy's "office," a cubicle in the raw-wood building closest to the ship. Everyone called the building "the command center," although the commander, Jonah Stubbins, and his second, David Chin, actually worked elsewhere. This cavernous, ugly building was filled with scientists and engineers, working furiously on computers or arguing tensely across cheap conference tables. There were a lot of arguments. Marianne, who had never been around so much as a garden shed being built, let alone a starship from plans nobody fully understood, had begun to think the *Venture* would never get off the ground. Not unless it could be fueled by sheer hot air.

She said, "You don't know how long it will take to get to World?"

"Wait just a moment . . . I just have to . . . there." Judy turned her attention to Marianne. Judy looked tired, the broad planes of her face drawn down in sags. She wore overalls and another of her exquisitely embroidered silk shirts; the effect was of the world's richest handyman. "We're pretty sure the star drive distorts the fabric of space-time and that it won't take much time at all to arrive at World. Of course, 'not much time at all' is a matter of debate, like everything else around here. But we don't know how long we need to be there, or who will stay on the ship, or what. There are sleeping cubicles in the design for twenty-one people, so twenty-one people go."

"From everything I've read, Terran space travel was planned with ships that were self-sufficient biosystems, at least as much as possible. Hydroponic tanks for growing food, algae-based air scrubbing, waste recycling. The *Venture* doesn't have that."

"There will be plants aboard," Judy said.

"But it won't be a sustainable closed biosystem."

"We never got that to work even on Earth. You know that, Marianne."

"So that means that nobody stayed aboard the mother ship when the Denebs came to New York seven years ago. It was empty."

"That seems to be what it means, yes." Judy grinned, a weary grin. "I know what you want to ask. So ask it."

"Okay. Who are the twenty-one?"

"Nobody knows. Stubbins isn't saying. Except, of course, for David Chin."

"Do you want to go?"

Judy gave her a *duh* look. "Of course I want to go. Everybody here—well, most everybody—wants to go. But I don't think my chances are good, not for the first trip. We're all hoping for subsequent trips. What we want is a bus route to the stars, with regularly scheduled commuter routes. Don't you want to go?"

Marianne said slowly, "I don't know. Noah is there, but Ryan and Elizabeth and the boys are here, and—"

"I forgot—you're a breeder. Well, that does tie you to terra firma, doesn't it?"

"Judy, why am I really here? What does Stubbins want with Luke and Ava and Colin?"

Judy grasped Marianne's shoulder. "Put on your coat and let's go on over to the mess. I'm starving."

Outside, Judy spoke in a low voice as rapid as her stride. For a short woman, she could move amazingly fast. "Nobody knows what Stubbins wants with those kids. Believe me, there's a lot of speculation. Luke's been here since site selection. So you tell me: What's special about these three kids? Is it true that they can hear in infrasonic and ultrasonic ranges?"

"It's true of Colin and Luke. I don't know about Ava. She doesn't talk to me."

"She doesn't talk to anyone but the other kids. A prickly pear, that one. But Stubbins wanted her badly enough to pretend he's going to marry her mother. He never will, of course. Why don't *you* ask him why he wants these kids? You're the one with a right to know."

"God, I've tried!" Marianne said. "I can't get to him. When he's on site, and I actually succeed in finding him, he's rushing off to somewhere else, hollering folksy crap at me over his shoulder. 'Catch you soon, lil' lady!' And Belinda—she's not here, either. She's off getting reconstructive surgery for her face, which was apparently her price for coming here. Ava's next."

"Well, that's good. That poor kid needs—What the *fuck*?"

Sirens sounded all over camp: three short blasts and one long, over and over. Security had conducted extensive drills; this pattern meant "not a drill"! Marianne, with Judy panting behind her, took off at a dead run for the underground bunker where Allison Blake would take the children. The bunkers were small and crude, except for communications, but they could protect everybody from anything less than ballistic missiles.

The attackers had ballistic missiles.

Packed into the rocky caverns, shivering without their coats, the four children pressed close to her and Allison. Marianne put her coat around Colin and Ava, the smallest two, without taking her eyes off the bunker's LAN-fed TV. The ground underneath her was hard and damp; moisture dripped along the walls; Ava clutched Marianne's arm hard enough that the girl's untrimmed nails drew pinpoints of blood. Marianne felt none of it. Her gaze never left CNN.

Minutes ago a short-range tactical missile—"possibly a Scud" said the visibly shaken newscaster—had hit the California site of SpaceX. Images of twisted wreckage, burning buildings. On the Internet, credit was being claimed by ACWAK, No Contact with Alien Killers.

Judy said raggedly, "A Scud! Those things can carry nuclear warheads. This one must've carried only conventional explosives . . . 'only,' Christ, listen to me . . . fuck them to hell!"

Marianne said, "How could an American hate group get a *Scud*?"

"Oh, fuck, Marianne, the Russians sold them to everybody. *Congo* had Scuds. They've been drifting around ever since, sold and resold on the black market. They can be launched from mobile launchers and their accuracy within, say, fifty miles isn't too bad. Although these fuckers got really lucky, the—"

Colin said in a small voice, "You're saying bad words."

"Sorry, kid."

Jason said, "Is that spaceship all the way wrecked?"

"Yes," Marianne said. She pried Ava's nails off her hand. *But we're completely safe*, she wanted to say—but was it true? She turned her full attention to the children.

"Listen, all of you. Mr. Stubbins has really, really good security here. You know that. I don't think any missiles will ever get to his ship. We're—"

"But you ain't all the way sure," Ava said, with a mixture of defiance and fear that tore at Marianne's heart.

"No," she said. "Nobody can know exactly. But I'm pretty sure, and meanwhile we're going to stay down here until the all-clear sounds."

Allison said, "Yes, and we're going to play a game. See—I've got the Fantasy Fighters deck right here. It's like online, only more fun. Ava, what character do you want to be?"

Ava said, "Snot Thrower."

Marianne watched Allison skillfully engage all four children, arranging them with their backs to the TV. Bless Allison. Marianne turned back to the screen. Initial reports put at least twenty-seven dead at the SpaceX site. The ship was a total loss.

There had been seven "Deneb ships" being built in the world. Now there were six.

The missile had been a modified SS-1e Scud-D, carrying a high-explosive warhead, fired from a mobile launcher twenty-five kilometers away. The launcher was quickly found. The three men on it were dead by their own hands. They wore ACWAK uniforms.

Judy and Marianne sat in the mess hall at midnight, the only ones there. The scientists, engineers, and workmen at the *Venture* site went to bed early, woke up early, worked long hours. Benjamin Franklin would have been proud of them. A bottle of scotch rested on the table between the women, and a salad plate overflowed with Judy's cigarette butts.

Judy said, "We should have anticipated this. The Russians sold Scuds to every third-world country they could."

Marianne said, "We're not a third-world country."

Judy gazed around the cinder-block mess hall, with its cheap metal tables and chairs, its scattered computers with their monitoring systems to spy on anyone who used them. "Are you sure about that?"

"Third-world countries can't build anything like the *Venture*."

"No. But then, the good old US of A isn't building it, is she?" Judy sipped her coffee. "Jonah Stubbins is."

Marianne didn't answer.

Judy said, "Oh, Christ, here comes Ahab. Look, say you were smoking these, all right? I'm in enough trouble as is." With a single fluid motion she was off the bench, across the room, and out the opposite door.

Stubbins didn't seem to notice her departure. Nor did he comment on the cigarette butts. He stood in the doorway, gave a small lurch, and then stumbled toward Marianne. Plopping heavily onto the bench, he fumbled for Judy's glass, knocked it over, and gestured toward the scotch.

He was, Marianne realized, toweringly, monumentally drunk.

"Gimme drink, sweetheart."

Marianne didn't want to be alone with Stubbins in this state. She smiled, pushed the scotch toward him—only a few fingers' worth remained in the bottle—and said good night.

"Stay a minute. Damn Scuds—next time that could be my ship."

The sudden pain on his face cut through his sloppy drunkenness like detergent through grease. Marianne suddenly realized this could be an opportunity to obtain information from Stubbins. *In vino veritas.* It had sometimes worked with Kyle, although the information she got from her alcoholic ex-husband never turned out to be anything she wanted to hear.

But before she could frame her first question, Stubbins said, "Sweetheart, you know why I'm so rich?"

"Don't call me that, please. We are not sweethearts."

He laughed, a loud bray. "No. But damn, I shoulda married somebody like you, not those bimbos I allus picked."

"Belinda is hardly a bimbo."

"No. She's a shark. Bes' negoti . . . negotit . . . bargainer I ever saw."

Marianne could believe that. Belinda had bargained herself into reconstructive surgery and probably a big financial settlement. Marianne said, "About the *Venture*—"

"Too bad I can't use Belinda on World," Stubbins said. "Might need good bargainers. Swee—Marianne, know why Earth's going to hell?"

There were several things she could have answered, but before she said anything, Stubbins was off. He held his glass—Judy's glass, which he'd filled with the last of the scotch—so loosely that Marianne kept expecting it to fall from his huge hands and smash.

"World going to hell 'cause-a Darwin."

She hadn't expected that. "Darwin? Charles or Erasmus?"

"Don' go cute-intellectual on me. Charles. Survi'al of the fittest. People don' take responsibility for themselves, expect everybody else to do it for them. Unfit don' deserve to survive."

"So you'd murder, or murder by neglect, people born 'unfit' who might turn out to be Beethoven."

"Beethoven—you liberals allus bring up Beethoven. Or Temple Grandin. No, thass not what I mean. Physically unfit is nothin', tech makes that irrel . . . unrel . . . don' matter. I mean unfit to take the risks and pay the price of movin' forward. Capitalism, I mean. The pure thing. And bringin' society along with you."

"Far too often," Marianne said, "the capitalist risk-takers have had other people pay the price. A risk to mine ore, but the miners get the cave-ins and black lung. A risk to finance a railroad, but Chinese laborers die laying the tracks through mountains and across deserts. A risk to finance nuclear power, but the officials and scientists don't live anywhere near the reactors. A risk to—"

"Would you rather be without the ore and railroads and power?"

She was silent.

"You're an honest woman," Stubbins said, somehow managing to sound both more articulate but no less drunk. "Naïve but honest. So answer me honest. Would the country be better oof—I mean, better off without steel and railroads and airplanes and power grids? Would you wanna live in a country without 'em?"

"No," she said reluctantly, "but—"

"No 'buts.'"

"Jonah, that's what people like you never see! There are always 'buts'! Every issue is complex, shades of gray, not black and white."

"Oh, I see that. I jus' don' get lost in gray."

"But—"

"If human beings gonna survive, it'll be because somebody took risks. Big risks. Your own speeches said that."

"Yes, but I meant the risks of building the government spaceship, of going to World—"

"Which I'm doin'."

"Yes, you are. But Jonah—what else are you doing? After we arrive? What risks are you going to take, and with whose lives?"

For a breathless moment she actually thought he was going to answer her. His face changed, going from the triumph of his supposed victory in their debate to an expression quieter, more somber. But all he said was, "That coulda been my ship blown up by those Scuds."

She said, "Pure capitalism is one of the most exploitive and inhumane economic systems ever invented."

He grinned. "Hobbled capitalism gets nothin' done."

"Depends on what you want to do."

"Absolutely right," he said. "And on somebody with the guts to do it."

"Ivan the Terrible had guts."

"But no vision." Stubbins stared into the middle distance—at a vision only he could see? Or merely at the squinty illusions of someone too drunk to make sense?

Then he added, with one of the lightning changes that so bewildered her, "I give back, Marianne. I do good while makin' profits. And 'profit' ain't a dirty word."

"I never said—"

"As good as said." And then, as if mourning a lover, "Poor bastards. And that coulda been *my* ship. No way. Never let it happen."

"Good night, Jonah."

"*My* ship. No way." He raised bloodshot eyes to hers. "Never."

Colin's dreams had gotten worse. Now he had three bad dreams: Daddy being more trapped underground than Brandon's elephant. Paul killed by Colin's tree branch. And now large purple monsters blowing up the *Venture*. If that happened, Colin would never get to ride on it. Jason said they probably wouldn't get to ride on it anyway, but Colin didn't believe him.

Daytime was a lot better, especially since Ava came. Jason was their leader because he was the oldest, but the other three could hear the ground and plants and everything. Colin didn't have to teach Ava how to arrange the noises in rows. She was better at it than he was. She could hear more sounds, too, and she knew what more of them meant. Colin was jealous.

But Ava couldn't read, not even the few words Luke knew. She was smart, she told the boys, but something was wrong with her brain. Letters and numbers just went "swimming" in front of her eyes and wouldn't stay still long enough for her to make sense of them.

Colin pictured the alphabet with fins and goggles, swimming all over the page. He could see how that would make reading hard.

Ms. Blake tried. She guided Ava's hand to draw letters in sand, so that Ava's muscles would learn the letters even if her brain couldn't. It didn't help, and school had finished with Ava throwing sand at everybody and screaming bad words at Ms. Blake.

On a clear, cool day the four children lay on a patch of weedy ground behind a building and a tiny woods. They were pretty near the inside fence, which had barbed wire on it but no electricity like the outside fence, where the guards walked. Colin, Luke, and Ava pressed their ears to the ground while Jason kept watch.

"Hear that sort of thump-thump-whistle-thump?" Ava said.

"Yeah," Colin said. "That's the biomass saying that something not-too-big is walking around."

"Us," Luke said proudly. A week and a half of comparing what they'd figured out about the plant signals going through the soil, and they all knew more than before. Even Luke, who had much less trouble remembering this than how much was six plus two.

"Duh," Ava said. "What else?"

Colin said, "That tree over there wants water."

"Duh again. Everybody knows that. You're such a baby, Colin."

"Am not!" Colin said. To prove it, he hit her.

"Stop that!" Ava screamed. "If you don't, I'll sneak into your room and dump gasoline on you and set you on fire, so help me Lord!"

Luke shuddered, but Jason just rolled his eyes. Colin was a little scared, but he said, "You can't."

"Yes, I can!"

"I'll . . . I'll make a tree fall on you!"

The three of them looked at him. Jason frowned—was he remembering the tree branch that fell on Paul? Colin said desperately, "I'm sorry, Ava. Look—I'll . . . I'll do those alphabet letters Ms. Blake told you to write for homework."

"She'll know it were you and not me, dummy."

"I'll write them all wobbly so she'll think it was you."

"And then when I cain't write them in school she'll *know* it warn't me."

Colin didn't know what to say next. But Luke did. He said, "The sounds can teach Ava her letters."

"What?" Jason said.

"That's how I learned. It's hard, but if you make lines when the sounds come . . . I can't say the words."

"Then show us," Jason said. He jumped up and found a discarded stick, one of the many splinters of lumber lying all over the camp. He handed it to Luke, who took it helplessly.

Luke said, "Don't look at me. I don't like it when people look at me."

"Okay," Jason said. He looked at the dirt beneath the stick. Colin and Ava, arms folded scornfully across her chest, did the same.

"Well," Luke said slowly. "Remember that whistle? From the tree past the fence?"

"Yeah," Ava said, "it wants water. So what?"

"I think that sound in my mind and I make these lines because Ms. Feldman said that it starts 'tree.'" Carefully, as if the two lines had no connection with each other, he drew a line and a top: T.

Ava said doubtfully, "But do those lines always start tree? Or do it change?"

"I think always."

Colin felt a sudden jolt in his head, like his mind sat down too hard. Luke couldn't sound out words, couldn't see how letters spelled things. Luke only memorized lines which didn't mean anything to him, because he'd made letters go in some sort of rows in his head, connected to sounds that weren't the letters' sounds. And Ava couldn't even do that, unless Luke could teach her.

Luke did, with enormous patience. After half an hour, Ava could draw T, V, and A, and write her name. Good thing it was so short! But when Colin, wanting to help, asked her to name things that started with T, she hit him again.

"Ow! Stop that!"

"Then stop trying to teach me! You cain't! Only Luke can!"

"Someone's coming," Jason said. Colin heard it; the subtle change in the background noise of air and ground. Footsteps. Colin even knew whose.

"Well, young'uns, here y'all are. Your grandma and Ms. Blake say to come on in, you're late for dinner. Having fun out here?"

"Yes, sir," Jason said.

"Good, good. Come on in now. Don't want the womenfolk mad, do we?" He lumbered off.

Ava looked after him with eyes sparkling with hatred.

Jason said. "Why don't you like him?"

"He's bad. Bad, bad, bad! He don't love Mama, he don't even like her, he said he'll marry her just so's he can get me. And he don't like me neither. He just uses me for all those tests while Mama's gone to the hospital to get her face fixed. I'm sick of tests all the time. Even if Devil Stubbins's gonna fix my face, too."

Fix her face? And her mother's face? Could Mr. Stubbins do that? Colin thought Mr. Stubbins could only build spaceships. And he'd never seen Mr. Stubbins do anything bad.

She said, "Just 'cause my mama's crazy don't mean he should treat her like he do."

"What does he—"

"Oh, shut up, Colin, you're such a baby." She stalked off. Colin didn't understand any of it. It was the first thing he didn't even want to understand.

Ms. Blake was sick with something. She was in the infirmary, which was a little hospital in camp, littler than the one Daddy was in or the one where Ava's mama was away getting her face fixed. Colin liked Ms. Blake and hoped she got better, but the great thing was that Grandma didn't know yet that the teacher was sick. So after some grown-up came to their classroom to tell them that and then left again, nobody told them where they were supposed to be.

"We should go find Grandma," Jason said.

"No!" Colin said. He was mad at Grandma today. She'd found them all playing *Ataka!* and asked them where they got it. When Jason said "From Mr. Stubbins," Grandma's mouth got all pressed together and she made them show her how to play it. Then she said it was too violent and deleted it off the player, and it was Colin's *best* game. He was almost to the third level.

Jason nodded. He was mad at Grandma, too. He said, "Then let's go on a hike. We'll take provisions."

Colin didn't know what "provisions" were but they turned out just to be food: apples and water bottles and some stolen cookies. The children slipped between buildings, trying to not be seen, until they were at the edge of camp. Then they crawled across a place with deep grass, pretending that bad guys were after them. Then they ran into the tiny woods and collapsed, laughing. Jason tossed everybody an apple.

Ava let hers roll away. She said, "There's people down there."

Colin, still holding his apple, tipped himself over and pressed his ear to the ground. Ava was right.

Jason said, "What do you hear?"

"People," Ava said. "In a cave."

Colin nodded. They'd all listened to the underground buildings all over camp, most of which were filled with machinery. They also listened to a few real caves, small spaces that Grandma said were mostly filled with mud. This cave was like the underground bunkers for attacks but bigger. Colin said, "People are down there—and mouses! I mean, mice!"

"Cool!" Jason said. "How many mice?"

"Lots," Luke said. "I wish we could see them."

"Well, we can't," Jason said. "Because then the people would see us."

Ava said, her ear pressed to the dirt, "Them people are mad."

They were; Colin could hear it, too. Not real words, but angry noises. He didn't like to listen to angry people, so he was glad when Jason said, "You know what—let's look for mice up here!"

"Yeah!" Luke said.

They walked around under the trees, Colin, Luke, and Ava as carefully and quietly as they could, listening hard. Jason kept lookout. Colin found a mouse first, not underground but scurrying across a little clearing. "Look, there!" But by the time the others turned their heads, the mouse was gone. Still, Colin had seen it clearly: a tiny brown mouse with a black stripe down its back, little ears, and a really long tail.

Ava said, "Over here!"

The boys raced to her. The only thing to see was a small hole in the ground, but when Colin, Ava, and Luke put their ears to the ground, they could hear them clearly.

"Six babies," Luke said. "They want their mommy."

"Let's wait to see her come home," Jason said.

They settled down around the hole and waited. Colin got thirsty, but he didn't want to move until Jason said to. Finally Jason said, "She's not coming home. And we have to go back."

They got to their feet. The walk back wasn't as much fun as the hike out. But still, it was a good day. Mice were a lot more interesting than people, even angry people underground. And Jason said they could come back every day to check on the baby mice. Maybe the mother mouse would even come home while they were there. Maybe the babies could be pets. And maybe he'd see that other mouse again, the striped one.

Colin was really glad that mice were back in the world.

Marianne visited Ryan every two weeks. A helicopter took her directly from the *Venture* site to Oakwood Gardens. Ryan never seemed either better or worse. Marianne carried on a mostly one-sided conversation with her son, although she could see he was trying to be present for her, trying to fight his way up from the dark cave into which he had fallen. When the effort exhausted him too much, she left, still smiling, careful to not let her face collapse until she was outside. On a day of wind, threatening snow, she was hurrying across the frozen lawn on her way back to the waiting chopper when Tim Saunders suddenly materialized at her elbow.

She gasped, "How did you get in here?"

"Climbed the fence. Security here is shit. Marianne, I gotta talk to you. It's urgent."

Looking at him, Marianne felt a faint echo of the desire that had propelled her for so long. Tim looked good: tanned, lean, his blue eyes intense as always under the tousled fall of mahogany hair. But the echo was faint. And nothing in his face said that he was rushing back to her out of unconquerable love.

"Okay. Talk." It came out harsher than she intended.

"Yeah, here is good. But first . . . just let me . . ." He moved toward her, his hands moving over her body. She jumped back, but then realized he was checking her clothes for trackers. He found one. Carefully he removed it, carried it several yards away, and laid it on the winter grass.

Marianne was outraged—how dare Stubbins? But then she realized she was not as outraged as she should be. A Scud had just destroyed the SpaceX ship. Stubbins needed every single precaution, and privacy versus security was an old, old story.

Tim returned. "Tell your chopper pilot—who's looking at us hard—that I'm an old flame still carrying the torch, okay? I'll say this quick. You know I never liked that Earth for Humans gunman outside your apartment right as you came home, or that kid who knew Colin's real name at his school—both just felt hinky. So I've been digging."

Marianne, already cold in the January wind, went colder.

"The gunman got caught on the building security camera and I—"

"How did you get access to those recordings?"

Tim didn't even bother to answer. "Got a photo of the guy, did some asking around. He does work for a man who sometimes gets things done for Stubbins. Okay, that's not much to go on. But the kid who knew Colin's name and all about you, Paul Tyson, his father is a vice president of something at Stubbins's Manhattan sales headquarters for the perfumes. And Tyson's a very old friend of old Jonah himself. And he—no, don't turn away, listen to me—just got promoted to head honcho on the research project Stubbins is running at his big pharma company in Colorado to find a drug to help all those kids born since the spore cloud. Even though Tyson has no research background."

"What drug? I didn't hear about this."

"Since when does Stubbins tell about his drugs until they're on the market? That's gonna be a huge market, a drug that can block unwanted sounds for those kids without turning them into zombies like Calminex does."

"If anything like that were in the works, Harrison would know about it."

"Maybe he does. Did you ask him?"

She hadn't. Tim made a gesture of impatience that she remembered all too well.

"Focus, Marianne. I'm telling you that I think Stubbins arranged both the gunman threat and the Paul kid in order to get you to the *Venture* site."

"Why would he do that? I could have gone on writing his web and broadcast content from Manhattan."

"I don't know why. That's for you to find out."

Marianne wrapped her arms around her body for warmth. "It all seems pretty circumstantial to me."

"Uh-huh. And you seem like the trusting idiot you've always been." His face softened. "The smartest idiot, though. Listen, I have to go—your pilot is barreling over here to rescue you. I just wanted you to have all the info." He ran off, faster than the middle-aged and overweight pilot could possibly follow.

Marianne intercepted the pilot and fed him Tim's romantic lies. Was Tim being paranoid about Stubbins? As her bodyguard, paranoia had been his job description. But . . . was he right?

She needed to have a talk with Jonah Stubbins. This time, she would keep hunting until she found him.

CHAPTER 22

S plus 6.5 years

The mice were disappointing. The mother mouse did not come home, the striped mouse did not reappear, and the baby mice stayed underground where Colin could hear them but not see them.

The children sat yet again around the mouse hole, waiting for something to happen. Colin was cold, even though he had on his parka and Grandma kept saying how warm this winter was. The trees above them had no leaves, except for the Christmas trees and one big tree with dead brown leaves that just stayed on it and didn't fall. The little woods had no color, not even in the sky, except for some red berries that Grandma said were poison. Maybe Ms. Blake got sick because she ate the red berries. But she was a teacher so wouldn't she know better? Colin was worried about Ms. Blake. She was still in the infirmary. Colin had gone there and pressed his ear to the building and he heard lots of things—people, machines, plants—but not Ms. Blake's voice. He missed it. And he never even saw any mice.

"This is stupid," Ava said. "We been here a really long time."

"You only came with us once before," Jason said, "but we've been here lots, waiting. So you can wait, too."

"It ain't my fault if Devil Stubbins needed me for more fucking tests!"

"Don't use bad words," Colin said.

"Will if I want to."

"Luke doesn't like it," Jason said.

Ava looked from Colin to Luke. It was true that Luke didn't like any kind of fighting or cursing. And it was also true that Ava liked Luke best, even though he was slow and Jason was their leader. Ava was always kind to Luke. Colin didn't understand that but at least it was something good. He went back to watching the mouse hole.

And then he heard it. "Shhhh! She's coming!"

All four children froze. Luke and Ava turned just their heads, their bodies still, in the direction of the noise. Jason followed their gaze. He couldn't hear what Colin heard, the high *screeeeee,* but in another minute they all saw her.

The mommy mouse staggered from a bunch of dead leaves toward the hole. She fell down, got up, fell down again. Her brown fur—no long stripe on her back, she was just a regular mouse—was all weird, standing up in patches. She was really skinny. All at once her body started to shake hard as she kept making that awful noise: *Screeeeeeeeee!* And then she gave a huge shake and lay still.

Nobody spoke until Jason said, "I think she'd dead."

Ava said, "I don't see no blood."

"Maybe she died of sickness," Jason said.

Colin didn't like that, because of Ms. Blake. What if she died, too? He stared at the dead mouse.

Luke burst into tears. "Without their mom, the baby mice will die!"

"No, they won't," Ava said. "We'll take care of them. Don't you cry, Luke."

"We don't know how to take care of baby mice," Jason said.

Then Colin had an inspiration. "We'll take them all to Grandma! She used to have mice at her work, she told me. She'll know how to take care of the babies, and maybe she can even fix the mommy mouse!"

Jason stared at the corpse. "I don't think so. It's pretty dead."

"Well, let's bring it anyway."

Luke said, "We haven't got a box."

"That's okay," Ava said. "We got clothes." She pulled off her parka. It was pink, but the mommy mouse was a girl so that was okay.

"Don't touch the mice!" Jason said. "Pick them up with clothes!"

Carefully, Ava scooped up the dead mouse with her parka.

Colin said, "We got to get the babies." He started digging dirt away from the hole.

The babies were deeper than Colin thought, but they got them out. There were six, but two were already dead. Jason put the live ones in his parka and Colin put the dead two into his pockets, lifting them with brown leaves. Luke took off his parka and made Ava wear it. The baby mice kept on crying for their mother.

Colin really, really hoped that Grandma would know what to do.

It took Marianne almost a week to find Stubbins. First he was "off-site" at one of his companies. Then she'd "just missed him" at the mess. There was a warm cup of coffee in his office but no Stubbins. Finally she ran him to ground on the bridge of the *Venture,* where she was not supposed to be but Judy told the duty guard it was urgent that they see Mr. Stubbins stat. The guard knew that Judy was a scientist, and she'd put on her most intimidating look. They went aboard.

So this was the twin of the ship that had taken Noah away to the stars. Marianne was surprised all over again at how small it was. She'd always imagined the Deneb mother ship to be even larger than an aircraft carrier, but the *Venture* wouldn't have filled a football field. A quarter of the interior was taken up by the shuttle bay, another quarter by storage. The drive machinery was encased in some sort of field that involved both quantum entanglement and dark energy. There may or may not have been an unknown version of wormholes connected to the star drive. That anybody would ride in this ship was an act of insane courage.

The rest of the *Venture* was divided into a small bridge at the bow and, behind it, a large living area. This contained partly unfinished seats, sleeping cubicles, kitchen, bathrooms, communications systems, none of which were specified in the plans. The basic machinery was Deneb but the fittings would be Terran. Marianne picked her way among crates, tools, and workmen listening to loud rock as they riveted.

Over the din Judy yelled, "You asked once if I'd go? In a New York minute. But my frustrations aren't the point today, are they? Good luck, Marianne." She left, running her hand lovingly along a gleaming curved bulkhead. All the beauty and grace the campsite lacked was embodied here, at least potentially, in the alien ship that humans were trying to make their own.

The door to the bridge stood open. Beyond it, Stubbins loomed large, listening intently to two engineers. If he was surprised to see Marianne, he didn't show it.

She listened to the rest of the engineers' report, unable to follow most of it. When they left, Stubbins followed. Marianne said, "A word, please, Jonah."

"Not now. I gotta—"

"It's about Carl Tyson and his son Paul."

Stubbins stopped, looked at her.

Marianne said, "You might want to close the door."

He did. Marianne told him what Tim had said about Paul and the gunman in Manhattan, making the connections sound more definite than Tim had actually found. She finished with, "I don't expect you to admit any of this. What I want to know, right now, is why you so badly wanted me here at the *Venture* site. Why you paid for apartments, bodyguard, the kids' school, Ryan's treatment, all of it. Why you brought me here."

He said, "Your insider's view as a force shaping public opinion about—"

"Bullshit. Two dozen people could have written those articles, and if we changed even one person's mind in this polarized political atmosphere, I've yet to hear about it. It was Colin you wanted, wasn't it?

Not me. The research on your new drug under hush-hush development in Colorado, the one to help the generation born with hyper-hearing issues—you wanted to run fMRIs and other tests on Colin's brain, to find out what is different about him that he can handle the auditory bombardment. How did you even find out he could? The testing company I first took him to, right? You were collecting that sort of data."

Stubbins said nothing, watching her.

"But then you found Ava. She's better at that than even Colin is, and you can get agreement from her mother for pretty much anything, including things that I might balk at. Just offer to marry Belinda."

"Marianne," Stubbins said, and now his voice had gone avuncular, "maybe it's good that we're having this conversation. If you are really unhappy here, maybe it's better if you and the boys go."

She hadn't expected that, hadn't been thinking far enough ahead. Where would they go? A laboratory job might be impossible to find, given her notoriety. Perhaps her old college would take her back. Most universities were, for various reasons, pro-Deneb. Even if she couldn't get tenure-track again, or at least not right away, maybe she could negotiate a year-to-year contract until something opened up.

"Maybe that is best," she said to Stubbins. "But I need a few weeks to make arrangements. At least. Can I stay here that long?"

"Of course. Stay as long as you like." He waved his hand magnanimously, a cheap fake-regal gesture, and she thought how much she disliked him. Then he made one of his chameleon changes of personality. "Marianne—don't judge me too harshly. If I can bring this drug to market, the one that suppresses the neural firings that respond to hyper- and subsonic sounds, I can help a lot of families. And I want to. As much as I want to launch the *Venture*."

Impossible to not believe him. She had never met such a complex person, such a mixture of idealism, ego, and crassness. She hoped to never meet one again. Jonah Stubbins bewildered her.

"Best of luck to you, Marianne," he said—with genuine feeling, as far as she could tell—and lumbered off the bridge.

She was in the mess, sending e-mails on her laptop, when Judy dropped onto the chair beside her. Judy's voice was husky and she held, against all rules, a burning cigarette. "Allison is really ill."

Alarm ran through Marianne; Allison dealt so closely with her pupils. "Not just a stomach virus? Is it a virulent strain of flu? This is flu season. Is anybody else ill?"

"Nobody else, which makes me think it's not flu. Everybody is supposed to get vaccines immediately. It'll be on the PA soon."

"Vaccines for *what?*"

"They're not saying."

"Judy, that's ridiculous. You can't vaccinate people without telling them what for. That's illegal."

"Oh, they'll tell us something. But will it be what Allison really has? If it were flu, somebody else would be sick. Especially the kids, since she works with them, and I saw them tearing toward your room just a few minutes ago, healthy as wild pigs. It's not flu. So what is it?"

Judy's innate paranoia? Maybe. "How do you know that Allison is that sick? And what are her symptoms?"

"Nurse at the infirmary is a friend of mine. Fever, chills, and nausea to start, now low blood pressure, vascular leakage, kidney problems."

"Couldn't that be a lot of different things? And if she were really ill, wouldn't they move her to a real hospital?"

"Maybe. My friend isn't nursing Allison, she's in isolation and the only doctor who's treating her does everything, including bedpans."

"Well, for quarantine . . ." Vivid memories flooded Marianne of her own quarantine aboard the *Embassy*. But that had been for *R. sporii*, a truly dangerous microbe. *"Or so we thought,"* she suddenly heard in

Evan's voice, ghostly across seven years. "But still, a vaccine requires full disclosure."

"If you say so." Judy ground the cigarette onto the concrete floor, left it there, and walked off.

Marianne picked up her laptop and went to her room. All four children waited there and Judy was right: They looked healthy in a wild, hectic sort of way. Two parkas lay bunched up on the table. One squeaked.

"Mice!" Jason cried. "Grandma, we got to show you something!"

Six pups of *Mus musculus*, two of them dead and the other four not looking good. A dead doe with thin and patchy fur lay stiffly in what looked like a convulsive position. No blood or other evidence of predation. She said as calmly as she could, "Did you touch the mice? Any of you?"

"No!" Jason said proudly. "I told everybody to pick them up with their clothes!"

Colin, looking more troubled, said, "Can you make the other babies stay alive?"

"I don't know, honey. Probably not." Most diseases did not jump species. But some could: rabies, avian flu, MERS. And rodents could be carriers of human diseases without being affected themselves, although these mice certainly had been. So not hantavirus, not bubonic plague, not a lot of things. Probably just a mouse disease, something else that, if it spread, would again complicate ecological recovery.

"I want you all to go take a good shower, with lots of soap. Wash your hair. Don't put the same clothes on again. Just in case you might get whatever disease the mice have, okay? Let's do that now."

Ava, staring at the mice, said, "I don't want to die."

"Nobody's going to die, honey. I promise."

Colin, focused on his main concern, said, "But can you make the babies well?"

"I don't know, Col. We'll try."

He stuck out his lower lip. "The other mouse was well. It ran fast."

"What other mouse?"

"The other one. The *striped* one."

There should be no striped mice in this part of Pennsylvania. She said, "You can draw me a picture later. First, a shower."

Marianne put Ava in her own shower and the three boys, one after the other, in theirs, carefully bagging their clothes in plastic and giving Ava some of Colin's, which fit her skinny little body well. Who had been looking after Ava since her mother went off-site for plastic surgery? Marianne felt guilty that she hadn't even asked. Stubbins must have found someone; he always did.

And what of Luke, now that Marianne would be taking her grandchildren away with her?

She pushed that thought aside for now. She didn't even have a position at the college yet. When the kids were clean and dry, the announcement came over the PA—Lyme disease had stricken a staff member. Everyone would be vaccinated, purely as a precaution.

Allison Blake's symptoms, as described by Judy, didn't sound like Lyme disease, which was tick-borne. Marianne examined the mouse pups, dead and alive. None of them carried ticks. And Lyme disease did not kill *M. musculus*.

Colin brought her the drawing he'd been working on while Ava, Luke, and Jason played something noisy on their Nintendo. Colin had always been an exceptionally good artist for his age. He'd used his colored pencils and worked carefully.

Marianne took the picture and her spine stiffened as if she'd never move again.

"What is it, Grandma? Why do you look like that? Is that a bad mouse? Did it trap those angry people we heard down in the cave under the woods?"

"Marianne, it's the middle of the night! What's happened? You look—Come in!"

Harrison stood frowzy and alarmed at the door of his—once their—apartment in the secure enclave near Columbia. She'd insisted that the gate guard phone him, just as she'd insisted that the chopper pilot take her immediately to Ryan's home because her son had tried to commit suicide. The pilot had of course checked with Stubbins, who'd okayed the trip. Marianne would feel guilty later about using Ryan's illness like that. The chopper departed and the cab she had waiting at Oakwood Gardens drove at crash-worthy speed south to New York.

"You're the only one I can trust, Harrison. There's something going on at the *Venture* building site and—"

He said sharply, "The kids?"

"Okay. I left them with Judy. This is—"

"Who's Judy?"

She'd forgotten his methodical, careful way of assessing a situation: dig out all the facts, arrange them in rows, study them. It steadied her. You didn't win a Nobel Prize with wild assumptions, nor with excesses of either trust or paranoia. She had always admired Harrison's mind, and now she needed it.

"Judy is a friend, a physicist at the site. I need to tell you all of this, but first let me show you some data points. Dead mice and a picture."

He looked at both. He said, "That's *Apodemus agrarius,* the striped field mouse. It's not found in the United States."

"It is now," she said grimly. Another invasive species. "And it carries Korean hemorrhagic fever with renal syndrome. You remember that German scientist did the initial work on HFRS infecting *Mus musculus,* probably from *Apodemus,* and then the American team led by Samuel Wolski extended it." From her bag she drew the six dead, plastic-wrapped pups.

Harrison studied them. "I'd need to do lab work on these, of course. Do you have live specimens?"

"Not anymore. Harrison, there's a woman at the *Venture* site ill from what I think may be HFRS. The rest of us have been vaccinated, but we were told it's for Lyme disease."

"Why do you think it wasn't? And that whatever killed these mice is in any way related to your sick woman?"

"I can't know for sure. But I brought you a vaccine sample—I stole it, actually." She'd pretended she couldn't breathe, sending the nurse out the room to summon a doctor, and had pocketed a vial of vaccine.

He frowned and ran a hand through his thinning hair in a gesture she remembered well. "I can do tests, of course, Marianne, but the vaccine for Korean hemorrhagic fever isn't even available in the United States. They use it extensively in China and Korea, but it isn't FDA approved."

"That wouldn't even slow down Jonah Stubbins."

"Stubbins?" Harrison grimaced. "No, probably not. But still . . . the disease is transmitted through inhalation of aerosolized rodent urine or feces. Transmission rates aren't high with proper pest control."

"That's another thing I want you to investigate," Marianne said. "To find out if the virus has been genetically altered to go airborne."

"Marianne—why on Earth would anyone—"

"Not on Earth," she said. "On World. As a weapon, or a threat of weapon. Find out. Please."

CHAPTER 23

S plus 6.5 years

Everything was bad.

The mice all got dead. Everybody had to get a shot in the arm, which hurt, and Colin felt sick for a whole day after his. Grandma said they had to leave the spaceship camp, her and Colin and Jason, and Colin didn't want to go. Luke wasn't going and Ava wasn't going—they got to *live* here. But Ava wasn't here now because she had to fly with Mr. Stubbins someplace for some more of those stupid tests. Two weeks had gone by since Grandma told them about leaving, and Ava had been gone that whole time.

"Everything's shit," Colin said, trying out the forbidden word. He only did that because Grandma had left her laptop to go to the bathroom, while Jason and Colin did math on their tablets and Luke struggled to read something to himself in the corner. His lips moved. They were the only ones in the mess hall because it wasn't time to eat and anyway why weren't they in their own room where they usually did lessons? Maybe because Grandma looked a lot at her laptop.

"Not everything's shit," said Jason, who liked math better than Colin did. Colin liked drawing and reading but not math. "Grandma said Daddy was getting better and pretty soon he can come live with us again."

Colin said nothing. He liked living here better than he'd liked living with Daddy.

"And Ms. Blake is getting better, too."

"She isn't better enough to teach us," Colin pointed out. "And when she is all better, we'll be gone and we'll have a new school and new kids to get used to and that'll be shit, too." He thought of Paul Tyson.

"Maybe it will be good," Jason said, entering an answer on his tablet. "There might be enough kids for a soccer team."

"I hate soccer," Colin said, although he'd never played soccer. Right now he hated everything. Everything was shit. And he couldn't figure out how many apples were left over if you divided seven of them up evenly for Pat and Pam and Cam. Who cared if those stupid girls got any apples anyway?

Jason said, "Why are you so grumpy?"

"I don't want to move away."

Jason sighed. "Col—"

"I'm going now." The idea burst in on him like a firecracker. He could walk out of this room! Grandma could make him leave the camp for good and miss the spaceship launch and everything, but she couldn't make him sit here and do this math. She had really disappointed him! That's what she said when he or Jason did something bad, they'd disappointed her, but this time *he* was the one who was disappointed. No camp, no mice, no Luke or Ava forever and ever. He had a right to be disappointed!

He got up and walked to the door.

"Hey!" Jason said. Luke stared with big eyes.

Colin opened the door and darted through it, real fast, before Grandma could come out of the bathroom. He knew where he was going and he ran as fast as he could. Behind him he heard Jason, still going "Hey! Hey!" and then Luke. Jason was taller and Luke was bigger and all three boys reached the spaceship at the same time.

Jason panted, "What . . . do you . . . think you're doing?"

Colin didn't answer him. The spaceship door was open, but two workmen inside were doing something to a door and they would just tell him to go away. So he walked—he was too tired now to run—around to the other side of the *Venture*, where there was no door. There was a guard but he was used to the boys and just went on reading his comic book. Colin slumped to the ground, his back against the side of the ship, which was called the "hull." It felt warm from sunshine. Then Colin heard it.

Luke did, too. Luke said, "There's mice in there!"

Colin pressed his ear to the hull. The sounds were clear and high. He rearranged the rows of noises in his head to hear the mouse sounds more clearly. "A lot of mice."

"They're mad," Luke said.

Jason said, "Let's go in and see them!"

The boys crept back around the ship. The door was still open but the workmen weren't there. Colin led the way through the airlock, into the big room where some seats were ready and some still in big boxes. To Colin's surprise, he heard Mr. Stubbins on the bridge. Did that mean Ava was back? Then why wasn't she at Grandma's school? Mr. Stubbins said to somebody, "Damn it, there has to be a door on that toilet! *Make* it fit!"

A workman—Colin could see part of him now, on the bridge—answered. "It won't fit, sir. It just won't."

Luke said, "We shouldn't be here."

Jason said, "Luke's right. Let's go."

But Colin didn't want to go back to math and to Grandma—who was going to be even madder than the mice—and to leaving camp forever. Another firecracker idea burst into his head. "I can't go! I have to rescue the mice!"

"Rescue?" Jason said.

It was like Brandon and the elephant in the basement! Colin was the hero who would rescue the mice, who were probably mad because they were trapped in their cages. But Colin didn't have time to explain that because the two workmen, frowning, came back from the bridge. Jason and Luke ran through the airlock and outside. Colin yanked open a door and ducked behind it.

The mice weren't here. It was a big empty space except for a smaller ship: the shuttle. The walls of the room had cupboards, mostly open and mostly empty. Colin climbed into one and closed the door. He just fit. Perfect—he could stay here until night when everybody left, and then he could go out and rescue the mice.

After a while it got cramped in the cupboard, but Colin stayed in there because that's what rescuers did. He could hear everything: the mice and the workmen and Mr. Stubbins rumbling to somebody else on the bridge and the ship making its metal-ship sounds and the underground machines and the real ground under that. All of it.

But it was cramped and he wished everyone would go home.

The e-mail arrived while Marianne was in the bathroom. She heard the laptop ping with the specific sound she and Harrison had set up as a signal, and she finished hastily and rushed out to the mess. The boys were gone.

"Jason? Colin? Luke?"

No answer. They'd run off. She was surprised because all three were usually obedient, but Colin and Jason had both been angry with her ever since the announcement that they were leaving the *Venture* site. She'd deal with them later. This e-mail was the reason she'd been teaching the boys here instead of in the classroom.

Her heart began a slow, arrhythmic bumping in her chest.

Harrison had written using the code they'd worked out, he skeptical that such *"cloak-and-dagger histrionics"* were necessary, she increasingly sure that they were. Each sentence meant something entirely different than its ostensible content:

My dear Marianne—

Not "dear Marianne" or just "Marianne." The dead *Mus* had tested positive for hemorrhagic fever with renal syndrome.

I find myself thinking about the time we spent together in the harbor, at Columbia, that day in Central Park . . .

Harrison's hybridization analyses of the postmortem material had found either antigens or the viral RNA itself in the mice's brain, liver and spleen.

. . . and, especially, that memorable boat ride on the Hudson.

A small groan escaped her. That was the worst. The virus's genes had altered so that it could infect via a respiratory route. Either that evolution had occurred naturally, or there had been a long, intensive effort to change the genome.

I guess what I'm saying is that I would like to see you again . . .

Colin's identification of the striped field mouse had been accurate. *Apodemus* had been imported to carry the virus here. Or rather, not here—to World.

She had no doubt now that Stubbins had imported and altered the virus, or that World was his target. *Apodemus* was an incredibly adaptive rodent, and Terrans already knew it was not killed by the spore cloud. Stubbins had stockpiled vaccine in case it was needed for just such an emergency as Colin's escaped mouse. World would have no vaccines, no natural immunity. Judy's speculations did not look quite so paranoid now. If Judy was right and World did not know as much genetics as Stubbins's scientists did, Worlders would be vulnerable to even the threat of the disease. This version of HFRS was the most deadly, with a kill rate of 15 percent—and that was not counting what other microbes the mice might carry as they slipped, silently and pervasively, into whatever World cities looked like. And even if alien microbes killed the mice, the rodents would leave behind droppings, urine, carcasses, all infected with airborne viruses.

Smallpox to the Indians.

But *why*? What could Stubbins gain? Not revenge. Whatever the Russians might want, Marianne didn't think that Jonah Stubbins was after vengeance. For that, you had to care about what you'd lost, and Stubbins cared for no one and nothing except profit. So—these mice were bargaining chips, threats, to obtain something from World. Trade, or tribute, or power, or maybe just survival.

There was one more piece to Harrison's message: *Eagerly awaiting your reply, Harrison.*

He was notifying the CDC.

Folded up in the cupboard, Colin suddenly had to go to the bathroom. Was there a bathroom on the spaceship? There must be because every place had a bathroom, even parks, although Grandma wouldn't let Colin use park bathrooms by himself. Colin wished he were in a park now. He crossed his legs.

There were less people in the ship now. Colin could hear every one of them, if he looked at the right rows of sounds. Closest was Mr. Stubbins, still on the bridge, rumbling at two men and Grandma's friend Dr. Taunton. Colin was supposed to call her Aunt Judy, she said so, but he never did because she wasn't his aunt. Aunt Elizabeth was his only aunt, and he hardly ever saw her because she lived far away in Texas, where she played with guns. She didn't like children anyway.

What if Grandma took Colin and Jason to live with Aunt Elizabeth? Well, he wouldn't go, he just wouldn't! So there!

Crossing his legs wasn't helping.

Marianne was still staring at Harrison's message when Jason and Luke burst into the mess hall, panting, their faces gleaming with sweat. "We lost Colin!"

Marianne grabbed Jason's arm. "What do you mean, you lost him? Is he hurt? What happened?"

"He ain't hurt, ma'am," Luke said, and belatedly Marianne saw that Jason was more excited than alarmed. Some sort of boyish adventure, then. But Colin was barely six.

She forced herself to calm. "Tell me what happened."

"We went to see the spaceship," Jason said. He propped himself with one arm against a table and pretended to pick a speck of dirt off his sleeve. Marianne recognized the attempt at casualness to cover transgression; she'd seen it in Ryan, just this same pose, all his life.

Jason continued. "There were people coming out of the bridge so we ran but Colin didn't come. Maybe he wanted to find the mice."

"Mice? What mice?"

Luke said in his slow, labored speech, "Mice on the ship. Lots."

Stubbins was stocking his weapons. Oh dear God. How close was liftoff? Who knew? "Where did Colin go?"

"We don't know," Jason said. "Maybe he's still on the ship? Or he ran away to hide? He's mad at you, Grandma, 'cause he doesn't want to leave camp." After a moment he added bravely, looking directly at her, "I don't want to, either."

"I know. We'll talk about it more. But right now I have to go find Colin. You two stay right here, do you hear me? I mean it. If I find out that you left the mess hall again . . ."

"Yes'm," Luke said. He hung his head. Jason did not, but he sat on a bench and halfheartedly picked up his tablet, still displaying math problems.

Marianne moved at a fast walk to the *Venture*. She was not seriously worried about Colin, who was only acting out his displeasure at leaving. But what Stubbins planned was bioterrorism. Harrison would, of course, think first of the CDC; he focused on pathogens. But if Marianne was right and Stubbins actually intended to menace World, if he was bringing infected mice to threaten or retaliate—

She didn't know how men like Stubbins thought. She never had. But others did know, the military and the FBI, and that's where the CDC would report. The president. The UN. What was left of NASA. Something would be done. It was out of Marianne's hands, and she knew that what she felt was, in part, a cowardly relief.

The door of the *Venture* stood open. Inside, two workmen were installing a door on a bathroom. Marianne was surprised at how complete the interior now looked. Seats bolted to the deck, tables, a wall screen that said "Sony," a giant coffeemaker on one wall. The interior was being customized for Terrans. Doors led to the bridge, the shuttle bay, the aft storage area. Were the mice back there?

"Well, hold the fucking door steady!" one of the workmen said to the other.

"I told you, it won't fit! No matter what the old man says!"

"Well, we need another one, then. We're done here for today."

Marianne went through to the bridge. Stubbins was there, along with Judy and the chief engineer, Eric Wilshire. Behind Stubbins stood his bodyguard, whom Marianne had never heard called anything but "Stone." He was huge, muscular, and blank-faced. Not usually around when Stubbins was at the ship, Stone's presence suggested that Stubbins had just returned from another of his off-site trips.

Judy carried an unlit cigarette and looked annoyed. "Eric, I've explained and explained. The plans are mostly pictorial and mathematical, so we're guessing at all the effects, and even though the shielding seems minimal there's evidence that the repulsion factor doesn't exceed the—Hey, Marianne."

"Hi. Jonah, is Colin here?"

"Colin? 'Course not. Why would he be here?"

Stubbins gazed at her, and Marianne felt a shiver in her brain, as if he could see directly into it. See her thoughts, know what she now knew. He was preternaturally insightful, as aggressors often were. Was her body language giving away her revulsion, her fear, her fury at what he planned to do? Or was she responding to one of his infernal pheromonal scents? No, that was fanciful; she was under too much stress; her suppositions were ridiculous.

No, they weren't. Stubbins knew she'd discovered something. He knew.

She said, "Colin ran away. I know he's fascinated with the ship so I thought maybe—"

Judy, oblivious but helpful, said, "He isn't here, Marianne. We're just winding down for the day."

"Okay, I'll just—"

Then everything began at once.

Aaarrrrr! Aaarrrr! Aaarrrr! Blat blat blat!

Sirens sounded, just like a fire engine but a lot louder. Colin had heard those sirens once before, when the bad guys fired missiles at the other spaceship and wrecked it. The *Venture* was getting attacked!

He burst out of the storage cupboard and fell, his legs wouldn't work right, they were all cramped up. A moment later he was up. He ran through the door from the shuttle bay just before it swung shut and made a locking sound.

The big door to the airlock swung shut and locked, too, but not the bathroom door because there still wasn't one. Colin bolted for the toilet and made it just before it would have been too late. Only the toilet didn't have any water in it or pipes; it wasn't hooked up yet. He didn't care.

Grandma's voice behind him—what was Grandma doing here? Nothing made sense! "Colin, what are you . . . oh my God!"

Colin finished peeing and turned around. The wall screen in the big room was filled with a man's face. He looked familiar, like somebody Colin had seen around camp. He also looked scared.

"Incoming, incoming," the man said. "Impact in ninety seconds. . . . Jonah, the *Venture* is the target! Eighty-five seconds . . ."

Bad words were shouted from the bridge, a very lot of very bad words. Mr. Stubbins. Colin didn't know what to do. Then Mr. Stubbins said, "I'm lifting," and Dr. Taunton yelled, "No!" and Grandma grabbed Colin and he screamed, too, because all the grown-ups were so scared.

The spaceship made different, new noises, coming to life.

Dear God, the Venture was *taking off.*

Marianne grabbed Colin, who stood with his jeans around his ankles, pissing into a pipeless toilet. Stubbins cursed from the bridge, loud raspy noises as if the very words choked his throat. Judy yelled something—

Judy. What had Judy said, months ago? *"A very real fact—no one knows what will happen the day we finish the ship and press the button to start her."*

But nothing seemed to be happening, not even motion. No press of gees on Marianne's body, no tilt to the floor, nothing to say the ship was lifting except the clanging shut of the airlock and shuttle bay doors and the two images on the wall screen, now split between the twisted face of the ground officer and the land falling rapidly, silently away beneath them.

"My pants!" Colin cried. "Let me go!"

"Twenty, nineteen, eighteen—" said the ground officer.

An aerial view of the building site, then the no-man's land around it, then the perimeter fence and guard towers.

"Grandma, my *pants!*"

"Thirteen, twelve, eleven—"

Hills and farmlands coming into view. Frightened cows raced away from the thing in the sky.

Marianne released Colin, who yanked up his jeans. On the bridge Stubbins still shrieked and Judy matched him in volume. The door to the storage bay flung open and a man stumbled out, his face ashen. *"Jonah—"*

"Seven, six, five—"

Marianne threw Colin into one of the seats—as if that would help anything! The ashen-faced man, she knew him, from somewhere. . . . *"No one knows what will happen . . ."* Incoming incoming. . . .

"Three, two—"

Far below them, something streaked white across the landscape, and then the place where the *Venture* had been exploded into light and flame, almost immediately obscured by thick smoke. Marianne forced her eyes to stay open, to watch . . . no mushroom cloud. The weapon had not been nuclear. But how much of the site had been taken out? *Jason and Luke—*

She dashed to the bridge. The ship rose steadily, light as a soap bubble. Stubbins stood in the middle of the bridge, meaty hands gripping the back of the captain's chair, with Judy and Eric Wilshire in the two side chairs facing consoles, studying data displays just as if they knew what they were doing. Stubbins said, "How bad?"

The ground officer's face, pupils dilated as if on drugs, said, "A direct hit, probably from a high-explosive Scud. Hard to see through the smoke but it seems . . . two buildings severely damaged. Casualties unknown. Havers, come in, Havers . . . Johnson . . . Olvera . . ."

But Wilshire, even paler than the man in the main cabin, said desperately, "Mr. Stubbins! What—"

"Stop the ship!" Stubbins roared. And then: "Do you know how to stop the ship?"

"No one knows what will happen—"

The ship stopped.

Marianne clutched at something, anything, to keep herself upright. Her hand found the back of Judy's chair. There was no lurch beneath her feet, no sound of grinding engines. The ship simply stopped; again her dazed mind thought of a soap bubble, gently hovering. A soap bubble with perfect Terran gravity inside it. . . . My God, what forces must be contained here! How had human engineers built this?

Below, in panoramic sweep and brilliant Technicolor, lay Pennsylvania as it might be seen from a jet liner thirty thousand feet up. Life-support machinery must have switched on somewhere; there was warmth and oxygen and light.

Stubbins began to laugh.

The sound was shocking, unreal—more unreal even than the alien ship around them. "We did it!" he cried. "We fucking did it!"

Marianne felt something clutch her legs. Colin. She found her voice, although it didn't sound like hers. "Jonah—the *children*? On the ground?"

Stubbins didn't hear her. She had seen faces like that in medieval paintings, on stained-glass windows. His broad features and small eyes shone, transfigured with unholy joy.

"Jonah! The children!"

She might as well have spoken to the bulkhead. But Judy, who'd been talking in low, rapid tones to unseen people on the ground, said, "The kids were nowhere near the impact, Marianne. Jonah, NASA codes coming in."

Stubbins took her seat. Judy grabbed Marianne and dragged her off the bridge, Colin still clinging to her. "You don't belong here. Classified. They don't need me in there. Kid, you all right?"

Colin nodded. The man who'd burst out of the storage bay stood uncertainly beside a crate. Judy said, "Who the fuck are you?"

"I know who he is," Marianne said because, all at once, she did. "Wolski. Samuel Wolski, the geneticist. You did that work on HFRS infecting *Mus!*"

Judy started back toward the bridge but stopped as if shot when Marianne said, "The infected mice. They're aboard, aren't they? To release on World."

Wolski, cowering, moved behind the crate, as if Marianne might attack him. Every organ in her body turned to mush. She'd been right, then—Stubbins had weaponized mice and was prepared to deliberately cause a plague on World if he thought it might help him get what he wanted. And now the *Venture* had lifted and was on its way to . . . oh, God, was the ship steerable? Or was its alien technology preset on one route, a sort of interstellar trolley on fixed and unalterable tracks?

Judy exploded, "Infected *mice*? Here?"

"Judy," Marianne managed to get out, "is the *Venture*—"

But Judy had turned away. She had heard, as Marianne had not, the shouting on the bridge, even through the thick metal door. Judy flung it open and bolted back to the bridge.

Marianne hesitated, then grabbed Colin and dragged him with her. She wouldn't leave him with Wolski. And if the *Venture* was about to self-destruct, or vanish into some other dimension, or plummet to Earth, she wanted to be holding Colin when it happened.

The *Venture* did none of these things. The bridge had the focused air of a high-stakes poker game, the shouting suddenly over. Stubbins sat in the captain's chair, facing a screen showing a room full of people in uniform. Wilshire occupied the second chair, Judy the third.

"No," Stubbins said, quietly. Yet the word had the force of an avalanche. He touched something and the room full of uniformed men and women, suddenly moving very fast and with faces rigid with anger, all disappeared. Stubbins's ground officer reappeared.

"Confirmed, Jonah. I'll put it on tracking."

The central screen in front of the captain's chair split into two, with the officer on one side and a graphic on the other. An arc of the Earth, looking like a blue marble—had the *Venture* resumed flight? Marianne had felt nothing. Beside the arc were two dots, one blue and one green, moving toward each other.

Judy made a low sound that Marianne had never heard anyone make.

Marianne's mind raced. Human communications systems on the *Venture*—and what else? As long as the drive machinery and life support and other technical aspects of the Deneb plans weren't altered, anything could be added to the ship. Military tracking systems? Military weapons? Yes, of course. If homegrown terrorist groups could obtain Russian Scuds, what couldn't Jonah Stubbins obtain on the international black market?

Or *was* it the black market? Had the US Army . . . No. That room full of angry soldiers had not approved of whatever Stubbins was up to now.

"Judy," Marianne said, because it was clear that no one else would answer her, "what are those blue and green dots?"

Judy didn't reply. She was rapidly typing on a keyboard and examining data brought up on her screen. But Stubbins heard Marianne and he said, still in that deadly voice, "Get off the bridge. Now."

Marianne stayed where she was. But she said to Colin, "Go back to your seat and stay there. Do you hear me?"

At her tone, he stuck out his lip, but he went. No time now to worry about Wolski.

"You, too," Stubbins said, without turning around. Marianne didn't move. Judy suddenly sank into her chair and her head snapped back as if she'd taken a blow, but a moment later she was back keying in commands.

"Stone!" Stubbins bellowed.

The bodyguard moved toward Marianne. Effortlessly, as if she were Colin, he picked her up and carried her, flailing pointlessly, to the door. He shoved her through and slammed the door to the bridge. A second later she heard the lock click.

Colin cringed in his seat, looking very small. Marianne, scarcely knowing what she was doing, went to him and he crawled onto her lap. Wolski had disappeared. Colin began to talk, but she didn't hear him.

She had caught a snatch of Wilshire's conversation with the tracking station on the ground. She knew what the two moving dots on the screen, so small beside Earth, were. One was the *Venture*. The other was the Russian ship *Mest'*.

The *Revenge*.

Colin was scared. Nobody was acting right. It should have been thrilling to be up on the ship out in space—especially since Jason and Luke and Ava didn't get to go, only him—but it wasn't. Grandma was holding him too tight and that big man who was always with Mr. Stubbins had locked them out of the bridge and Colin had peed in a toilet with no pipes so that he couldn't even flush his pee away. It was just sitting in there for anybody to see because there was no door on the bathroom.

And the big wall screen had nothing on it to look at.

But at least that changed. Somebody on the bridge must have done something because all at once a picture of Earth—Colin was proud that he knew what it was—came onto the screen, with two dots moving near it.

"Grandma, is that a video game? Can I play? Where's the controller?"

Grandma didn't answer. A second later sound got added to the picture, but it was just Aunt Judy and Mr. Stubbins and that other guy on the bridge. Aunt Judy whispered, "Marianne, one-way comm," and then there was only the other two grown-ups, saying things Colin didn't understand.

But maybe Grandma did, because she got even weirder. She went all stiff, like the mice that had died, and for a horrible minute Colin was afraid that Grandma was dying, too. But she wasn't, so he said again, "Where's the controller? Can I—"

"*Be quiet,*" she said, so mean that Colin was shocked. Grandma was never mean to him! Nothing was right!

He jumped off her lap. She said to him, "Sit down and don't say anything." It was her obey-me-or-else voice, so he did. But he picked a seat behind her so that when she wasn't looking he could leave the room and go hide again. That would show her!

Tears prickled his eyes. He hated everything.

After a moment he got up and moved—carefully, soundlessly—toward the storage bay. He could hear the mice someplace in there. Right now, mice were nicer than Grandma. Quietly, Colin opened the door, slipped through, and closed it behind him.

Judy had routed audio-visuals to the screen in the main cabin. Marianne listened, and looked, and found she could barely breathe.

The *Mest'* had lifted because the *Venture* did. To the Russians, it must look as if the *Venture* was going to beat them to World. Or were they afraid of some other kind of attack that these ships were capable of but ordinary weapons were not?

She knew nothing about weapons, ordinary or alien. But Noah and Ambassador Smith had both told her that the Denebs were peaceful, did not engage in warfare. Had Noah been deceived and Smith lying? Or had Stubbins's engineers, as well as those on the *Mest'*, discovered ways to use the drive machinery as a weapon? Dark energy, Judy had told her. Quantum entanglement.

No. There was no reason for this much paranoia. The *Venture* had lifted because of the Scud, and the *Mest'* lifted because the *Venture* had. In a moment the *Venture* would set back down in Pennsylvania, and the *Mest'* would set back down at Vostochny because even if vengeance was the Russians' motive for building their ship, they weren't any more ready for an interstellar voyage than Stubbins was. The UN would be working on this mess right now. Vihaan Desai was no longer Secretary-General, but the newly chosen Lucas Rasmussen of Denmark was a man of peace. In just a moment the *Venture* would return to Earth . . . dear Lord please let Wilshire know how to actually control this thing. . . .

Stubbins's voice said over the open channel, "Eric, get close enough to fire."

"Yes, sir," Eric said.

Marianne's throat closed so suddenly she couldn't breathe. *Fire? Fire what? Why?*

"How long?" Stubbins said.

"Assuming they don't return to Vostochny—"

"They won't," Stubbins said grimly. "Not until we do. They don't want us warning the Denebs what's coming. Those Russky sons of bitches aren't going to destroy my trade partners, much less my ship. We'll get them first. Maneuver into firing range."

"We don't know the range of anything they might—"

"Do it!"

"Yes, sir."

Breath whooshed back into Marianne's lungs. Why didn't Judy object?

Then she knew. Judy had opened the channel so Marianne could hear all this. She had not objected because she did not want to be thrown off the bridge and have it locked behind her. Judy's paranoia had paid off—she suspected this might be Stubbins's course of action. And now she and Marianne would have to stop it.

Three men on the bridge, two of them big, Stone a trained fighter. Wolski somewhere aft. The chances of she and Judy—middle-aged, unathletic, female—overpowering the men was nil. What did Judy expect her to do? Judy was the one on the bridge! But over and over Judy had told her *"I'm a physicist, not an engineer."* Marianne had no idea of how well Judy understood the human equipment Stubbins had installed on the ship, or what Judy could or could not do with the *Venture*. And Marianne had far less understanding of the ship than Judy did. So what the fuck could Marianne *do*?

She could use her brains. It was all she'd ever had.

And . . . *Where was Colin?*

Marianne pressed her hands hard against the sides of her face. Then she tried the door to the storage bay. Inside the vast space were pallets of boxes and crates; the liftoff had been so smooth that they had not shifted a centimeter. Marianne said softly, "Colin?"

No answer.

Neatly stowed against the wall on hooks and in straps were tools for opening wooden crates. Marianne freed a crowbar, then tried the door at the far end of the area. It opened.

Exactly what she had expected: a small genetics lab. The familiar equipment—autoclave, sequencer, thermal cycler—looked jolting in this unfamiliar setting. But it was she who was the jolt, who was unfamiliar even to herself. The thudding of her heart melded with squeaks and rustles from the mouse cages lining one wall.

Wolski, bent over a bench, turned. "You! What are you doing—"

"Lie down on the floor," Marianne said. "Right there. Or I'll hit you with this."

Wolski didn't move. His eyes slid sideways, looking for a weapon of his own. He stood maybe five foot eight, not muscular—could she overpower him if she had to? A close call.

"I said lie down!"

Her tone, so effective with undergraduates and grandchildren, made no impression on Wolski. He started toward her. At the look in his eyes, she struck him on the shoulder with the crowbar.

He cried out and went down, grabbing at her legs. One of his arms got around her knees and she felt herself wobble. Fury filled her. This man—this son of a bitch travesty of a scientist who would set a plague free on strangers, on Noah, for potential profit—this *insect* would not get the best of her. Even as she was collapsing on top of Wolski, she swung the crowbar at his head.

A sickening crack.

He slumped to the floor and she fell on top of him.

Marianne scrambled away, still clutching the crowbar. Blood streamed from Wolski's head. But head wounds always bled a lot, that didn't mean he was that badly injured, didn't mean he was dead. . . .

She crept back toward him, took his limp wrist in her hand. He was dead.

She, who opposed the death penalty even for serial murderers, had just killed a man.

Weirdly, in numb shock, a line from an old novel came to her: *"I won't think about that today. I'll think about that tomorrow."* Who? What book?

Then she pushed Margaret Mitchell's potboiler out of her mind and staggered to her feet. This was an animal lab, which meant mice were sacrificed for autopsy, for tissue extraction, for DNA sequencing. What she needed would be here, somewhere.

She began opening cupboards and drawers. None were locked. Wolski had not anticipated anyone in here who might be a threat.

Colin heard Grandma call him, but he didn't answer. He had wedged himself between two big mountains of boxes in the storage place, and he was still mad at Grandma. Let her look for him!

But she didn't. He heard her open the door to the room where the mice were, then close it. The spaceship was so strange—Colin could hear every sound it made, but never in his whole entire life had he not also heard noises from the ground and the plants and the clouds. There wasn't any ground or plants or clouds. He didn't even have to put the sounds he heard in rows. The sounds in here—

The sounds got ugly.

Low talking, then louder talking (although he couldn't make out any words), and then a scream! A crack! Something heavy fell to a floor.

Colin whimpered and shrunk back into his hiding place. But— Grandma had gone in there! What if that mouse man had hurt Grandma? Colin would have to rescue her, just like Brandon rescued the baby elephant in the basement. It was his job.

Still, he wished Jason and Luke and Ava were here to help.

In another minute he would go.

Somebody was slamming doors around in the mouse room. Then, a really loud smash.

In just one more minute he would go, as soon as he remembered just what it was that Brandon had done to make a rescue.

There it was. In the last cupboard she opened, the only one locked. She smashed the lock with the crowbar, smearing Wolski's blood onto the metal door.

A part of her mind noted that she had become somebody else, somebody who could do these things without flinching. Adrenaline. Cortisone. Amygdala activation.

Necessity.

She had expected the ketamine and other anesthetics, although not in such large quantities. What she had not expected was the large, zippered leather case. But it made sense. Stubbins had not known, because nobody knew, what fauna might exist on World. And Stubbins was a man who believed in thorough preparation.

SURE-PRO VETERINARY TRANQUILIZER SYSTEMS said the lettering on the leather case. Inside were two pistols, syringe darts in graduated sizes, CO_2 cylinders, and a puff sheet with maximum hype and minimum directions.

> Best and most versatile dart pistol ever made!
> Allows user to safely inject an animal without close and dangerous encounters!
> Fingertip muzzle velocity control!
> Rotating rear barrel port for quick and efficient loading!
> Virtually silent!
> Made in America!
> "The best product I know—I use it all the time!"—James R. Strople, Chief Animal Control Officer, Colorado

And in much smaller letters:

> Individual response to tranquilizing agents may vary widely.
> Proper certification is necessary to administer any type of chemical immobilization.

Strangled laughter rose in Marianne; she recognized it as hysteria. A second sheet of paper included a table of suggested doses for various tranquilizing agents on different animals. Hands willed into steadiness, she followed the directions to load a CO_2 cylinder, good for six shots, and a dart with the ketamine dosage for a black bear. She practiced ejecting and loading darts, then put four more in her pocket.

How long did she have? How long did it take for a blue dot launched in Russia to get within firing range of a green dot launched in Pennsylvania? When both "pilots" had to learn how to steer their ships?

Nonetheless, she took the time to practice-fire a dart. She was startled by the force with which the syringe left the pipe and buried itself in Wolski's dead arm.

Bile rose in her throat.

No time, no time.

She reloaded and ran from the lab through the storage bay. Carefully she cracked the door to the main cabin and peered out. Empty.

On the wall screen, the blue and green dots closed in on each other.

Grandma walked past real fast, without seeing Colin peeking out from behind the pile of boxes. All the air went out of him. Grandma was okay! He didn't have to rescue her, and she was okay!

He waited to see what would happen next. But all that happened was Grandma went out of the storage place back to the big cabin, holding something that Colin couldn't see very well.

When everything was quiet again, Colin crept out from behind the boxes. Behind the other door, mice squeaked and moved. He wished he knew what they were saying to each other. Something had happened in the mouse room, and curiosity took him. He tiptoed to the door and opened it.

A weird smell, not mousy. He inched into the room.

A man lay on the floor. Blood ran out of his head in little rivers. So much blood! It was the same man Colin had seen before in the big cabin. Somebody had killed him. It must have been Grandma, because nobody else had been in here.

If Grandma had killed the man, then he must be very bad. Maybe he was going to hurt the mice.

Colin crept closer. He'd never seen a dead person before. But it wasn't really gross because this had been a bad man. Colin squatted on his heels, looking carefully, so he could tell Jason and Luke exactly what a dead bad person looked like. He had a thing sticking up out of him; it looked like the little blue things that popped up on a turkey when it was all roasted and ready to come out of the oven. Did everybody have those things in them, to pop up when they died? Maybe Jason would know.

But what had the man been going to do to the mice that made Grandma kill him? It must have been really bad. Colin left the corpse and went over to the mouse cages. The mice weren't *Mus*, they were like the other one that Jason and Colin and Luke and Ava had seen in the woods: grayish-brownish-reddish with long black stripes down their back. Their cute little ears twitched.

What if the bad man had other bad people to help him hurt the mice? Pretty soon, probably, the *Venture* would go back to Earth. More of Mr. Stubbins's people would come aboard. Some of them might also be mouse-hurters. And there weren't enough mice left on Earth— *everybody* said so!

Colin stood on one foot, chewed on his bottom lip, and thought hard. He hadn't had to rescue Grandma. But he needed to recue something. Mice shouldn't be hurt just because they were little. And probably they didn't like the smell of the bad man's blood any more than Colin did.

One by one, Colin opened the mouse cages. Some mice stayed inside but some, especially those in the cages closest to the floor, scampered right out. Then, because they were so cute, Colin scooped up two mice and put them in his pocket. They just fit.

He opened the door and made it stay open with a stool he dragged across the floor. A few mice ran out the lab door, toward the smells of food farther into the ship.

Softly Marianne tried the bridge door: locked from the inside. She would have to get Judy to open it. But how? Over the wall screen Marianne could hear what was said on the bridge, but Judy had told her that was one-way communication. And of course, Judy had no idea what Marianne was going to do. Judy just hoped Marianne would do *something*.

Beyond the door, Stubbins said, "Time until we're in range?"

Wilshire said, "Another half hour, if everybody holds speed and direction."

"Judy—any indication that this boat is gonna jump into hyperspace or anything like that?"

"I told you, Jonah, we have no fucking idea. I'm still trying to figure out what the drive is already doing, let alone what it will do."

"Well, keep trying," Stubbins said, and Marianne heard the dangerous edge in his voice. "Eric, NASA still jabbering at us?"

"Yeah, but we can arrange it so we have credible deniability."

Stubbins grunted. Marianne thought: *He's actually going to do it.*

This man was going to shoot down a Russian spaceship, despite what had to be a barrage of data coming at him from NASA, from the military, from the White House, from the UN. Maybe even from the Russian ship itself. How did Stubbins think he would get away with this? Would "credible deniability" be enough? Or was his massive narcissism so out of control that he thought nothing on Earth could stop him?

Nothing was.

Or maybe he planned on not going back to Earth afterward. If Wilshire and Judy could fly the *Venture* from here to World, there would be no human rivals to challenge Stubbins's trade plans. Stubbins would arrive with only a fraction of the specialists he'd planned, but maybe he thought he could still negotiate—or wrest through terrorism—whatever he was after. The energy shield that had protected the *Embassy* so completely? With that, he might well be nearly invincible.

Judy said, "Jonah—I need the bathroom. Now. I really cannot wait."

"Stay where you are!"

"All right," she said, "but in about twenty seconds this bridge is going to stink of diarrhea and you're going to choke on the stench. I'll be gone maybe a minute. Nothing is going to happen in the next minute."

Wilshire said, "Christ, Judy, we don't even have a working bathroom."

"There is," she said with great and patently fraudulent patience, "a commode. Better than a pile on the bridge deck. A very loose and runny pile."

"Oh, go!" Stubbins said. "Women!"

Marianne moved quickly from the line of sight from the bridge. She raised her loaded dart gun. If Stone accompanied Judy . . .

He didn't. Judy slipped out alone and closed the bridge door behind her.

"I'm here," Marianne said, gun raised. A sudden panic took her. What if she was wrong, if Judy hadn't opened that one-way communications channel in order to gain Marianne's help, if Judy was actually *aiding* Stubbins. . . .

"Oh, thank God—what is that?" Judy said.

"Tranq gun."

"You couldn't get real firearms?"

"No!"

"Okay," Judy said. "What's in the gun? How long does it take to work?"

"Ketamine. About two minutes."

"Two *minutes*? That's your plan? Those fuckers can pull out a dart in two minutes!"

"Plan? You think I've had time to put together a plan? Judy!"

"Okay, sorry." She wrinkled her face into a fantastic topography of determination and fear. "We can make it work. Give me the gun. I'll bet you've never fired a pistol in your life."

True. Marianne said, "If you can hit the neck, that's best. If—"

"No, wait," Judy said. She darted to the bathroom and picked up a heavy wrench left by the workmen. "I'm going in first, and you fire. I'm going to hit Stone in the knees, break his kneecaps if I can. Hold the door open a tiny bit until you hear that, then rush in and fire at him first, then at Stubbins. Keep firing—do you have to reload?"

"Yes."

Judy groaned. "Well, Stone first, then Stubbins. Eric's a wuss. We have surprise on our side. Let's go."

"Judy—if we take them out—then what? The *Mest'*—"

"One problem at a time. Ready?"

Marianne nodded, lying. She would never be ready for this. A sense of unreality fogged her mind: *I'm a geneticist, not Delta Force.* Then she crowded close behind Judy to go in.

The rest of the mice wouldn't leave their cages. Probably they were scared. Colin was. The smell of the dead bad man was making his stomach all funny, so he left the lab and walked carefully through the storage place. The two mice stirred in his pocket but they couldn't get out.

"I'll keep you safe," Colin whispered to them. "We'll find Grandma."

The mice made mouse noises, but that didn't help.

He opened the door to the main cabin. Grandma was by the door to the bridge, her back to him, but before Colin could say anything, she rushed through and the bridge door closed behind her.

The door was left open only the smallest bit, but Stone saw it. "Shut the door," he said to Judy. Marianne heard them not through the door but through the open channel of the wall screen.

Judy said, "God, that hurt. My ass—hemorrhoids—"

"I said—Arrhhhh!"

Marianne flung open the door. Judy had succeeded in whacking Stone in the knees, and he'd fallen back against the bulkhead. Marianne fired. The dart hit him in the neck. His face twisted into an expression she'd never seen on a human face. He roared, yanked out the dart, and threw himself toward her. Judy whacked him on the back of the head with the wrench and he went down.

But now Stubbins was on Marianne, wrenching the dart gun from her hand. He shouted something she couldn't hear, something was wrong with her hearing, all sound blurred into a single noisy buzz. Jonah had the gun in one hand and his other came up and backhanded her across the face.

Words emerged in her head from the general buzz: *If that had been his fist, I'd be gone.* But it hadn't been his fist and although the pain was incredible, *But not as bad as childbirth*—what a time to think of labor now—she rolled away. Judy tried to hit Stubbins with the wrench but he batted her away. She fell to the floor and threw it at him. It hit him in the face and his bellow filled the bridge like a gale.

He picked up the wrench and advanced on Judy.

Marianne had not the slightest doubt that he would beat her to death. Stubbins had dropped the tranq gun. Marianne crawled over to it and began reloading. But there was no time, no time—

Wilshire, who'd sat frozen in his chair, came to life now that the odds were so heavily in Stubbins's favor. He jumped up and pinned Judy to hold her against the bulkhead just to the left of the door, so that Stubbins could better attack her.

"Stop!" a little voice cried. Colin stood in the doorway. "Don't hurt Aunt Judy!"

Stubbins turned his head briefly, saw Colin, and turned back to Judy. He raised the wrench high above his head.

Something hit him in the face, then another something.

Mice. Colin had thrown two mice at Stubbins. Where had Colin gotten . . . oh God. . . .

The soft squeaking projectiles distracted Stubbins just long enough for Marianne to stagger up and fire. The dart lodged itself in Stubbins's neck. He groped to pull it out.

If Wilshire had still been holding Judy, Stubbins's momentary pause wouldn't have made any difference. But Wilshire shrieked, "Those mice are infected!" and let go of Judy. The mice, dazed, ran around on the floor. Wilshire pushed past Colin and ran off the bridge, slamming the door behind him. Judy rolled away from Stubbins.

Marianne loaded again and fired.

Stubbins pulled out the second dart and started toward Marianne. Judy leaped onto his back. She didn't have the wrench, but she reached around his head and gouged at his eyes. He roared and reached behind him to throw her off. She didn't let go, wildly jabbing at his eyes, and they spun in a crazy tarantella around the bridge. While they struggled, Marianne reloaded and fired her last dart. It hit Stubbins in the shoulder, easily penetrating his shirt. Judy shifted from her unsuccessful attempt to reach his eyes and instead grabbed his arms, trying to keep him from pulling out the dart. Marianne rushed over and hit Stubbins with the empty tranq pistol.

He struck out with his fist, connecting with Marianne's left shoulder. She gasped with pain but kept hold of the pistol in her right hand, striking him with it until with a huge final roar he grabbed her arm, flung her across the room, and threw Judy off his back. He pulled out the dart.

Colin was trying to catch his mice. Before Marianne could even yell, "No, Colin—don't touch them!" Stubbins had the boy in his arms.

There was sudden quiet on the bridge.

"Sit in that corner," Stubbins said, "both of you, or I'll kill him."

Marianne cried to Judy, "Do it!"

Judy crept to the corner. Marianne followed her. Colin whimpered but didn't cry. Marianne focused on Stubbins. His last words had slurred a little. How much of the ketamine had gotten into his bloodstream?

Individual response to tranquilizing agents may vary widely.

"You . . . you . . . ," Stubbins said.

Keep him talking. "Jonah, don't hurt Colin. We'll do whatever you say, go wherever you want, are you taking the *Venture* to World, do you know how long the voyage—" She had no idea what she was babbling, she just wanted him to respond, to do anything except hurt Colin—

"Let me go," Colin said clearly.

Stubbins's eyes rolled in his head. His big body slumped. Just before he fell over, Colin slipped from his arms and landed upright on the deck, as neatly as if climbing out of bed in the home he didn't have.

With Stubbins and Stone both down, pain rushed back into Marianne. For a moment blackness took her, but she fought it off. There was no time now for shock.

"Colin, are . . . you . . . okay?"

"Yes," he said. "Are you hurt, Grandma?"

"No," she lied. "Judy?"

"I think my arm's broken."

"I'll get first aid and—"

"No!" Judy said. "Lock the bridge door."

"I'll do it!" Colin said. "I know how!"

Yes, of course—Wilshire was still somewhere in the ship. Marianne did a quick body check on herself. Bruised and hurting but nothing seemed broken. She said, "I have to go out there, Judy. We need rope to tie them up. I don't know how long Stubbins will be out."

"Don't tie up Stone," Judy said grimly. "He's dead."

That made two men they'd murdered. Marianne pushed away the thought and turned to Colin. "You sit up on that big chair, you hear me? Don't touch anything, including the mice!" The two mice still ran frantically around the bridge, which lacked crevices to hide in. One settled for cowering under what had been Wilshire's chair. Marianne, Judy, and Colin had all been vaccinated, the supposed "Lyme disease" vaccine—but what if the mice carried something else besides Korean hemorrhagic fever? Did Wilshire know; was that why he was so afraid?

Everything on Marianne hurt. But she picked up the wrench and cautiously opened the door. Both mice ran out. Wilshire was not in the main cabin. Marianne tore open random lockers: no first-aid kit or rope but she did find duct tape.

When she returned, locking the door behind her, Judy had dragged herself into the chair she'd occupied before—the communications chair?—her arm hanging limply by her side, her face twisted with pain. "Can you tie up Stubbins?"

"Yes." She taped his hands together. As she started on his ankles, Stubbins twitched. Before she'd finished, his eyes opened.

They stared at each other.

Stubbins tried to buck his huge body toward her, but it was a feeble motion. Some ketamine still remained in his system. Then he started to curse, language so foul that Colin's eyes opened wide. Marianne ripped off her shoe and then a sock and stuffed the sock into his mouth.

Judy laughed, the sound shaky but shocking. She did something else to the controls in front of her and all at once the cabin was filled with Russian voices.

"I have a channel open to the Russian ship," Judy said unnecessarily. "Can you speak Russian?"

Marianne had only the phrases she'd learned to address a cleaning lady she and Kyle had once had: *Please to clean stove today* and *Need more soap?* She understood nothing of the sentences swirling around her. "No!" she said to Judy.

"Well, one of us better try. Look."

Marianne glanced for the first time at the blue and green dots on the wall screen. They had moved much closer to each other.

Judy said, "I don't think they can see us. Go."

"Can they fire on us?"

"How the fuck should I know? *Go!*"

Marianne sat down in the seat Judy vacated, the drop into the chair a harder jar to her aching body than she expected. She said loudly, "*Mest'*! This is Dr. Marianne Jenner."

Sudden silence. "I am on the *Venture*." Maybe if she used simple words, someone aboard the *Mest'* would know enough English to understand. Although the *Mest'* had taken off as suddenly as the *Venture* and so was probably without a linguist. "We will not fire. This is a mistake!"

A torrent of Russian answered her.

"I don't know what they're saying!"

"They're moving closer," Judy said. She had taken Wilshire's chair. And then, very softly, "I can fire first."

"What? No!"

"Marianne, I'm not getting blown up when there's a way I can defend myself."

"You have no reason to think they'll—"

"Why else are they moving closer?"

Marianne's guts churned. She hadn't known, hadn't suspected this side of Judy. The Russian torrent became more insistent. Marianne said, "Nyet! Nyet! We will not fire! We will land our ship!"

More Russian.

Then Colin said at her elbow, "Say this, Grandma: 'Sdayus.' It means 'I surrender.'"

"What . . . how do you know that, Colin?"

He hung his head. "*Ataka!* The game you wouldn't let me and Jason play."

A tremor shook her whole body. "Can you say, 'I will not fire'?"

"You said that was a bad game."

"Tell me."

"It might not be right."

"Tell me anyway! 'I will not fire.'"

He screwed up his little face. "I think . . . maybe . . . it's sort of like 'Strelyat' ne budu.' That's what Ivan says in level two when he puts down his gun."

Marianne repeated the strange sounds, twice.

No response.

She turned back to Colin. Can you say, 'We both should land now'?"

He shook his head.

"Try, Colin! Maybe 'We go back now'?"

"What if I get it wrong?"

Then we all die. Her six-year-old grandchild looked at her from clear gray eyes. Colin's little body stood stiffly beside her elbow. His lip trembled. She had no idea how much of this he understood.

She said gently, "Do the best you can, Col. 'We go back now together.'"

"Maybe . . . 'Poshli obratno umeste'?"

She said to the unseen Russians, "Poshli obratno umeste," and held her breath.

A long silence. At the other console, Judy did something. Arming warheads?

She cried, "We go back together now! Poshli obratno umeste!"

Another eternity, and then a heavily accented voice said, "You first."

Judy didn't know how to land the *Venture*. However, she didn't need to. As soon as she opened the communications frequency, NASA ground control took over. People who had worked on the United States Deneb ship destroyed by the superstorm three years ago were hastily brought online. It seemed there were hundreds of people who understood how to control the Deneb crafts, if not the underlying forces that animated them.

Not, Marianne thought, unlike human minds.

Stubbins, lying on the cabin floor, worked steadily and ineffectively at Marianne's duct tape and made noises around the sock in his mouth. Both women ignored him. Marianne sat in the captain's chair, Colin on her lap. Judy, in what had been Wilshire's chair, followed instructions from NASA—*push that button, then these two simultaneously, then*—and the ship took over. The *Venture* landed lightly as a butterfly in the no-man's land between the inner and outer fences of its building site. Immediately the ship was surrounded and besieged.

Judy sagged in the chair, her broken arm dangling at her side. Once the ship was down, she allowed her face to contort in the full assault of pain.

"*Venture*," said a man's voice on the encrypted channel that served the building site, "this is the FBI."

Stubbins groaned.

"Who am I talking to?" said the FBI—Marianne incongruously pictured the entire Hoover Building squatting on the Pennsylvania scrub—in a calm, subtly reassuring voice. "Jonah Stubbins?"

"No," Judy said. "This is—" She moved in her chair and gasped with sudden pain.

"Let me," Marianne said. She put Colin down as far away from Stubbins as possible in the cramped space and stood behind Judy. Public speaking was what she did. "This is Dr. Marianne Jenner. Dr. Judith Taunton and I are in control of the bridge, and Jonah Stubbins is in our custody for assault, attempted murder, and bioterrorism. Dr. Taunton is injured."

"This is Special Agent in Charge Jack Warfield. Are you coming out of the *Venture*, Dr. Jenner?"

"Yes, of course we are. But first we need help. An engineer, Eric Wilshire, is somewhere else in the ship, I don't know where. He may have found weapons. I have a child with me here. I can't open the door from the bridge to the main cabin until I know we'll be safe."

A long pause. Then Agent Warfield said in that same hostage-negotiator voice, "I see. Why might Eric Wilshire be a threat to you?"

Because we've hog-tied his boss and killed two other men. Marianne didn't say this. Whatever she did say now was going to be very important. There were going to be investigations, hearings, maybe even trials for murder. She needed to present everything in the best possible light.

She said, "Has the Russian spaceship returned to Earth? We made an agreement with them that both ships would land and avert any kind of international problems. That was our first concern."

Another long pause. Warfield was conferring with someone, probably several someones. The wall screen showed the people and vehicles around the ship, and a larger mob, probably press, beyond the outer fence.

"Yes," Warfield finally said. "The *Stremlenie* has returned to Vostochny, Dr. Jenner. We can send in people to protect you and to tend to Dr. Taunton's injuries as soon as you release the door lock to the *Venture*. Can you do that from the bridge?"

"I don't know how. Judy?"

Judy shook her head.

Colin said, "Some machines are coming."

"I'm sorry," Marianne said. "We don't know how."

"We have experts here who will explain it."

Marianne followed NASA's instructions. They didn't work. She said, "The lock must be customized."

"Is Mr. Stubbins conscious? Can he tell you how?"

"He has a sock in his mouth," Marianne said, and all at once was conscious of her one bare foot. It felt cold. She had to get control of this situation.

"Agent Warfield, I'll take the sock out of Jonah Stubbins's mouth, but I don't know if he will cooperate. But before we do that, I want to tell you for the record exactly what happened here. Step by step. Can I do that? Will you please record this?"

"Certainly," Warfield said. "We very much appreciate your cooperation, Dr. Jenner. Go ahead."

Marianne took a deep breath and began. Two sentences in, bullets exploded against the door of the bridge.

"Stop shooting!" Marianne screamed. "Stop!" She ran to Colin and stood between him and the door.

"We're not shooting," Warfield said. "It's not us. Dr. Jenner, are you all right? Can you hear me?"

More bullets, a spray of missiles against the outer door. *Wilshire*. Could the bullets pierce the door? It was heavy metal, and the lock on this side, Marianne realized for the first time, was a manual bolt because Stubbins's paranoia had wanted a shield against the digital dexterity of his own crew. A last-ditch fortress. Just in case.

She shouted over the din, "It's the engineer! Wilshire! He's firing at the door with some sort of heavy-duty gun, you need to come in and stop him!"

No answer. But then she heard the high-pitched whine of a laser cutter, and the bridge wall screen went dark and shattered. They'd been ready for something like this. They were cutting their way onto the bridge, careful to destroy not the consoles that controlled alien forces nobody understood, but only the human communications devices that everybody did.

Wilshire must have heard it, too. The hail of bullets stopped.

It took an astonishingly short time for the SWAT team, in full armor, to burst through the jagged metal hole onto the bridge. Marianne, with Colin in her arms, said, "I'm Dr. Jenner." Judy gave the men surrounding her a weary, pain-filled grimace.

Marianne said, "There are mice loose in the ship, infected with a very contagious version of a deadly virus. Do not let any of them escape. I repeat—*You cannot let any of those mice escape.* Jonah Stubbins was stockpiling dangerous and illegal living weapons of bioterrorism."

Stubbins, his mouth still stopped with Marianne's sock, closed his eyes, and every muscle in his huge body sagged with epic, monumental defeat.

CHAPTER 24

S plus 6.9 years

Ryan and Marianne sat in wing chairs in the day room of Oakwood Gardens. The day room looked, Marianne thought, more like a living room in Georgetown than a mental-health center. The distinguished, dark-toned portraits on the wall could have been nineteenth-century ancestors of some senator or congressman. A bouquet of June roses sat on the mantel. The Chippendale bookcases, worn oriental rug, and nautical pillows looked like they belonged to the sort of people who summered at Newport.

They were the only occupants of the room. This was a special visit and the other patients were at lunch. A nurse hovered in the doorway, but the room was so big that her presence didn't feel obtrusive. Warm rain beat sideways against the tall windows. When Marianne had first arrived, Ryan had seemed troubled by the weather, but now his full attention was on his mother. Because he had seemed so distracted, she had begun to talk.

"The boys are with me, and Luke, too. You don't know who Luke is, do you? He was living under some murky arrangement with Jonah Stubbins. When Stubbins was arrested for domestic terrorism, I took Luke with me. We're all living near my old college. The boys are doing fine, you don't have to worry about them."

Ryan said nothing. But he looked, for the first time since he'd come to Oakwood, as if what she was saying genuinely mattered to him. She didn't dare stop talking.

"Judy Taunton will stand trial, too, for killing a man named Andrew Stone. You don't know about that and I won't explain it now, but Judy's attorney is positive that she'll get off. Actually, a whole bunch of Stubbins's people are being detained until the FBI sorts out who knew what about the mice."

Ryan didn't ask about the mice, and Marianne didn't explain. Nor did she tell him that no charges had been filed against her for Wolski's murder; the district attorney had decided it was self-defense. Marianne had no idea how much Ryan understood, or had been told, of what had happened aboard the spaceship. Maybe nothing. She was now talking as much to herself as to him, saying aloud all the things that had kept her awake nights during these last painful months. Once she'd started, she couldn't stop.

"The *Venture* has been taken over by the government. Some law about seizing property involved in terrorism. I doubt Stubbins will ever get it back."

"But you know the strange thing, Ryan? The thing that doesn't fit? Stubbins's pharmaceutical company just released the drug he developed for children born after the spore cloud. It fast-tracked through the FDA trials without a single hitch. It blocks ultrasonic and infrasonic hearing, so that those who can't do what Colin and Luke and Ava can, won't need Calminex. Won't be little zombies. Stubbins did that. The same Stubbins that could commit an atrocity like weaponizing HFRS."

Ryan didn't even blink. His steady, sharp gaze was a beacon, or her need for a beacon.

"I was wrong," she said. "Completely wrong, a hundred eighty degrees wrong. But I thought that by urging the spaceship to be built no matter what, I was helping promote human cooperation and brotherhood. That's how I felt when I was researching aboard the *Embassy*. When Harrison and I were running the Star Foundation. When I was helping Stubbins get to World. I thought that because Worlders and Terrans are both human and not separated by much evolutionary time, we should just establish open communication."

She let her hands rise, then fall back to her lap. Ryan's gaze stayed on her face.

"But I was wrong. It can't be that simple. We can't have an open highway between Earth and World. It has to be . . . oh, I don't know, a toll road. With checkpoints so that not everyone with the money and expertise can just drive past. Because you were right, Ryan. You were right all along."

His eyes, so completely without Noah's and Elizabeth's beauty, sharpened.

"No," Marianne corrected herself, "you weren't completely right. You were right to say that on World, we would be an invasive species. An organism not in its native ecological niche, infecting the Worlders with pathogens like Jonah Stubbins. He *was* a pathogen, yes. But the answer isn't to never go to World, or anywhere else. The answer is to do what Noah did, to slowly infect each other. In a controlled way. With restrictions on who can go to World, and why. And on who can come here. A slow journey toward brotherhood. Like any two clans would have done when our species was still whole, on the savannah, before Worlders left us in the first place."

Ryan said something, very low.

"I'm sorry," Marianne said, "I didn't hear you? Ryan?"

He said, "I did it."

She didn't ask what he meant. She knew. Knew, too, that this secret was what had been destroying him ever since the *Embassy* bombing. Marianne's heart shattered and rose into her throat; she couldn't breathe. Her son had arranged for Evan's death, for the deaths of the other scientists—

He said, "I gave them the layout of the *Embassy*, that you told me about. I never thought they'd bring in a bomb. It was supposed to be just a group of spokespeople, with all our arguments against the Denebs' presence, I never thought they'd . . . but that doesn't change my responsibility. I told them. I did it."

Marianne breathed again.

"No, Ryan—no. If you believed it would be only a peaceful protest, if you didn't know about the bomb . . . You can't destroy yourself with guilt because you were wrong! Everybody is wrong sometimes!" And then, as much to herself as to him, "You can't control everything."

Not ecologies, not economies, not superstorms or spore clouds or invasive species. Not one's own children.

Ryan said nothing. Marianne tried to calm herself; she was shaking. The silence stretched on and on.

Finally Ryan said the same words he'd been uttering for months. This time, however, he said them not as a cry for an uncapturable past, but with their real meaning. "Mom . . . I want to go home."

Marianne gazed at him. She saw Ryan the sturdy little boy, tagging after Elizabeth. Ryan the quiet, secretive teen. Ryan the angry conspirator, holding his anger inside. Ryan the invalid, ravaged by his own failure. This was the way it was with one's children; all the versions of them lived simultaneously in your heart.

"Yes," she said. "Let's go home."

EPILOGUE

Everything old is new again.

—songwriter Peter Allen

S plus 9 years

Sunday evenings always bustled, she thought, no matter how much planning had gone into the next week. No matter how much relaxation had taken place over the weekend. No matter how lazy the weather, like this warm August sunset of still air, humming crickets, sweet fragrance of lilies.

She sat on the front steps of her rented house, a half-eaten peach juicy in her hand, a stack of textbooks beside her. The children played in the cornfield next door, some game that involved a lot of running and shouting; occasionally one of their bright T-shirts flashed through the stalks, a pink or red or orange comet. Harrison came out of the house, suitcase in hand.

"All packed?" Marianne said.

"I travel light." He put down the suitcase and lowered himself to sit beside her. "Preparing your syllabi?"

"Nominally, anyway." The semester started in two more weeks, and she would be teaching two classes she'd taught before and one for the first time, all in evolutionary biology.

He took her hand, a little awkwardly. Their relationship, simultaneously old and new, was still finding its way and, contrary to what Harrison had just said, neither of them traveled light. Too much had happened.

She said, "Good luck with the speech in Chicago."

"Thanks." And then, "I wish you were going with me."

She squeezed his hand. She wrote Harrison's speeches so he didn't have to take too much time from his research, but she could not give them herself. No one wanted to hear Marianne Jenner talk about careful screening and control of interaction with World, not after she had spent eight years advocating just the opposite. *Flip-flopper* was the kindest of the invectives hurled at her now. Most people didn't, or maybe couldn't, understand that experience modified political stances, or that isolationism and brotherhood were not a dichotomy but two ends of a continuum, with many viable points between them. She had always fought to protect Earth, but now World needed protection, too. Everything was intertwined—Terra and World, profit and idealism, ecology and progress—and the only way forward was to respect those sometimes inconvenient connections.

Harrison, unlike Marianne, could make these points, and did. His work in neurology had earned him that. The SuperHearers—the media's dumb name for children born after the spore plague—were now contented pre- and elementary-school kids. Harrison had blended his careful work in neurochemicals and cranial electrical mapping with the hastier research of Stubbins's pharmaceutical team. The result was Audexica, one of the most successful drugs ever known. Public pressure combined with sheer volume kept the price low. Humanitarian groups had cooperated to manufacture, ship, and distribute it around the world. Eighty-nine percent of Terran children now took Audexica.

"I wonder what 'normal' really means," Marianne said.

Harrison didn't have to ask why his affectionate statement had led to musing about statistics. They followed each other's unspoken thoughts. No one else had "got" her in that way since Evan, nearly a decade ago. It felt nice. The sex was nice, too, and if it was no more than that—well, nobody got everything.

Harrison said, "Whatever definition of normal you use, we're not it."

She laughed. "See you on Friday?"

"Yes." He kissed her and stood. Weekdays he spent at Columbia, weekends here. She wondered how long it would be before they decided to get a place together, probably in New York. Or maybe here. Harrison was well over sixty—surely he would retire some day?

No, probably not. No more than she would, until they had to.

Jason burst out of the field, spiky corn leaves and silky tassel fibers festooning him like ornaments on a Christmas tree. Colin, Luke, Sara, and Sam trailed behind him. "Grandma! We found a ditch with a lot of frogs!"

"Wow!" Marianne said. "How big are they?"

"One is big!" Colin said, panting up behind his older brother. "I heard them first!"

Of course he did. Neither Colin nor Luke took Audexica. Stubbins's drug had induced methylation to turn off the genes responsible for hyper-hearing—the same genes that *R. sporii* had turned on. But the drug had had unpleasant side effects. Audexica, however, didn't block hyper-hearing. Instead it strengthened neural pathways that let children filter and, eventually, classify ultrasonic and infrasonic noises the way children like Colin and Luke had learned to do by themselves. As kids matured, more of them could do without the drug but keep the hyper-hearing.

Luke, his broad round face glistening with sweat, said, "Two kinds of frogs. Little ones in trees and big ones in water."

Jason said, "I caught a little one and held it!"

"Be careful," Marianne said. "Those tree frogs are really fragile. You don't want to hurt it."

"'Course not!" Sam said indignantly, at the same moment that Sara said, "They're cute!"

Marianne smiled at the twins, who lived on the other side of the cornfield. They were just a few months younger than Colin. None of that generation hurt animals. Eight now, Colin was a self-elected vegetarian. He'd insisted that his father hire a "plant doctor" for a tree infected with oak wilt. He watered parched wildflowers. He put out salt licks for deer. There had always been kids like that, but now there was a whole generation of them, everywhere, and eventually they would grow to adulthood, still sensitive to Earth's biomass.

They were, Marianne allowed herself to think, the best hope for the planet.

A car turned off the road and pulled into the driveway. The twins' father leaned out the window and called, "Hi, Marianne. Kids, time to go home."

"Not yet!" Sara cried.

"Yes, yet. Come on, get in."

Sara and Sam went to the car, feet dragging. Marianne said, "Go on inside, you two, and wash your hands. With soap."

"Race you!" Jason said.

"No fair! You got a head start!"

Marianne ate the rest of her peach. Ryan came out onto the porch. "Mom? What are you doing out here? The mosquitoes are starting."

"I know. I'm coming in. I was just thinking."

"About what?"

She turned her head to look up at him, backlit by light from the house. Too thin, still, but here.

"About Jonah Stubbins. His trial starts next week. But . . . he did this, you know. Along with everything else, he contributed a lot to this great thing for the world's children."

Ryan didn't answer.

"Did you catch the news earlier? About that girl in Indonesia who heard the tsunami coming just the way the animals did? She warned her whole village to get to high ground and saved I don't know how many lives."

"I heard," Ryan said tonelessly.

"And that kid in Russia who rescued a nest of mice from a cat because he heard their ultrasonic cries? *Mus* is returning to Ukraine and Kazakhstan, too."

"I heard."

She had to stop. Ryan was still fragile; too much information connected in any way with the spore cloud brought an edge to his voice. She changed the subject.

"When does Elizabeth's plane land tomorrow?"

"Noon. I'll go get her."

"No, let me go. You stay with the boys." It would be better if Elizabeth got to rant to Marianne before they reached the house. Because there would be a rant about something; there always was.

For the first time, she realized that Elizabeth was fragile, too. Her anger was how she protected herself, just as Ryan's deep depression had been how he punished himself. Maybe Noah, her drifter, had been the strongest one, after all.

She gazed upward at the "summer triangle" of stars emerging in the navy-blue sky. Altair, Vega, Deneb. Would she ever see Noah again? Maybe. Neither the *Venture*, now government property, nor the *Mest'/ Stremlenie* had yet taken off for World. The United States and Russia were "in negotiation," a polite word for a standoff. Meanwhile, other nations' ships were finally nearing completion. Then what?

Nobody knew.

"Mom, the *mosquitoes*."

"Okay, okay, I'm coming."

She rose from the porch, dusted off the seat of her jeans, and went into the lighted house.